A Man of Respect

A Man of
Respect

A Novel

Darryl London

Lyle Stuart Inc. Secaucus, New Jersey

Revised 1986, copyright © Darryl London
Copyright © 1982 by Darryl London

Published by Lyle Stuart, Inc.
120 Enterprise Ave., Secaucus, N.J. 07094
Published simultaneously in Canada by
Musson Book Company,
A division of General Publishing Co. Limited
Don Mills, Ontario

Address queries regarding rights and permissions
to Lyle Stuart, Inc., 120 Enterprise Ave.,
Secaucus, N.J. 07094

Manufactured in the United States of America

Library of Congress Cataloging-in Publication Data

London, Darryl.
    A man of respect.

    I. Title.
PS3562.0485M3   1986   813'.54   85-30740
ISBN 0-8184-0390-X

To My Friend
Mr. Cohen
May You Rest in Peace

Thanks for the Inspiration

נ͟פְֿשִֿ֯י בְּקָֿ אֱלֹקִֿ֯י֯ יֵֿהֿוִֿ

I Am in Thy Care O God

A Man of Respect

Prologue

1939, BOSTON, MASS.

A bright light glared out of a kitchen window overlooking Fishermen's Wharf. It was at the bottom end of Fleet Street. The old man, Gustavo Menesiero, sat on a wooden chair facing his youngest grandson, Bephino.

The ten-year-old boy stared into the eyes of his grandfather as tales and fables, mixed with truths and wisdom, were passed down through the reflections of blood-ridden history—a moment of closeness for both the man and the boy.

Gustavo was short, stocky, and powerful. His white hair, brown eyes, and unshaven face gave him an innocent look. The young boy's red lips and absorbing eyes were set off by a nest of curly brown hair. He watched and listened silently and with fascination as the old man casually stopped to puff his twisted black cigar, which emitted a harsh smell of burning seaweed. Like all immigrant grandfathers, he talked about his youth in the Old Country.

It was a Friday night, after the customary Italian fish dinner overly complemented with the rich thickness of homemade wine. Gustavo was proud to be the baby-sitter and the one to get his youngest grandson's undivided attention for the evening. He began to cut a pear, and in between laughs fed a slice into the young lips of the boy, who seemed to be adoring him. Sixty-five years of wisdom were being funneled into the young boy's mind. Gustavo's voice penetrated the young boy's soul. A passing of the wisdom was important to the old Sicilian, but it had to be passed on carefully. A heavy Sicilian tone filled the room as the old man spoke in broken English.

"Remember, *figlio mio,* in Sciacca, a Sicilian must have honor and respect to be a true Sciacchitano. You must be loyal to your people. There should be only *uno padrone, uno presidente,* only *uno capitano, ah capito?* Understand, Bephino?" he repeated, demanding the boy's attention.

"Si, io capeesh, Nonno."

"Fai il buono, figlio mio. Buono." The old man rewarded the boy with another slice of pear. Then he whispered, as if he were telling a secret to his grandson, "The men and women of Sciacca, theya obeya the unwritten law in one worda." He raised his voice. "*Ah respecto* means respect and loyalty to our people." Exposing his tobacco-stained teeth, he grinned at the boy.

"*Ah respecto,*" the boy repeated in a low voice. "*Ah respecto* means respect," he whispered. It was Sicilian slang for *rispetto.*

"Grandpa, Grandpa, did you ever fight with other men in Sicily?" he asked, chewing his fruit. "The older boys told me you fought a lot in Sicily."

The old man's thick lips pulled back, once again revealing his stained teeth as he smiled at the question. In a rough but gentle voice he replied, "Yes, Bephino. I fighta, but only when my honor and *rispetto* were being taken from me; then I fighta very hard. I fighta to win, never to lose. But otherwise, I avoida to fight. But sometimes we need a good fight to cleara the air, to keepa respect. Don't let people confusa your goodness with weakness. They do that very easy, you know. And thatsa very bad."

"Grandpa, are we in the Mafia?"

The old man's eyes widened at the question as he sipped his wine. He asked harshly, "Who tella you Mafia? Why you talka Mafia?"

"The kids in school, they say I'm Mafia. Am I in the Mafia, Grandpa?"

"You're ten years old, *figlio mio,* you're a . . . a young boy. What kids in school saya that to you?"

"The Jewish kids. They call me Mafioso. What does that mean, Grandpa?"

The old man's face flushed with anger. He thought for a moment, then whispered to himself, "*Eh, ejewda.* The Jewish boys." Raising his voice, he said to Bephino, "*Ejewda,* they lika to teasa you. You tella them you gonna be the *presidente* someday. You tella them you gonna be . . ." He hesitated, then looked into Bephino's innocent eyes. "Sometimes, Bephino, you gotta smacka their face to keep them boys nice. *Ah capeesh,* Bephino?"

"Si, io capisci, Nonno."

Gustavo slipped another slice of pear into his grandson's mouth.

A moment later, the boy spoke again, "But, Grandpa, I would like to know . . ."

The old man, afraid of the next question, quickly interrupted him, reaching into the pocket of his well-worn work pants. "I got something for you today, Bephino. Special for you."

10

Bephino's question remained unasked as he waited in eager anticipation for his surprise. His eyes followed his grandfather's hand searching deep in his pocket.

The old man pulled out a few coins, hoping to find a shiny nickel. "Ah, see what I gotta for you? Special for you, Bephino. A shiny nickel with the Indian and buffalo on it."

The boy's eyes lit up. "Thank you, Grandpa. I'll save it. Thank you very much." The boy hugged his grandfather with a loving affection that passes through one's life so quickly—a love that becomes a memory, like a dream that ends too quickly. The old man kissed the boy's forehead, his unshaven face rubbing against the smooth skin. A spark of love ignited in both, a moment only death can obliterate.

Gustavo, tired and trying to stay out of the line of questioning, told Bephino, "Put the radio on, Bepy. There's a fight tonight. We listen to it."

"What station number, Grandpa?" Bephino asked, moving toward the large wooden radio standing in the corner of the room.

The old man sprawled quietly on the sofa. "You searcha, *figlio mio*, you searcha."

Book I

1944–1945

1

The Menesiero family had come to Boston in 1929 from the small fishing village of Sciacca, Sicily. In 1944 they moved again. Still seeking the American dream of a better life for their children, they decided to try their luck in New York City. They settled in Bay Ridge, Brooklyn, and began to work in their trade, fish peddling.

Using wooden pushcarts, the Menesiero men moved from street to street calling out to the people living up in the apartment buildings: *"O pesce! O pesce!"*—their Sicilian "Fish for Sale!" Their continuous calling sounded almost like begging—begging for a customer to buy some fish before they began to spoil. Long after dusk *"O pesce!"* was the cry that echoed through the narrow alleyways.

During the long hot summer days, the ice would melt quickly, and the fish would start to smell. On a bad day for the immigrants, the rotting fish were not enough. The New York City police would be busy handing out two-dollar tickets to the poor fish peddlers for disturbing the peace or peddling without a license. The Menesiero family soon learned the meaning of the English word *harassment*. Some of the cops just loved to harass the newly arrived Italians, who were struggling to feed their children. It was tough enough to survive in New York, but to have to endure the police trying to deprive them of the right to survive was almost too much. But what really hurt was that these cops did it with a red-faced smile!

Gustavo and Nina Menesiero had three sons and two daughters. Their oldest son, Pasquale, married a girl named Finametta Poluccina, who was from the same town in Sicily. The wedding was a prearranged agreement made by their parents in Sicily. Pasquale and his wife worked hard in the fish business and began to raise a family. They had two sons. The older son's name was Mario; the younger was named Bephino. This story is about Bephino Menesiero.

In 1944 the United States was at war. Bephino was fifteen years old and hanging around the streets of Brooklyn. His lifelong search for financial success and respect began one hot summer night in July of that year.

It was 9:30 P.M. Bephino arrived home in a hurry. He had something "hot" on his mind as he approached the six-unit apartment house his family lived in. He heard music coming from the back yard; the sound of mandolins mixed with the beautiful warm summer breeze. He walked to the rear of the long, dark alleyway that opened on the lighted back yard. His heart beat faster as he walked excitedly toward the music. There were about twenty neighbors, including his mother and father, singing Italian songs. A few of the older men were playing mandolins or guitars, and everyone was swaying back and forth to the rhythm of the music. The men strummed their instruments and smiled at each other each time they hit a fine-sounding chord. They were happy people. The tables were filled with food and hot homemade pizza. Some men stood in a circle guarding a barrel of beer. Everyone saw Bephino walk into the yard. His young face was glowing with joy to see his people so happy. Most of the men were feeling extra good from the beer. Excitement filled the yard. Bephino's eyes looked over to his father, who was sitting at the crowded table pouring wine out of an old gallon bleach jug.

Bepy was a handsome boy, very Italian. He always looked real sharp. At times he wore a pea cap tilted to one side. The older Italians were always impressed when they saw a young boy like Bepy carry on the Italian ways and style of the elders. The men and women began to smile and embrace Bephino. This was their way of showing respect to Pasquale and Finametta; to embrace their sons was the ultimate respect.

Bephino moved through the crowd, trying to get his father's attention.

"Hey, Papa, *scusi*, please. I need a quarter. Please do me a favor, Papa, and lend me a quarter. I gotta date, Papa," he whispered

But his father only laughed at one of the other men's jokes and didn't answer. After a moment Bepy leaned over and whispered directly into his father's ear. He spoke in Italian, trying to soften him up. He knew his father liked his sons to speak Italian to him. *"Papa, piacere lasciare mi avere un venticinque sorta."*

Pasquale answered, *"Venticinque sorta? Ma duza pazzo?* Who's got a quarter? Bepy, I don't have no quarter. I haven't seen a quarter in two days."

"Come on, Papa. It's important to me. I need it. Please don't say no to me."

"Forget it," Pasquale whispered. "And don't ask me no more. *Ah capeesh?"*

Finametta, observing what was going on, knew that once Pasquale said no, that was it. Case closed. Smiling so the neighbors wouldn't notice Bephino's unhappy face, she moved right into action.

16

"Bephino, have a piece of pizza. You gonna like it. Rosie, the napoletana, she made it. *Bella mangiare, figlio mio.*" She stroked his face and fixed his hair, hoping he wouldn't respond disrespectfully to his father in front of their friends.

"Yeah, go ahead, eat. Have a glass of wine," Pasquale said, reaching under the table to get the homemade red wine, which he offered to his son.

"Have a drink. It make you sleep tonight. It's good for you, Bephino. It take your mind off 'important' things."

"Papa, I got a girl. She's like a cat. *Una bella creatura, Papa. Una bella creatura,*" he repeated.

His father turned to the man next to him and offered him wine.

Bepy, realizing that he was not going to get the quarter, took the pizza his mother was waving in his face, kissed both parents, and walked slowly down the alleyway. As he walked and chewed he thought about how poor his family was. He knew his father must have been totally broke to say no in front of all those people. He felt both sad and angry for his father. I never want to be poor, he said to himself. Never. Never. Never. Vehemently, he threw the remains of crust in the street.

Looking up he saw Charlie the Horse, a guy from another neighborhood, walking arm in arm with the reason he needed the quarter. Her name was Irene, and she was shaking her famous ass all over the avenue. Bephino had her lined up for the night, but now Charlie had got her. He felt miserable, and Irene looked so good. He was uncomfortable—horny and deprived—that hot summer night.

Irene was sixteen years old and was proud of her plush bustline and well-curved buttocks. She was a young man's fantasy and an old man's dream. It was said around the neighborhood that if you bought Irene a large lemon ice and a salted pretzel, she would let you count the freckles on her body all night. She had blue eyes, blond hair, and was completely freckled from her toes to her nose.

She was a Brooklynite American, a real New York citizen. A professional plumber by trade, she practiced her profession in the parks of Brooklyn. They said it was like fucking some kind of leopard. They also said she even screamed and whimpered like a feline for hours just at the sight of a well-endowed male. She was to have been quite an experience for young Bephino, and he knew it. He reached into his pocket, pulled out a coin with a buffalo and an Indian head on it, then put it back.

Irene's passion for sex was undisputed throughout the neighborhood. The Italian ladies whispered that she had inherited her sexual desires from her mother. They called the mother *Gaila Puttana.* The kids, investigating the mother's and father's roots, had discovered that Irene came from an amorous family of bisexuals, exhibitionists, and swingers. Fortunately, the older fellows, who were banging her mother, were discreet about her sex life, so the kids never found out if the mother also screamed like a feline at the sight of an erection. Some said that her father was the screamer; he screamed like a cat at the sight of a cock.

Bephino was young and ripe. And he wanted to have her. He kept thinking about her sexual habits and he wanted to be a part of them. One of the guys from the poolroom had told Bepy he fucked her four times one night, and that to stop her screaming he had to stuff her jaws with paper. "She chewed my cock like a beaver, without taking a break. Then she started that meow shit when we walked by the parkway, but we had to go home, because people were driving by on their way to work. This broad's got some lungs and some muscles in her neck," the guy said. "She's no quitter, Bep. You gotta feel her neck; it's so strong. She's like a bull. You gotta be careful, though. She's rough on a dick."

Bepy wanted to feel her so bad, and all he needed was one lousy quarter.

Charlie the Horse had the money and was already heading for the park. He was even carrying a blanket under his arm. Bepy's heart beat faster as Irene walked away down the avenue. That ass. It's so beautiful, he thought. If only I had that rotten quarter, I could have got the lemon ice. And I'd have gotten her.

That was the moment he decided he would never be a poor bastard again—no matter what it took. "We ain't got nothin'," he murmured. "We ain't got no respect."

Bepy crossed the street to Louie's Candy Store and Luncheonette, where his friends were watching him. Half-heartedly he greeted Monkey, Red, Alley Oop, and Little Pauli.

"I thought you were getting laid tonight, Bep," Monkey said, with a knowing grin on his face.

Bepy smiled back and said, "I did. I just got fucked by Charlie the Horse." They all burst out laughing.

The next day, Bepy walked his daily two blocks to the local poolroom. As he entered, the owner, an old man the boys had named Pop, stopped him at the front counter.

"Hey, you! How old are you?" he asked.

"Whatta ya mean, how old am I?" Bepy asked.

"Thatsa right, I aska you your age."

"Hey, Pop, you gotta be kiddin'. I've been shooting pool here for six months now. I swept the floors for you last night. Remember? I'm the guy who helped you clean up. Why are you breakin' my balls now? Whatta you got, your balls twisted today or what?"

"Never minda twisted balls. I breaka your head you talk like that to me."

The old man got off his stool and started to push Bepy out. Bepy was embarrassed in front of the other guys.

"Pop, what the fuck's wrong with you? I'm in here every day. I cleaned up for you last night. I can't believe this crap." Looking over at his friends for support, Bepy yelled, "I swept the fuckin' floors for this guy; *now* he wants to know my age." He turned back to look directly at Pop. "How come last night you acted nice to me, huh? Whatta ya, nuts or what?"

"Hey, Johnny," the old man suddenly called out to his son. "We gotta wise guy here." He kept shoving Bepy toward the door.

Bepy felt like dirt. All the guys were laughing now. "Keep ya hands off me," he yelled at the old man. "You stink of garlic. I hate that fuckin' smell. Don't touch me. The raw garlic you eat is fuckin' up your head."

John came to the front, rubbing a cue ball with a rag and eying Bepy. "What's the matter, Pop? You got a problem with this little punk?"

"Throw this bum out," the old man said.

"Hey, whatta you guys, nuts?" Bepy yelled.

John grabbed Bepy's shirt and threw him out the door. Bepy's shirt was ripped, and he had a burning scratch on his neck. He knew about John—about how short-tempered he was and how tough he was supposed to be. And he knew about John's connections with the Mob. Bepy didn't want to be disrespectful to those important people, but he'd just got kicked out of the poolroom and had lost face in front of his friends. Something had to be done to correct this wrong. He was tough and he didn't take any shit from anyone. But John was older, and Bepy was expected to have respect for him. So Bephino Menesiero had a big decision to make: respect or disrespect? Which was it going to be? Bepy straightened up and tucked in his shirt and thought about his embarrassment. I can't believe these people! They threw me out in the street for nothing! I gotta do something about this. I should get a gun and blast that bastard!

The kids in the pool hall were not surprised when the door opened a few minutes later and back came Bephino. The old man, though, looked up shocked. He had just been laughing about the way John, who was forty-two, threw out the fifteen-year-old kid.

"Hey, Johnny," Bepy called out, "I wanna talk to you."

John slowly walked up to the front with a smirk on his face. "Hey, the porter is back. Come back tonight. You can sweep then. OK, punk?"

Bepy casually moved closer, and when in perfect range, swiftly kicked John right in his balls. The kick was so hard that everyone heard John's asshole snap. He fell to the floor, moaning—really hurt. He turned blue in the face and was unable to get up.

"You son of a bitch!" the old man cursed Bephino.

Bepy just turned and walked out. His friends had known he would do something; they just hadn't known what.

John had to be taken to the hospital, where they kept him a week. He had a dislocated testicle and a torn sack. His asshole was fine. John told his visitors that he was going to kill "that kid" when he got out. Bepy heard this and found it amusing. He soon started his own rumor: when John got out of the hospital, he was going to kick him in the balls again; so John had better be expecting him.

All the older Mob guys on the block were buzzing: "That kid Bepy is a real Sciacchitano." "He's got balls." "He hurt John, the poolroom guy." Sciacchitano meant, for them, men of a tough and faithful breed, men known to be strong fighters to the finish; truly loyal and honorable people from Sciacca. These were men who had commanded respect in the old days of the Sicilian Vespers.

Two weeks later, with John still limping around the pool hall, Bephino decided he wanted to shoot pool. He opened the door and entered. Pop stared at him in amazement. He couldn't believe his eyes. Bepy walked over and put a large clove of garlic on the counter. "Here," he told the old man, "*pazzaella, mangiare aglio.* I think you need a good worming."

The old man was numb. He sipped some wine, staring in silence at Bepy.

"I'm shooting pool. Give me a table," Bepy demanded in a cocky voice. Then he grinned and looked around the room. "Where's Johnny One Ball?" he asked with a grin.

Everyone in the joint cracked up. John had been watching him and couldn't believe what was happening. "This kid's crazy," he said, but he started to laugh with everyone else. Even the old man started to laugh.

"This guy's a real Sicilian," Pop told his son. And Bepy smiled. Pop smiled, too, showing that peace had been made. Bephino had gained their respect the hard way.

Every day when Bephino left home he would walk past the neighborhood bar and grill. It was the hangout for the Mafia Boss, Don Emilio Morrano, *Capo di Tutti i Capi.* Boss of Bosses. He was, in fact, the top of the five New York City heads. The Don was sharp as a tack. He dressed in three-hundred-dollar tailor-made suits and an expensive hat, smoked dollar cigars, and bought a new Cadillac every year. He stood in front of the bar acting like he owned Brooklyn. And he did. He was the Boss. No one would defy him or his men.

Don Emilio was a very hard, stern-looking man. The ladies considered him handsome; the men considered him dangerous. His suits, topcoat, and fedora all matched his dark-gray personality. His olive-skinned face had a smooth boxy look. You could tell his mood from the set of his jaw. His eyes were black and piercing, and they vigorously expressed his high authority as a leader of men. His word was law in the world of the Mafia.

When he looked at you, it seemed his thoughts were focused exclusively on your future. This made people uncomfortable in his presence. He puffed long, thick, expensive-looking cigars crunched between his teeth. Even when he spoke, the cigar never left the center of his lips. His love for beautiful women was his weakness; his love for his wife was his treasure. And Emilio Morrano was born in Sciacca, Sicily.

Bepy greeted him every day when walking past the bar. "Good morning, Mr. Morrano," he would say respectfully.

The Don never answered. With his cigar crunched between his teeth, he simply gave Bepy a nod. He knew Bepy had moved there from Boston. He also knew the Menesiero family from the Old Country. Don Emilio Morrano, as a boy, used to hang around Gustavo Menesiero's café on the wharf in Sciacca.

Bephino's grandfather had used large boat hooks to fight with other men, and Morrano had seen this. He knew the quality of Bepy's Sicilian blood. He kept an eye on Bepy, but never talked to him.

One hot summer day, after an early-morning rain, when the sidewalks were still steaming and the hot and humid smell of Brooklyn was in the air, Bepy went to the schoolyard. That was where all the kids hung out when school was closed for the summer. It was late morning, and all the kids had already left for Bay 15 on Coney Island's beach. Bepy, sitting on the school steps alone, knew he didn't have the money to go swimming anyway. As he sat feeling sorry for the poor bastard that he was, he noticed Bob McAteer's 1942 Buick across the street in front of the big apartment house Bob and his wife lived in. The car was beautiful, one of the best in the neighborhood. It was dark green, but it was so dirty it looked gray. Bepy suddenly thought that maybe he could wash it and earn a buck, then meet the guys at Coney Island.

Bob McAteer was known to all the people on the block as "The Rebel," because he came from someplace down South and talked with a Southern accent. He had married Margie, a neighborhood girl who was half Italian and half German. Margie was built like something in a Hot Book cartoon. None of the Italian fellows would marry her because she was too conspicuous to live with. Italian mothers would be ashamed of such a voluptuous daughter-in-law moving around in the kitchen. It could be an embarrassment to the younger children's friends. So Margie had to marry a hick, a guy who didn't know any better. Even Bepy thought Margie was so sexy and beautiful that it was a shame to waste her on a guy who didn't seem to realize what he had. But he was only fifteen and it was none of his business, and he knew that, too.

Thinking about washing the car, Bepy walked over to the apartment building and rang Bob's bell. The door buzzed. Bepy climbed the steps to the fifth floor. It was such a hot day, he was soon sweating. When he got to the top floor, Margie was waiting, her head hanging out the apartment door.

"Can I help you, Bepy?"

"Hey, Margie. Can I speak to Bob?"

"Bob went to visit his family down South, and won't be back for a week."

"OK. Sorry to bother you, Margie. I'll run along."

Margie, noticing the sweat on Bepy's face, said, "Would you like a cold drink? You look overheated, Bepy."

"Thanks, Margie. I think I *would* like something cool. It's so clammy today." As he moved toward her, he said, "My friends already left for the beach, so I had nothing to do. I figured maybe I could wash Bob's car today." He followed Margie into the apartment, letting the door slam shut behind him. Margie was wrapped in a large bath towel, and he watched her move gracefully in the slightly wet covering.

"Excuse the way I'm dressed," she said when she realized he was watching her. "I just finished my bath when the bell rang."

"Don't worry about me," Bepy answered. "I like wet towels on women."

Margie grinned. She told Bepy to help himself to a soda in the refrigerator and went into one of the bedrooms. As he drank a ginger ale and browsed around the living room, he heard the sexy sound of French singing through the door, which she had left open about ten inches. Bepy looked at a wedding picture of Bob and Margie. What a hick this guy is, he thought. But he's got some broad. I've got to give him credit; he's got guts moving to Brooklyn and marrying her in a tough neighborhood like this. Boy, she's got some body. He must be fucking her brains out.

The room was quiet except for the soft music. After a few minutes he heard Margie's voice from her bedroom. He thought she said, "Did you get your soda OK?" or something to that effect. I wonder why she's talking without coming out of her room? he thought. Maybe she's trying to get my attention? Maybe she wants me to go in there and bang her? But Margie was about thirty-four years old.

Again he heard her voice. This time he really couldn't understand her. So, being the type of guy who always moved toward trouble and not away from it, he pushed open the door and entered. "Are you calling me, Margie?"

Margie, nude, was standing in high-heeled bedroom slippers combing her hair in front of a three-way, full-length mirror. She spun around, holding her hands between her thighs to cover herself. But it was hopeless. Her bust was totally bare, and when she turned, her ass was fully exposed to Bepy in the mirror. Her red plum nipples matched her long red hair. He noticed that her collar and cuffs matched. She's a genuine redhead—a ruby in the rough, he thought.

"What are you doing in here, Bepy? Get out!" she yelled angrily.

"I thought you called me for something. I heard your voice. I thought maybe you needed me."

"Are you kidding?" she answered. "I only asked if you were enjoying the French music. Get out of my bedroom. You've got some nerve walking in my bedroom without knocking. Ya know that?"

"I didn't know you were nude, Margie. Ya think I wanna see you nude? I'm sorry. I thought you called me. I couldn't hear you so good with the music playing."

Margie stopped complaining and laughed sarcastically, "Called you? Needed you? Why should I call for you? You're only a . . ."

Bephino couldn't take his eyes off of her. He was glued to the spot he was standing on. His eyes were bulging out of his head. She felt his youthful excitement glowing all over her, but he felt a bit scorned when she laughed at him. "Gee, Margie, I don't know what to say. I'm sorry. I didn't mean to see you naked like this. Boy, Margie, you look so beautiful!" He smiled tentatively. His voice thickened. "I never seen such a beautiful woman as you in my life."

23

Her long red hair hung down to her hips. Her breasts were large and firm, and her nipples were exactly like two plums, taut and ripe for his lips, he thought. He stared at her voluptuous body with a hungry look. Margie's high-heeled slippers gave perfect balance to her shape. Her loins seemed to be inviting him to enter her. His mind ran wild with the thought. He had never seen such a bright red pussy before.

Margie realized he was overcome by this sight of a woman more than twice his age.

She gave him a slight teasing smile. "So you think I'm a beauty, huh, boy?" she said, emphasizing boy.

"Yeah, Margie, you're a beauty. I'm tellin' ya, you're a beauty. I love the way you look. You got more curves than a race track. Ya know that?"

Margie now seemed to be more comfortable with her nudity. She thought for a brief moment, then began raising her hands, casually exposing herself completely to him. Standing with the seductive posture of a model as he watched every move, she slid her hands up and down her thighs very slowly and stared back at him.

Oh, God, she looks so inviting, he thought as she teased him. Praying frantically for this to be the real thing, he swallowed deeply and finally moved closer. He could smell the clean fresh scent of her soap-bathed body. Sensing her acceptance, he touched her, missing nothing.

Margie was amused by the eagerness and boldness of this young boy, and his smooth, strong touch was exciting her to wetness. She smiled softly at him, acknowledging her passion. She reached out and touched his smooth, whiskerless face, running her fingers over his features, stopping gently on his lips.

"How old are you?" she asked in a thick whisper.

"Fifteen."

"You're only a boy." She grinned nervously but anxiously.

"Yeah, I'm only fifteen."

They stood in the three-way mirror as Bepy reached down deep between her thighs. She smiled, weakening. "You're so young and you want me, don't you? You're only a kid and you got the hots for me."

Then turning around, exposing her rear to him, she struck a soft, relaxed stance.

"I want you, Margie," he whispered. "You're so sexy-looking. I'd do anything to make love to you."

"Anything?" she asked, and looked at him in amazement. He just stood there fondling her and bulging in his pants. His throbbing was more than evident, and she saw this. It began to excite her. As his hands roamed between her thighs and back up to where she wanted them to go, she rubbed her body against his probing fingers. "You're a good-looking guy," she whispered, running her hands through his curly hair. Slowly she kissed his young mouth and licked at his lips with oncoming lust.

Bephino's heart was beating wildly. Now he put his hands on her hips, then slowly and awkwardly moved them down to her buttocks, rolling his palms around with his fingers, feeling her beautiful softness.

Her eyes closed, and opened once again in amazement at his tender moves. She looked so beautiful to him as he contentedly pawed her buttocks. He could tell she loved this, so he kept it up to please her.

Watching his roving hands in the mirror, Margie squirmed in fiery passion. "Touch me, touch me all over. Please touch me," she directed him, staring intently at his face. She spread her body, fully giving herself to her young lover. "I'm so wet, Bepy. I'm dripping."

Her voice was that of a bewildered nymph, and she gasped as he now stroked her between her voluptuous thighs. She suddenly began tearing at Bepy's clothes. She impatiently unzipped his pants, and her eyes widened with pleasure and surprise at the size of him. His thin, boyish body intensified his endowment. She dropped to her knees, pulling at his pants. She began lubricating him with her tongue, then her lips, becoming more passionate with each lick. She tried to devour him completely with one hard thrust of her head. He smiled, thinking of her laughter and her sarcastic "Why should I call you?" Only a few moments before, she had called him a boy. Now she was gagging on his large cock.

He tried to stop her and move to the bed, but she wouldn't stop. Her tongue was like a feather with a light coating of sandpaper. She impatiently unbuckled his pants, dropping them to the floor as she lowered his drawers. Placing her hands on his small backside, she ran her long fingers down the valley of his ass, then grasped him passionately. He tried to unplug himself from her mouth, but he couldn't leave the delicate feeling that had taken hold of him. He was a prisoner of passion as he began to climax. Her large green eyes widened. His knees and legs trembled as his body yielded to rapturous delight. He shook and trembled, trying to control his body as he continued to come. He held her head and watched her lips, waiting for her to finish, hoping to gain control of himself. She took him to the end.

Finally he pulled away in total exhaustion, raising her from her knees. He led her to the bed, stripped completely, and lay on his back relaxing. Margie stood near him smiling. Her red pussy was soggy but still glowing.

"How was that, you little devil?" she asked.

Bepy smiled, "Fantastic! My body couldn't stop shaking. It felt so good."

"Now you must return the favor."

"What kinda favor?" he asked.

"I want your pretty face on me," she said, smiling. "You must return the favor to me." She began to mount him.

Later that day, Bepy began to dress. Margie was still in bed, on her back. She turned to him and said, "It was really fantastic, wasn't it? You're really great, Bepy. You're welcome to my bed anytime, provided my husband is working or away. OK, love?" she asked; then added, "You understand that, don't you?"

Tucking in his shirttails, he replied, "Of course I understand."

"Why don't you sleep with me tonight?" she asked. "I'm all alone. I'll make dinner for us."

"I feel great, Margie, but I don't feel that great. I gotta get some raw clams in me. I'll come back tomorrow. OK?"

"What time?"

"About ten o'clock tomorrow morning."

"I'll be waiting."

Bepy leaned over the bed and kissed her. As she grabbed for more, he said, "Hey, wow, I'll be back tomorrow. Rest up; take a nap." Then he left.

He felt so good to have such a woman at his beckoning. He couldn't wait to tell the boys in the poolroom about her. Then he started to think about it. I'd better not say a word to anybody. If I open my mouth, that apartment building will be like the Italian army on maneuvers. *"Silenzio,"* he said aloud.

His leather heels clicked on the sidewalk as he walked toward the pool hall. His stride was rhythmic, and he moved with graceful confidence. His thoughts were of Margie. Grinning over her comments, "Get out of my bedroom" and "Call you? Why should I call you?" Bephino laughed as he strutted up the street.

2

A few weeks later, Bepy was at Louie's Candy Store, next door to the bar owned by Don Emilio. The luncheonette was a good hangout for Bephino and his pals. At night they would try to con the girls into spending their money on malts and the jukebox. Then, if the girls were real nice people, the guys would take them to the park. That evening, Bepy was sitting in a booth with a few neighborhood girls, Monkey, and Red when some guys from another neighborhood walked in.

The girl Monkey was sitting by sighed. "Oh, look. That's Butchie Mazzola. He's a senior at New Mountain High." She continued running at the mouth about this guy, and Monkey was starting to get burned up.

Red, seeing this, told the girl, "Look, ya little cunt, you're sitting with us now, right? So have some respect. After we fuck you, Butch can have ya. OK?"

The girl wanted to die when Red opened up on her like that. She stopped watching Butchie walking around the store like a big shot, eying all the girls, and flexing his muscles.

"Get Louie over here," Bepy told Red. "I wanna talk to him."

Red called, "Hey, Louie, Bephino wants a few words with ya."

Louie, the owner, about forty-six years old, came over to their booth. "Whatta you guys want?" he asked

Bepy said, "Hey, Louie, you'd better straighten out this guy Butch before we gonna do a *dota della* on his head. He's got big eyes. He's eyin' up our broads, and Monkey here is gettin' peeved."

Leaning over the table, Louie snapped at Bepy, "Oh, is that right? Monkey's gettin' peeved, huh? Don't think you're gonna make trouble here like you did in the poolroom, you little punk. I'll kick your little ass right out of here. All three of you."

"I'm suprised at you, Louie—callin' me a little punk, and protectin' the Dukes. Them guys are the 86th Street Dukes gang. Why do you talk to me like that? I'm a good customer. I live in the neighborhood, don't I? We ordered three malts tonight. The broads played the juke ten times. We're spenders, Louie. *Ah capeesh?* I always respect you, Louie, don't I?"

"Just keep your ass shut, Bephino, or I'll throw you out. You *capeesh?*" Louie answered and walked away.

The girls smiled over Louie's snappy remark.

"What the fuck are you smilin' at, ya little douche bag?" Red asked.

27

"Get yourselves ready," Bepy said to Monkey and Red. "We're gonna dance. This fuckin' Louie's got no respect. We gotta teach him. Imagine that shit! We bought three malts and he treats us like animals. And, we don't like that. So now we gotta do the two-step on Louie's head."

"Hey, Bepy. Are you sure you wanna wreck this place?" Monkey asked. "It's right around the corner from your mother's house. You know Louie's a wild man. He's gonna go crazy."

Red replied. "Bepy's right. We gotta teach this bastard some respect. He's outa line, and these fuckin' broads are outa line. The Dukes is outa line. So we gotta dance tonight. First we dump this creep Butchie and his boys, then we all cripple Louie. Go for the kneecaps. If you hit the floor, do damage to the knees."

The girls were shocked. One said, "Butchie is eighteen. He's the toughest guy on 86th Street. You're gonna have trouble with him."

Bepy blasted her, "Trouble with him? No shit! I been having trouble all my life, and now he's gonna have trouble with me! Watch Butchie's eighteen years go down the fuckin' drain, ya prissy little bitch!" He got up and, turning to the girls, said, "Sit tight, 'cause when this is over, we're gonna finger your little asses good tonight." He told Monkey and Red, "Make like we're leavin', then grab those large soda bottles off the rack and start crackin' heads. When we finish off Butch and his boys, all three of us go for Louie. OK?"

They nodded. Monk whispered, "I wish Alley Oop was here."

Bephino was too involved mentally to think about help. He was still giving out orders and thinking of ways to handle this unexpected battle. He said, "Use the full soda bottles. They're heavier. Keep your heads cool." He was totally into the fight, not thinking of possible defeat. He pushed full speed ahead.

The three went into action. Butchie was the first to go down; because he was eighteen, they treated him with extra special respect. He got hit from all sides. Louie ran from behind the counter and quickly attacked Bepy like a wild beast. He hit him with a blackjack from behind; miraculously, it just missed his head, but caught his left shoulder. Louie was out to kill Bepy, it seemed. Bepy felt the club hit again and again on his back, and he knew he was hurt, but he kept moving, trying to shake it off. Blood was all over the place. Butchie and his boys were down, and Red and Monkey were swinging at everything that moved.

It all happened so fast. Then suddenly Louie got hit by Red from behind. In the confusion Bepy stopped and walked over to where Louie was huddled on the floor. With his shoulder pounding and hurting, he yelled to Red and Monkey, "Come on. Let's dance again. Beautiful work.

28

I'm proud of you guys. You danced well. Now we *dota della* on Louie's rotten head. He japped me from behind. He's a real Jap motherfucker!"

"Yeah, let's kill this rotten bastard!" Red agreed, and the three attacked Louie like animals.

The fight ended with an ambulance carrying Louie and Butchie to the Coney Island hospital. Red, Monkey, and Bepy, watching from across the street, thought it was beautiful, really beautiful, to see the two allies, Butchie and Louie, on stretchers side by side.

"Let's get them girls," Monkey said. "They're waitin' for us across the street."

The next day the whole neighborhood was talking about the fight. It was reported to Don Emilio that Bepy's gang had put Louie in the hospital; everyone figured Bepy's ass was in trouble. They watched the Don as he stood outside his bar when Bepy walked by.

Bepy had awakened late that day, but he greeted the Don as usual: "Good morning, Mr. Morrano."

"It's afternoon, not morning, and get in the car," the Don answered, speaking around his long, thick cigar. "I wanna talk to you."

Bepy, seeing all the kids watching from the corner, tried to act cool and not worried or embarrassed. He got in the Don's car, and they drove off together.

Don Emilio spoke. "So you like to fight, huh? You make a lot of trouble here last night. I understand you like to break heads, huh?"

Bepy answered, "They were guys from another neighborhood, looking for trouble. We had to do whatever we had to do to keep the peace."

"So you kept the peace? And how about Louie? Why is he in the hospital? Was he disturbing the peace?"

"Louie is a traitor," Bepy answered. "He needed his lumps. He was backing those guys from 86th Street. They're outsiders. This is our neighborhood, right? We gotta protect our neighborhood. That's what I always thought."

Don Emilio smiled, shaking his head. "I think you're like your grandfather. He always liked to fight. In the old days nobody could control him. He never would walk away from a fight. I know your family from Sicilia. I'm Sciacchitano, too."

"My grandfather would never avoid a fight?" Bepy smiled. He had heard a different version of this from his grandfather.

"Your grandfather was a credit to our people; I'm sorry he died. He was a very fair man, but a man who'd not back down from anyone. I remember him from when I was your age." His eyes focused on Bepy's.

29

"You like to fight. OK. Come see me next Wednesday, at 2:00 P.M. I let you do something and you can make a few bucks. OK kid? And don't sleep late. Your eyes are too puffy."

Bephino's eyes lit up. "Make some bucks? Yes, sir. I'll come next week. I sure can use the money."

"I said next Wednesday, at 2:00 P.M., not next week."

"Yes, Mr. Morrano. Wednesday, at 2:00 P.M. I'll be on time."

Bepy got out of the new Cadillac. He felt good about his first real contact with the Don and the ride in a beautiful car with such an important man. His first business with Mr. Morrano. He was going to have the best things in life, and he was willing to do whatever it took to get them. That Cadillac was so posh; it rode so smooth, Bephino thought. I got to be important someday. I want to be a man who's respected.

Meanwhile, the kids waiting on the corner yelled over to him, "Hey, Bepy, what did he say? Is he mad at you?"

"Why should he be mad? I protect the neighborhood, don't I? He's happy, not mad. Next time he's gonna give me a gold medal. Today he only gave me ten bucks."

"Come on, Bepy. Tell us what he said."

"He told me to keep things under control around here. So keep your noses clean. Don't make unnecessary trouble in the neighborhood! Understand? I'm in charge around here."

They were beginning to believe him. "OK, Bepy. You know we're with you. Whatever you say, you're the Capo."

The next day Louie was out of the hospital and in the store. He was peeking through the broken glass window, watching Bepy on the corner with the other kids. "I can't understand why that bastard kid Bephino is acting like a hero. Look at him, smiling at everyone," Louie said to his wife, "Morrano was supposed to straighten his little ass out. What happened? Look at the punk. Look at him, Edna. He looks like he's a young Don standing there. That son of a bitch! I don't believe it! Them goddamn Sicilians stick together. Morrano lent me the money to buy this store. Now it's all busted up."

"You're bleeding again, Louie," Edna said.

"I hate them fuckin' Sicilians. They're fish people, that's what they are," Louie said, banging his fist.

"Louie, what part of Italy are *your* people from?" Edna asked.

Louie, still pissed off, turned to her. "Go make your egg creams and don't break my balls. I don't know what part they're from. I know it wasn't Sicily, that's for sure. I'm not like them double-crossers."

Next week, Wednesday, at 2:00 P.M., Bephino was waiting in front of the bar for Mr. Morrano. The Don arrived with two husky men, his captains or lieutenants. All three men were well dressed; they looked important to Bepy. He greeted them. "Good afternoon, gentlemen."

The Don, cigar in mouth, nodded; the other two did not respond.

Bepy followed them to the rear of the bar and sat at the table with them.

One of the men asked, "Who's this kid?"

Don Emilio said, "He's from the neighborhood. I'm using him on Fatman."

"You're using this kid on Fatman?"

"Yeah," Morrano replied.

"Fatman will swallow this kid up for lunch." The Capo laughed.

Bepy's face flushed with embarrassment.

"Are you sure, Emilio?" the other man asked, eying Bephino.

Morrano looked at the kid, smiled, and said, "He can handle it. His grandfather was Menesiero from Sciacca."

The two men laughed. "Ah, Schiacchitano. Well that's another story. We knew your grandfather," the Capo said.

"I heard from Mr. Morrano that you did," Bepy replied.

He felt better now that the men seemed to accept him. He never knew his grandfather commanded so much respect.

The Don proceeded to give Bepy his instructions. "This is what I want you to do. There's a fellow on 3rd Avenue and 29th Street. I want his legs broke good. He's called the Fatman. He owns the Blue Note Café. Everyday at 4:00 P.M. he's there, before the café opens. Maybe he eats or does paperwork or something in the back room. You make this look like a robbery. I want it to look like he's been harassed by young robbers."

"I understand. Don't worry, I can handle this. That's my racket. It's easy," Bepy replied nonchalantly.

"Nothing's easy. Don't be too sure of yourself. Be careful, *ah capeesh?*"

"How much does this job pay, Mr. Moranno?"

"Two hundred bucks."

Bepy was stunned by the amount of money—just to beat up a guy. Trying to hide his reaction, he asked in a businesslike manner, "Can I have it now? I usually get paid in advance, and I can use the cash."

"Yeah, I pay you now," the Don said, and handed Bepy two one-hundred-dollar bills. Bepy had never seen a one-hundred-dollar bill; he had never even seen a fifty-dollar bill. A few months ago, he couldn't raise a quarter to buy lemon ice and a pretzel for a piece of ass. Now he was holding hundred-dollar bills in his hand. Life can change overnight in America, he thought. I'm almost rich.

He told Mr. Morrano, "OK. You want this to look like a robbery and you want this guy in a coma? Am I right?"

The Don smiled. "That's good, a coma. It sounds nice, a coma." He liked Bephino's style. "Now be careful and don't be too cocky. He may be packing a gun, or the bartender may be with him and may have a rod under the bar. So be smart. Think. Use your head, and don't get hurt. The Fatman drives a blue 1942 Cadillac. Check around; see if it's outside. Oh, and kid . . . if you get caught, don't mention my name. Just say you were robbing the place. You gotta take what comes then. You understand, kid?"

"I understand. I did it on my own. Don't worry, Mr. Morrano. I would never talk. Can I keep whatever I rob from this guy?"

"Yeah. Whatever you rob, it's your gravy. You can go now, but be careful. I don't want you to get hurt. And if you get caught, remember you're on your own. Don't let us dream about you. *Ah capeesh?*"

"*Si io capeesh.* Don't worry, Mr. Morrano. I'm like my grandfather. I can handle these kinds of situations."

Bephino excused himself and, as he left, he turned and said, "OK, gentlemen, you can order the Fatman's flowers. I'm going to work." He laughed to himself. Boy, I hope Fatman's got some money on him; I could get loaded working for these guys. What a score! Squeezing the two hundred-dollar bills in his pocket tightly, he walked quickly up the street.

The three men talked after Bepy left. "This kid's really something. He has respect and class for someone so young. Did you notice he had the brains to ask if he can keep whatever he robbed from the Fatman?"

One man said, "Yeah, but can he handle it? He's only a punk kid. If he gets caught, he'll open up. I'm not sure we're doing the right thing using him. Fatman may hurt the kid. Did you think of that, Emilio? You know Fatman's a bad guy to handle, and he's wild when he gets cornered."

The Don answered in a strong voice. "That's the kid who put John Filippo, the poolroom guy, in the hospital eight weeks ago with crushed balls. And Louie, next door, also checked in the hospital last week. This kid's a killer at heart. He takes after his grandfather. Don't let that baby face fool you guys. Remember how *we* started? We were only twelve years old when we made our first hit in Sciacca. Let me worry about the kid. He's got good breeding behind him."

That night Bepy contacted Red and Monkey. He told Monkey to steal a car, bring it to the poolroom at three o'clock sharp the next day. Then he told Red to get a couple of his uncle's guns and meet him at the poolroom at the same time.

"Why do we need guns?" Red asked.

"I'll tell you both what we're doing then. We got something important to handle for some important people. So be cool, OK?"

Later that night, lying in bed, Bepy thought about Red and Monkey. What if we have to kill Fatman? Can I trust Red? Maybe I should use Crazy Mikey instead of Red. He's pure Sicilian; Red's not. Bepy trusted only Sicilians with his secrets, but he made an exception for Red. Red was a heavy hitter, but could he kill? His grandfather had always warned him against northern Italians, because they were weak-gutted people and prone to Communism. He called them Mussolini people. Bepy had always obeyed his grandfather.

Red, whose parents came from Milano, had a strong personality. He'd been called Red since he was a baby, because he had bright red hair and fair skin. He was baptized Louis Biancosquardo. He was a charmer, always turning on the charm and affection at the right time. He used this as a weapon, to get his way. His hair, combined with unusual gray eyes and yellow teeth, made him look untrustworthy. His bright red face would flush at times, however, and expose his thoughts. He was big and husky and sported a fat ass. He was a hard puncher and a good pipe man. Although not Sicilian, he tried to look one. All through junior high school he had ideas, ideas that always needed financing. Smart in school, sometimes too smart for his own good, he was an opportunist, sometimes at the expense of his friends. It was said by his teachers that Red could charm the Grim Reaper at death's door.

Aldo Pastrona was known as Monkey. He was a short, shabbily dressed guy with round shoulders. His nose was wide and rested high above his lips. His eyes bulged, and his hair was straight and jet black. Although his family was very Italian, from Adrano, Sicily, if Aldo ate a banana, it would cause one to have second thoughts. His hobby was stealing cars. His loyalty was unquestionable. For his size, he could fight vigorously. He had guts and, above all, respect. An only child, he lived with his widowed father.

On Thursday, at 2:00 P.M., Monkey went over to Abe's Deli, a busy eating place. People were running in and out, picking up coffee-break snacks. Monkey saw his car. The guy left the motor running. This was

33

going to be a snap; no wires to cross or anything. Monkey got in and drove off. Meanwhile, Red had got the two guns his uncle kept in the wine cellar.

At 2:20, Bepy was at the pool hall waiting for his men. He had the job figured out, and had gloves for him and Red and nylon stockings to cover their faces and hands. Red showed up forty minutes early with a paper bag containing the two rusty guns. Huddled in the corner, Bepy looked them over and remarked, "Hey, Red, these guns are shit. They look like your uncle hung around with Bluebeard." He discovered that one gun had no bullets and the other had only two shells. "You got empty guns, Red. We better not get in a shootout. These guns are crap. Look at them; they're rusty."

"That's all he had," Red explained. "They were down in the cellar. It's damp down there."

"OK. I understand," Bepy remarked, trying to keep things calm and running smoothly. "I'm gonna do this thing so fast they won't know what hit them."

At 2:30, Monkey pulled up with the car. Bepy and Red jumped in, and they pulled away.

"You guys were both early. That's what I like to see," Bepy said, praising them. "Hey, Monk, you got gas?"

"I didn't check the gas gauge. I never thought of it."

Bepy looked over at the dashboard, "You're lucky; you got half a tank. From now on, always check for gas. Understand? Never steal an empty car. It could cause you lots of problems. You still got a lot to learn, Monkey."

"Well, I'm only fifteen years old and I only been stealin' cars three years now. Time is on my side."

"Look, we've got a lot of work to do, and I don't want anybody makin' us look bad. So let's be serious for a change. I think we got a lifetime contract with a very large firm. And we gotta impress the board of directors."

Red and Monk looked at each other. Bepy was really talking big now—lifetime contract, board of directors. They had seen him in action before, and they knew he had the balls to do anything he said or promised, good or bad. But what board of directors?

"OK, pull over. There by the junkyard," Bepy told Monkey. "I gotta get a pipe. I'll be right out; leave the car running." He returned with a short pipe and told Red, "Keep this with you through the whole job; we're gonna need it."

"What are we gonna do this time?" Monkey asked. "Fix a bathtub?"

"Look, Monk. Don't ask stupid questions. The less you know, the longer you'll live. Your job is to drive. You do your job, nothing else. OK? Let's stick to 'business is business' and forget the bathtub bullshit. You're the driver. Me and Red gotta do the plumbing."

Bepy spoke to Red, "You do like you always do. Stay by me, break heads, or whatever. Use the pipe like you normally do. No changes, OK?"

"Yeah, no changes," Red answered as the car moved away.

"You know, fellows, we're semideprived people. We're getting half a hump out of life. We have no choice; we gotta make hits. We gotta crawl out of the gutter; we gotta get to the top! We're only hitting Mob guys for other Mob guys, so actually we're cleaning up the neighborhood for the good people. We're doing the right thing. So don't ask me questions about these contracts, OK?" He smiled at his friends.

"OK, this is it. Red, you come with me. I have the gun with the two rusty bullets. You got the empty gun."

Monkey interrupted. "What?" Your gun has rusty bullets, his is empty? Are you guys really nuts? You're better off using a frying pan."

"Listen to me good," Bepy blurted out. "These guys may have rods hidden behind the bar or in the office. We'll bluff them with ours, then grab theirs. Red, I want you to search the joint good. But first, lock the door behind us when we walk in. I'll cover them and check out the situation. Pull your nylon over your face quick. I don't want this guy to see our faces. OK?"

"OK."

"When we get close to them, keep your rod trained on their heads. Keep them scared and off balance. The more scared they are, the easier it will go for us. Red, I want you to move your fat ass today and keep moving. I don't wanna get caught in there. Work fast. Get everything. Cash, guns, rings. Fill this potato sack with everything you grab. If you find their guns, drop yours in the sack, so you'll have a gun that's loaded. I'll keep my gun trained at their heads. If they move, I'll kill 'em," Bepy said, watching Red's eyes for a reaction.

"Yeah." Monkey laughed. "They'll die from rust poisoning."

"Look, this is a snap for us. We're pros," Bepy said. "We've done this shit before, so be calm. OK, fellas?"

"Yeah, we did it before—once to a dentist, and to a couple of porno business guys. But not Mafioso," Red proclaimed, his eyes watering. "This sounds like Mafioso."

Bepy looked at him angrily. "Whatta ya mean, Mafioso? We're the Mafioso, ya schmuck! This is where the big money is. No more dimes and quarters for us. Not so long ago, I didn't have a buck to go to the beach. I had to hump that big-ass broad Margie to stay in her air-conditioned apartment all day. Them days are over. *Finito*."

"Listen to this bullshit. To stay in her air-conditioned apartment all day!" Monkey laughed. "What a way to brag about humping Margie. The whole neighborhood is having wet dreams over her, and he says *finito*."

"OK, we're here. Cut the shit. Pull over there," Bepy told Monkey. "That's it. The Blue Note Café; that's the joint. Fatman, please be there. See if you see a blue '42 Caddie."

They checked the area. "It's not around. I don't see any blue Caddies. Maybe he's driving another car today," Monkey said.

"We better be careful," Bepy told Red. "Maybe he's not in the joint yet. They told me he drives a blue Cadillac. I'll look through the window. If I wave, come with the sack and the pipe. Walk quick, but don't run. My wave means he's in there."

"Yeah, don't forget your pipe," Monkey reminded Red.

"Don't joke, Monk," Red said, acting a little nervous. "This guy's dealing with Mafioso." Turning to Bephino, he asked, "Do you know what he looks like?"

"Yeah. He's short and fat. They call him Fatman. I want the car parked over there, in front of the dry cleaner's, twelve feet from the hydrant. Keep your engine running. Don't leave if you hear shooting. Give us a chance to run to the car. OK, Monk?"

"Don't worry. I'll never leave you guys," Monkey answered.

"I know, kid. I know that." Bephino looked back at Monkey. "We'll be out in a minute. OK, let's do it."

Bepy strolled up to the café window. It was hard to see, but he made out a fat man's figure sitting at a table in the rear. He waved for Red to come. They walked in. Red tried to lock the door behind them, but it needed a key.

"I can't lock the door. It takes a key," he told Bepy.

"Fuck it. Let's move. Here's your nylon. Keep movin'."

Red paused when he saw a hanging sign on the table. It said CLOSED. He picked it up and hung it on the door to keep customers out.

"Come on," Bepy insisted. As they walked to the rear, they quickly slipped their nylon masks on. Bepy, walking fast, held his gun up to Fatman's face and said, "I'm glad to see you, Fatso. If you move, I'm going to blow your head off. Understand? Don't stop eating and don't move your eyebrows. I don't want to kill you, Fatso."

Fatman, eating Italian celery and wearing a napkin around his neck, began to choke at Bepy's words. Bepy spotted the appetizer on the table and figured there was another guy in the joint preparing the main course. So he had to wait and see who was in the kitchen.

Red ran behind the bar and scooped up all the loose change. He came across a money bag full of cash. Then he found a new blue .38 snubnose, and quickly threw it in the sack.

Bepy, with one eye on Fatman and the kitchen door and the other on Red, yelled, "I gotta have three fuckin' eyes with you. I told you to put yours in the sack and keep theirs handy. Don't let me have to make speeches, OK?"

Red, feeling stupid, put his empty gun into the sack and took the other out. He checked to see if it was loaded.

Bepy had been right. Suddenly, a guy walked out of the kitchen smiling and carrying a plate of hot fried shrimp.

"Ah, here's your cook, huh, Fatso? I knew you had a cook around here." Bepy ordered the cook to sit down and start eating the shrimp, or it would be his last supper.

"What's going on? What's goin'..." The cook realized the seriousness of the situation when Bepy pointed the gun at him. Quietly he sat down and began to eat.

"Don't make me kill you guys," Bepy said. "Be smart. Stay quiet."

Red moved into the kitchen. On his way to the back office, he opened drawers and closets. He found another bag of money in a drawer in the desk and two more loaded guns. He also found rolls of tens and twenties in a sugar can. He stuffed his jacket pockets with the green bills. He knew Bepy could not see him, so he took the opportunity to rob everyone, including Bepy. Quickly returning to the front room, he said, "OK. We got it all. Let's go."

Bepy said, "Hold it. Search this fat bastard. Get all his cash."

Red went into action again and found another big roll, enough to choke a horse. All hundred-dollar bills. Red's eyes opened with greed at the sight of the husky bankroll. He reluctantly put it into the sack. Bepy noticed Red's sluggishness, but was nervous and didn't detect disloyalty.

"Now get that diamond ring and his watch," he ordered.

Red also cleaned out the guy who was eating the shrimp. Bepy glanced at the simple-looking guy and told Red to give him back his wallet. "He can keep his money."

"How come?"

"Let him keep it, I said. He's only a poor bastard. Leave him alone. The guy's a fuckin' cook. Let him be, will ya?" he demanded.

"No, I'll keep it," Red insisted.

The cook was choking on his cud, he was so afraid to stop eating. His eyes darted from Red to Bephino. Bepy ordered him to go into the toilet and not come out or they would kill him. "I got three kids," the cook said. "Please don't shoot me. Keep my money. I didn't see nothing, right? All I do is cook here and clean up. I'm not connected. I got kids, pal. Please don't hurt me."

Red walked the guy into the men's room and whispered, "Lay down and don't come out. Fatman's in real trouble. Stay here for one hour or we'll kill you."

When Red returned, Bepy said to him, "Give the pipe a workout."

Trying to keep Fatman calm, he told him, "You're lucky. We were going to kill you today, but I'm only gonna whack you once or twice. So you can finish your *finocchio* in the hospital."

Fatman didn't know if he should feel relieved or not. He looked at Bepy as he pleaded, "Come on, fellas. You took the cash. Why you gonna bust heads for? There's no point in busting heads. Let's call it ev..."

Red slipped behind Fatman and hit him over the head. He crashed to the floor.

"Keep hitting him," Bepy ordered. "He's gotta be hurt real good. Cripple him good. I don't wanna look bad to my people."

Red belted the hell out of Fatso.

"OK. That's it. That's enough. Stop, for Christ sake! You don't follow orders, huh?" Bephino asked. "What the hell's wrong with you? I don't want him dead. That's two orders you ignored today."

"I was just warmin' up," Red said.

"Oh, yeah? Remember, scumbag, when I say that's enough, that's enough. Let's get the fuck out of here. Don't forget anything," Bepy reminded Red.

As they walked to the front, they saw two men reading the sign on the door. They tried the door, and when it opened, they entered.

"Holy shit. What now?" Red asked Bepy.

"Relax, don't panic! We'll do the same thing to them. We'll destroy these dumb bastards. They can't read; so we'll teach them." He told Red to get behind the bar. "Be cool, OK?"

"OK," Red answered. "But make it quick. I wanna get outta here."

As the two guys walked in, Bepy quickly trained his gun on them. "OK, boys. We've been waiting for you. Why are you late?"

One of them said, "Vot do you mean, late? Late for vot? We thought you vere closed."

"Oh, yeah? Then why did you walk in? Huh? Get the fuck over there and empty your pockets, ya stupid bastards, or I'll blow your heads off. And be fast," Bepy ordered.

Red dumped their wallets, cash, and jewelry into the sack with the other loot.

Bepy moved the men to the rear. They couldn't help but see Fatman on the floor in a pool of blood. He made them lie down near Fatman. "Stay down, be nice, and I'll spare your lives," he hissed. "Now, both of you Swedes put your hands in that pool of blood and play patty-cake with each other. Ya fuckin' dummies, next time read the sign. Come on, soak 'em good, fellas. That's nice. Get 'em bloody. Rub your faces, too."

Red asked Bepy in a low voice, "Why the hands in the blood? Whatta ya, crackin' up?" Bepy gave Red a look, but no reply.

The two men were afraid. They believed Fatman was dead and thought they were next. "Please, fellows, ve only stopped for a drink. Don't kill us," they begged.

"OK," Bepy hissed back through his nylon. "We won't hurt you, but don't move. Stay on the floor half an hour. If you get up, we will kill you." He turned to Red and began to walk fast toward the front.

"Come on, let's get out of here. Don't forget!" he yelled back. "If you guys move before a half hour, we have your wallets and we know where you live. You'll be hearing from us." Bepy and Red ran out the door and simultaneously removed their masks and gloves.

"Get this car moving."

"What the fuck took you guys so long? I almost ran out of gas. The fuckin' car was almost overheating. You guys took so long. How did it go?" Monkey asked.

"Perfect," Bepy answered. "Perfect. Drive nice; don't be reckless. Let's get home safe."

Red, with his pockets full of stolen cash, began his con job on Bephino. "Boy, that Bepy is cool. He's smooth. Every move he makes is just right. But I can't figure the hands-in-the-blood deal. How come ya did that?"

Bepy refused to answer Red; he was pissed off at him for insisting on taking the poor cook's money against his orders. After a while he spoke. "OK, drive slow. Drop me and Red off at his house. We gotta count up. Are your mother and father eating over at your grandmother's candy store tonight?"

"Yeah. The old lady's sick. They gotta help out. It gets busy when the evening papers arrive," Red replied. He took a deep breath before continuing. "I couldn't see givin' that cook back his wallet, Bep. You know what I mean?"

"No, I don't know what you mean. You took it; it's yours. Don't mention it anymore. I don't wanna talk about it. We ain't partners. You're a worker. You get what I give you. No profits; only pay. Fuck you, wise guy! Keep that poor guy's wallet, with pictures of his wife and kids. Who cares! You made your decision. Now I'll make mine. We go to your house and count up. Monk's gotta wipe all the prints off the car and dump it. Monkey, you should always wear gloves, like we do, especially in these hot cars. We can't afford to fuck up. From now on that's the rule. OK, Monkey? The cops go to the steering wheel first for fingerprints."

"Yeah, you're right. I'll rub everything off. Don't worry."

Everything had gone smoothly. The job made front-page headlines. Mr. Morrano was happy to learn Bepy was qualified to handle such matters. Because of Red's greed and refusal to follow orders, Bepy controlled the cash and also took the guns, to be held for the future. The total cash taken was just over twenty-one hundred dollars. Bepy kept fifteen hundred for the bank, and paid his men two hundred dollars each for their day's work. The balance was his pocket money. He went home and hid it in a closet in an old shoebox. So much money at one time was unbelievable! He had never seen such a pile of money in his life! His first big score. That night he couldn't sleep. But as the days passed, he began to adjust.

Red did very well for himself. He skimmed sixteen hundred off the deal, and no one knew it.

Bepy advised the boys not to spend the money loosely and not to be conspicuous about the change in their financial status. "Keep the nickel-and-dime look," he said.

Three days later the Don waved Bepy into the bar.

"Good morning, Mr. Morrano."

"Good morning, kid," the Don answered. "I like the way you handled that thing for me. Very nice and clean. I understand you did pretty good with the cash, huh?"

"Yeah, we did OK, Mr. Morrano."

"Sometimes you can make a good score on these jobs?" Morrano asked, his eyes wide.

Bepy tried to play low key on the amount of cash involved. "I know. I sure can use some scores. It's a nice opportunity for me, Mr. Morrano. I appreciate the work."

The Don smiled, crunching his cigar, "Yeah. Some bonus—about four grand worth. I said you could keep it, so it's yours. Now keep your nose clean. I call you again when I need you. You did a perfect job, Bephino. It couldn't have gone better. I'll be in touch with you."

"Yes, sir. You let me know when. I'm always ready." Bepy left quickly. He didn't want to talk further about bonuses or money. He heard four grand and he began to think: I wonder if Red pocketed some of that loot? We only counted twenty-one hundred, and that's a big difference from four grand.

3

After strong pressure from his father, Bephino took a part-time job at a meat market. Every day after school he cleaned up around the store and delivered orders.

His brother worked for a newspaper called *Brooklyn Empire*. He was a route planner, and he also unloaded the trucks. Mario was very bashful and at times had a slight stutter. But if he became upset or nervous, he could hardly talk and turned as red as a Chinese apple. He was a nice chubby kid, loaded with freckles. He was seventeen, two years older than Bepy. The other kids who worked at the paper were seventeen and eighteen, and most of them were tough guys who were envious of Mario's easy job.

One Monday evening Bepy was home early. In one of his rare quiet moments he was listening to "Superman" on the radio as he waited for dinner to be served. His mother was cooking one of his favorites, *carne polpetta e pasta*. Pasquale was washing up in the bathroom. He had just arrived home from the markets after ordering his week's fish.

Suddenly the door opened and Mario walked into the apartment. His face was covered with blood. Blood was coming from his mouth. Finametta started screaming, "Mario! What happened?"

Mario, between the blood and the stuttering, was a mess. He tried to speak, but he couldn't be understood.

Pasquale and Bephino ran into the kitchen. They saw Mario and began to yell, "What happened? What the hell happened?"

Pasquale, seeing the blood coming from his son's mouth, told him, "Rinse your mouth out with cold water until it is clear. And wash your face, so we can see what happened to you."

Finametta got Mario cleaned up and settled down. He had a bad cut in his mouth, but she managed to control the bleeding with an ice-packed washcloth.

Mario said, "A b-bunch of Irish kids from the newspaper j-jumped me. I'm going to get them tomorrow after school. I'm going to ge-get them one by one with a b-baseball bat over their skulls."

But Pasquale was fuming. "We got to get them now. Tonight, while it's fresh. They have to pay for this! Otherwise we can't sleep tonight."

"Them sons of bitches! They hit my brother," Bepy cursed. "I'm going to kill them for this." He patted Mario. They never got along too well, but they were brothers, and Bepy loved Mario. He wasn't kidding when he said he was going to kill for this. "Don't worry, Mario. I'll get them for you. I'm gonna get them for this. Tomorrow I'll take my gang there. Alley Oop will strangle them."

Pasquale was furious. He wanted vengeance that night, but he realized he couldn't go out and hurt kids only seventeen and eighteen years old. Being an adult Sicilian, he turned to his only immediate choice for revenge. "I want you to get them bastards! You get them *now*!"

It was like turning a wild dog loose. Bepy ran to the closet to get the only weapon in his mother's house, a hammer from his father's toolbox. With it, he ran down the steps two at a time to the street.

Finametta was screaming at Pasquale, "What are you doing? They will hurt Bepy, too. Don't let Bephino go. Please, Pasquale! He'll be hurt. Them boys are much bigger than him."

Pasquale was too upset to argue with her. "Bephino will get them. He'll get them for this."

"Pa-Pa-Papa," Mario said, shaking his head and trying to speak. "Don't let Bepy go. Them guys are big."

Bepy ran the six blocks to the newspaper office. He got there puffing and excited. He saw about eight boys sitting on tables smoking and spitting on the floor. They were laughing and kidding around.

Bepy, with blood in his eyes, ran into the office without saying a word and began to break heads with the hammer: direct hits, skull-crushing blows. He was out to kill. He ran from guy to guy like some kind of a wild beast. He was whimpering, "You hit my brother? You hit my brother?" in a low voice, almost like he was crying. The office was soon bloody. Everyone was screaming and trying to punch Bepy. The guys were running for their lives. Bepy got as many as he could. He was punched in the head a few times, but was not bleeding.

After the blood bath he walked home, hammer in hand. His father was waiting in front of the building for him. Pasquale, seeing Bepy messed up from a battle and the hammer covered with blood, said in a choked voice, "How'd you do?"

42

Bepy answered, "They want blood? I give them blood. I hit everybody in the office. Now there's plenty of their blood on the walls and floor. It's all over the place down there. How's my brother?"

"The bleeding stopped. He's OK. Let's go eat—the macaroni is ice cold."

"Tomorrow I know Mario's gonna go to that newspaper office and finish the job I started," Bepy said. "He'll beat the shit out of those guys. They caught him off guard; that's why he got hurt. I'm gonna take Alley Oop and the boys. We're gonna cripple them guys good tomorrow. Let's eat. I'm starved."

An hour later the doorbell rang. It was Mr. Johnson, the man who ran the newspaper office. He wanted to talk to Mr. Menesiero. Finametta greeted him and allowed him to enter the apartment. Pasquale and his sons were still sitting at the table. Finametta offered Mr. Johnson a piece of fruit. He politely refused.

"Why the war?" Mr. Johnson asked. "What happened to cause such a bloody war? My office looks like a hospital!"

Mario started to explain. Halfway through, Pasquale interrupted and said, "That's why Bephino had to do what he did. And that's why there was a war. Tomorrow Mario finishes the war that his younger brother started."

Mr. Johnson read the names of the boys hurt badly by Bepy. "They're all at the hospital getting stitches."

Mario, again trying to speak, began to stutter. They waited for him to get the words out. Finally, he said, "P-P-P-Papa . . . B-B-Bepy hit the wrong guys."

The table went silent. Finametta put her hands to her head, then put a bottle of Scotch on the table. She knew it was time. Mr. Johnson had a double in one gulp.

One day in October, Don Emilio Morrano sent for Bepy at the pool hall. He was most warm toward Bepy, and Bepy returned the warmth. The Don spoke. "Bepy, I want you to do something special. I need a kid with the balls of a giant but the size of a tough midget for this job, someone that I can trust to keep his mouth shut. Do you know where I can get such a guy? I believe you're my man, Bephino Menesiero."

"I got the balls but I'm five eight. I ain't no midget."

"Good. You're my man, Bephino." The Don grinned.

"Whatever you say, Mr. Morrano. You know I can handle it. Just tell me what you want me to do."

The Don smiled. "I want you to report to one of my soldiers in downtown Manhattan at ten tonight. He owns a café. He's doing something important for our family. *Ah capeesh,* Bepy?"

"*Si, io capeesh.*"

"You're to report to him and do whatever he says. He's a tough fellow, this Sally, so be careful. He'll instruct you on your duties. This is a sudden decision for me. It must be carried out tonight. It is very, very important for us to make sure it's done tonight. A lot of things depend on this."

"OK, sir. How much does this job pay? And who will pay me?"

The Don, surprised at Bephino's discussion of payment, nevertheless replied, "You get five hundred for your end. OK?"

"Yes, sir. That's fine."

"I guess you want it now, huh?"

Bepy smiled, "Yes, sir. I always like to get paid in advance."

"Why in advance?" the Don asked.

"Well, just in case I get knocked off, my mother will get my money. I keep it in a hiding place in my room, and she'll find it. If I can't have it, maybe she can enjoy it."

Don Emilio smiled again. "You're smart, Bepy. I like that. That's a reasonable answer. You're a kid who thinks about the future. I like that very much."

"But don't worry, Mr. Morrano. I'll do my job. I'd like to make some hits for big money. I'm interested in the big money."

The Don looked at the kid and said, "OK, Bepy. You'll get some big hits and the big money. Just keep it under control. Don't go too fast for me. You're kinda young; you got time. So go slow; be patient."

"Yes, sir. I'll wait a while."

The Don looked at Bephino and shook his head over the ambition of the boy. "The guy you report to is Sally DeMatteo. Like I said, he's a tough fellow, loud and rough. But he knows you're with me, so don't get scared. I told him to go easy on you. Sally is bad. He handles heavy stuff. You can learn from him. Listen and don't talk back; just learn.

"I promise you I won't get too scared," Bepy said jokingly. "I'm willing to learn all I can."

"And don't talk too much to them; they'll get weary of you. You're on a real big job this time. Don't let Sal worry about you. He gets nervous about young people. Sally is a very important man who's moving up in our organization, so have respect for him, OK? I repeat this to you because of the type of man Sally D is. I don't want you to get hurt, Bepy.

The guy has a very bad temper. Come to me when the work is done. We talk some more."

"OK, Mr. Morrano. I'll report to Sally tonight at his place. And don't worry, I would never embarrass you. I'll have respect for Sally D."

That evening, about ten o'clock, Bepy rode the subway to Manhattan. He was dressed sharp as a tack, wearing his dark blue suit, white-on-white shirt, white tie, black shoes, and his white suspenders.

When he tried to enter the café, the guy at the door refused to let him in because he looked too young. Bepy explained that he was there to see Sally DeMatteo. Sally came to the door. After some sarcastic questioning, he escorted Bepy toward his table. Bepy heard smart remarks about how he was dressed: "Is this kid with you, Sally? Is he your new bodyguard?" "Who's the little dapper, Sal?" "That's some suit he's wearing." Bepy felt like crawling under a table.

Sally replied to his men, "I don't even know this kid. He's with the old man. He was sent here personally by him."

Sally then looked over at Bepy and said, "Sit down, kid. And don't be afraid to wrinkle your suit."

The men quieted down as the band started up. The music was loud, and a girl came on the stage and danced to a sexy hot beat blowing from the band's horns—a Latin-style beat that matched the atmosphere.

Sally yelled over to Bepy to have a drink. "Kid, are you old enough to drink?" he joked. When Bepy ordered a Scotch sour, Sally told the waitress, "Give the little dapper a double."

"No, miss, please, only a single for me, thank you," Bepy told her. She smiled at him and nodded. "I'll make it a single," she whispered.

Bepy thought, Boy, these guys are full of smart remarks. Dapper? The waitress came back with the drinks and eyeballed him, but not knowing whose girl she might be, he didn't respond. He didn't want a knife in his back over a strange girl, even though he thought the waitress looked cute and tempting, very tempting.

The music had a seductive quality that made Bepy's blood perk. He kept staring at the dancers; then realizing he was being watched by the entire table, he looked away and sipped his drink.

The waitress asked him where he was from, but Bepy showed no interest or emotion. He remained quiet. Don Emilio had told him not to talk too much. He was there to do a job and had already gotten paid for it, and he was not going to get beaten up over some wet-lipped waitress.

Sally ordered another round. "Give the kid a double," he yelled out. He noticed that the waitress had the hots for Bephino, but the kid wasn't responding to her. Feeling good from the booze, he looked over at Bepy and in a snappy but drunken tempo blurted, "Whatsa matter, kid? You don't like girls? You keep looking away. How come?"

"Sure I like 'em. I love 'em. But tonight's not the night for this. We got business to take care of," he replied, trying to speak over the music.

"Oh-h-h, you got business to take care of, huh?" Sally said loudly, turning to his girl, who was seated next to him. "Listen to this, little pussy. He's got business tonight.

"Oh, tonight's not the night..." Sally continued taunting him. "What are you, on the rag? Or are you a little fag? That's a good one—the fag's on the rag."

"Come on, Sally, what rag?" Bepy responded. "Morrano sent me here to do something for you. Why are you pickin' on me?"

"Because you're full of shit, kid. With that fancy blue suit, you're a little cherry. I bet you never got laid," Sally boisterously shouted across the table. "He's probably still a cherry. I guarantee you this punk's a cherry."

Bepy smiled in embarrassment as everyone around the table began laughing at him.

Sally whispered to the girl sitting by his side. She was his personal girl friend, Anita, and it was understood they were getting married soon. She was Puerto Rican, beautiful and well built, with a perfect fine-featured face. A very sexy-looking lady. She seemed to be disturbed by what Sal was saying and argued heatedly with him. Sally began to shove her. He was drunk, but not drunk enough to be excused for his actions.

Sally told her in a rough voice, "Go ahead, I said. Cock-tease the kid. Let's have some laughs. Play around with him, Anita. Make him come in his pants."

She balked at the idea. "He's only a kid. Are you loco?"

The music was so loud Bepy couldn't quite hear all of what Sal was saying. His sense told him that Sal was trying to make a fool of him. The evening was no longer pleasant. Bepy felt like he was stripped naked. He began experiencing waves of anxiety.

Anita drank a straight double in one gulp and stood up. Curling her lips from the aftereffects of the drink, she looked over at Bepy. Public dancing was on. The band was playing a merengue, and the sound was enchanting. Excitement filled the place. Anita, looking back at Sally, reluctantly walked over to Bepy and began to rub her hands through his hair, saying, "Come on, sonny boy. Come to mama. Let's dance."

Bepy refused outright and smoothed his hair. "I don't feel like dancing."

The table burst into laughter, as she began rubbing herself all over him. Then she sat in his lap, saying, "You make me horny; you know that, honey? Come hold mama; dance with me." She was making a joke out of him.

Again, this time showing his annoyance, Bepy refused. But she kept on. Sally and his boys and the other girls were laughing so hard they had tears in their eyes. Seeing this, Bepy felt very small and very embarrassed. He gave in. The music was beautiful, and Anita definitely was beautiful. He thought, Fuck you, Sally. I'll squeeze your girl's ass around the dance floor until she gets tired. So a decision was made to play the Boss's game.

Bepy and Anita began to merengue. Her breath smelled of Scotch, and her eyes were glazed. The band went wild, and the music got hotter and hotter. It rang through the place with such excitement that everyone stood up to watch the dance floor. Bepy cut a fine figure and was a very good dancer. His rhythm enticed Anita. Sally's face paled as the crowd cheered. Bepy kept her moving smoothly to the beat, and she felt fine dancing with him. Gradually everyone began to grin at each other, confirming the wickedness of Anita's movements. She was shaking her ass and rubbing herself all over him, dancing away from him, then dancing back, pressing her body against him, rubbing her pussy on him. He could feel her pelvis digging at him. He was feeling so good that he almost totally forgot about Sally watching them.

"Your're a good dancer. You know that?" she whispered.

"So are you," he replied, kissing her ear.

Every time he faced Sally, he tried to back away from her, as a matter of caution. But when they were buried in the crowd, he let her know it wasn't Mickey Mouse she was dancing with. He rammed her between her loins, and she loved it. He grabbed her ass, and she loved that too. He pressed his throbbing dick to her and kept it throbbing between her thighs until her eyes confirmed his endowment. The crowd was so thick that Sally couldn't see them, and Anita knew this. She decided to enjoy being molested by this crazy kid. Her bright eyes spoke her thoughts. As she nonchalantly reached down and felt his crazy dick, her eyes widened with pleasure at the thickness of him. She looked deeply into his fiery eyes and saw a very horny boy. Watching her facial expression change to the feel of his prick, he smiled at her and whispered, "Come to daddy."

The music stopped, and they returned to the table. Bepy sat down quickly, trying not to expose his throbbing prick. Sally began acting even worse than before. He became more ruthless and senseless, because he was embarrassed by their erotic dancing but didn't want to reveal any weakness. He knew Bepy and Anita had enjoyed themselves. He had no choice but to show his friends that he could go all the way with his game. He continued coaxing her to play with Bepy to prove his decision right.

There were five other guys and five other girls at the table. Like one big happy family. The guy sitting next to Bepy seemed pleasant and told him he danced well. So Bepy, reaching for a friendly ear, asked, "Why is he pushing his girl on me? What the hell is he getting out of this?"

"Relax, kid. That's his way when he's drunk. He likes to make people look bad or punk. Just be cool. You'll be all right. Do whatever he says and you won't get hurt. Just do what he says and don't give him reason. Sally's rough people. Let him save face."

But Sally again pushed Anita around to Bepy's side of the table. This time, though, she wasn't so reluctant, and Sally detected it. She quickly grabbed Bepy's hand and said "Come on, let's dance, horny."

Being called "horny" annoyed Bepy, so he refused her—a bit too harshly. Sally raised his eyes and yelled, "Take him upstairs. Take the virgin upstairs!" He laughed, looking around the table for support for his madness.

She looked back at Sally, questioning his request. He repeated boisterously, "Yeah, take the punk upstairs. See if he's a man." Sally was sorry for that remark. He was also testing Anita, to see how she'd react. And she definitely failed the test. She was too eager.

She blurted out, "Come on, Bepy. Take me upstairs." Then she whispered, "I've got a hot cat for you."

Bepy, disgusted with the whole situation, thought, Hot cat? The cunt finally blew her class. She's got a hot cat for me. I got news for her. I'll fuck her brains out. That's what I'll do. Then, looking at her smiling at him, he thought, Look at her sweaty face. She's in heat. She really expects me to go up there and fuck her? What the hell's wrong with these people? Look what I'm involved in!

Sally yelled across the table at him, "Let's see if you've got a cock. Check him out, Anita." Sally watched Anita's eyes for her reaction. Everyone at the table looked away in embarrassment, but they still laughed, so as not to displease Sally. He was in too deep, and everyone knew it.

In a last effort to stop the game, Bepy spoke out angrily to Sally across the table. "I'm here for business. When does it start?"

The guy next to him touched his arm and whispered, "Look, kid, when Sally gives the orders, we move. Don't mess with him. He'll hurt you. Let him make a punk out of you. Keep quiet. You keep talking like that, you'll wind up flying off the roof tonight. Be calm. You'll live longer."

48

"What am I supposed to do?" Bepy asked him. "Go upstairs and fuck his Spanish fly girl to keep him happy?"

"Are you crazy, kid? Just play along and don't be stupid. You fuck her, you're dead. You'll never see tomorrow."

Feverishly, Bepy thought the situation over. Looking around the table, he saw everyone was still laughing. The beautiful Spanish woman's white teeth were glittering at him, like a dream that was really happening. The laughter, almost at screaming pitch, rang through his ears. A cold sweat seeped through his skin. It had become a matter of respect or disrespect. There was that very thin line staring at him, and he knew it. His predicament was serious, so he made a decision. I'm gonna fuck her. Then I'll kill that big-mouth bastard. That's the only way to handle this prick. I'll hump his spick girl in her ass! Then I'll wack that fuckin' screwball. I'll tell Mr. Morrano the way he treated me tonight. He'll understand.

Anita had moved onto Bepy's lap, coaxing him to take her upstairs. Bephino's nerves were shattered. He was upset; he had made a very tough decision too quickly. Are these people nuts? he thought once again, trying hard to escape from a bad dream. Look at this shit. The guy's a big man. He wants me to hump his girl. I don't believe this. How did I ever get involved this deep?

Anita was now moving him to the open stairwell. Sally, unaware of Bepy's decision, was still laughing at the kid. Bepy reluctantly let himself be dragged to the pad upstairs, acting unwilling and moving slowly.

With her beautiful Spanish smile showing her perfect white teeth, Anita kept looking back at Bepy. She whispered in broken English, holding his hand like he was a little boy, "Mama only gonna play with you. You'll be OK, honey. I won't hurt you, honey." This turned his stomach further, so he glared at her.

In the apartment above, he looked her over and noticed that she was wearing a tight two-piece knitted dress. No bra, no panties, he knew from feeling her up on the dance floor. The apartment was hot and had only a small bulb lit in one corner of the room. Bepy never imagined he would be in such a situation with a Mafia leader's woman, the guy, half crazy from booze, sitting downstairs drinking. He felt uneasy and vulnerable, and in a highly dangerous position. Yet he had made his decision.

He put a chair behind the door to discourage anyone from coming in. The minute they approached the bed area, Anita moved into his arms, kissing him like a barracuda. She was all tongue. He responded to her love-making with manhandling moves. He knew she liked his touch. He kissed her passionately, then in one motion pulled her sweater up over her head and off. Her tits were huge, hard and sweaty. Her body was wet and slick from the mounting tension. She seemed to be relieved to have her top off. She sighed and kissed him again. There was no stopping now. She began to grunt anxiously and make passionate sounds. He reached down under her skirt, and she whimpered as his fingers deeply entered her moist cunt.

She began to whisper to him in Spanish. Her hot breath mixed with Scotch was sexy. He paused and stared at her as she fondled her own breasts passionately and sighed. Unfortunately, he was in a hurry, probably the biggest hurry of his life. Otherwise he would have watched her play with herself all night. It was a pretty sight to see. She was so hot and erotic-looking. But he had to move quickly. It was his big chance to get even with the scumbag downstairs. He removed his jacket and pants in one quick motion, leaving his shoulder holster and shirt on. He raised her tight skirt fully above her plump ass, exposing her black hairy cunt. He stood throbbing between her thighs.

Unexpectedly, she balked, her eyes flashing at the door, but only momentarily. The fear of Sally must have entered her mind, until she felt his huge warm organ slip deeply between her thighs, rubbing feverishly between her swollen lips of love. Anita stepped back for a moment, just to admire his enormous erection. She touched it with grinning pleasure, stroking and admiring him. Then, grasping at his balls as he also nervously watched the door, she lost all control. The whole ball game had gone beyond everyone's expectations. Lying on the bed, she urged on his passions. He crawled to her. Unsophisticatedly, she directed his organ in deeply, speaking passionate love words to him. Bepy mounted her like a young stallion and took full command. Anita's eyes shown white as he thrust harder and harder. "I'm coming," she whispered. "I'm coming. My God!" She felt his warm juices mix with hers. Her eyes dilated as she entered oblivion. He gave her all he had, ramming hard into her slurping nest. She was half out of her mind with passion. With her face drooling wetness on the pillow, she had the expression of an incoherent nymph.

Half over her body, pushing himself upward and looking at her, Bepy whispered, "Not bad for a cherry, huh?" He would never forget this unexpected erotic experience of fear mixed with orgasm.

After the tremors subsided, Bepy quickly dressed. Anita, watching him, asked him to do it again. "Bepy," she whispered, "please, again. Let's make love again."

"Are you nuts?" he replied. "That fuckin' dog downstairs is probably having puppies by now."

She sat up in the bed and began fondling her breasts seductively, trying to entice him. It looked beautiful to him, but he really had to go.

He headed for the door, and never looked back at her. Holding his jacket in his arms, he intentionally exposed his shoulder holster, and he purposely waited to raise his suspenders over his shoulders until he walked down the stairs in view of the occupants of Sally's table. This enabled the people who had been laughing at him so heartily to read between the lines and form their own opinion of him. And that was just what they did. There was a great pause and complete silence at the table. Their opinion of Bephino Menesiero was formed: the kid had to be totally nuts. He had defied Sally DeMatteo; he had fucked Anita; and he had crossed the Mafia's very thin line between respect and disrespect. Bepy's eyes darted around the table and showed no emotion.

Sally stared directly at him and said nothing. No more laughter. Not a word. Bepy straightened his shirt and tie at the table, always keeping his hand in the area of his shoulder holster and his .38 snubnose. He watched carefully, hoping against hope that he had made a livable decision. Sally kept his eyes on him. He gave him the look of death. The guy sitting next to Bepy got up and changed his seat.

The waitress offered Bepy another drink. He accepted and became a little more relaxed. She was smiling warmly at him, and he nervously returned a quick smile, but he was feeling very much alone.

About ten minutes later, Anita came down the stairs, trying to look like a girl who hadn't been fucked. But it was impossible. Bepy looked up at her and sipped his drink and waited for his orders from Sally. He began to think about the stunt he pulled. He had fucked the headman's woman, and no comment had been made, yet. Sally stared at Anita, looking like he was about to blow up, but he did nothing.

Then, sending all the girls away, Sally spoke in a low voice. "We had a terrible disturbance here tonight, but I can't let it interfere with our important business. We'll settle it later on. Let's get this thing over with." He pointed to Bepy with an evil look in his eyes, "The old man wants you to go into the bra factory on 4th Avenue like the little fuckin' worm that you are. He wants you to crawl around like a worm and sneak through a vent; go to the second floor; come down the stairs, and open the door for us. If anybody grabs you, tell them you're looking for a girl or something." Sally's face changed, red with embarrassed anger as he said the word *girl*, betraying the fact that he was bitter about his failed efforts to exploit Bephino as a cherry. He continued his instructions. "We will be outside waiting for you. Let us in the building, and we'll do the rest. Don't fuck up like you already did tonight. I'll deal with you another time over your little episode with Anita. She'll tell me exactly how you acted toward her. I promise you, punk, this evening will not be a loss to me. Your fuckin' virtue belongs to me now."

Bepy, trying to change the subject, asked, "What do you guys have to do in there?"

Sally whispered, with a false grin, "Kill Pete Lungo. He's ordered dead. He's in room 208. That's his office. He always works nights because his factory is open all night. So we know he's there. The old man wants him dead tonight, so he can't attend a meeting tomorrow on Long Island. OK, Bephino, any more questions? Now you know everything that's going on. . . . In other words, Bephino, you know too much. *Tu capeesh?*"

"*Io capito tutto, molto bene, Signore Salido,*" Bephino replied, starring back in defiance.

Bepy realized that Sally had told him too much for a good reason—probably to have an excuse to knock him off, too. A real boss, he thought, would never talk so vividly about such matters. Maybe he'd tell Morrano the kid had to go. He knew too much, so they had to hit him, too. Bepy had to devise an alternate plan, to detour Sally's brain, so he would think differently about Bephino's life.

It was 2:00 A.M. The café was closing. Sally spoke. "OK, let's go do it. Get the door open for us, Befumo—or whatever the hell your name is."

Bepy got in their car, and they drove to the factory. They dropped him off and pointed out the building and the doors they wanted opened. Bepy moved around to the alleyway and looked for the air vent. He was also thinking about his nice blue suit. He didn't want to ruin it climbing through a vent, but the job must be done, and tonight.

He spotted a window on the second floor with a light on. Three windows over from that room was a room that was dark, with a window open. It was hot for October, like Indian summer.

The open window was a lucky break for the blue suit. There would be no crawling through a vent. Bepy easily climbed up the drainpipe to the second floor and through the window. Once inside, he got himself straightened out. He was unable to see his way very well, but he moved slowly toward the light that crept under the door from the hall outside.

Once in the hallway, instead of going down to open the doors for Sally, he walked quietly down the hall, looking for room 208. He spotted the door and walked in. A man was sitting behind a desk. Bepy said, smiling, "Excuse me, sir, I'm looking for a Mr. Pete Lungo."

The man said, "I'm Pete. But who let you in here?"

Bepy pulled out his gun and moved toward the man quickly. "Mr. Lungo, I'm not here to kill you, only to rob you. Don't make a sound or I will be forced to kill you. I want all your money now, and fast. If you move or make a sound I'll pump lead. Simple as that. OK, Pete, get the fuckin' money out fast."

Pete looked shocked. "Don't shoot. Don't be stupid. Do you know who I am? I'm a capo, I'm Pete Lungo. Don't fuck up, kid. I'm heavy stuff."

"You're heavy stuff and I'm a fuckin' gypsy," Bepy answered. "Just give me your money and you will remain a capo. If you don't give me enough cash, I'm gonna kill you now. Believe me, mister, I'll kill you. So don't fuck with me."

"OK, OK. I'll give you plenty of money. Don't do anything crazy."

"OK, Pete, I'm waiting. Hurry up. No sudden moves. Hurry but no funny stuff. I'll start shootin' if you pull shit."

Pete's moves were quick but seemed like slow-motion. He opened a box and took out several bundles of bills. "Here," he said, "that should keep you happy. There's six grand there."

Bepy stuffed the cash in his pocket. "Now empty your pockets. Give me your rings, watch, and wallet." Pete stared at him, trying to show Bepy he was making a big mistake, but he handed everything over. Bepy stuffed the jewelry into his pocket with the money. "OK, Pete, lie down on your belly. I'm going to tie you up."

Pete, a bit relieved, lay down on his belly. Bepy took Pete's jacket off the chair and covered the gun to muffle the sound. He placed the gun close to Pete's head and quickly pumped two shots through it. The sound was not too noticeable. Bepy then pulled Pete's pockets inside out to make it look more like a robbery.

He left the building fast, wiping doorknobs on the way out and opening the front door of the factory by kicking the safety bars. Then he walked across the street where Sally was parked. He had figured that if he killed Pete himself, he would take away Sally's opportunity for revenge. Sally would not be able to justify a hit on Bephino to Morrano. Because Bepy had done the hit himself, he couldn't talk about it, so there would be no reason for Sal to justify a hit on him. It was insurance for Bepy, something he had to do to stay alive. He had to keep Sally off balance and in his night of confusion. Bepy was pretty young to have gotten himself into a position to commit murder.

As he reached the car, Sally got out, saying, "Get the fuck in the car and wait for us. We'll be out in a minute."

"It's all over, Sally," Bepy told him excitedly. "I knocked off Pete while I was in the building. It's all taken care of. Let's get out of here. Come on, let's go before we're seen."

"Are you bullshittin' me?" Sally asked. Enraged, he turned to his boys. "If this kid's bullshittin' us, what a time to get shitted."

"Look, Sally, I don't bullshit. I shot him twice in the head. I took care of it. I was there, so I saved you the trouble. Let's say you owe me one, OK? Now let's get out of here before the cops come."

Sally stared at the kid in astonishment. "I hope you realize how important this hit was tonight, you impudent little bastard. You got no respect," Sally yelled. "Are you sure it was Pete Lungo you hit?"

"Yeah, I'm sure."

"Are you sure he's dead?"

"His fuckin' brains are all over the floor. What do you think? Do you wanna go check his heartbeat?"

"I hope you're not a bullshittin' kid, that's all I hope."

Bepy looked at Sally's face and said coldly, "You know I don't bullshit, don't you, Sally?"

"Get in the fuckin' car and let's go," Sally yelled angrily.

They all jumped in the car and drove away.

"Would you believe this? I gotta explain this shit to Morrano—that this fuckin' kid made the actual hit. Do you believe this? This fuckin' kid's a curse on me tonight!"

Bepy started talking. "The old man sent me here, right? I must know what I'm doing then. You wanted Pete dead. So now he's dead. The job is done. How come you're still complaining? Go tell Morrano I did it for you. Go tell him I did everything for you tonight."

Sally reached over the back seat and grabbed Bepy by the throat. "I oughta kill you right now, you little bastard. I oughta..." Then Sally released him and became very quiet. His boys seemed pleased the job was already done, and they made no comments.

Fixing his shirt and acting strong, Bepy asked "Are we all done now? Can we go home?"

"Yeah, we can go home. But are you sure you hit Pete Lungo? That's all I gotta know. I gotta be sure," Sally shouted.

"If he shows up at Long Island tomorrow, I'll give you a refund," Bepy answered, maintaining his position of strength against Sally.

"Ya know, punk, I gotta kill you. Maybe not tonight, but I gotta kill you. You're a wise little bastard. You got me confused bad tonight, but I'm gonna think better tomorrow, Bephino," Sally threatened. "And you can bet your ass you're a dead little punk!"

"Drop me off at the nearest subway to Brooklyn," Bepy answered. "The guy's as dead as a doornail, Sally. He's got a fuckin' hole in his head the size of Anita's cu... Two holes he's got in his head, two holes not one. And you're still worrying about it? Drop me off, I'm going back to Brooklyn."

The guys in the car were snickering at Bepy's remarks. One said, "This fuckin' kid's nuts. Drop him off fast. He's a fuckin' wacko."

As the car pulled up to the curb to let Bepy out, he made this last declaration. "Sally, remember how you treated me tonight. You provoked me into the entire ordeal. You're a big man, but you're not a respected man. And you can bet your ass I think I'm gonna kill you before you kill me." He ran quickly down the subway stairs. Sally stared into the night as the car pulled away from the curb.

Two days later Bepy reported to Don Emilio. The Don embraced him. Bepy was proud he was being honored by the Boss. The Don spoke. "Bepy, I heard you handled it yourself perfectly. I heard all about it. You're a proven man now. The newspapers say it was a robbery. So it doesn't reflect on us. Everyone thinks he was robbed and killed by a burglar."

"Mr. Morrano, he was robbed," Bepy said. "I did rob him before I killed him. I cleaned him out."

The Don looked at Bepy and smiled, "I know your style. You robbed him. Good for you. That's a good style; you combine things to work out for you and me. Very nice, Bephino. Oh, Sally DeMatteo came to Brooklyn yesterday. He told me you made the hit against his orders. He made a big speech. He was very upset with you. He threatened to kill you. But I told him to forget it, because you're under my protection. I heard you annoyed his girl. Is this true?"

"Yes, sir, it's true. But he asked me to in front of everybody, so I obliged him. He forced her on me. He tried to make me look punk and *that* I won't let anyone do. I didn't want to hurt his feelings. So I porked her one time."

Morrano laughed. "You porked her? What d'ya mean? Sounds like you had a very busy night over there, my boy. You better go slow, I told you to go slow. You're becoming too old too fast, Bephino. These people will come after you. They'll sneak around us and hurt you. We don't want you in that position. I'll talk to Sally again about this. I didn't know it was that serious. I'll try and make peace for you."

"Yeah. While you're at it make peace for him, also." Bephino said, smiling.

Book II
1945–1947

4

Bephino had achieved young "hit man" status. He fulfilled a duty that beckoned him from his family past. He was accepted in the eyes of the Mafia as a person commanding respect—a proven killer at such an early age. Destined to take the ruthless way of life, he began his two lives.

Schooldays were not pleasant for Bepy, Monkey, and Red. The school they attended was getting ready for graduation exercises, and all the kids in the neighborhood were excited. Parents were buying new suits and dresses for their children to attend the prom and graduation. Signora Finametta Menesiero spoke to her son Bephino during dinner one evening.

"When are you going for your graduation suit, Bepy?" she asked.

Bepy kept eating his *pasta lendica* to avoid answering. Then, trying to con her, he said, "Boy, Mama, I really enjoy your *pasta lendica.* You're the best cook around. *Lendicas* are good for us, right, Mama?"

Pasquale stopped eating for a moment and said, "I taught your mother how to cook. She couldn't fry an egg when I met her."

Finametta, taking up her own defense, said, "I was a very young girl when I married your father. But I learned fast."

Bepy hoped the subject of graduation was over. But he was wrong.

Finametta once again asked, "Bepy, I asked you about your graduation suit. I saved the money for you myself, so you can pick out something nice. Huh, Bepy? You always like to be a 'sharpy.' Maybe a nice brown plaid suit, like your cousin Jerry got."

"Mama, I don't need a suit."

"Why not?"

"Because I'm not invited to the graduation exercise or the prom. So I don't need a suit. We're lucky. We save money, Mama," Bephino said.

"Lucky? We save money? What do you mean, not invited to the exercise and prom? I don't understand this. Everybody and their families go to see their children graduate. We went to see Mario graduate. He looked so beautiful on the stage. Me and your father were so proud of him."

"Mama, I know. But I'm different from Mario."

Mario quickly interrupted. "Thank God, I'm not like you, Bepy."

Bepy answered back. "Thank God, I'm not like you, Blubber."

"You know, Bepy. You know why you don't do good in school?" Mario taunted.

"Why? Why, Fat, why?"

"Because you're too busy, plowing that Margie, that's why."

Pasquale hit the table and said in a loud voice, "When I finish my espresso, I speak to Bepy about this school business. OK, Finametta? Now, everyone be quiet. We gotta eat. I don't want no *acido*."

Finametta obeyed but started crying while she ate, sobbing that Bepy was her cross. She kept repeating, "This boy, he always has a surprise for me." She said she couldn't take it anymore, she was getting sick. "All my nieces and nephews they graduate!" she lamented. "But not my youngest son! He's gonna be a big shot!"

After dinner was over, Pasquale, chomping on a toothpick, spoke to Bepy. "What do you mean you're not invited to the graduation or prom? Are you getting promoted or not? You're almost sixteen!"

"Papa, I made a good deal with the principal. He said he could leave me back because I'm a borderline case. But if I agreed not to attend the prom or the graduation, he would help me go to a high school of my choice, if they accept me. I asked him why can't I at least attend the graduation activities. He said I'll get into a fight or make trouble. The guy is nuts. I never fight. I'm too busy learning in school to fight. He's a Jew, and don't like Italians. He thinks Italians like to fight all the time."

Pasquale slowly removed the toothpick and, squinting his eyes, asked, "Are you the only one who made this deal with the principal?"

"Yeah. I made a good deal, huh, Papa?"

Suddenly, Pasquale moved in for the kill. Finametta screamed, "No, no, you'll ruin his beautiful nose! Please don't hurt him. You're too rough! You hit too hard. Leave him alone, Pasquale."

Despite her pleading, Bepy caught two good punches to the head and was dazed. Normally, he would fight back, but it was his father throwing the punches, and Bepy was prepared to take the beating with honor. He would never raise his hands to his father or mother. That's the Italian way. *Ah respecto.*

Finametta excitedly washed the blood off Bepy's lips and looked him over, checking his ears and eyes, as only a mother would do, and secretly admiring her son's face. She asked him, "So whosa this Margie you plowing around with, *figlio mio?* And what does this plowing mean?"

Bepy looked at his mother and said, "Don't listen to Mario, Mama. He's nuts. He's a joke! He better go on a diet. He split his new pants yesterday."

Two weeks later, Bepy, Monkey, Alley Oop, and Red were talking about high schools. Monkey asked, "What school you going to, Bepy?"

"My father's on the warpath. He don't want me to go to New Mountain. He says I gotta be a tailor like Mario. My brother goes to Eastern Needle Trade High in Manhattan, so I gotta go, too," Bepy replied.

"Are you kiddin'? You a tailor? I don't believe you. You're gonna be a hit man—not a tailor."

"What ya talkin' about, hit man?" Bephino yelled. "I'm only sixteen years old. I could be a famous tailor someday. What d'ya think of that? I'd only take a hit for the big dough involved. We gotta be financially strong. We gotta get out of this fuckin' gutter. It's choking me. We may have to step over a few people on the way up, but we got no choice." Then he lowered his voice. "It's a business. As far as the school goes, I ain't got no choice. My father is still the boss, and I love him. I gotta keep the peace, even though I don't think it will work out. But I'm gonna give it a try. At least I gotta do that for my ol' man."

"Yeah, I understand," Monkey replied. Then, looking over at Red, he asked, "How'd ya like to book a bet that this guy becomes a tailor. Make odds for me; I'll take any odds. You, too, Alley Oop; give me a bet. I say he lasts two weeks in a sewing class. Make odds."

Red smiled at Bepy. "Monkey's right. It's a good bet."

"Hey, look, our business still goes on as usual. When I get the call, we go into action. Nothing is changed. We gotta keep the business going. We got more contracts coming, and that's where the money is. Look, fellas, we committed our services to the big guy. The contracts are good business for us. We're gonna hit guys that are rotten bastards anyway, scumbags. We're doing our country a favor. Mr. Morrano keeps Brooklyn clean. Right?" Bephino reassured his friends, then asked, "Am I right, Red?"

Red didn't reply. He looked over at Monkey.

"Yeah, Mr. Morrano don't like scumbags in our neighborhood. I'm with you, Bep," Alley Oop said. Pointing to Red, Alley Oop continued, "These fuckin' Milanese are afraid to commit themselves."

During the next weeks, Bepy attended Eastern Needle Trades High School in Manhattan. He traveled by subway alone, while Mario traveled to the same school with his girl friend, Gloria. Mario didn't want his brother around, because he liked to keep Gloria bullshitted and Bepy might say the wrong thing. But Bepy understood.

Traveling alone on the subway can be quite an experience in New York. The subway from Brooklyn to Manhattan was another world in itself. Some of the people who used the subways were of such unique character a zoologist could watch them move through the crowded trains for hours, like busy ants traveling back and forth, looking and staring at one another. There were little old ladies and big old men and, of course, mothers stuffing chewing gum in their kids' mouths to keep them from vomiting.

There were tough hoodlums and religious groups of all faiths and nationalities sitting or standing next to beautifully exotic people from all over the world, including gay blacks, gay Orientals, gay Jews, even some very suave, three-piece-suited gay Italians from Milano, with umbrellas under their arms, all traveling on New York subways.

The early-morning scene was the same every day. The rocking trains were crowded with commuters, people going to work or school, guys meeting their girl friends to go to work together. And the subway had a special magic, like music, that churned some people's groins to follow their demented brains. The groper—a special breed—would pick out a pretty girl standing alone, and she would become his morning glory or his morning prey. He would maneuver through the crowd, always apologizing and smiling, but constantly moving toward her. Then there was the female groper, who sits and waits for her prey to come to her. Sometimes, if your luck was running bad, you would get stuck with a male groper, instead of a horny lady groper, trying to pet your cock. So a subway ride was all part of growing up in beautiful New York City.

One day, Bepy was in the boys' room when a tall blond fellow entered. He was at least six four and hugged a basketball.

"Hi, guy." A voice loaded with femininity echoed through the tiled room.

Bepy looked up at the blond giant staring at him, not knowing what to say. "Hey, what's up, blue eyes?" he finally asked.

The guy, who was smiling broadly, holding the ball to his chest, replied, "I hope you're up."

Bepy glanced around. "Today's one of them days, isn't it?"

"Yessss, it sure is, isn't it?"

Bepy smiled then said smoothly, "Sorry, Blue Eyes, I'm late for my sewing class."

Accustomed to the schools in Brooklyn, he hated this new school. It was eighty percent black. Suddenly, he was a minority and didn't like the idea. He missed all the crazy guys in Brooklyn. They all hung around the candy store and ate meatball sandwiches and sausage heroes, while he was now with total strangers, wearing an apron like a shoemaker. It was another world for him. His friends all had short nicknames. But these guys had proud names, like important politicians. John Earl B. Valentine, Charlton Theodore J. Washington, Oby Lee Williamston, and

Robert Livingston Parkinson were among his new classmates. At this school, Bephino had no support, no friends. It was like being stranded in a concrete jungle. He hated the atmosphere.

One day a boy told Bepy, "Hey, you guinea bastard, suck my dick. Come on. Suck my dick, I said."

"OK," Bepy replied, "Take it out! Take it out."

The boy turned and ran like the wind, with Bepy doggedly pursuing him with a knife.

The next day war was declared by the blacks. The few Jews were worried. Three of them were talking excitedly after being jumped in the boys' room. "Who started this war and why? They threaten to kill all the whites in the school. The percentages are against us," one boy insisted.

Bepy, trying to rally the Jewish kids to fight back, replied, "We can beat them! Fuck the percentages and fuck them niggers. Who the hell do ya think started it? Let's get our men together and finish it. We can fight them," he yelled, "even on their turf."

A vote of confidence was not in the cards. They explained to Bepy. "We're only twenty percent of us white. We can't win in an all-out war. We don't have the numbers. How could we win? The percentages are against us."

"We're entitled to protection, aren't we?" one boy asked.

"You're entitled to shit," Bepy yelled in disgust. "That's what you're entitled to. Ya want protection, ya gotta fight for it."

But they were reluctant to rally behind him, insisting that the school should be made responsible for handling the matter. And Bepy knew they were right about the percentages. The rhythm was missing for a victory. He knew he needed some Brooklyn boys for support. He couldn't handle this battle alone, and he realized he was about to face his first disaster in that school.

From then on, Bepy carried a gun to class. He had to piss in corners outside the building. On one occasion two black guys had jumped him in the toilet. He battled them for fifteen minutes. He was a good street fighter, and although he got punched around and beaten up, he got lucky and hurt one of them badly. The fight was finally broken up by other boys, and classes resumed, but the uptown boys were still on the warpath. They spread the word through the school that they were going to get him after school and kill him. He was threatened all day. The blacks walked through the halls during class changes yelling, "We'll be waiting for you, Guinea!"

When school let out, Bepy hid in the building, trying to stay calm. He looked out the window and saw an army of them waiting for him.

Sneaking into one of the vice-principal's offices, he called Red. There was no answer. He called Red's girl friend to see if he was over there. Red usually banged her after school, either at his house or over at her house before her mother came home from work. Norma answered and said he had gone to the poolroom about fifteen minutes ago.

"How come he's not there with you today, Norma? I need him bad."

"Because I got my friend. It's that time of the month," she replied.

"Norma, do me a favor. Run to the poolroom and get Red to call me at this phone number right away! I'm in real trouble. Please do it now. It's important. I'll wait by this phone. Hurry. I'm in real trouble."

"But I'm all padded up. I got cramps. I can't . . ."

"Hey, Norma," Bepy interrupted her, "fuck the pad and the cramps. Get Red for me *now*. Don't talk stupid. Hurry! It's a matter of life or death. Some niggers wanna kill me."

"OK, Bepy, I'll go. Stay by the phone, and I'll run and get him."

"Thanks, Norma."

It was four o'clock in the afternoon. Bepy felt very alone in the empty school. Even though he packed one of the guns he had stolen from Fatman's café, he knew he had only six bullets. There must be forty or fifty guys outside. They knew he was in there hiding. But he didn't want to shoot one of them in front of the whole mob. He was too smart for that.

Fifteen minutes went by, but it seemed like hours. The phone rang. Bepy quickly picked it up. Red said, "What's the emergency, Bepy? What niggers wanna kill you?"

"Red! I'm fucked good over here. Fifty niggers are waiting for me outside the school. I'm on the uptown side of the building. I'm watching from the window. They're doing a fuckin' war dance now. The only entrance still open is on this side. All the other doors are locked. Get as many guys as you can. Quick! Bring your guns, pipes, pool sticks, and come and get me out of this fuckin' place before the drums stop. When I see you pull up in a car, I'll come out shooting. OK, Red? Make it quick, before these coons eat me alive."

"We'll be right there, Bepy. Don't worry. As long as they keep dancin', you'll be OK," Red replied.

Forty minutes later three cars pulled up to the school. Bepy saw his friends from Brooklyn piled one on top of another in the cars. Pool sticks were hanging out the windows. Even the older guys from the neighborhood were there—guys twenty and twenty-one years old from the Fort Hamilton poolroom. It was a sight to see.

Look at them bums, Bepy thought. They're beautiful. He felt good; his friends had come for him. He owed Red for this one. As planned, he ran out with his gun blazing. He was like Billy the Kid. He wasn't trying to hit anyone, but to let them know Bephino Menesiero was packing. It was unbelievable how fast everyone could run.

The next day, after hearing about the trouble, Pasquale agreed that Bepy would not be a tailor, or a shoemaker, or a violin player. He had had dreams of his sons becoming tailors or shoemakers, and at one time he had asked Bepy to learn the violin. He always said, "Back in the Old Country, the tailors and shoemakers never went hungry. And I lika the violin."

But Bepy had different dreams. He wanted to be in big business and big money, and he was not afraid to do whatever it took to get there. He remembered how the Italians were pushed around in New York City in the early years and he never forgot the hurt look on the faces of his parents. The Italian people were said to have been treated like rubbish by the other ethnic groups. Bepy wanted his life to be different. His father worked so hard pushing a cart and selling fish in the neighborhood. After pushing the cart all day in the hot sun, in the ninety-six degree heat, he might have earned only two or three dollars.

"What do you think happened?" Bepy said to Alley Oop as they reminisced one afternoon. "An Irish cop gave my father a two-dollar ticket for pushing his cart on the wrong part of the gutter. Ain't that some shit? That's the way life's been for some Italians, Alley. But not for us! Remember that, Alley, not for us! There's a few men, like Mr. Morrano, who don't take any shit! You know what they push, Alley? They push big-titted women and fine wines. And that's the pushing I wanna do."

"I think ... that's what I want, too, Bepy. Same as you. No pushcarts for us." And they shook hands on that.

In 1946, as Bepy was approaching seventeen, he got himself a job as an office boy in a Wall Street brokerage firm. His salary was thirty-nine dollars per week. The senior partner was Giuseppe Gustini, a very rich Italian from Rome. He was in charge of the International Division of Jules Hart and Company and took a liking to Bepy, and Bepy had great respect for him. Bepy had quickly realized that the brokers worked at a hectic pace, so he knew that extra speed would be appreciated. In order to impress them more, he would come into the office twenty minutes early every day to sharpen all the discarded pencils he had collected. He even straightened up the brokers' desks and filled their pencil holders before the opening of the stock market. He liked his job and wanted the brokers to think well of him.

One day Mr. Roberts, one of the partners, asked bluntly, "Who the hell is sharpening these damn pencils?"

Bepy replied, "I am, sir. It's a shame to waste good materials."

"I'm glad somebody is using his head on Wall Street. Give the boy a five-dollar raise," he ordered Bernie Melvin, office manager, who was Bepy's immediate supervisor. Bernie Melvin grunted to Bepy, "Ha, you're becoming a big shot already. So now you're in the pencil business."

Bepy looked straight at the little eyes behind the heavy horn-rimmed glasses sitting on a head that reminded him of a dwarf egg and said, "Mr. Melvin, why don't you like Italians? Tell me, will you?"

Melvin nearly crawled out of his baggy wool suit and under a nearby desk, because he suddenly remembered that the senior partner was from Rome. With his small hand, he patted Bepy on the head. "I'm only playing with you, boy. Don't be so loud already."

Bepy smiled knowingly at him.

Two weeks later, an insurance company bonding report came down to Melvin from Personnel. The report read, "Bephino Menesiero is a possible risk to the firm. He was kicked out of school for fighting..." Melvin proudly presented the notice to Ziggy Faulgaten, who was a junior partner.

Faulgaten, originally from Germany, read the report and immediately decided that Bepy would have to leave the firm. The report made bonding Bepy questionable. "Jesus Chris-s-st, boy, what the hell did you do in school?" Ziggy asked.

"I live in Bensonhurst, Brooklyn. I had no choice. The kids fight every day in school. It's either fight or get stepped on," Bepy calmly answered. "I chose to fight and stay alive."

The two management types huddled for a moment and then turned around to Bepy. "You're fired," Faulgaten declared.

Bepy got up and walked out. Deciding to go over Faulgaten's head, he went straight to the executive offices and knocked on Mr. Gustini's door, which was half open.

"Oh, come in, Bephino. How are you?" Gustini greeted him warmly.

"Mr. Gustini, I just wanted to say good bye. I'm leaving the firm."

"Why are you leaving our firm?"

66

Bepy explained the situation, and Mr. Gustini listened with interest. He held his chin in a concerned fashion and squinted his eyes when Bepy mentioned the fighting in school. He was trying to be as understanding as possible about a life he had obviously never lived himself.

"Coma. Coma with me, Bepy." He briskly led Bepy back to where Faulgaten and Melvin were still congratulating themselves on getting rid of the office boy. Mr. Gustini furiously confronted them, speaking in broken English, "Do you knowa that boysa like Bephino are very hard to finda? Don't you knowa he's wortha his weight in gold?" He stood tall, with one hand on his hip. "I'ma surprised at you! How can you letta him become available to our competitors? I have a brother still in Italia. He's *presidente* of a bank, and his name is Bephino, too!" he said with a proud grin. "I order you to putta Mr. Menesiero back to work with a better job and a raise in pay. This was an insult to Italia, and I won't have it! That's *finito!*" Without waiting for an answer of any kind, he left and did not look back at anyone, including Bepy. Bepy stood there. He couldn't believe it was Bephino Menesiero, that Mr. Gustini had been talking about. To Bepy, Mr. Gustini looked like a roaring lion, but at the same time like a delicate dancer doing a slow ballet.

Turning to Melvin and Faulgaten, Bepy remarked, "He has a brother named Bephino. What d'ya think of that? A million-to-one shot and I win. I thought I was the only Bephino in the world!"

"So did I," Melvin said, walking away.

Bepy was moved to the trading desk and given a raise.

A few months later Gustini whispered to Bepy, "Bephino, tell your family to buy OJA Oil Company. The stock will rise in two months."

Bepy went home that day and said to his father, "Papa, I got a tip on a stock. Mr. Gustini said to buy it."

"I don't have any money to gamble," Pasquale replied. "I can't afford to take the chance, Bepy. You know our money problems."

Bepy understood his father's financial situation very well and backed off.

That night, about nine o'clock, Bepy saw Don Emilio, Big Bubber, and three beautiful women getting out of a brand-new Cadillac. The women were real sexy, four-star rating.

Bepy said, "Good evening, Mr. Morrano."

The Don smiled at Bepy. "How are you, kid?"

"OK," Bepy answered. "I'm working on Wall Street now."

"Come in and have a drink with us," Don Emilio offered.

"OK, Mr. Morrano. Thank you." Bepy followed them into the bar.

"How's your mother and father doing?" the Don asked.

"They're very well, thank you." Bepy went on to tell him that though he was working on Wall Street for a brokerage firm, he was still available in case something had to be done.

"As a matter of fact, I got something for you coming up, kid," Morrano leaned toward him and whispered.

"I'm always ready. Just say the word," Bephino whispered back.

"Come see me here next Thursday night. Same time."

They then began to talk about how beautiful the ladies looked. Morrano said, "Always have the best, Bepy, never second best."

Bepy looked at the women and agreed rapidly, nodding his head. Then he told the Don about the stock tip. The Don listened with interest. "How much is it a share?" he asked.

"Around nine and a quarter."

Morrano turned to Big Bubber, "Make a note to buy one thousand shares of OJA Oil tomorrow for one of my corporations."

After Bepy had left, Big Bubber asked Morrano, "Do you really wanna buy them shares? What the hell does a kid like that know about stocks?"

"Of course I wanna buy them. I got confidence in Bephino, and don't forget it. He wouldn't steer me wrong. If he got a tip, he wouldn't lie about it. You buy those shares for me, Bubber, first thing tomorrow."

Bepy had, in his shoe box, about seven thousand, two hundred dollars, left from the Fatman deal, the Pete Lungo hit, and other small jobs he had done. This was his chance to invest in something he believed in. He took his entire savings and bought OJA Oil.

One week later, he kept his appointment with Mr. Morrano. From the bar, they went to a scheduled meeting with a Queens boss. The meeting was held in an Italian restaurant popular in Bay Ridge. Everyone who walked in could see Bepy sitting and eating with Don Emilio.

During the dinner meeting, after a lot of small talk and smiling back and forth, things got very serious. Bepy was offered five thousand dollars to hit a guy in the Bronx. His name was Joe Tortello and he was connected with the family of Nick, the other man sitting at the table. Don Emilio explained, in a whisper, that Tortello was organizing against Nick, who has been the Boss of Queens for eight years. Bepy was never told Nick's full name, but Morrano made it known that he and Nick were very good friends. Bepy listened carefully and didn't ask questions or show a personal interest. He remained quiet and enjoyed the dinner. The men seemed to like his silence. It signified a strong sense of responsibility and gave more credibility to his being able to carry out such an important hit.

Don Emilio explained further. "Nick can't trust his own people to make this hit. He doesn't know if any are loyal to Tortello, so I help make the arrangements. My people and Nick's people eat together. So we can only use someone like you, a person with no close ties to any of the men in our families. *Ah capeesh?* No one will spot you, Bephino."

"*Si, io capeesh,*" Bephino said, staring at both men.

Don Emilio then told Bepy, "So you make the hit. You have two days to do it. Here's his picture. He owns a used-car lot in the Bronx—Happy Joe's Motors. He goes there once a day. He never drives the same car, and his bodyguard is a pro. So be careful, Bepy. OK? Don't be overconfident. A lot of guys don't come back from being too sure of themselves."

"Do you know where he lives or any special place he eats?"

"No. He recently changed his style. That's why Nick thinks he's ready to move on him. Tortello's a changed man all of a sudden," Morrano explained. "Bepy, we only charge Nick five grand for this contract. He's a good friend, a *paesano*. You keep it all on this one, Bephino. It's yours for the job. Next one, we pay you even more, OK? Like I said, we can't use my men because Tortello and his bodyguards know them, so we use you. No one knows you yet," Morrano repeated.

"I understand," Bepy answered. "That's fine. I can use the money." He shook hands with both men.

Nick put an envelope on the table and said, "It's all there, kid. His picture's in there too. Good luck. You understand I need this done right away. I smell something bad coming and I don't want him to get me first."

"Don't worry. I'll get to it right away. Good night, gentlemen," he said, excusing himself politely. Then he whispered, "You can order Happy Joe's flowers now." He knew the two Dons needed to talk alone.

Morrano smiled at Nick. "This kid's the best. He's like the unexpected. He handles these things with style. Who would expect to be hit by a kid like that? He's got big balls, this kid. I'm telling you, Nick, he's young but I got confidence in him. He's got a future ahead of him."

Nick looked amazed and remarked, "But he's only a kid."

Morrano, puffing his cigar, said, "Yeah, some kid. That's what they all say before they die. He's the boy who ate the people, then had the fuckin' lion for dessert. He's seventeen going on thirty-seven. And he loves cash!"

Eight o'clock Friday morning Bepy called Jules Hart and Company and told the secretary, "I've got a fever. I won't be in today."

She replied, "See you Monday, cutie pie. Hope you got a pretty one and she makes your fever go down!"

At 8:15, Bepy called Monkey. "Get the fuck up and get a car right away. I'll meet you at the Greek diner on 4th Avenue. We'll have breakfast together. We gotta talk."

Monkey arrived at the diner forty-five minutes later. "I got the car, and it's full of gas. What the hell's goin' on this early in the morning? Why ain't you on Wall Street?"

"You got the car full of gas. Very good. You're getting better and better."

"Yeah, better my ass. If I don't get a steady job, my father's gonna put a contract on me. So if you hear of one around, please don't accept it."

"Come on, Monk, let's eat. Order fast. We gotta get going to the Bronx."

"What for? Oops," Monk said, catching his mistake. "I know, I know. Don't ask questions, right?"

"Right."

"Can I ask one?"

"Yeah."

"Is Alley Oop or Red coming?"

"No. I handle this one alone. It'll be better with fewer people to notice. Alley Oop is working at the fruit store and he can't take off on Fridays anyway."

After breakfast, they drove to the Bronx and arrived at Happy Joe's Motors. Monkey parked across the street from the car lot, and Bepy cased the area and noticed there was only one salesman working the lot. He told Monk to stay with the car. "If you hear shooting, start the engine and wait for me. Don't leave. I'll be out shortly."

"Of course I'll wait. I always wait, don't I? You think I would leave you behind?"

"I'm just reminding you. It makes me feel better, that's all. I'll hit this guy quick if he shows up, but if he don't, this may take hours. I don't know. So relax, but don't sleep. OK, Monk? Keep your eyes open and this gun handy, in case we have trouble and anybody tries to sneak up on us. I want you to watch the streets. I don't want you to go to sleep on me. Look all over the place. Keep your eyes moving around—but not your head. Head movements look suspicious," Bepy instructed him.

"We'll be in a hurry when we leave, so be ready, Monk. I'm going to work."

He strolled into the Happy Joe's Motors office to ask if Mr. Tortello had arrived yet.

The salesman answered, "No. Who wants to know?"

"I do. Mr. Tortello said if I ever wanted to clean cars, I should come to see him."

"Clean cars? I don't know, kid. We already have a spick who cleans cars. You'll have to see the boss."

"I know I gotta see him. I'm just hoping he can use me. I clean cars real good. What time will he be in today?"

"Ya never know. It could be anytime. Hey, wait just a minute. I think I see him now." He looked through the window, then smiled. "Hey, you're lucky. I see him getting out of his car across the street now. I thought I saw his car pass, but he's been using different cars lately, so I wasn't sure. He seldom comes this early. You're lucky."

"Why does he park across the street and not in the car lot? You have plenty of space."

"What are you a reporter or something? He has his own reasons. For a kid who wants to wash cars, you even wanna know the floor plan, huh?"

The door opened, and Tortello walked in. He was a heavyset man in his late fifties. His pitted face was hard and tough-looking. He wore a navy blue coat, gray hat, and shiny pointed black shoes.

"Joe, this kid wants to see you. He says he washes cars."

Bepy confirmed that Tortello's face matched the picture he'd received last night, and quickly pulled out his gun. "Mr. Tortello, I'm not here to kill you, so don't make me shoot. Just lie down on the floor, hands behind your back. I'm only gonna rob you. I need money bad. All I want is your money. Empty your pockets nice and slow. Don't make me shoot." Bepy acted nervous, waving the gun, but checking on the bodyguard still in the car across the street.

Tortello looked at his salesman and in a deep, rough, gravelly voice asked, "Who the fuck is this kid?"

"I don't know, Joe. He said he knew you and wanted to wash cars."

"Wash cars?" Tortello yelled and looked directly at Bepy. "Who the hell are you? Do you know who I am? I'm Joe Tortello."

Bepy, slowly pulling back the hammer on his gun and pointing it at the man's face, said, "Joe, say one more word and I'll blow you away. Just one more fuckin' word and you're a dead Tortello. I told you to lie down on the floor, ya mutt! Get down on your belly. All I want is your money, you scumbag, so don't get yourself killed for a few lousy bucks. Empty your pockets. Be quick or I'll kill you with one shot in your ugly face!"

The terrified salesman was shaking and trying to hold back his bowels. Tortello reluctantly crawled to the floor. He just lay there, stalling for time and hoping for an interruption of some sort. Bepy, watching both Tortello's bodyguard and the two prospective hits, said to the salesman, "Empty his pockets and wallet fast. And yours, too. I'm robbin' both of you bastards. Don't make me shoot this scumbag."

Tortello turned and looked up at Bepy. The last word made him stare deeper into space. He didn't like to be called a scumbag by this kid. He knew it was Bensonhurst talk and, because scumbags usually go down the drain, the idea of a contract on his life from the Brooklyn people became a reality in his mind.

The salesman knew Bepy's face clearly now, so Bepy knew he had to go also. Their pockets were emptied. A big stack of hundred-dollar bills came out of Tortello's pockets, which Bepy stuffed into his jacket pockets.

"No wonder you were so slow in emptying your pockets. Look at all the green you had," Bepy said. "Give me that ring. Take his ring off. I want that diamond. It's big, ain't it, Joe?"

Still watching the bodyguard across the street, he ordered the salesman, "Lie down next to your boss, and move quick. Don't make me pump lead. I don't want to hurt you guys. Face down, hands behind your back." He leaned over and said, "Look, boys, I'm only going to knock you out. So don't move. When you wake up, you'll be happy you're alive. Now, happy motoring."

He quickly belted the salesman across the head with his gun. The salesman wasn't out, but to avoid getting hit again, he made believe he was. Bepy smiled, thinking, What a phony bastard. He then pointed his gun at Tortello's head and blasted one shot right through his temple. Tortello's brains splattered all over the salesman's face. Screaming in terror, the salesman tried to roll away from the blood and skull fragments. In one quick motion Bepy put one in the salesman's chest and another through the top of his head. He knew both men were dead. There was no doubt. The bullets were .38 hollow points, which made holes as large as a man's fist.

The hit was complete. Now to get out and head back to Brooklyn. Bepy glanced out the window. The bodyguard was looking in the direction of the office, as though he thought he had heard something.

72

But with the sound of the city's truck traffic rumbling over the cobblestones, Bepy knew he couldn't be sure of what he had heard.

The bodyguard glanced at Bepy as he left the office and kept his eyes on him every step of the way, as he crossed the street.

Bepy's mind was racing for a solution to this new problem. Did he hear shots or not? Did he get a good look at me? What should I do now? He's a pro. If I fool with him, maybe he'll nail me. If I run, he'll know who made the hit. Then, having made a tough decision, Bepy walked up to the bodyguard sitting behind the wheel. "Hey, mister, Joe Tortello told me to bring his cigars in from the glove compartment."

The goon began to reach for the glove compartment, then said, "Joe only smokes cigars after lunch. . . ." Realizing he was caught off guard, he carefully turned his head and looked up into the barrel of Bepy's gun. His mouth gaped in a silent scream as Bepy blasted away—two quick shots. The man's head was almost completely gone; blood was all over the dashboard.

Bepy ran a few parking spaces up the street to the Monkey's car. "Let's go."

Monkey turned on his radio and drove off.

"What's with the fuckin' radio?" Bepy asked.

"I like to listen to music while I drive."

One week later, Nick requested a dinner meeting with the kid again. Bepy asked Don Emilio, "What does he want now?"

"He wants to talk to you. I don't know what it's about yet. We haven't talked much since the hit."

The dinner was at the same place as before. During the meal Nick asked Bepy, "Did you have to hit the salesman, too?"

"Of course I did. He was there, big as shit, staring at me. He had to go. And the bodyguard was a gift. I threw him in free. Now he's out of your way, too. You got three for the price of one." Bepy acted very sure of his actions—not like the first meeting. He knew he had made a successful hit and he was not about to act doubtful about it.

Morrano's eyes flickered back and forth from Nick to Bephino.

"Yeah, I know you did a good job, Bepy. But the salesman was my brother's son-in-law," Nick said.

"Your brother's son-in-law?

"Nick, how am I supposed to know these things? When I work, I work, and anyone who gets in the picture has gotta go, right? The guy talked to me for ten minutes. He saw my face. He could pick me out in a full house in Ebbets Field. How was I gonna let the guy walk?"

In support, Don Emilio interrupted. "You're right, Bephino. You had a job to do and you did it very well and very cheap. He cleaned your house, Nick. Three for the price of one. The kid worked well."

Nick backed off, "Of course, of course."

"Look, Nick, I'm sorry, but that hit got a bit crowded. The only place I could make contact was the car lot, and I only had two days to do it. I was lucky he showed up there," Bepy said. "The Tortello guy was acting pretty cocky with a .38 to his head." In a strained voice, Bepy continued. "He wanted to know who I was before he died. I knew it was important to you, so I cleaned house up there."

The two Dons grinned.

"Look, Bepy, I'm not complaining. I should have told you not to hit the salesman. You saved me a lot of trouble, I realize that. The case is closed. OK? It was my error. You did a great job. I give you a bonus. Two more grand. How's that?"

"Thank you." Bepy put out his hand to receive the cash.

Don Emilio smiled at Nick and at Bephino's quick acceptance of the cash.

Nick suggested that Bepy do another job for him "in the near future."

Bepy replied, "When?"

"I'll let Emilio know when I'm ready. I have a few soldiers who were loyal to Tortello. When they think it is over, that's when I remove them from this nice world."

5

One day at his favorite coffee shop, Bephino met a beautiful Italian girl named Dana Viccione. She had long black hair and was built just the way Bepy liked a girl to be. Her eyes were green and complemented her oval face. She worked in an investment banking firm a few blocks up the street. They ate lunch together several times and began dating.

Dana also lived in Brooklyn. She worked part time and was only fifteen years old. Dana also dated other boys, and Bepy dated other girls, but he felt she was really something special.

One night, Bepy asked Dana to go to an Italian festival in Bay Ridge. She also loved Italian festivities. Dana's parents, who came from Naples, were not too happy about her dating a Sicilian boy. They were afraid he would be involved in the Mafia, through his heritage.

Bepy arrived to pick Dana up at her apartment house. He was greeted by her mother and father and older sister and brother. The brother recognized him from the poolroom and knew his reputation for being a fighter, but he was cordial anyway. Five years older than Bepy, he didn't have too much to say to him. Dana's sister kept staring at Bepy; her nostrils were so wide apart you could stuff a silver dollar in each hole. Dana was smiling and purring like a kitten. Her mother had a special look on her face that said, "I don't know if I want this boy to take my daughter out."

Her father spoke with a heavy accent. He asked Bepy, "Whatta is your nama? Please."

"Bephino Menesiero."

"Ah, *Siciliano,*" the father said.

Si, io Siciliano," Bepy replied.

"Bene," her father replied with a smile.

"You're all Sicilian?" the mother asked. "Your mother and father are both from Sicilia?"

"Yes. Both of my parents are from Sicily. From Sciacca."

Her eyes started blinking like flickering light bulbs. Bepy understood right then and there where he stood with her mother. He wanted to leave.

"Come on, let's go," he whispered to Dana. "Your sister's blowing smoke from her nose, and it's burning my neck. She's like a dragon with tits." He smiled at everyone, trying to be charming.

They excused themselves and got up to leave. The mother, still blinking, followed them out the door into the hallway. She asked, "What time do you intend to come home?"

The father interrupted his wife. "What are you worried about? That boy will take good care of her."

"Did you ever think of getting your mother a set of blinkers at the racetrack?" Bepy asked Dana later.

"What do you mean, blinkers?"

"Nothing. Forget it."

At the festival, they played different games and ate sausage and peppers on Italian bread, and zeppoles with powdered sugar. Dana loved zeppoles with sugar. While walking around and saying hello to people they knew, they passed a gang of boys on a corner. One wore a dark blue fedora. He was one of the other guys Dana dated. His name was Johnny

Amado, a tough guy from the 86th Street gang. Bepy held hands with Dana while they walked past. Johnny smiled at Dana, then said something that made all the other boys laugh.

Hearing the laughter, Bepy thought, Look at that shit. They're laughing at us. Now I gotta bust the bastard's face. And I was really having a good time tonight."

Dana sensed that Bepy was going to do something and she got worried. She didn't like trouble. She came from a quiet family. "Please, Bepy, let's keep walking. Don't stop," she pleaded. "Don't make trouble, please. I can see it in your face. You're gonna make trouble."

"Me? Trouble? They made the trouble. See that fuck with the hat? Watch his head closely. I'll only take a second. OK?"

Dana was scared as Bepy strolled casually over to Johnny. "Hey, Fat Face! Were you talking to me?" he asked.

Johnny began to laugh and talk at the same time, but Bepy didn't wait for the words to untangle themselves. He hit him with a haymaker. The punch was so quick and hard that as Johnny went down, his hat flew in the air and landed on St. Jude's statue behind him. Johnny stayed down, his right leg contracting in muscle spasms.

"Dana, you like St. Jude?" Bepy asked.

"I love St. Jude. He's my favorite saint."

"Good. He just got himself a nice blue fedora."

"Bepy, you hit him too hard," she pouted. "Look at his leg; it's shaking. Something's wrong with him." She pointed. "I'm getting upset. Look, Bepy, look."

"Nothing's wrong. He just can't take a punch. Usually, I make them tap-dance."

Dana chuckled nervously. "Bepy, you're crazy," she said, speaking out of the side of her mouth.

As they walked slowly away from the crowd that had gathered, they heard one of Johnny's friends saying: "That's Bephino, from Bensonhurst. What a punch he's got!"

When they arrived back at Dana's apartment house, it was just before midnight. Bepy wanted to love her up a little on the front steps, but suddenly Dana's mother appeared at the front window four floors up. "Dana, are you coming up? Up, up, up," she repeated.

"In a minute, Ma, Ma, Ma." Dana answered back, acting smart.

"I want you up now, Dana!"

Bepy, looking up at the mother and then at Dana, said, "I better go, go, go. Gargantua's up there roaring and she might wake up that big-

76

breasted dragon that's sleeping in the wings. It's late anyway." They laughed, kissed, and said good night.

The next day after work, Bepy arrived home to find a commotion in front of his house. His friends told Bepy that his father just had a fight with two guys. "Bepy, you should've seen him. He was like a wild man," one of them said excitedly. "He kept punching them both at one time. He was punching like crazy."

"Is my father all right?" Bepy asked.

"Yeah. But the two guys aren't."

"What d'ya mean?"

"Bepy, your father threw them down the stairs. He beat the shit out of them."

Bepy, relieved that his father was all right, started up the stairs to his apartment. "What happened?" he asked as he entered the kitchen.

"Your father's *pazzo!*" his mother replied, pointing her finger to her head. "He's a crazy man!"

"Why?"

"He fights like an animal, that's why. He should talk, not hit."

Pasquale was soaking his hand in a pot of water.

"Tell me what happened?" Bepy asked him.

"Eh, what happened? I bought a TV last week. You know, I used that money Grandma left me when she died. Well, you know that *focha bruta* guy Eddy, at the TV store? He told me to pay twenty bucks more and I can get an extra fifteen foot of pipe for the antenna, so we would get a clearer picture. Today, these two guys come to install it and they know nothing about an extra pipe. They already had the job almost finished, but I see no extra fifteen foot, and they wouldn't take it apart to satisfy me. I told them I spent six hundred forty-five dollars for a beautiful Dumont TV and I wanted it to be right. They got nasty with me and told me to see Eddy. Then, Mr. Ruffo, the landlord, comes up on the roof and he wants a two-dollar raise in rent because the antenna is on his roof. These two guys started laughing at me, so I kicked the shit out of them. That's all that happened. And your mother makes a big deal out of it. So now tomorrow, I'm gonna fix Eddy."

Pasquale flexed his fingers in the water and said to his wife, "Finametta, please, why don't you go watch TV, huh? You'll feel better."

"Now I know why you're a *spostato,*" Finametta told Bepy. "Because your father's a *spostato.*"

"OK, Mama. Let's eat. Whatta you have tonight?"

"You're lucky I have anything after the way your father did. The whole building was in our apartment trying to calm him down," she lamented, holding her face with a dish towel. "I'm so ashamed . . . All the neighbors . . . "

Bepy, while eating, noticed an electric drill on the floor, a big commercial type. "Papa, whose drill?"

Pasquale replied, "Those dopey guys left their drill on the roof."

"Sure, after you start punching, they're lucky to get off that roof." Finametta laughed sarcastically, then she made the sign of the cross. "Dear God, what did I do to deserve these men? I was always a good girl."

Bepy began smiling at his father, shaking his head, admiring him. "You still got a good left hook, huh, Pasquale?"

"I got a letter from Mario today," Finametta said. "He arrived in Germany. He's now a PFC. He's a good boy, my Mario. He looks so nice in his uniform."

"Is he still fat?" Bepy asked.

"Shut up and eat. Is he still fat? What kinda talka is that? You're too skinny, and I know why, too. I seen that Margie woman up the street. Mrs. Torino told me you sneak to her apartment once in a while. The girl is married! Why you go there, Bephino? Why you bother people?"

"I don't bother her, Mama. She bothers me. She loves my style."

"You better stop plowing around, *figlio mio*. Be careful," Finametta warned him. "She has a big husband like a cowboy."

Pasquale called from the parlor, "Hurry, look. Look at the TV!"

They joined him and laughed together.

Two weeks later, the news came to the neighborhood that Johnny Amado had been killed. Shot two times in the head and found in an alley.

Dana felt terrible. Johnny had been so young and handsome. Talk began in the neighborhood that Bepy had done it. But Bepy never talked about it and was never questioned by the police about it.

One day Dana asked, "Bepy, did you kill Johnny?"

"What do I look like? A fuckin' nut or what? Why should I kill him?" Bepy asked. "You ask me like it was a common thing to do. What the hell is wrong with you?"

At Dana's home that evening, her sister, Gina, began a campaign against Bepy. "He's too tough," she told their mother. "He's a gangster. I heard stories about him. He's no good for her. I have my doubts about him."

The mother lapped this up like a bloodhound, "Me, too. I felt the same way from the beginning," she said.

Dana's father, though, held firm, "I don't want my daughter to go out with some stupid, weak boy. That's a good fella. I lika him."

"He's not my type, Dana. I like a more manly type," her sister kept saying. "He looks like a boy, to my eyes anyway. My boyfriend is more of a man."

Dana looked at her sister, who was ten years older and still not married, with a smirk and asked, "You don't think Bepy is manly enough? Do you think he's without courage? I doubt that very much, Gina. You're wrong, my darling sister. He's too much of a man, I would say."

Gina said, backing off a bit, "I mean he looks like a boy. I don't know if he acts like one."

"I don't know about these men. They too rough. I don't like a rough man," Dana's mother added.

At least Dana could always talk to her father about Bepy, and her father would laugh at things she said. He knew Dana cared for Bepy, so he interrupted Gina and said, "I lika the boy."

"We gotta keep making money. It's very important for us," Bepy said later that week to Monkey. "I'm piling it up. I bought shares, oil shares, but I keep very quiet about it. My mother and father don't know my financial status."

"Neither do I. I don't even know my own status." Monkey laughed. "I'm glad somebody's piling it up. I'm not. I still don't have a job."

"What are you talking about? You've earned several grand from us, Monk. What are you doing with it?" Bepy asked.

"I flashed a roll to my uncle one day to show off. The next thing I knew he was on my doorstep asking for a loan. I lent him three grand. He said he needed it for an operation. So, he tapped me out."

"He probably conned you, the old fuck. Did he have the operation?"

"Nah, not yet."

"Jesus Christ, Monkey. You can't give the money away, especially not to uncles! They fuck you the hardest, and the quickest, too. They go to the track with the fuckin' hard-earned money. You know what we have to do to get that kinda cash, Monk? Do you realize it's blood money?"

"I know," Monkey replied, "but I already gave it to him."

"You know we never had money before," Bepy said. "We were always broke. A fuckin' quarter was a lot to us. I never fucked that hot cunt Irene. I missed out because I was broke, remember? I ain't going to be a semideprived adult, too. Ya gotta save and invest."

"And you ain't never gonna forget Freckles, are you, Bepy?"

"I wanted that freckled-ass broad. See, it takes money to have a good life in America. We gotta do whatever it is we gotta do to make it."

"Yeah, you're right, I know. You gave me plenty of cash, Bepy. I'm not complaining. I'm blowing it on the family to keep them alive. That's my stupidity."

"We gotta keep making money, understand? It's the only way guys like us will survive. It takes a lot of cash. And we gotta save it."

Wall Street was booming. The stock Mr. Gustini told Bepy to buy shot up from nine and a quarter to fifteen and a quarter in one day. Something was really happening. Trading was halted by the Floor Commissioners. The exchange announced that so many OJA Oil buy orders were coming in, they could not handle them. Finally, five hours later, the stock reopened at twenty-five and one-eighth. It kept going up, to thirty and a quarter. Bepy was wild. He had the shits for three days. He asked Mr. Gustini if he should sell his stock.

"Yes. You sell it at ninety dollars," Mr. Gustini answered.

Bepy bit his fist. Ninety dollars! "I'm rich. I made it." He tried to figure his profit in his mind, but he was too nervous.

As he was calculating, a secretary walked by and saw Bepy with his fist in his mouth. "What is it, lunchtime, Bep?" she kidded.

"Nancy, my stock is up! I'm gonna sell it at ninety bucks a share, and I only paid nine and a quarter. I think I'm gonna be rich, Nancy!" Feeling good and easy, he asked, "Can I sleep with you tonight? I feel excited about my success. I need someone to talk to. I need a cushion"— looking up at her large breasts—"to put my head on."

She smiled. "Give me two days, Bep. My husband goes back to Fort Dix. Then we can discuss your wealth and the cushions you need. OK?"

"OK, Nancy," he answered, staring off into space like an imbecile.

That evening he stopped to see Don Emilio. The Don was in a conference with a few of his soldiers. Bepy was greeted warmly by the Don, and the soldiers stood up to shake his hand. It seemed as though they had heard of Bephino Menesiero. One of the men, a fellow in his late sixties, spoke to Bepy in Italian for a while. Then he turned to the others and said, *"Mi piace questo compagno Sciacchitano.* I like this fellow Sicilian. He will be an important man someday." Bepy knew that a compliment from the elderly is a great honor to receive.

Everyone left after a few drinks, but Bepy stayed to talk in private with Mr. Morrano. He asked him about his OJA Oil shares.

"Yeah, I bought one thousand," the Don said. "But I never checked to see what it was doing."

Bepy told him that the stock had jumped to thirty and an eighth.

Morrano could not believe his ears. "Should we sell, Bepy?" he asked.

"Yes. We sell at ninety bucks," Bepy answered.

"What . . . ninety dollars?"

"Yep. Ninety dollars. I'll let you know when to sell, OK?"

"You gotta be kiddin' me!"

"*I* kid *you?*" Bepy smiled.

"You're unbelievable! You know that, kid?"

Bepy's spirits were raised by his success in the stock market. He began to feel at home on Wall Street. At night he would go wining and dining among other white-collar people. He tried to fit in, but he felt out of place—and like a sore thumb with Alley Oop at his table.

The bars were loaded at night, with everyone boozing and talking shop. From time to time, the conversations would turn to money and where to get some. By using a little muscle in the right place, Bepy became known as another Wall Street lending institution. He would lend money, take bets on ball games, fights, and horse races. He was a loan shark. Red became a forty-percent partner and handled all of these transactions, but the Street knew that Bepy was the boss. And it didn't take people long to realize that Bephino Menesiero was the head of the newly organized crime family in the area. Many became eager to be considered his friend.

Don Emilio gave Bephino carte blanche to do whatever he wanted on Wall Street. He even lent him five grand without interest to start up until he sold his stock. Such intrusions into the public domain take the approval of a Mafia capo to get a territory in New York. They must be certified and on record with the Mob. The Don gave Bephino the approval and the loan without discussion.

Business was small at first, but slowly it began to build. For example, one customer, Tom O'Malley, borrowed two hundred dollars and had to pay back three hundred at the end of the month. Business on this scale looked proportionally good and the future bright for Bepy and Red. Bepy never turned down a deal. He always listened to what they had to say. After a few months, things were going smoothly on all fronts, and they were raking in plenty of money.

Dana called Bepy one afternoon and asked to see him. She said it was very important. Over lunch, she explained that she was having problems at home. Her mother wanted her to go out with other boys, not just him.

"They want me to go out and get some experience in life, to see if I'm really in love or not."

Bepy got very angry. That evening he went to Dana's home and raised all kinds of hell with her mother and sister. Getting absolutely nowhere with them, he left, slamming the door. This did not make things better. No doubt about it: Bephino Menesiero had a temper, a very bad temper. And even Dana was having second thoughts about him.

As the weeks rolled on, Dana dated other neighborhood boys. Bepy didn't like these guys. He thought about handling them, but he shelved the idea, believing it would only make things worse.

One day in the office, while talking to Red on the phone about the day's bets, a tall, dark guy from the order department walked in and started raising his voice at one of the office boys. Bepy, now the head of a small section of boys, heard the yelling.

"I gotta go," he told Red. "Some guy who looks like Sabu is making a riot in our office. Call me back, OK?"

Bepy approached the fellow. "Hey, what's going on here? Why are you yelling so loud? You're in an office, not a bar. What's your problem, Sabu?"

Sabu, waving two stock order blanks, screamed something about the brokers leaving off the "buy" or "sell" on the order and when the market opened he couldn't catch the opening price because he didn't know if he should buy or sell. So now he wanted to know who would be charged for the error.

"Hey, calm down, fellow," Bepy said, "and stop waving your arms in my face."

But Sabu got nastier. Bepy moved up real close to him and just stared at him. Then suddenly, with an open hand, he slapped him across the mouth lightly, turned him to face the door, and kicked him in his square ass. The guy wasn't hurt but he was shocked over being handled so abruptly. He walked slowly back to the order department wiping the blood off his big juicy lips. The entire office started to laugh.

About an hour later, after a meeting, Bepy was approached by Mr. Melvin. "I heard you're becoming violent and throwing punches at people now, Bepy," he said. "What's next?" He smirked, in his cold, brittle style.

Bepy, thinking he had handled Sabu beautifully, became defensive and answered, "Sir, do you know what I do for a part-time job?"

"I can't imagine," Melvin replied, removing his glasses and cleaning them with a tissue he pulled out of his pocket.

"I accept contracts," Bepy whispered calmly.

"Contracts? What do you mean by contracts?" Melvin slid his glasses back on his face.

Bepy back-pedaled. "You know, soybeans, cotton, corn, knishes ... anything like that. That kinda contract."

Melvin walked away shaking his head. Then suddenly it hit him. Turning back and subconsciously removing his eye glasses once again, he stared at Bepy with fear in his puffy eyes. He tried to look as if he were laughing at the joke, but his nervous frown made him look ugly and scared.

The phone rang. It was Red. "Is everything OK?"

"I guess so."

"What's the matter up there?"

"Ah, everytime Mr. Gustini takes a trip to Europe, all hell breaks loose around here. It'll be all right. I took care of it. Let's talk about business, our business. How're we doing?"

"Good," Red said. "I got an idea for a new business. Let's meet for lunch."

"What kinda business? And how much will it cost me," Bepy asked.

"It's a food business."

"A food business? What the hell do we know about food?"

"Don't worry. First listen to my idea, OK? Let's meet," Red replied.

At noon, while they were waiting to order, Sabu walked in O'Brien's Café. "There's Sabu, the guy who fucked up a beautiful day for me," Bepy told Red. "Hey, Sabu, come over here," he called out.

"Gee," Red said, laughing, "he really looks like Sabu."

"Sabu, where did you park your elephant?" Bepy asked.

"My name's not Sabu. It's Joey D. And I don't have an elephant."

"Joey D, eh?" Bepy said, jokingly. "Hey, his name's Joey D. Fancy, huh, Red?"

"Yeah. He's a fancy guy, this Joey D."

"OK, Sabu. What's your full name?" Red asked. "Gunga Din?"

"No. It's Joey Desporto."

"Desporto?" Bepy asked. "You're Italian?"

"Of course. What ya think?"

"I thought you were a spick or an Indian ... or maybe an Arab. I never figured you for Italian. You're Italian? And you made me smack you and kick you without a fight? What kind of Italian are you?"

Joey D answered simply. "I'm a peaceful Italian."

"Peaceful Italian? Ha. The way you were yelling in the office?" Bepy laughed, "OK, Joey D, the peaceful Italian, have some lunch with us.

You're invited to eat with us, and from now on you take my orders or I'm gonna break your kneecaps. *Ah capeesh?"*

"*Si, io capeesh.*" Joey D grinned knowingly.

"Hey, Bepy. You wanna talk about this idea I got in front of this guy?" Red asked impatiently.

"Yeah. It's about food, you said. Right? And it's getting late, so let's talk. I can't stay out late today. That fuckin' Melvin is watching me like a hawk."

"Let's order and talk."

"OK. I think we should expand our partnership into new ventures. We can't take bets in other guy's areas because we'll have problems with the big boys. You know that," Red explained. "So our business is limited to the Wall Street area, right?"

Bepy, frowning at Red said, "We were supposed to talk about food, not limited area." Turning away quickly, he looked at Sabu, and pushed the pickle bowl towards him. "Have a pickle, Sabu," he murmured.

"Go ahead, Red. I'm listening."

"I want us to open up sandwich shops in the Wall Street area. We could even take the action in these stores, and these bums will go nuts for Italian sandwiches—meatballs, sausage and peppers, veal and peppers, on Italian bread. Fat Nicky will supply the bread from his Mulberry Street store. I asked him already. He said we'd get wholesale prices. He's got some bread, that Fat Nicky, huh? People could eat and bet. It's a perfect setup."

"Yeah. It sounds good."

"That is a good idea. I like it," Joey D said, while chewing on a pickle. "Hero shops—that's what he's talking about, hero shops. They do good. They all make money."

"Look, Sabu," Bepy said sharply, "don't talk while eating your food. Don't be a *cafone* around me. Have some manners at the table. Chew with your mouth closed."

Joey D quietly put his head down almost to his plate and kept eating.

Bepy looked over to Red, "OK, Red. I love the idea. Get a store and set it up, using the money we have in the kitty. If you need more, let me know. Keep a record of every penny you spend, so I can check what's going on. I don't want to have nightmares. Same cut, sixty-forty. Understand, Red?"

"Of course. Same cut, Bepy. Sixty-forty."

Red proceeded to open the hero shop, and six months later business was great. Profits were high. So Red suggested opening another shop.

84

"Go ahead," Bepy agreed. "But Monkey must be the manager of store number two. Take him off the food line of store number one. He gets to the top with us. Agreed?" Red did not respond. "Your cousin can keep his job as manager of our first store. From now on, I want Monkey always to be a boss. Do you agree? I'm waiting for your answer, Red."

"Of course I agree. I fully agree. You know, Bepy, you got class."

"Yeah, why?"

"You're cool. I like the way you say 'store number one,' 'store number two.' I can see you saying 'store number twenty-nine' and 'thirty' someday."

"Someday I will, and you'll be with me if you do the right thing, Red; not like the Fatman deal. You pulled a switch on me that day. I got bad thoughts about the cash take on that job."

Red looked at Bepy with a red, flushed face. "It'll never happen again, Bepy. You're talking about the cook's wallet, ain't ya? Well that's over. Now I always do the right thing." Red tried to sound convincing. "Have you dated Dana lately?"

"Don't change the subject, Red. You better do the right thing, because I'm still bothered by that split. I'm having nightmares over it. And you know that's bad," Bepy said, turning away.

Red nodded in agreement, but still tried to change the subject. "So tell me about Dana. I heard she's dating other guys."

Reluctantly, Bepy gave in and said, "Her family is still mad at me. But I met her father the other day in the street and he invited me up to the apartment to eat. Of course, I didn't go. 'Don't worry,' he said, 'you and Dana will get together again.' The old man likes me and I like him. She's going out with a guy called Mousey. He's supposed to have a good job. He's a printer or something like that."

"Mousey? What a name he's got!"

"You know him, Red. He's a half-a-hump guy from Bay Parkway. If you see him, you'll know who he is. He's about twenty years old and has a nice car. He's a little short bastard. I dreamed of him twice this week, and it's starting to bug me. I have been very patient. I really like Dana, so I think I'm gonna have to get crazy again and rip his lungs out."

A few months later, at the 602 Club in Brooklyn, where the boys went dancing and drinking, a pretty girl approached Bephino. "Hi, Bepy," she said, leaning over the table to kiss him. He'd dated her about a dozen times.

"Hi, Sandra, what's up?" Bepy said, smiling.

"Let's dance, Bep. I have to talk to you."

"Sit down, rest ya feet, and have a drink," he replied cheerfully.

"No, Bepy, let's dance. I wanna talk, and they're playing our song. Come on, Bepy. Dance with me. Please."

"Dance with Alley Oop. That's his song, too. Go ahead, Alley, dance with her." Bepy laughed.

"Forget the dance, Mr. Smart Guy," she snapped, her voice dripping venom. "We'll talk right here. You've been seeing me off and on for the past five months, Bepy. Only it's been more off than on. You take me out when you wanna get laid. Am I right?"

"You're absolutely right. So what, Sandra?"

She leaned over real close. Lowering her voice, she said, "You know I'm crazy about you. I do whatever you ask me to. Right?"

"You're right again, Sandra. Keep trying, I'll tell you when you're wrong. Try me one more time."

"Now I'm pregnant—two and a half months."

"That's it!" he yelled, jumping out of his seat. "That's it! You're wrong, baby, you're wrong. I can't be the guy. I had my balls tied when I was a child. You got the wrong fella, honey."

"I'm pregnant, Bephino," she said emphatically.

"OK, OK. So you're pregnant. Just be cool and tell me who's the lucky guy?"

"You, ya bastard. You know that," she answered angrily. "You never wore a rubber when I asked you to..."

"Look, Sandra, you're a nice girl. But don't try to corner me with that shit. I told you I had my balls tied. Anyway, how do you know I'm the guy? You said it yourself, I see you off and on. More off than on, right?" He looked around the table at his buddies for support.

"I know you're the father because I only go to bed with you," she said, glaring at him. "You're the father. And you've been neglecting me, Bephino, and I don't like to be neglected. You know that, darling, don't you?" Her voice full of sarcasm.

"Listen to this shit. You're neglecting her, Bephino, when you should be home humping her," Red said, laughing.

"Mind your business, Red," Sandra snapped. "Look, Bepy, I love you and I know you love me. You always tell me that. And I'm pregnant." Sandra sighed, "You're the father and you know it. So what do we do?"

"You're the guy," Red said, grinning. "She knows it, but do you know it? That's the question."

Bepy thought for a moment. "What do you mean you love me? I love you? What kinda bullshit is that? What do I look like, a fuckin' moron? You're knocked up, so now you love me. I must look stupid or somethin'.

We both loved each other when we were coming. Everybody says that when they're coming. You want me to put it in writing? Forget it."

"But I'm only putting out for you, Bepy. I was a cherry, remember? You were my first."

"Yeah, but was I your last? That's the big question. Right, Red?"

"You ain't kiddin'," Red agreed. "The last guy gets the kid. That's the law in Brooklyn."

"OK, I know what to do," Bepy said, in a more serious manner. "We'll get you an abortion. You happy now? We clean you out nicea nice, and you'll be happy again and outta love with me."

"Nicea nice, my ass. I'm not happy. I'll never be happy. I told you I love you, and I want to have this baby. Marry me; that's what will make me happy and nicea nice. We'll have your baby together."

Bepy looked at his friends around the table and stopped at Alley Oop. "This girl is crazy," he said. "She wants a baby at sixteen years of age, and she's only a baby herself." He looked at Sandra. "Why do you want a baby to take care of when *you're* still a baby, Sandra? It don't make sense to me. Don't make this mistake," he yelled at her. "Think about it."

"You didn't think I was such a baby when you spread me on the bed, did you, Bepy? You told me I was great. Look, Bepy, I can take care of you and me and a baby. Stop trying to squirm out of it," she said, glaring at him.

Bephino stared at her, stopped cold. After a moment, he yelled, "What the fuck do you want from me, huh, Sandra? I'm too young to be a father. I'm still an adolescent. I'm young ... Why the hell you wanna talk about marriage. You just ruined my night."

The other two boys cracked up. Alley leaned over and asked, "He's an adolescent? What does that mean, Red?"

"That means he's still indulging in masturbation," Red whispered into Alley's ear. "He can't be the father, Alley, because he's a very private person. A very private person," he repeated.

Alley stared at Red silently, confused by his explanation. Red realized this, so he made a hand job sign. "You know, Alley. He's still jerking off," he whispered, shaking his hand up and down.

Alley collapsed on the floor with laughter. Bepy had to laugh at their antics.

Sandra sang the same song. "I want to get married. I'm a Catholic girl, and my family will flip over this if they hear it."

"Ohhh, I understand," Bepy said sincerely. "You want a husband, so you come to me to help you out. OK, kid, I'll get you a husband. Have no fear. Bephino will be here."

87

"What do you mean, you'll get me a husband? Who ... you?"

"Look, Sandra, you're an Irish broad and I'm a Sicilian fellow," he explained coldly. "All we could do is fuck together; we can't get married. I gotta marry an Italian, only an Italian. You better understand this, and don't make me any more upset than I am."

Alley Oop handed Bepy an antacid pill. Bepy thanked Alley for thinking of him, patting him on the neck. Then he addressed Sandra. "I said I'll get you a husband, and I mean it. You'll have one in two days. I treated you fine, Sandra, and you know that. I always held you like a lady."

"Yeah, Sandra," Alley Oop interrupted, "Bepy always treated you like a lady, I remember."

"Oh, yeah. He held me like a lady and fucked me like a whore," she replied, tears running down her pretty freckled face. "You're a prick, Bephino," she whispered. "OK, get me a husband. But you're a bastard, Bephino. You know that?" She ran out crying.

The next day a meeting was called at hero shop number two: Red, Monkey, Joey D, Augie the cook, Little Pauli, Alley Oop, and Crazy Mikey. It was four o'clock in the afternoon, and the lunch business was over. They sat around a table drinking and eating as though a celebration were taking place, but no one knew the reason for the meeting. Joey D was employed as cashier in store number two. He had left his job at the brokerage firm at the request of Bephino.

Suddenly Bepy raised his glass and began to make a toast. "Attention, everybody," he yelled. "I'd like to make a toast to Joey D."

Everyone laughed. "A toast to Joey D?" "Why Joey D?" They couldn't understand it.

"Silenzio," Bepy said.

"How come you didn't invite my cousin Giulio?" Red interrupted.

Bepy looked down at Red and replied, "One Milanese is enough in my family. This is my family, and I like it the way it is. If you don't mind, Red? I wanna continue my ovation to these fine gentlemen bestowed upon my table and motivate them by my toast to our very distinguished friend Joey D."

Red made a face at the awkward use of the words.

"Can I get back to my toast?" Bepy asked. "Are there any more interruptions? I'd like to make a real toast to Joey D. Gentlemen, Joey D is getting married." Then he added, "Tomorrow."

Joey D began foaming at the mouth from laughter, thinking this was a joke. But he really was getting married, and tomorrow was his wedding day, Bepy explained. Joey D couldn't believe what he was hearing. But it soon dawned on him that Bepy was serious. This had to be the reason for the meeting. He listened to the men screech with laughter as Bepy told them to prepare fat cash gifts for Joey's reception tomorrow. Joey's large lips were parched as he stared at everyone around the table.

When Bepy finished his speech, Joey asked to speak to him in private. They moved to another table, and Joey D tried to speak firmly. "Suppose I refuse to marry this girl? I mean, it is a girl you want me to marry, isn't it?"

"Of course, it's a girl," Bepy said. "She's a very pretty girl with hot rocks. She loves to fuck. You'll enjoy her, Joey, believe me."

"What'd you do, Bepy, knock her up, and now you're dumping her on me?"

"Nah. The girl only thinks she's knocked up. She didn't even see a doctor or nothin'. She just wants to marry an Italian fella, so I picked you. You're gonna love this kid, Joey. She's cute."

"Yeah, but I don't even know her. How do you expect me to be happy with her? She's a total stranger to me. Who the hell is she anyway? I can't marry her. What do you think I am, nuts? Huh, Bepy?" he asked.

"Sabu, here are your options," Bepy said in an ice-cold voice. "Either you get married tomorrow or you ride in a parade on Sunday."

"Parade? What parade?"

"Yeah," Bepy mumbled. "You'll ride in a nice parade, Sunday, lying in a basket with six white horses pulling you through New Utrecht Avenue to the cemetery. Take your choice. It's either fuck a sexy, beautiful girl or take the parade."

Joey D, who knew what kind of a guy he was dealing with, thought for a moment. "I hope she's a good hump," he said finally. "I guess I'm a married man. Wish me luck," and he held out his hand to Bepy.

"Do the right thing, kid," Bepy told Joey D. "You'll be taken care of."

That evening Bepy took Joey D to meet Sandra, who was anxiously waiting at the club. Bepy ordered a round of drinks to make everyone more relaxed. He said, looking at Sandra and placing his arm around Joey D., "Meet your new husband."

Joey D was smiling and shaking his head at Bepy's way of doing things.

Sandra looked up at Sabu and continued to sip her drink nervously. After a few moments she leaned over to Bepy and said drily, "I'll take the fuckin' abortion."

Bepy had played his trump card and won. "OK, I'll make the arrangements. Give me two more days. I'll let you know the time and place. All expenses will be paid. So don't worry about anything."

Sandra grinned at him and whispered, "You're a prick, Bephino Menesiero. I just want you to know that."

After they'd left, Joey D told Bepy, "Boy, she was something! Huh, Bepy?"

"Yeah, not bad lookin'. I told you, didn't I?"

"Not bad lookin' at all. I thought she was cute. She had some big ass for such a small waist. Huh, Bep?"

"Yeah," Bepy answered. "But she's Irish. Who the hell wants to eat Irish stew all his life? I got to get my head together and stop banging all these broads in these bars. They're closin' in on me. Anyway, I still like Dana too much."

"Hey, Bepy," Joey D asked jokingly, "why don't you let me marry that cartoon-lookin', big-titted redhead? You know, Margie. Let me use her for a few weeks. I heard she's a real beauty. I wouldn't mind that broad for a while, hmmm."

"Who told you about Margie? You never met her."

"Monkey told me you been bangin' her since you were fifteen years old. Is that right, Bep?"

"That broad, she'd kill you, Joey, believe me. She smothers you with pussy. Margie is making me an old man. It's been three years now. She's sucking my brains out. My dick's got wrinkles all of a sudden. I can't say no to her. She keeps calling me from her window right in the street. People in the neighborhood, they talk about it to my mother. And I think her husband knows I'm humping her. He looks at me funny like. I always feel like he's gonna attack me from behind. Forget her, Joey. She'll destroy you. She'll loosen up your eyeballs with those big tits banging at your face."

Two weeks later Mr. Gustini arrived back at the Wall Street office from Rome; OJA Oil was selling at fifty and a half now. Bepy greeted Mr. Gustini warmly and thanked him for the stock tip. Mr. Gustini, in broken English, said, "You remembera my client Rupert, Prince of Wallenburg?"

"Yes, sir, I do."

"Well, Rupert and his group are now gonna make a tender offer to alla available OJA stock. They will offera the public sixty dollars per share. Don't sell! We sell atta ninety dollars in twoa months. Tell your father to hold."

"Thanks, Mr. Gustini. We appreciate your help, sir."

"Keepa up your good work. You're doing well, Bephino." Mr. Gustini patted him on the back.

Bepy owned seven hundred shares of OJA. If the tender offer really came through, he was made. No one knew he had the stock. He had told Mr. Gustini it was his father's purchase. He didn't want people to think he had such funds at his disposal. That's why he kept his job, though it paid such a small salary compared to the profits from the hero shops and the gambling business. He would be safe on Wall Street. He figured he'd stay with the brokerage firm until he got rich, then retire, wealthy, to some island paradise. He often thought, pityingly, of the way his father held a two-dollar bill like it was two hundred; the way his father rubbed a dollar with love and affection. He remembered the pushcart parked in the alleyway at night, smelling of old wood and rotten fish. He had felt so poor. Now he feared that poverty might grab him back like quicksand.

Early one Saturday afternoon in Brooklyn, Bepy saw Dana getting out of Mousey's car. She had her hair set in rollers and clips, like she was getting ready for a Saturday-night date. He began boiling over as he watched. He approached the car as Mousey leaned over to kiss Dana good-bye.

His heart pounding, Bepy interrupted them. "Dana, I wanna talk to you."

She was surprised to see Bepy standing there, but seemed sort of happy at the same time.

"Dana, go wait for me by your building. I'll be there in a few minutes," Bepy said.

Dana walked away slowly, afraid that Bepy would cause trouble.

Mousey, still sitting in his car, asked angrily, "What d'ya want, punk?"

Bepy opened the door of the car, a white 1946 Ford. Mousey was sitting on two pillows behind the wheel. Bepy reached in and quickly pulled the pillows from under Mousey's ass. Suddenly Mousey looked like a midget behind the wheel of his four-door sedan.

He was embarrassed. "What the hell are you doing?" he yelled.

Dana watched this through the window of Morris's grocery. She couldn't believe it. One minute Mousey was behind the wheel; the next minute all she could see was his nose. She began to laugh.

Bepy climbed into Mousey's car, pulled out his Sicilian stilleto, and stuck Mousey in the ribs, just enough to put the fear of God in him.

"Look, you little scumbag, if I see you near Dana again, I'll cut you from your asshole up to your neck," he said loudly. "Do you understand? And tell those other scumbags you hang around with that the same goes for them." He cut just a little notch in Mousey's ribs. "Do you feel the spirit, Mousey? Tell me, ya little bastard. Do you feel the spirit?"

"Yesss," Mousey gasped, and pissed his pants right in the car. "You cut me," he moaned. "I'm bleeding." He opened his eyes in fear.

"No shit," Bepy hissed. "I cut ya? Gee, you wet yourself and ruined your velvet upholstery. You better get plastic seat covers, because the next time I'll make you shit."

Mousey pulled away holding his side. He knew Bepy meant business.

Bepy walked to the corner where Dana was waiting nervously. He entered the store, walked over to Morris, and ordered two ham-and-cheese sandwiches on Italian bread and two Pepsis. Then, turning to Dana, he said in a low voice, "Tell your sister to get used to me."

Dana smiled. "Let's talk, Bepy. We have a lot to say to each other."

After they left the store Dana walked a few steps and then grabbed Bepy's hand to hold it. She smiled again and said, "Bepy, I love you. I've missed you so much."

"And don't you forget it, Dana. You give me a lot of problems, you and your stupid family. Problems that I don't need. Why the hell were you going out with that half-a-hump Mousey? He must be four feet tall?"

"He's the same height as me," she said. "He just looks short because he lifts weights. He's all muscle. And he's got a good job. My sister works with him."

"You'd have midgets for kids! Dana, don't listen to your sister. She's steering you wrong, Dana. Believe me." Bepy appealed his case while Dana stood quietly listening to him go on and on.

"Anyway," he concluded, "from now on, you don't go out with anybody but me. That's it. I don't care what your sister says or what kinda job Mousey's got. I'm the boss, and you're my girl, and that's it. Case closed."

Dana smiled, "OK, Bepy."

Several months went by, and OJA Oil hit ninety-two dollars. The market was going wild; there was talk that it would hit one hundred dollars soon. Bepy sold his shares at ninety-one and a half.

That evening he went to look for Mr. Morrano. The bartender said he was home sick with the flu, so Bepy went to his house, after first stopping and buying a gallon of homemade red wine, the best in the neighborhood. He didn't want to go empty-handed. His mother always said never visit a sick person empty-handed.

When he arrived at Mr. Morrano's house, the Don's wife opened the door. "Aren't you the boy who worked in the butcher shop a few years ago?" she asked.

"Yes, ma'am, that's me. I'd like to see Mr. Morrano."

"Come in. You've gotten so big now. Emilio is in the bedroom. Go on in. It's the last door on the right."

Bepy walked down the hall to the bedroom.

Mr. Morrano, lying in bed, was surprised to see Bepy, but greeted him.

"I brought you homemade wine," Bepy said proudly putting the gallon bottle on the cedar chest.

"Thanks, kid. You're number one in my book."

"I came to tell you to sell the stock. At the closing of today's market, it was ninety-two. They say it's going to hit one hundred, but I advise you to unload now. Sell tomorrow, before profit-taking starts. That could have a tumbling effect. The stock could drop to the seventies. Then it may go back up to one hundred, but you'd better sell now, Mr. Morrano."

"Kid, you're unbelievable. Thank you for the tip. I'll make a good score, thanks to you. I'll clean up on that one, won't I?"

"You've been good to me, also, Mr. Morrano," Bepy answered. "Here's the five grand you loaned me. And thanks for the territory. I appreciate it. I used it to start the betting operations on Wall Street. Thanks for getting me started."

"My pleasure, Bephino, my pleasure. Did you buy any stock?"

"Yeah."

"So, you did all right, huh?"

"Yeah. I did very well. So don't worry about me. I'm fine. I gotta be rich one way or the other. You always told me to have the best, so I'm working on it."

"Bephino, something big is coming up. Do you want it?"

"How big?"

"This one is a connected guy who's gotta go. The Syndicate, we all chip in a total of twenty-five grand to send him away. Are you sure you want the contract? With your job on Wall Street and all the other things, can you handle it?"

"Twenty-five Gs tax free? Sure I can. That's a good score."

"OK. When I'm ready, I send for you. I give you all the information then."

"I'll see you then, Mr. Morrano. Get well fast, and enjoy your wine."

A few days later, while Bepy was shaving, his father approached him. "Bephino, how are you doing with Dana?"

"Very good, Papa. She's having dinner with us Sunday. Do you like her?"

"Yeah, me and your mother both like her. Napoletanas, you know, they make good cooks. You know that, huh?"

"Yeah, like Mrs. Russo, the Ravioli Queen of 13th Avenue. She's napoletana."

"But be careful, Bephino. Those people have a bad habit—they like to spend money. You understand, huh? Be careful. They love to have charge accounts."

"Yeah, Papa. I understand."

"One more thing. I know you work on Wall Street and you make sandwiches with Red, but I hear from your uncle Pietro that you are involved in some big deals with the Mafia. You know my father was a big Mafioso in the Old Country. But that's no life for you. *Ah capeesh?*"

"*Si, io capito,* Papa. Don't worry. I'll keep making the sandwiches. OK?" Bepy answered smoothly. "Hey, Papa, what does that big-mouth Uncle Pietro call big deals?"

"He didn't say. He just told me to keep my eyes open."

6

"Do any of your men know you asked me to accept this thing?"

"Not yet. Why?"

"Can we keep this one private? I don't want anyone but you and me to know that I am handling this one."

"How come?" Morrano asked.

Bephino looked at him. "Well, you said this involves the Syndicate. I assume you mean the five New York families. There will be a lot of talk among the soldiers of all the families on this hit. I prefer no glory, no talk."

"You're a smart boy, Bephino. I like that," Morrano said, shaking his head. "That's a good one. 'No glory, no talk.' OK, Bephino, we'll keep it quiet, but understand that only the five bosses know about this one. They all had to agree. Only they know I gave it to you: Menesiero, the Sciacchitano. The bosses don't talk about a hit to their soldiers unless one gets the contract. Understand? They would have no reason to. It could hurt them somewhere down the line, and they know that. Your glory and fame will be minimized, I assure you."

"Yes, sir. That's fine," Bepy answered, but he still had doubts. He knew how after a hit there were always whispers about the hit man who did the honors. It was a tradition in Brooklyn, a matter of respect, you might say.

They spoke in a huddle at the end of the bar. A black man was mopping the floor. As he came close, Bepy automatically switched to Italian. "Please give me all the information I'll need. Let's speak in Italian so the eggplant won't understand us.

The Don replied, also in Italian, "Yes, that's a good idea. Here are some important facts and his picture." He admired this young Italian speaking their native tongue so well.

The janitor heard the foreign tongue flicker and knew they were up to no good.

"You get the twenty-five thousand now, today," the Don continued. "I take nothing. It's all yours. This must be done with some style. We don't want it to look like a family rub-out or a family war. That's why I'm giving this to you and not one of our regulars. You have a good imagination. I feel you can handle it better. Whatta you think?"

"I think you're absolutely right," Bepy said. "I can handle it. Don't worry, I'll come up with something exotic. Watch the newspapers."

"Good. You put something together real nice, take a few days—even a week. Plan it well, and I'll watch the newspapers for the good news.

"The man's name is Vince 'The Hawk' Gacolido. He's maybe fifty-nine years old, about one hundred forty pounds, short, with gray hair, and always very well dressed. He has a mole on his right ear. It's a small brown mole, but it sticks out like a little lump. You can see it in the picture. Look at it close. So don't hit the wrong guy. Always know your man. We don't ever want to hit innocent people. It's happened before."

"Yes, I understand, Mr. Morrano. That would be bad."

"Now listen. Everyday he stops at his hangout, a candy store in East New York at this address. It's a bad neighborhood; so be careful. He always drinks a strawberry malted out of the can. Remember, a can, not a glass.

"The guy's like a little animal. We don't want you to hit anyone else—just him. If he's got soldiers with him, and if you're stuck and you have to save your own life, then kill them all. But try to avoid extra trouble. Make it a clean job and, like you said, make it something exotic, something confusing." He handed Bepy the cash in a bag.

"Bephino, this is very important. We don't want it to look like we're at war. The police, they gotta be confused for at least a few months, until the story quiets down." When Morrano finished, he seemed a little uncomfortable. With deliberation, he said, "This is a big one. I hope you can handle it."

"Mr. Morrano, you can order his flowers now. The Hawk is almost on ice."

Morrano smiled and kissed Bepy on both cheeks, then offered him good wishes: *"Buon viaggio e buona fortuna, amico mio."*

During the next few days, Bepy left Wall Street early to case the East New York section of Brooklyn. It was a whole new neighborhood for him, and he explored the terrain carefully. He watched the candy store. Each time, he wore some different hat or outfit or make-up, so he would not get spotted too often. He knew how important this hit was to the Don, and knew he could not afford to mess up. He also thought maybe the five families would kill him if it went wrong.

The third time in the store, he was browsing through some comic books and peeking around—it wasn't too crowded at three o'clock in the afternoon—when the door opened. A well-dressed man walked in, a little guy, who looked like Vince the Hawk. Bepy took a deep breath and looked for the mole via an overhead mirror. The guy sat down and ordered a malted and cookies and began to drink it out of the can. Finally, Bepy saw the brown mole. It looked like a little bug on his ear.

What an opportunity to knock him off right now, he thought. But he knew the setup was not ready yet. But he now knew his man, and the next time it would be sure and quick. He felt confident as he clocked the Hawk. He was a 3:00 P.M. malted drinker, with a side order of Oreos.

Bepy had left the candy store before The Hawk finished drinking and went directly to his hero shop number two. It was Friday and Monkey was cleaning up. "Drop everything you're doing," Bepy told him. "You're finished for the day. I got something for you."

Monkey took off his apron. "What's up, Bep?"

"On your way home, I want you to stop off at 18th Avenue and 54th Street. Go into the synagogue, but don't be seen. All the Jews start praying around sundown on Friday. Wait till they start singing and humming with their heads down. They'll be wearing their skullcaps. Steal two of their big hats, the kind with all the fur on them, and get two black coats from the closet area.

"Find a rabbi's car in the parking lot, too. Remember the make, color, and model. Don't take the car, Monkey, just take the license plates and exchange them with another set. Take 'em off another car, OK? The Jews will never realize the plates have been changed. After we use the plates, we'll return them to the car. We can get the rabbi's home address through that girl Marilyn at the license bureau and return them during the night if we have to. I'll see you tonight at the poolroom, OK?"

"How can I tell if a car is a rabbi's car? They have a sign on it?"

"Any car in their parking lot at five in the afternoon on a Friday is a rabbi's car, believe me. We gotta take a gamble. Pick one out without chrome. Them guys hate chrome."

"OK, I'll see you tonight." Monkey walked a few feet, then turned. "This is a big one, huh, Bep?"

"Yeah, Monk. Don't ask me, please. I told you—I hate to explain what's going through my mind. It spoils my train of thought. Just follow my orders exactly, Monk. I'm getting butterflies in my stomach, and I hate that feeling."

"OK, I'll get your fur hats and coats, and see you tonight."

"Monk, I said hats, coats, and license plates. Don't forget the plates. Be careful. Don't be seen by anyone. Tomorrow is my debut, so I can't fuck up. It's like a confirmation of my heritage. OK, kid?"

Monkey smiled broadly, "You got some line of shit, Bep. You should've been a lawyer."

Later that evening, Monkey arrived at the poolroom. He motioned Bepy to a dark corner in the rear. "I got your hats and coats and changed the plates on a rabbi's car. And I know exactly what car we need tomorrow. So don't worry. Everything went smooth. It was a snap!"

"You know, Monkey, you're beautiful. You are beautiful. You handle everything so smooth."

"Yeah, but them rabbis are gonna go berserk looking for their hats and coats," Monkey said.

"I don't care about them. They'll get their stuff back. I only care about the hit. Monk, tomorrow morning, you take the train to the race track and rob a car exactly like the rabbi's car. Same color and model. Put the rabbi's plates on the car you take at the track. I want those plates on before we make the hit. Then meet me off the Coney Island and Bath Beach exit. You remember that exit? Meet me there at 2:00 P.M. sharp. I'll go by bus. I'll be waiting for you when you come off the highway."

"OK, I'll be there," Monkey assured him.

"Get to the track early—about eleven—and watch the cars come in. Follow the car we need to its spot and get it fast. Gas it up if it needs gas, then stay out of sight until you meet me. If you're running late getting the car, I'll wait. Don't talk about this to anyone. And don't forget, make sure the car is the same as or close to the rabbi's. That's important. All these things are important to this hit. I realize you don't understand, but everything comes together for me at the end like a puzzle. You know what I mean?"

"Yeah, you're a pro. I know, Bep."

Later that evening, Bepy looked through the arsenal of guns the boys had collected and found just what he needed—an old .44-caliber rust-pitted gun. It would definitely be the wrong type and caliber for any professional hit man to use. It was like shooting a cannon. It would blow apart anyone it hit. The gun looked like an antique. It could add to the confusion that Bepy was trying to prepare for the police. He loaded it and tested it by shooting into the dirt mound at the construction site on 8th Avenue. It worked.

The next day Monkey picked Bepy up right on time, in a 1947 black four-door Chevy, which didn't have an ounce of chrome on it. It looked like a real rabbi's car to Bepy: a very plain model.

"What a hard job it was to get the same car!" Monkey said. "I didn't think I was gonna find a dupe out of all those cars, but finally one came in. A priest and two nuns from Long Island were driving it. I didn't know nuns went to the track?"

"There's a lot of things holy people do we don't know about. Hey, Monk, do you remember the lot number you got it from? And how do you know they were from Long Island?"

"I checked in the glove compartment. I saw some church papers that said Farmingdale, Long Island. The lot number's thirty-eight, Section Y.

"Did you change the rabbi's plates to this car?"

"Yeah. I parked off the highway and put the rabbi's plates on this car. Don't worry. I learned all the detail work from you. It rubs off, Bepy."

Bepy looked at his friend and spoke to him in Italian, maybe for good luck. *"Ah ecco perche tu impari presto."*

"Bene cominciamo sono pronto, Alfredo," Monkey replied. "Yeah, I'm ready, Freddie," he sang.

"Monkey, let's pull over here and put these coats on. It's nice and quiet on this street."

They arrived at the candy store dressed like rabbis. Bepy even wore black pants, shoes, and gloves.

"Ahh, there's a bunch of kids hanging around in front—perfect. That's perfect," Bepy said.

"How come ya happy about the kids?"

"I like that. I like to see kids out in front of the store. Only a kid would take the license plate number of a car and open his yap to the cops. Kids like to play Dick Tracy. You know, they wanna be heroes," Bepy explained. "When we leave, I want the plate and the car description to be seen and reported. Then the police will blame the rabbis for the hit. If it goes all right, Monk, two and two will make twenty-five grand for us."

Bepy quickly fixed his fake beard, with curls hanging by his ears, his fur hat and black coat with velvet collar. He was a very sharp-looking rabbi. He handed Monk a beard, too. "Put this on, Monk. There's tape on it already."

Monkey looked at Bepy in amazement. "Boy, you look good. These beards look real."

"Monkey, fix your hat. It's crooked. Look in the mirror and fix your beard. Do it nice, Monk. I practiced last night in the bathroom. My mother thought I'd cut my hair, because she saw hairs in the sink. Pull in front of the store on the avenue."

Monk made a turn and double-parked in front of the candy store. The kids turned to watch them.

"Keep the motor running. I'll be right out. Blow your horn once in a while. Act crazy. Act like one of those excitable Jews who are always in a hurry, with nothing to hide. You know what I mean? Keep this car noticed by those kids. The whole ball game is right out here in the street."

"It's about time I got the important job." Monkey laughed, then leaned over and squeezed Bepy's neck. "Good luck, Bep. Be careful."

Bepy left the car at three sharp—malted-milk time, he hoped. The kids standing around were amused to see rabbis in an Italian neighborhood. They stared at him and the car.

Vinney the Hawk, please be here, Bepy said to himself.

As he entered the candy store, he looked toward the soda fountain. He spotted an empty Oreo wrapper on the counter and then he saw The Hawk. The guy had his little face in a malted can, trying to suck up the last chunk of ice cream at the bottom.

What timing! I'm a fuckin' pro, Bepy thought. A perfect plan. The fuckin' hit is drowning himself in the can on the dot.

He walked up to the counter. "What ya havin', bub?" the soda jerk asked Bepy in a nasty tone.

"I'm thinking, I'm thinking. Don't rush me already with the bubs," Bepy baited him.

The soda jerk looked like a rough, tough character. He had a burly body, a bald head, and obviously very little class.

"Well, while you're thinkin', don't stand too near the counter with that fuckin' beard." He leaned over and sneered at Bepy. "We have people to serve," he said, looking over to The Hawk for acknowledgment. "I don't want hair from that fur hat on my counter. So move back."

Bepy acted highly insulted, but was happy the soda jerk was leading the way to the fiasco that was coming up.

"Is that the way you talk to a man of God? . . . Hair from my fur hat? From my beard? You, you're a disgrace to humanity."

"Man of God, my ass," the soda jerk spat back. "Move the hell back, you Jew bastard. We don't like hair in our food."

"Dummy, you dummy!" Bepy yelled back.

The Hawk, amused by the rabbi standing up to the soda jerk, stopped sucking on the malted can.

Monkey blew the horn. Everyone looked toward the store window.

Bepy yelled back at the soda jerk, "You—you bum. Don't you talk to me like that! I'm a man of God, a man of God!"

The whole store was watching now. "Get the fuck out of my store, you crazy bastard!" the soda jerk hollered.

Bepy pulled out his big antique pistol, waved it around crazily and acted very inexperienced and excited. He pretended he'd gone mad and was going to shoot the soda jerk. He threw a wild shot into the mirror, which missed everyone but shattered the glass, sending The Hawk and everyone else to take cover. In the confusion, Bepy looked straight at Vince the Hawk, who was ducking down next to him, and put one directly in his head. The head split like a melon, and The Hawk's brains splattered all over the counter. Then Bepy fired another shot, trying to wing the soda jerk in order to convince everyone the jerk was the guy he was really trying to hit—not The Hawk.

Bepy ran out screaming, "I'm a man of God! I will not be damned by you!"

The soda jerk crawled out from under the counter. He had been hit in his shoulder and bleeding badly. He saw The Hawk slumped down, with a two-inch slit in his skull. The broken mirror was splattered with blood and brains. The other customers were screaming.

The soda jerk moved to the window and watched the car pull away. "Can you believe a rabbi would do this?" he asked in shock and surprise. "Them fuckin' Jews! Look what they've done. Look what they've done to us. They've destroyed us. The fuckin' guy's nuts, I tell you!" he screamed out.

The children outside got the plate number and car model. They couldn't figure out why the rabbis pulled away so slowly from such a shoot-out. But an old man watching said that religious people always pull out slowly. They never drive fast. They don't want to get a ticket.

"OK, Monkey, keep driving to the track. Don't stop."

They removed their get-ups and stuffed them in shopping bags. By the time they reached the track, they looked normal again. Monkey pulled in and parked the car in the same spot he took it from, then quickly put the original plates back on. He took the rabbi's plates and the hats and coats and consolidated everything.

"Wait here. I'll get us a car," Monkey told Bepy. He grabbed a new Cadillac from a different section and drove back to where Bepy was waiting. Bepy was quiet, trying to regain his composure and return to sanity.

"I took us a Caddie. They always steal Cadillacs at the track. They'll think it was one of them car-ring guys."

Bepy agreed and watched Monkey's keen, sharp movements during their exodus from hell.

They returned to the rabbis' House of God, slipped in, and mixed the hats and coats up with the other clothes hanging in the entrance closet. Outside, they were in luck again. The original rabbi car was in the parking lot. Monkey removed the plates and gave the car its own plates back, the plates the police would be looking for.

Bepy took the pistol and laid it on the front seat of the car, so when the real man of God got in and sat down, he would feel the lump and reach under and pull it out. In so doing, he would handle the murder weapon, thus putting the only prints on it that would count.

The news did not hit the papers until Monday morning. The newsboys throughout Bensonhurst cried out: "Extra! Extra! Read all about it! RABBI KILLS THE HAWK IN A VIOLENT RAGE!" The paper explained that the police had the killer, a rabbi, and that the bullet was not meant for The Hawk; he got hit by mistake. The soda jerk told the police about the argument that took place and identified the rabbi as the killer.

Don Emilio couldn't believe the way the kid had handled this contract. The police would never solve such a bizarre crime. The Mob people went deep into their conclaves to whisper.

With the twenty-five thousand dollars for the hit, Bepy had piled up some serious dough for a guy who had just turned eighteen. He was secretly rich. But even though he had wanted no glory on the hit, word leaked out.

"Who the hell is this kid they say is the hit man from Brooklyn? They call him the Sciacchitano." Capos and soldiers whispered such things while eating in their favorite Manhattan cafés. "They say this guy is something special. They say he's only a punk kid, but he's already a specialist. The kid's got class. When he makes a hit, nobody knows what's coming up. Like an executioner."

"I'm glad somebody's got class around here," another man said, chewing on a roll from the basket in front of him. "I'm tired of the sloppy shit that's been going on. Last year we sent two soldiers out to hit three of Al Poscoe's guys who were drinking in a bar. The dumb bastards hit three vacuum-cleaner salesmen by mistake. Can you imagine that? Then we brought in some new soldiers from Sicily on their first job. They were sent to the Bronx to rough up a guy and they spent two days on the subway asking the police for directions. When they finally got their man, they were so fucked up and confused, the guy beat the shit out of them and sent them home to Cherry Street."

They laughed and drank their black coffee.

Bepy had become the subject of good conversation. Everyone spoke well of him, even though they did not know they were speaking of Bepy. All they knew was that Don Emilio Morrano had a good young man in his service. The Morrano family was known around the country. If any of the out-of-town families from Boston to Los Angeles needed a special hit, they would contract it through the Morrano family in New York. Once the contract was accepted, the client could consider his enemy one of St. Peter's roommates.

Book III
1947–1960

7

When Pasquale came home one evening, Finametta was pale as a ghost.

"What's the matter, Finametta? You look *tutta bianca.*"

"Come. I have to show you something." She led him to Bepy's closet, opened the shoe box, and showed him the money.

"E'una fortuna! Pasquale said, picking up green bundles of neatly rubber-banded cash. "Too much to count." He covered the box and said, *"Aspetta,* Finametta. I'll talk to Bephino when he comes home. Maybe he's holding it for somebody."

"I'm worried Pasquale. That's why he's been buying us so many things lately, eh?"

"What things? He buys a toaster, an orange juice squeezer...that's nothing," Pasquale said, attempting to reassure her. "Don't get *pazza.* He's a businessman. He makes money on Wall Street and through other things."

"What other things?"

Unable to explain, Pasquale just stared at her.

When Bepy arrived home later that night, his parents were sitting at the table waiting.

Pasquale got up and picked up the shoe box. "Bepy, we wanna talk to you."

"OK, let's talk," Bepy said, and started to remove his shirt.

Pasquale showed him the shoe box. "Where did this come from, Bepy?"

"Oh, the box? From Florsheims," Bepy answered with a smile.

"We're talking about the money inside." Pasquale opened the lid, then asked in an anxious voice, "How much is here? Why is it in the closet? What kinda business you in? Tell me, Bephino. I like to know the truth."

"I always tell you the truth. About eight-five grand. I made money from a few deals."

Finametta was listening. "What kinda few deals?" she asked.

"Different deals. We book bets and numbers on Wall Street."

"And you earn this kind of money doing that?" Pasquale asked.

"Sometimes we lose and we gotta pay off, so that's not all profit. It's like a bank, Papa. If we lose, we need it to pay off the betters. Anyway, forget it. I make good money with my sandwich shops. I bought you a beautiful new car today—brand new, not used. It's a beauty. You're gonna love it."

"You bought me a car?" Pasquale asked in disbelief.

"Yeah, Papa. A brand-new Pontiac. It's on order. It'll be delievered in two months. It's a four-door, with plenty of chrome, like you like, huh, Papa? Let's be happy. Maybe our life is beginning to change."

Pasquale was stunned. He had always dreamed of having a car. "What color?" he asked meekly.

"Never mind the color," Finametta blurted out. "You're just as crazy as your son. He thinks he's a *banca* now." She began wailing. "What do I do with this box? I'm too nervous to enjoy things. And don't buy me no more toasters and juicers."

"Put it back in the closet, Mama. But in case of fire, grab it and run."

"How can I sleep now? I'll feel like I'm on guard duty, watching this thing. You always make me worry, Bephino. Now I got more things to worry about."

"Next month I got a big soap box full of money coming. So you can guard them together. OK?" Bepy chuckled as his mother walked toward her stove talking to herself. "Mama, make me some hot chocolate, will you? You got any pound cake left? I feel hungry."

"Why don't you put it in the bank and get interest on your money?" Pasquale asked. "Then your mother won't worry so much. The bank is safer, Bephino."

"We'll talk another time about interest. I'm sleepy and hungry. It's late. OK, Papa?"

Pasquale, sitting himself down at the table, said "Finametta, make two hot chocolate, please." Then, turning to Bephino, he whispered, "Tell me, what color is the car?"

"Maroon. And those new cars smelled so nice inside, Papa." Both smiled. It was Pasquale's favorite car color.

Thirty days later, Bephino was drafted. The brokerage firm promised that his job would be waiting when he got out of the service. Red and Joey D were 4-F, and Alley Oop was considered a family hardship case, or a mental case. Monkey got drafted into the navy; Bepy was assigned to the army.

Bepy was forced to make a decision about the cash he had piled up, so he made bank deposits in different banks, totaling ninety-two grand. He gave the books to his mother. "Mama, you're off guard duty, and your name is on these books. If anything happens to me, it's all yours. OK?"

"Don't talk like that, Bepy. I don't want money. I want my children. I'm happy the way we are."

"If I die in the army, buy Mario a new Buick, on me. He likes Buicks. It's a gift from me to my brother."

She smiled and hugged him.

"But only if I die, OK? Tell Papa if you need any money. Just take out whatever you need. It's OK. I have a lot more money, a lot more," he whispered to her. "I'm rich, Mama. But I can't tell anybody yet."

She stared at him as though he were nuts.

Speaking softly and moving his hands Italian style, he continued. "I bought IBM and telephone stock. Papa knows about that. It's a lot of money. He knows where the certificates are, so don't be afraid if you need money. OK, Mama? I'm loaded."

"How come you so loaded now, Bepy?"

"Mama, our life has changed. Believe me, our life has changed. It'll take a few years before I can act like a guy with lots of money and *ah respecto*. Right now I gotta be a bum and struggle for the public. *Tu capeesh?*"

"I'm in the dark about the whole thing. Please be careful, *figlio mio*," she said as she held her forehead.

"OK, you stay in the dark until I get home, and then we go to Miami Beach," Bepy said, laughing.

His mother began to relax and laugh at his joking.

The following six months, Bepy was in training in South Carolina. Then he was shipped to France. His brother was by then already discharged and back home in Brooklyn.

Bepy and Dana got engaged before he left for France. They had a party and gave diamond rings to each other. Her family was happy now. Peace at last. The promise was made and would be kept. It was the Italian way. Good or bad, a promise is a promise.

While in France, Bepy hustled like crazy. He found ways to make even more money . There was no betting and only very small gambling games, but the GIs always needed money to spend on whores and they were always short of cash four or five days before payday. So Bepy set up business fast: ten dollars for twenty, all notes payable on payday. Even if it was three days before payday, the price was the same. He recruited a few guys from New York City to help him collect. They were reliable hard-hitters who listened to him and did what was expected of them.

The French whores loved his style. They would tease the American soldiers, and when the soldiers didn't have the money, they'd say, "Go see Menesiero, the Bank of Italy. He'll lend you the money."

The soldiers, hot and horny, were happy to get instant cash. Bepy even had his own table for business transactions in a local bar. He recorded each GI's serial number, company, and barracks. Then on payday he and his men went around in an army jeep and collected. The setup was perfect, and Bepy was making plenty of money. It was wall-to-wall pussy for him and his buddies and small mortgages for the rest of the guys.

Even the lieutenant in charge made life easy for Private Menesiero. He came from Long Island, and Bepy promised him that if he gave him any trouble while in the army, he would be waiting when the lieutenant arrived in New York after his discharge. At first the lieutanant didn't believe him. He called Bepy a "greaseball" out of the gutter, and gave him kitchen duty three days straight. Bepy wrote and told Alley Oop and Crazy Mikey to deliver flowers signed, "Love, Bephino" to the lieutenant's wife on Long Island. It blew the lieutenant's mind. Being a smart fellow, he quickly accepted the force of Sicilian promises. He realized Bepy could be for real. Therefore, he decided to make life easy for a fellow New Yorker, so easy it almost became a joke. He thanked Bepy for the flowers and said, "If you need anything, just let me know."

Bepy had to unload some of the French francs he had piled up, so he sent Dana money orders every month and told her to save it for their wedding. Her family could not understand how a GI could save that much money from a soldier's pay. "He's only a private!" her sister said. Her brother remarked, "Maybe he's protecting the general against the Mafia in Italy. That guy's unbelievable."

But her father still liked Bepy. "That's what I call a man," he'd say. "He knows what he's doing. He's a hard worker, that boy."

One evening in a bar, U.S. soldiers and French soldiers got into a fight. The French used knives and clubs, and a lot of heads were broken on both sides. It was a battle royal. Bepy got arrested because a French civilian picked him out as the one who broke a bottle over a French soldier's head. The soldier was in critical condition at the hospital. No one mentioned that the French soldier had stabbed a GI in the stomach with a long knife, and he was also critical. They only talked about the bottle incident.

Before the Army could take him under its jurisdiction, Bepy was confined in a maximum-security cell block of an old French prison, built in the sixteen-hundreds of stone. It was deep, dark, and damp—a real dungeon.

When Bepy entered, his cellmate greeted him. The man was a tall, heavily built, very muscular black with bushy hair and a face that looked like it had been chewed up by a school of piranhas. The guards locked the heavy door and left him without saying a word.

The black man smiled eagerly at Bepy. Then he stood in front of him, hands on his hips, and looked him up and down. He didn't say a word; just smiled. His white teeth glowed out of his horrible face in the dimly lit cell. Finally, he said in a snappy tone, "Why ya in here for, Babyface?"

Bepy moved to the vacant bed, unrolled his mattress and didn't bother to answer. He was shocked by what he was to room with.

"I'm talking to ya, honey," the man snapped, "An ya bess answer Big Yom, understand, Babyface? Cause Big Yom gonna be your man soon enough."

He walked over to the center of the room, picked up a set of barbells, lifted and began to pump about four hundred pounds of weights, groaning and puffing as he lifted the weights over his head ten times. When he lowered them to the stone floor, sweat dripped from his face and shirtless body. He flexed his enormous muscles in a show of masculinity.

"See, that's the way I pump. I pump real hard when I gets uptight." Bepy looked at the guy and couldn't believe his eyes. Then he glanced quickly around the room, looking for anything to protect himself with. But there was nothing.

"Where you from, boy?" Big Yom asked.

"Brooklyn. Where you from?" Bepy replied anxiously.

"North Carolina, that's my home," Big Yom answered with a grin. "I bet you're real smooth, ain't ya, boy? I bet ya don't have a ripple on your ass, huh, white boy? Yeah, you're gonna be smooth as silk. I can smell that baby ass right now. I'm very anxious for ya, honey. It gets real lonely in here. I always enjoys smooth things in the dark." Moving his hand around, he continued. "I runs my hands all over smooth things in the dark. I'm gonna be your man. Whatcha think of that?" he snapped.

"How come you're talking like that to me when we're both men?" Bepy asked.

"I'm the man. You're the woman. Whatcha think of that?" A broad grin spread on his face.

"Did you ever get your fuckin' eyes plucked out in the dark? What'd ya think of that?" Bepy asked.

"Sure enough?" Yom answered. "You think ya can take my eyes out, woman? I'll slap ya into tomorrow, boy. I'll slap ya into eternity," he said angrily. "Ya see these arms? I can tear your skinny legs off your body if I want to. I can rip ya apart like a boiled chicken."

Bepy knew he was in real trouble, but he forced a weak smile. "Who named you Mr. Yom? That's an interesting name."

"Some ol' white wife of mine. He got sick in his head."

"Your wife was a he?" Bepy asked in disbelief.

"Sure. Sure enough. All wives are he's in the French tombs."

"What happened to him?"

"They tooks him from me. He was a skinny little fellow, an ol' crow. But I had nothin' else. I needed somethin' bad—had the fever in my body real bad—so I tooks him for my wife." He laughed as he thought about it. "The little ol' crow fought me until I had no choice but to hurt him. He fought me and bit my shoulders until his false teeths fell out, but finally he became my wife. He named me Mr. Yom, the little ol' crow. He was funny but tough as an ol' turkey. I'm tellin' ya that turkey was tough."

"Where was he from? Was he from Brooklyn? Are you sure he wasn't calling you *molinyom?*"

"Yeah, I think he was from Brooklyn. He talked about New York a lot. Ya see, one day the little chipmunk was bitin' me. See my shoulder?" He turned to show Bepy. "See that scar? He bit me there. So I stepped on his false teeths and broke them in pieces. His voice then sounded so dribbly and rough. So I thinks he calls me Mr. Yom. He was old, but I took him fine, real fine, till he started talkin' to himself. The damn crow went stir crazy, and nearly drove *me* crazy with all that mumblin' day and night with no teeths. I hurt him one night just a little, and the guards moved him to the next cell. But I sees him through them bars up there. Them goes to the next cell. I climbs up there and talks to him."

The prison walls were thick stone; an opening at the top with bars was the only ventilation. Green moss, like carpet, crawled along the floor and spread over the walls.

"I climbs up there and talks to my bride sometimes when I feels right. I tells him how good he was to me and why did he fight me so. But he mumbles, he always mumbles."

The huge black man smiled, his white teeth and pink tongue seeming to glow in the dim light, like a horrible dream.

"Could I see this guy? Where is he now?" Bepy asked.

"I don't know if I want ya to see my woman. You girls may fight, and I don't like my girls to fight." Mr. Yom looked at him suspiciously.

Bepy swallowed hard at that remark, but, challenging the seriusness of Mr. Yom's remark, he replied, "Don't worry Mr. Yom. We won't fight. What's his name?"

"His name is Hank. Hank Morrellioo."

"Do you mean Hank Morelli?"

"Somethin' like that. That little dago fought me day and night," Yom said, shaking his head in a sort of admiration for Hank.

"I knew a master sergeant in my division who was from my neighborhood in Brooklyn. His brother, Ralphy, owned a lemon-ice stand. Their name was Morrelli. I wonder if his first name was Hank? How come he's in jail? What did he do?"

"He tried to rob the gold bars from headquarters." Yom reached out to touch Bepy's ass. "You're gonna be nice. Ya know that, honey? Ya look fine. I like your shape. You're cute. Take your shirt off and let me see ya better."

Bepy protested. "Hold it, hold it! What're ya, fuckin' nuts with that bullshit? I'm a stud. I ain't no cunt. So get off that bullshit, OK, ya fuckin' *tutzone?* Keep your paws off me before I pluck your lights out, ya black bastard. Ain't you got any respect for a man's privacy?"

He started to walk around the cell in a nervous circle, tightening his fist. But the big man suddenly grabbed him, pinched a nerve in his neck, and held him tightly, like a kitten. The paralyzing hold seemed fatal to Bepy. Yom eagerly screamed out as he smacked Bepy's face twice. He yelled again, menacingly, as he continued to hit Bepy's face. "Don't ya never call me a black bastard. I'll kill ya, white boy! I'll kill ya. Don't ya know that?" he threatened.

Bepy couldn't believe this. He had heard about such things happening in jail, but never dreamed it would happen to him. He knew the muscle-bound man had him good and was gonna fuck him in his ass soon enough and sure enough.

Yom held him securely with only one hand, sweat dripping from his dark, shiny body and his pitted face wet and slick. He pulled Bepy up close against his chest, turning his face upward. Bepy's eyes, the only part of his body that still had the ability to move, spread wide in protest as Yom slowly kissed his lips with passion. Bile rose in Bepy's throat, and his eyes bulged in shock as the black man's tongue orally fondled him.

Using only his left hand Yom pulled Bepy's pants down in one motion, almost ripping them off. Suddenly Bepy felt hot meat poking at

111

him from behind. As the nerve pinch was slowly being released, Yom began kissing Bepy's back and shoulders.

Bepy, still numb from the pinch and the heavy blows, tried to regain his composure. He was surprised when his voice sounded high as he spoke up for his virginity through his bleeding lips.

"Let's do this right, OK? If we're gonna do this, let's do it exotic, Mr. Yom," he proposed. "You gotta put me in the mood. Don't force me like this. Get me hot, OK? If you're gonna fuck me, fuck me right."

Yom's eyes lit up as he knelt down and kissed Bepy's bare hips. Then, raising up, he kissed him on his shoulder, like a man drooling over a sexy woman. "Ya wanna hot time, don't ya, boy?" he asked, seductively grasping Bepy's firm young ass. "OK, let's have a hot time. But ya better be good."

Bepy quickly pulled his pants up, trying to calm himself. Look at this shit. He's treatin' me like a cunt. What the fuck am I gonna do now? he thought. The fuckin' coon kissed me on my lips; I even felt his prick against me. I think I'm gonna vomit. This guy is bad. He's like steel. He's a fuckin' black superman. I need a gun, a knife, even a bottle, to stop him. His eyes darted around searching for something to use as a weapon.

Yom began to rub him again, his still exposed cock throbbing and pressing against Bepy's thigh.

"Hold it! Wait a minute, will ya?" Bepy yelled. "Let me catch my breath for a minute. This shit takes time. I'm a slow starter. Let's talk for an hour or so. Pick your pants up, will ya? Until I figure out how we gonna do this thing." He turned away, muttering, *"Disgraziato molingiana* bastard, *disgraziato molingiana ganudo."*

"What ya say? What ya talkin', boy?"

"I'm talkin' love talk, you big *pungolo,* love talk."

Yom chuckled. "OK, sounds cool, boy. My old crow talked like that to me sometimes. It sounds cool."

"First, tell me about Hank. Let's get to know each other. Whatta ya say?" he asked, stalling for time. "I'd like to see this guy Hank. You say he spoke words like that to you?"

"Ya wanna see the old crow? Get on my shoulders, honey, and I'll lift ya up. Ya can see him in his cell. I think I'm gonna like the feel of ya sittin' up on me with your legs wrapped tight aroun' my neck." He grinned at Bepy in anticipation.

Bepy shook his head in disgust and climbed up on Yom's massive shoulders. For the first time in his life, he felt physically small, as he was lifted up near the ceiling. He peeked into the next cell. A skinny old man sat on a cot with an army blanket wrapped around his shoulders. He was mumbling and looked very bad. Poor Hank, Bepy thought. He was talking to the walls.

"Hey, Hank," Bepy yelled. "Are you Ralphy's brother?"

Hank looked up in surprise but didn't answer.

"Is your brother Ralphy the lemon-ice guy in Bay Ridge, Brooklyn?"

"Yeth," Hank mumbled in a slightly lisping but very polite voice, hampered by his lack of teeth. "Yeth, that'th my brother, Ralph. He knowth all the right people in Brooklyn. My brother knowth the right people. He knowth all the..." Hank continued to mumble, repeating the words over and over, seemingly unable to turn himself off.

"Hey, Hank, do you remember me? I'm Bephino Menesiero from 13th Avenue. I live near Ralphy's store. My father had the fish wagon."

Hank looked up again. "Yeth, I think I remember you. Are you all right? Are you all right? Are you all right?"

"Am I all right?" Bepy asked incredulously. "I'm in jail with this fuckin' *molingiana* next door. He's a fuckin' sicky, this bastard."

"Be careful, he'll hurt you. *Si botza, si botza, si botza e molingiana.*" Hank mumbled repeatedly, "Are you all right? Are..."

Bepy had forgotten he was on the shoulders of Yom. Carried away at seeing a guy from the neighborhood in such feeble condition, he'd said too much. When Yom heard the words "fuckin'..." he dropped him.

Bepy hit the floor hard, his face scraping the wall as he fell, his knees cracking as he landed. He lay there in pain, his thoughts running wild. I'm dead. I'm dead. Not only am I dead, but this guy is gonna fuck my corpse. Whatta nightmare this is. I gotta make a move now or I'll be talking to walls like Hank the rest of my life.

Yom lowered his pants and this time stepped out of them. He stood over Bepy balls naked, smiling. Bepy couldn't believe this was actually happening. A fuckin' nightmare, he thought. Wake me up, Ma, I'm late for school. I must be dreaming this shit. But it was real. The only thing within reach was the weights, and he knew he couldn't even roll them, much less lift them.

Thinking hard, Bepy struggled to his feet and did the only thing he could to save his life: he smiled at Yom and began running his hands over his chest and stomach. "You're starting to look good, you know that?" he said in a choking voice. "Yeah, you look strong and sexy."

A survival plan, a do-or-die plan, was slowly developing in his mind. With limp-wristed submissiveness, Bepy looked up at him. "You're gonna be good to me, ain't you, Tutzone?"

"I sure is woman. I'm gonna make your asshole blink back at me when I gets ya. Ya calls me Daddy from now on and I calls ya Smooth Ass. Now come to Daddy, Smooth Ass. Come when I calls ya."

Bepy knew his ass was grass, and this guy was the lawn mower. Keeping up his pretense, he asked shyly, "If we fool around, will the guards see us?"

"This is the French tombs, boy. The guards only bring us meals and dinner was two hours ago. We gots the whole night for ourselves. We gonna have a real honeymoon. I got the honey and you got the moon."

Bepy looked at Yom in total disgust but carefully tried to keep his true feelings from being revealed on his face. Look at those liver lips, he thought. He kissed my lips, my ass, and my shoulder already. Now he's gonna crawl over my body and tear out my organs. What a fuckin' nightmare I'm having. No weapons—nothing. *Dota della* is the only way. That or be banged for the first time in the ass.

"OK, big fellow. As long as we're not gonna be disturbed, then this is it," Bepy said. "Let's get down to some exotic sex. Let's play sex games that turn me on. Once I get turned on, you got it made, big boy. You lift weights until I tell you to stop. I'm gonna work you over like you never been worked over in your life. I'm gonna *dota della* on your big prick."

Yom was pleased. "Sounds good. That *della* thing, what is it?"

"You'll see. It's like a hot leather dance the Italians like to do. All over your balls," he whispered. "It will outdo any climax you ever had. While you pump your weights, I'm gonna play with you, OK?"

"OK, baby, OK. You're gonna be a fine wife." He put his arm around Bepy's neck. "Not like that ol' crow next door. He fought me day and night for two weeks. He never stopped fightin' me, that ol' turkey."

Bepy smiled at the thought of Hank hanging in there for two whole weeks. What a tough guy he must have been. "So get your weights and start pressin'. Don't stop till I get turned on," Bepy directed him. "Do you have any more weights to add to your bar?"

"No, that's all I have." The totally naked Yom picked up the barbells and began to press. Poof, poof, poof. He blew air from his mouth. After eighteen times he was still going strong. Every muscle glistened, and his body was so well formed that he looked like a black marble statue.

Bepy, hoping to keep the guy pressing and reassured, began to rub Yom's chest and shoulders, always smiling. He stroked Yom's hips and belly down to his balls. "Keep pumpin' them weights, Daddy. I'm gettin' turned on. I feel fine. Keep pumpin'," Bepy whispered, thinking with revulsion, God, what I gotta do to keep this man off me. I gotta kill this guy somehow. I gotta kill him. But how? How will I get the power to destroy such a big man?

Yom was performing to his fullest for Bepy. It was like an exhibition in hell. Every muscle on the black man's body bulged, dripping with sweat.

Bepy's eyes opened at the size of him, thinking of the big fuck that could take place if his scheme failed. The guy's balls looked like two hairy coconuts. They were big and full and were a great target for attack—the only place a hundred-fifty-pound man could hit and hope to stop such a powerful and passionately determined man. Once again, Bepy found himself hoping against hope.

"Come on, Daddy, just one more time," Bepy taunted Yom as he lowered his hands firmly to the man's groin, teasing him.

Yom looked like Goliath, a nude giant, every muscle in his beautiful body protruding to its shining fullest. His organ was now fully erect, rising high above his testicles. Bepy couldn't believe that this totally exhausted man was maintaining an erection. Imagine if he wasn't tired, he thought. This guy is deadly.

"One more time, please!" he coaxed, acting the part of the gay wife. "One more time. I feel so fine," he whispered. "I'm almost ready."

"Touch me again. Rub my body, woman," Yom whispered in an exhausted voice. "Get me ready. Don't ya come without me. Don't ya dare. Ya come with your man. Come on, touch ya Daddy."

"I will. Press. Lift. Just one more time for your woman," Bepy said as he wrapped both hands around Yom's prick. Yom was shaking and trembling with the effort. His muscles seemed to be ripping apart. Bepy stopped to measure up, then kicked the black man square in his balls. Then he kicked again, two more very hard kicks with his combat boots.

Yom just stared. His face expressed total surprise, but he was still standing tall, holding his weights above his face.

Bepy panicked. "Holy Christ!" he yelled, and began kicking and kicking like a machine gun. *"Dota della!"* he was yelling. *"Dota della!* Ya mother fucker! You wanna fuck me, OK. Fuck me if you feel like fuckin' me! Right now! I'm in the mood now."

The kicks were right on target. They were heavy, massive kicks to his balls. Bepy's boot tips were crushed. He quickly lowered his pants and mooned Yom as the big man tried to prevent himself from toppling over backward. Finally, with a groan, he fell with the weights. He hit the stone floor hard, and the weights landed on his face, ripping his chin off.

Bepy walked nervously around the body as he pulled his pants up around his waist. He was ready to launch another attack should the large man attempt to get up. Yom began to moan. He was hurt badly; blood was pouring out of his face. His head was partially crushed by the tremendous impact against the floor, his balls were totally displaced from

Bepy's wicked attack. Bepy couldn't determine the extent of the damage he had done. He sat and watched the body bleed into lifelessness. It had been a matter of survival for him.

The next morning the guards carried Yom out. He had died during the night, killed by the weights falling on him, the guards determined.

"Hey, Hank," Bepy yelled up to the opening at the top of the wall. "The *molingiana,* he's with St. Peter. He got fucked good last night."

"Are you all right? Are you all right, kid?" Hank mumbled.

Two months later, Bepy had his court-martial. He was charged with attempting to kill a French soldier while off base without a pass. The five judges were NATO officers, all colonels. Bepy faced a heavy sentence.

The trial lasted three days. The prosecution's main witness was a French civilian named Jean Chaval. He testified strongly against Bepy, determined to see him convicted. He explained in great detail what he saw Bepy do to the French soldier, smiling at the right moments, frowning when he described pain. He was like a lawyer himself, and the court seemed to be captivated.

Chaval's tongue rang a horrible sound in Bepy's ears.

Corporal Menesiero's turn finally came to take the stand in his own defense. He began to explain what happened. Inside he was boiling over Chaval's story, but he managed to appear calm. Suddenly, he referred to Monsieur Chaval as Monsieur Cocksucker. The remark came out so cooly, right in the middle of his testimony, that the courtroom reacted instantly. The English and American GIs went crazy and started to cheer. Even the judges couldn't hold back their laughter.

The defense then produced a pretty French whore who swore that Chaval was so drunk himself that night that he couldn't fuck her, so how could he see who had the bottle that struck the fatal blow? The court seemed impressed with her testimony. She also described the scene very vividly and convincingly. As she left the stand, moving her body and lips in a seductive manner, she looked at Chaval as if to say, "There's something wrong with that man."

Chaval, a married man, whose wife was present, showed shame and embarrassment. The defense attorney saw this, capitalized on his weakness, and asked him the fatal question: What he was doing in such a bar, with whores? Chaval smiled a small smile and struggled to find an answer, but his sharp tongue had come to a halt. Bepy whispered to his attorney, "Look at his French pride being shoved up his ass by a little whore. I told you it would work."

Then Chaval noticed several more whores waiting to testify. Bepy had him on the ropes. Chaval asked to be excused. He said he was ill.

It was obvious that Chaval would not return as a witness, and since the court was eager to discharge the case of attempted murder, they charged Corporal Menesiero with disorderly conduct: fourteen days' hard labor with no loss of rank or pay. The sentence was suspended.

Later on that year, Bepy took a thirty-day leave with a friend and went to his grandfather's hometown, Sciacca, Sicily. He rented the town hall and treated one hundred fifty people to a sit-down dinner in honor of his grandfather. It was a great experience for Bepy. The stories that were told about his father and grandfather were enjoyable and made him proud.

One day, Uncle Bruno took him to Palermo. He was a well-known Mafioso in Sicily. They went to see a very important man, Charlie Lugano, who was a former Mafia boss from New York. He had been deported to Sicily by the Senate Rackets Committee, and was living in a beautiful villa overlooking the sea. He greeted Bepy and his uncle warmly, kissing them on both cheeks.

Bepy greeted him and started to talk in Italian, but Lugano interrupted him.

"Let's talk English, OK? I have been deported twelve years now and I don't like it here. I miss New York," he explained.

"Why? You have such a nice place. It's beautiful here in Sicily. I think it's great."

"Bephino, you know who I am, don't you?"

"Yes, sir, I do. Uncle Bruno told me of your importance, Mr. Lugano, and I heard your name often in New York."

Lugano smiled. "Ah, my father and mother went there from Sicily when I was only three years old. I lived in America all my life, and I never learned to speak Italian very well. My mother and father, they practiced English twenty-four hours a day, so I really didn't learn to speak the Italian language. This place isn't for me. I'd rather be back in Brooklyn. That's where I grew up, in Red Hook."

"I understand now," Bepy said. "They deported you because you were born in Italy, even though you only lived there three years."

They were interrupted by a servant pushing a brass cart filled with wine, fruit, and cheeses.

As they ate and drank on the terrace, Bepy asked him if he knew Don Emilio Morrano.

"Yes, of course," Lugano replied. "Emilio was one of my soldiers when he was a young fellow. Now, of course, he has his own family in Brooklyn, a very strong and well-respected family. Don Emilio is a fine and honorable man."

Bepy said nothing about his relationship with Morrano.

Lugano also knew of Bepy's grandfather and said he was a very respected man. "No one dared defy him on the wharf," he said, much to Bepy's pleasure.

On the ride back to Sciacca, Uncle Bruno said, "Lugano is still the bigga bossa, even back in America. He's the real bossa. He's here, but he's still respected as the Boss of Bosses."

After eighteen months in France, Bepy was sent back to the United States for discharge. He had turned twenty-one and was a man of the world. His last six years had held more than a lifetime of experience. Dana was waiting for him when his ship arrived in Brooklyn. Corporal Menesiero removed his army clothes the day he arrived, so the guys in the neighborhood wouldn't see him in uniform. No one but Dana and his mother and father had seen him in uniform.

8

His first home-cooked dinner was rigatoni with meat sauce topped with ricotta cheese, meat, poultry, fruit, and *finocchio*. It felt so good to be home, he thought.

The first item on Bepy's list was to give Dana the OK to set a date for their wedding. They loved each other and were anxious to get married. She picked May 7, 1952, which would give them almost a year to get the arrangements made for the wedding and select an apartment.

Dana wanted to live near her mother's neighborhood so she could see her family at least a few times a week. Bepy liked the idea, too. Italians like to see each other during the week for dinners, and on Sunday aunts and uncles come to visit. He asked his aunt Anna to find them an apartment. She had more housing connections than the mayor. She could handle this for them.

After his welcome-home party, and after being with his family for a few days, Bepy got down to business as usual. First, a meeting with Red. He and Red had not seen each other for over eighteen months. They were sixty-forty partners in five stores now, plus the numbers and betting rackets.

When he called Red to tell him he was home, Red didn't seem overjoyed to hear from him. Bepy sensed something wasn't right. He told Red he wanted to pick up his end of the take and see all of the company's records, to compare sales figures of all five stores while he'd been in the army. He wanted to be sure that everything had been handled the same way it had been before. Red didn't say much.

They met the next day. After they talked a while, Red's face began getting as red as a tomato. Bepy sensed that Red wasn't feeling too good. "What's the matter, Red?" he asked. "You look sick."

"Sick? I'm not sick, Bepy. What makes you think I'm sick?" Red said, trying to smile.

Bephino smiled back, "Just as long as you feel all right. Red, tonight bring me all the cash you put aside for me while I was away. I'd like to have it tonight. I'm ready for my share."

"What cash?" Red asked, pretending to misunderstand.

"What d'ya mean 'what cash'? The money we always skimmed from the stores and our betting profits. My share." Then, with more emphasis, "You know, *my share*. Like we always split; I'm sixty; you're forty, remember?"

"I invested in two more stores," Red replied, nervously. "I got hit bad on the bets. We been taking a beating. I don't have any cash, Bepy. It's been a tough two years for me."

"You had a tough two years? Is that right? We go back a long way, Red. I hope you never forget about us. It's gonna be a terrible thing, Red, believe me—a terrible thing." Bepy smelled a big fat red rat. He thought a while and then spoke. "OK, Red. You say you have no cash. How about the profits, huh? What about them?"

"Things are bad in this country. What d'ya think, you're still in France? This is Brooklyn!" Red snapped at him.

"OK, Red. I understand clearly. You don't have anything for me. I left you in charge of the business, and you felt you inherited it from me. You felt my absence turned into weakness, huh? Well, you may be right, and you may be wrong. If you're wrong, them old ladies in church are gonna sing your fuckin' song."

Bepy walked away, then stopped and turned back to Red. " 'Ave Maria,'" he said. "That's your song. You stupid bastard! Did you think I

119

would accept this bullshit story? I can't believe you even tried it on me! You'll be hearing from me, Red. Go buy yourself a dark suit."

Red acted annoyed, but he was worried. They sang 'Ave Maria' at funerals. The rest of the day he kept thinking about every word Bepy had said.

That night he called Bepy. "Hey, Bepy, why don't you look over the records? See for yourself. Then you'll feel better."

"Look over the books? Of course I will. I'll be at the office first thing tomorrow morning. Have everything ready. I'm curious to see what you've been up to and how you hid the company's revenue. I can't believe you would try to pull such phony shit on me. We're friends a long time and I trusted you, scumbag. Don't you know that? I trusted you."

"What phony shit are you talking about?" Red asked.

"Forget it," Bepy answered and hung up. I can't believe Red had the balls to fuck me out of my share, he thought. He must've clipped a hundred grand from me in two years. You never know who will move against you in this world. Unbelievable. The guy's my partner and he fucked me outta everything. I gotta kill this Milanese. My grandfather must be turning over in his grave about this.

That same evening, Bepy went over to see Don Morrano at the bar. The Don saw Bepy walking toward him and stood up to greet him. He embraced him with true warmth and kissed him on both cheeks.

The two men seated with the Don got up from their chairs smiling and shook hands with him. "Hey, Bepy. You're back."

"I heard you visited Palermo, eh?" Don Emilio said.

"Yeah, it's beautiful in Sicily. How'd you know I went to Palermo?"

"We're always in contact with our people in the Old Country. We heard Lugano really liked you, enjoyed your company. He was surprised to find out you were with me. Whatsa matter, you ashamed of being with me, Bepy? You didn't mention to him you work for me. How come?"

"Mr. Morrano. I didn't want Mr. Lugano to think I was bragging or something, so I made no mention of my business with you. I just said I know you from the neighborhood."

Don Emilio smiled. "I know, kid. That's why we all like you. You play low key. Lugano was surprised when he heard you were a preferred person. We told him the little soldier boy had balls greater than Mark Anthony."

Everyone at the table laughed. Bepy then told them he was getting married May 7, next year.

"I want two tables, ten at each table," the Don quickly said. "I'm bringing the heads of five families and their wives and the captains of all the families to your wedding. They'll be my guests. After that day, you will be respected by all. Don't forget, two tables. OK, kid?"

Bepy was surprised and pleased that the Don felt that way. It would be an honor to receive such people. "I really appreciate the way you welcomed me home," he said. "Thank you, Mr. Morrano."

"Anything you need, you got. You know that. Just let me know, OK, kid? Keep in touch with me. Welcome home. Take this and get yourself a hat," he said, and handed Bepy five hundred dollars.

The next morning, when Bepy went to Red's office, only the secretary was there. After a little hassle with her, he sat down and checked the records. After about two hours, he came to the conclusion that Red was fucking him good. He had used the company's good name to get financing for the new stores. He hadn't invested any money from the profits. He had used company loans spread over ten years, made small payments, and then had skimmed out the profits. But business looked better than usual, based on the company's ordering of materials.

Red walked in. "Hi, Bephino, *come sta?*"

"*Come sta,* my balls. You fucked me good, Red, and I want you to know I'm fully aware of it. Maybe you think I don't know figures because I quit school at sixteen, but you're only fooling yourself. You're buying an early ticket to the grave. I started making plans for your future this morning."

"Come on, Bepy. Don't talk that way. What the hell's wrong? You never trust anyone. You're still the same old Bephino."

"What the fuck ya' want me to be, the same old screwball, like you? You're sick, Red. Something's wrong with you. I always thought you were smart. Did you say trust, you Milanese cocksucker? I'll trust you after I bury you," Bepy threatened. "You wanna know what's wrong? Yesterday I talked to Monkey, Alley Oop, Joey D, and Little Pauli. They watched out for me. Joey D is like a fuckin' computer; he shits out figures when I press his pointy nose. For the new stores, four and five, you completely financed the deal, every penny. None of our company's ready cash was invested. It was all notes. Also, the records show that when I left, we bought one thousand dollars of paper goods for each store per month. For the last year you bought two thousand dollars of paper goods per month. That means business had to be increased double. Either you're skimming real big or you're in the fuckin' paper business. Which is it, Red? You're a crook, and a dumb one at that. I always thought you were smart, but I was wrong, Red. You're a fuckin' dummy. And if the IRS checks our records, they'll see the skimming, too. Any idiot could see it. You're a stupid crook. The money fucked up your mind." His anger pushed the words out faster and louder.

"I also checked with Little Pauli, our runner. He says you cleaned up on the bets and numbers last year. You know, you scumbag, this is a shock to me. What did you think, that I was in combat over there and would get knocked off? I can't believe you didn't hand me a bag of cash—something, anything. I never figured my friend Red, the bookie, would try a long-shot deal and lose. You robbed ME—the guy who financed everything for us."

Bepy stopped to catch his breath and his temper. "I'll let you know in two days what I decide. I gotta think."

He pointed to the secretary, a blondish girl with very large tits packed into a tight polo shirt. "Oh, yeah, another thing. Who's the broad?"

"She's the secretary and bookkeeper," Red replied.

"Oh, she's the secretary, huh? She doesn't look like a secretary to me. She's only a kid, and all tits at that. For your information, that little cunt told me to sit outside and wait till Mr. Franco arrives. Who the hell is Mr. Franco?"

"That's me." Red grinned. "That's my new business name. How d'ya like it?"

"On you? It's shit. It sounds cheap. She also wouldn't give me the key to the file cabinet. And didn't have a key to your office."

"She never had a key to my office," Red said. "But you got the books, so what's the difference?"

"Yeah, I got them after I slapped the shit out of her big tits. Tell her to be out of here by Friday. She's fired. I don't like to be disrespected in my own office."

"Come on, Bephino," Red yelled. "She's my broad. She stays."

"Oh, she's your broad now? She stays? I thought she was the bookkeeper. How much are we paying your broad?"

"Two hundred a week."

"Well, in that case I want her out of here right now." Bepy walked over to her. "Look, big tits, you're fired. Go home and powder your ass. Beat it. You're out. *Finito.*"

"Bepy, cut it out," Red yelled, and banged his fist on his desk. "I told you she's with me." Big tits remained at her desk.

Bephino turned to Red and yelled back across the room, "Do you realize, Red, that you're paying her a hundred and twenty dollars of my money and only eighty of yours per week. In other words, you're a sport with my money. I'm paying for your whore." Turning back to look her in the eyes, he said, "Look at her grinning. Don't spend any money, Red. You'll need it. You got expenses coming up one way or the other. I got that semideprived feeling again in my life, Red, and you know what that means."

Two days later Bepy got a call from Red. He wanted to meet at the Italian Club in South Brooklyn.

"Why South Brooklyn? That's not our neighborhood," Bepy said.

"What's the difference?" Red replied. "We gotta talk. We gotta straighten a few things out. South Brooklyn is as good as anyplace."

Bepy hesitated, then said, "I agree, Red. What's the fuckin' difference? In that case, let's meet at Mr. Terrazano's Funeral Home. You can make it real easy for me to drag your body in, you son of a bitch. I'll make you come off with that bullshit, you wanna meet me in South Brooklyn. Whatta ya got, a cousin there?"

"I don't like the way you talk, Bepy. You're getting out of line," Red replied.

"*I'm* getting out of line?" Bepy asked. "Listen to this shit. You know, Red, this has gotta be a fuckin' dream. When we were kids, I knew you wanted a partnership. I broke my grandfather's rule, *uno capo*. Not to mention that you're a Milanese bastard. My grandfather must be turning over in his grave. Now you're telling me that I'm getting out of line. OK, I say no more on this matter. A decision has to be made."

They agreed to meet at a luncheonette in another neighborhood. Red was still acting strong and tough when they met. His actions told his story. He thought Bepy would back off and make a deal.

Bepy sensed this, so he spoke first, formally and emphatically. "I thought this over very carefully, Red. I made a decision for you. You give me fifty grand to cover this embarrassment and defiance on your part—which includes your disrespect for me for the past two years—and I'll let you go on living. If you say any word but OK, I'll kill you before you take your next shit, which is gonna be any minute now."

Red stared at Bepy. He knew a decision had been made and he knew Bepy didn't bluff. He thought it over for what seemed to be long minutes and decided it was best to keep the peace. A death decision had been made, and he felt Bepy was still crazy enough to carry it out. "OK, Bephino, but under one condition. No, I mean two conditions."

"Ah ah, what are you trying to say? Conditions? I make no conditions, Red. I made *uno* decision, remember? Nothing's changed. Either you do the right thing or you get the parade."

"N-n-no, Bep. Hear me, hear me out," Red stuttered. "I'll give you the fifty grand tomorrow, but everything must remain the same between us. No vendetta, promise me. No bad blood, OK? Business as usual. Partners the same way. Oh, and my broad stays. She stays, OK?"

"You know, Mr. Franco, a few minutes ago you were acting like a boss. Now you act much nicer. I hope you realize my capabilities." Bepy banged on the table, "OK, Mr. Franco, get my cash. You gotta deal." Bepy got up. "Tomorrow morning, ten o'clock, my house," he yelled on his way out the door. "Be on time. I don't like tardiness."

As he walked to his car, he thought, You mother-fuckin' son of a bitch. You bastard. I'll fuck you and your broad, too. He got in his father's maroon Pontiac and drove off. Red has really changed, he thought. He seems to have lost his respect for me. Everything the same? Bullshit. It could never be the same. He's not Sicilian like me. He tried to fuck me. The balls on this guy. I'll wait a while, then I'll cut his balls off. I'll make Alley Oop hold him good for me, then I'll operate like a Jewish surgeon.

The next day Bepy got his fifty grand. The money was all in small bills, and it smelled like it came from the hero shops. The smell was like tomato sauce and garlic. There was no doubt about it; Red had skimmed the hero shops. Bepy was boiling over. His blood would take weeks to cool down. He had been screwed. Now he was sure Red had skimmed even more from the betting business. I'll never know the truth, he thought. I really got fucked by him. If Red hadn't punked out, I would have had to kill him right there. I'd of been convicted of his murder, sure as shit. It could have been a real mess if he hadn't agreed to come up with some cash.

The next few days he spent with Red at the shops. He took control of all the businesses again. Red's girl kept staring at him. She sensed the change of command. What a bad deal Bepy had made agreeing to let her stay. Red was still paying her two hundred dollars a week. And Bepy was only getting ninety-five bucks a week before he left for the service. She knew nothing about office work. She was dumb, and she was getting two hundred bucks because Red loved tits.

When Bepy felt that his hero shops were running smoothly, he went back to Wall Street to see Mr. Gustini. Bepy's salary—nothing compared to what he had made on the betting operations and the hero shops—had almost doubled in the few years he had worked with the firm, but it was still peanuts compared with his other professions, and with what Red was paying his secretary. He wanted to leave the job with Julius Hart and Company, but that was his only cover. He needed a good cover for the Morrano jobs. It was important to show he was a hard worker and not connected with the Mob.

Mr. Gustini was glad to see him and asked if he was ready to return to work.

"Yes, I need the job," Bepy told him. "I'm getting married May 7."

"Wonderful!" Mr. Gustini congratulated him. "In thata case, you get a twenty-dollar raise: ten dollars for eacha year you were in the army."

"Thank you, sir. I really appreciate this. I can use the money," he replied.

Mr. Gustini smiled. "You'va done very well on the stock tips, Bephino," he said, reminding Bepy that he wasn't too poor at that. He walked him around the office and said to the staff, "You all remember Bephino Menesiero? Well, hesa back and starts working Monday morning."

Mr. Melvin came over to Bepy and shook his hand. "Welcome back, boy," he said, smiling. "Thanks for defending our country."

The months rolled by, and soon things were back to normal. Mario had gotten married while Bepy was in France. Bepy and Dana were getting things ready for their wedding, ordering tuxedos for the men and gowns for the bridesmaids.

Bepy set one day aside to talk to Monkey, Joey D, and the rest of the guys who had been loyal over the years. "Are you fellas all right?" Bepy asked, "Have you been treated fairly by Red? Are you getting enough money? Is there anything I can do for you now that I'm back?"

All of them worked for the hero shops or the betting business. They were Bepy's family, and they knew this. They worked hard, and their loyalty seemed very much in order. They could get anything from Bepy if they needed it, and they knew that.

The only one who wanted more money was Joey D. He was never satisfied. Like a glutton, he always wanted more. But Bepy saw something in Joey D that he liked very much: he was loyal and honest. He would never steal.

Joey D had a problem—a parent problem. His mother and father were good people, but real pain-loving people. They had to keep receiving pain to be happy. They were always pushing Joey not to work late, to ask for days off, and to get more money—always more money. Joey D always got more money, and he was satisfied, but his mother and father were not. For some reason they were under the impression that Joey was a boss and partner in the company and that he was not getting his share of the profits. They thrived on this pain.

Joey D's older sister explained to her parents that Joey was just the cashier and assistant manager, but they wouldn't believe it. They told her to mind her own business. Once they even called the police, got lawyers, and when this didn't produce a partnership for Joey, they threatened that they had a cousin in the Mafia who would straighten this thing out. Joey D kept telling them that he only worked for the hero shops and was loyal to Bephino as his friend. His mother asked, "Loyal to who? For what? Who do we owe loyalty to?"

Everyone liked Joey D, so Bepy didn't want to cut him loose. But when his mother called the district attorney's office to say her son was kidnapped, that was the last straw. Detectives came up to the brokerage firm, embarrassing Bepy. No charges were made, but in Bepy's heart a scar was formed. Joey D explained to the D.A. that his mother was a sick woman. The D.A. thought he was joking.

Finally, Bepy called Slim, Joey's father, to a sit-down. Slim was always watching your throat when he talked to you. He was told to lay off and to put a halt to his wife's bad breath, but he responded with very abusive language and told Bepy to go to hell.

Bepy didn't like people who didn't understand respect, and used foul language on top of it. So he very carefully told Slim that a decision had been made on his behalf.

That night he told Monkey that he wasn't sure if he was doing the right thing but nevertheless he hoped he could smarten up the Desporto family. The order was given to Alley Oop and Crazy Mikey to crush Slim's body a little. "Don't put him to sleep. Just let him ache for a week or two," Bepy said.

Alfredo "Alley Oop" Opolito's appearance spoke for itself. His head, the size and shape of a large coconut, looked strange sticking up between his massive shoulders. His thick neck and body were strong and powerful, and he walked with a wide giant step to keep his enormous testicles from rubbing his thighs. His skin was pitted, probably from teen-age complexion problems, and he had large teeth. He wore his hair in a pompadour and combed it quite often. His hands and arms were deadly weapons.

When he was eleven years old, he strangled a man, to avenge his father's death. He was sent from Trevelina, Sicily, with his mother and two sisters, to America. Alley and Bephino became the closest of friends. Alley spent most of his time working to support his widowed mother and younger sisters.

Michael "Crazy Michael" Lastrano was about five foot nine with black curly hair, a handsome face, a born "mustache Pete," a head crusher, and a soprano if Bepy asked him to be. When he was a young boy, he had sent a crushing blow to his own father's head with a stickball bat. Thus he became known as Crazy Michael. His parents were from Messina, Sicily.

126

Bepy only wanted Slim to cry a little. "I want him hurt, like a little bird. Break his fuckin' wing," he said to Alley Oop and Crazy Mikey. He felt bad that it was Joey D's father. It was hard to hurt a friend's family, but this was an unusual case. The disrespect was uncalled for and unbearable.

Slim was hurt and he cried out in pain. But, he also grinned at them. It seemed like he enjoyed getting the shit kicked out of him. Watching from the car and seeing Slim's smiling face after each blow, Bepy felt his stomach turn. He changed his order, yelling from the car window. "Kick his fuckin' teeth out. Just leave his molars, so he can chew his cavatelli tonight."

Two weeks later Joey D reported to Bepy that his mother had called her cousin, a button guy in the Mob. Slim had once again allowed his wife to create trouble.

Bepy was contacted at his office by the cousin, who said he wanted to see him. Bepy knew he couldn't have these types call the office, couldn't have Mob guys calling for sit-downs. His peace was at stake.

"See what you put me through?" he screamed over the phone to Joey D. "You're like a fuckin' black dream. Now I gotta pluck your cousin's eyes out and feed them to my uncle's dog. Can't you handle your own mother, you stupid bastard!"

"She's nuts, my mother," Joey D answered.

"Your mother's nuts?" Bepy said with a smirk in his voice. "You're all nuts!"

The meeting with the cousin was in a Sheepshead Bay schoolyard at eight o'clock. Bepy took Alley Oop with him, and the cousin showed up with his man. They were in their early forties and wore hats and suits, like Al Capone.

As they walked toward the two men, Bepy told Alley, "If I go into action, put your guy to sleep fast, then hold the cousin for me. I really wanna do a job on this guy. He sounded real nasty over the phone. I'm gonna pluck his fuckin' eye out with this ice pick. This has gotta be the end of the Desporto family and their bullshit. I'm getting fed up with that cow and her son Joey D."

"Whatever you say, Bep. Just go into action—I can use the exercise."

When the four met, the cousin tried to intimidate Bepy, who listened quietly. "You gotta do the right thing, kid, or it's broken bones for you guys," the cousin said. "Understand what I'm sayin'? Joe Desporto gets half of all your action from now on."

Bepy smiled, "Half of all my action!"

"What are you smilin' at, kid?" the other guy asked.

"You, ya rubber," Bepy replied.

"Do you know who I am?" the cousin asked.

"What's with you guys? Do you know who I am; do you know this; do you know that?" Bepy laughed. "Yeah, I know who you are. You're a couple of douche bags. I looked you up in the dictionary. You're *disposable* douche bags, also known as a coupla fuckin' throwaways."

The cousin was stunned. His friend quickly jumped Bepy and cut him on the neck with a razor blade. Bepy tried to back away fast, but he saw blood gushing from his neck and down his shirt and became still for an instant in surprise. The cousin saw an opportunity and quickly moved in for the kill. He punched Bepy twice, in the eye and the mouth. The guy was fast for a big man. Bepy was now spurting blood from his mouth *and* his neck.

Alley Oop, momentarily stunned by the man's speed, went into action like a steamroller, punching and kicking both men like a jackhammer. One of the men was soon down.

Bepy, holding his throat to try to stop the bleeding, ran over and began to kick the man's head. Blood spurted out of the man's ears and nose. He was completely unconscious. Bepy yelled to Alley Oop, in a thick voice, "Get that other bastard ready for me. I wanna pluck his eye out. That's Joey D's cousin." He ran over to where Alley was holding the cousin. "Hold that son of a bitch steady. I gotta pierce his fuckin' eyeball. He's my man," he said as he stuck the ice pick in his eye. The cousin screamed like a woman being raped. "My eye! My eye! Don't! Not my eyes!" he screeched. Then his body went limp with pain.

Bepy whispered in his ear, "The only reason I don't pierce your other eye right now is that I want to enjoy this fuckin' party again another time. When I hear from Joey D's mother, I'll come for your other eye." Then he wildly bit the man's left cheek and quickly spat out a chuck of his face on the ground. "Your friend cut my neck deep, the bastard! I should kill you for that!"

Alley resumed kicking both bodies in wild anger.

"Stop dancing! Take me to a doctor before I bleed to death," Bepy told Alley. "I don't know how bad I'm hurt. He got me good. I feel weird. The guy was fast. I didn't expect him to use a blade. They really meant business, those bastards! But we got them, thanks to you, Alley. You saved me. I didn't expect that old guy to be so quick. I almost froze. He surprised me. The bum really hurt me, didn't he?" Bepy lifted his handkerchief from the wound to show Alley.

"Yeah! It looks about six inches long and deep."

"Six inches? Holy shit, he really got me good. We shoulda killed both of them. We fucked up."

Alley whispered, "I'm takin' you to Coney Island Hospital. You're bleeding too bad. I'm gettin' worried. Stop talking, Bepy. Every time you talk the blood pumps out like a water fountain.

After that incident, peace on earth was upheld in Joey D's household. The cousin was afraid to lose his other eye over Joey D's mother's mouth. Joey D said his cousin resigned from the Mob and read the Bible all day in his new notions store. His bodyguard's brain had been kicked loose, and he walked around with a portable radio on his shoulder playing loud church music and laughing at his own reflection in store windows.

Bepy's neck took eighteen stitches. The wound healed well but left a scar. Dana kept asking him how his neck got cut.

But as the wedding day neared she thought less about his scar and concentrated on preparing for her big day. Arrangements were being made every day for something else for the wedding. While Bepy was recuperating and trying to get ready, he got word to report to Don Emilio.

"Bepy, I need this done right away," the Don told him. "It's a guy who stole big money from the union hall. The contract pays ten grand. Do you want it?"

Bepy hesitated.

"If you don't want it, Bepy, say so. Don't stall me," the Don said. "I offered it to you first, but I got other guys who will jump on it. It's an easy hit. The guy's a nobody. And nobody will even look for this bum. He's from a few blocks up the street. It's a good contract. I figure, with the wedding coming up, you can use the dough." He smiled.

Bepy was thinking fast. He really didn't want it. He didn't want to hit a nobody from the neighborhood. Too close to home. Suppose I know this guy, he thought, and I have to kill him. Suppose I know his kids? I just wanna hit big, bad guys I don't know who are better off out of the way. Besides, the timing was wrong for him. His head was cloudy, but he didn't want the Don to think he was getting soft. The truth was that the wedding had him dizzy, going to church to practice walking down the aisle and all that stuff. Also he liked the business-world way of life. Making hits was not a priority any more.

The Don broke the silence. "What are you thinking about? Yes or no?"

"Yeah, I'll take it," he snapped. "I can use the money. Things are too slow anyway around here." Bepy tried to think of ways to show that he wanted the contract. "Thank you, Mr. Morrano. I'm really happy you called me first. I appreciate the business."

The Don looked Bepy up and down in a deliberate way. "Come with me," he said. They walked into his office, where he showed Bepy a picture of the guy to be hit. "Destroy this after the hit. This is his home address. This is his place of work and his car style. Here's your money. When this is done, report to me as usual. And I want it done tomorrow. OK?"

Bepy noted that Morrano's tone of voice was different. "Sure, Mr. Morrano. You can go ahead and order the guy's flowers," he said, trying to regain his credibility.

"This bum don't even get a tulip. Just do it fast and perfect."

Bepy left with the ten grand in his pocket. This is my first hit for the Don since my discharge. Maybe he thought I was getting soft, he thought. Nah, he must realize I'm busy with the wedding.

At home, Dana called him. "We gotta be at the church office to sign papers at nine o'clock tonight. And tomorrow we gotta be ... and the next day we gotta be ... "

Bepy's brain was traveling at high speed; he was listening to her and making plans for the hit. "OK, Dana, I'll meet you at eight-thirty at your house." He hung up and then called Alley Oop and Monkey. He made an appointment to see them at the poolroom at seven-thirty.

When they met, they went for a walk. Bepy told Alley, "I want you to make a hit, and Monkey'll drive for you." They looked at each other and nodded in agreement. "This is his picture. I want it back, so don't lose it. Use your gloves. I'll give you my best gun, with a silencer. Get up close and make sure he's your man. Whatever you do, Alley, don't hit the wrong man. No errors, OK, Alley?"

"Yeah. No blunders. I know."

"When you get close, empty the gun in him, all six bullets in the head. I can't have this guy walking around the neighborhood tomorrow. He can't live through this. This one's become very important to me for some reason. Alley, I'm giving you and Monkey five grand to split."

"Yeah, that's good, Bepy. Five grand's beautiful, huh, Monk?"

"Go now. Hit him tonight and call me when it's done, no matter what time it is. I'll be waiting. My fuckin' brain is all messed up between Wall Street, the hero shops, gambling, Dana and the wedding—now this shit. You gotta do this right for me! Call me when it's over."

Bepy went to meet Dana to go sign papers at the church. He was still very jumpy, which Dana noticed.

"What's the matter, Bep? Getting cold feet?" she asked.

130

"Nah. I got business problems."

"Are you sure?" she giggled.

"Come on, Dana. You got a clear head. And I don't. So cut the bullshit. We're getting married, so let's talk about screwing or something like that. I told you, I got business problems."

She became very quiet as they headed toward the church. Later on he took her to an ice-cream parlor. Then, when he saw his chance, he took her home. But he didn't want her to realize that he was unloading her early, because Dana got bent out of shape easily. But he had the hit on his mind.

"Go upstairs, and I'll call you when I get home. OK?" he told her.

"Where are you going now?"

"I'm gonna go home now. Where do you think I'm going? I'll be there in fifteen minutes. I'll call you, so relax."

"OK. I'll wait for your call," she said.

He kissed her and headed home, in case Monkey and Alley were looking for him. When he arrived home, his mother and father were watching television, so he took a shower.

While he was drying off he heard his mother calling, "Bepy, Dana's on the phone. She said you were supposed to call her in fifteen minutes and it's now thirty minutes."

"Did you tell her I'm in the shower?" he yelled back.

"Yes, but she wants to speak to you anyway."

"Tell her I'll be right there." He wrapped a blue towel around his waist and went to the phone. "Hello?"

"I thought you were gonna call in fifteen minutes," Dana pouted.

"Yeah, but I figured I'd take a shower first and talk to you nice and clean."

"Boy, you're really something! You got some line of BS."

"Did I ever tell you how pretty your head is? The shape is exotic. I love it. It's like an egg."

After an hour on the phone with Dana, the doorbell rang. He opened the door and looked down the stairs. It was Monkey and Alley Oop.

"Should we come up?"

"No, I'll be right down." Bepy got dressed and ran downstairs.

The landlord, Mr. Ruffo, yelled from the top floor. "Hey! Easy on the staircase, Bepy? You run like a horse."

They went around the corner to a lonely spot to talk.

131

"How'd you guys make out?" Bepy asked.

"We made out good," Alley replied. "His car was in front of the house. Thirty minutes later he came out and got in. I ran over and looked at him real close to make sure it was him. The guy was looking at me like I was crazy. He asked me what the hell was I looking at. I knew it was him, but I had to make really sure, so I asked him his name, and the jerk told me. I was very close to him, Bep. I put three in his head. He was a mess all over the car. The guy's with St. Peter by now. What kinda bullets were in that gun?" Alley asked.

"Hollow points."

"Boy, they really make a mess," Alley said. "Next time give me a gun that makes smaller holes. My stomach was empty. You said hit him with all six, but after three only his neck was still there."

"You gotta be kidding. Only his neck was there?" Bephino asked, surprised.

"It felt strange using a silencer. I expected noise, but all I saw was his face blow away each time I pulled the trigger. So I stopped shooting him," Alley explained. "I was two inches from his head. On an empty stomach, things can't look worse."

"You guys did good work for me," Bephino said. "I won't forget this. Monkey, old reliable, what did you do with the car?"

"I put it back in the lot we took it from. No one was there, so I figure no one will know it was gone." Monkey smiled at Bephino and put his arm around his neck. "Don't worry, *goomba,* everything went fine!"

"Sounds like you guys did good work. Did you use gloves?"

"Of course," Alley said, and handed Bepy the gun and the picture with the address and other information.

Bepy counted out five grand and handed it to them. "OK, go home, eat, and go to sleep. Don't talk to anyone. Good night. And stay off the streets. Go watch TV. There's a good movie on tonight—Edward G. Robinson."

Bepy walked around the corner to see Don Emilio. He walked in the bar. The Don was at his table with a lady friend, a real plush broad with tits like two smiling pumpkins.

Bepy made eyes at Morrano, trying to get his attention.

The Don quickly understood and excused himself. Bepy followed him into the back office. Once the door was shut, the Don greeted him, and Bepy told him the guy was already with St. Peter, watching Morrano's eyes.

"That was quick," the Don said, patting Bepy's shoulder.

"I hit him quick," Bepy explained. "I'm so tied up with this wedding business. That's why I'm a little confused. My girl, she's got me in church every day for rehearsals! Up and down the aisle—like a pinball."

"Good work, kid. You do real good work for me. I like that. You're a proven man now. We may have something big coming up. If it comes, I want you to do it. You're the man for the job. I'm sure of it. It's a big one, and it pays very big bucks."

"I need a big one," Bepy replied, trying to act humble and appreciative. "You let me know when. I'm always around the neighborhood. By the way, I have your two tables reserved at my wedding."

"Good," Morrano replied. "Everyone wants to meet you, so they'll be there. We'll have a nice Italian wedding. It's a beautiful time of year for a wedding. Good night, kid. Talk to you tomorrow. I got this broad waiting out there for me. Understand? We'll read the papers tomorrow. Should be interesting, huh?"

Bephino felt good again, knowing Mr. Morrano had full confidence in him. He was now twenty-two years old and Mr. Morrano was fifty-one. Their friendship seemed to be destined for larger-scale "things" ahead and to last for a long time.

Now Bephino's men were also proven. He knew they could follow orders and do a job when called upon. They were strong-minded people. They had the guts it takes to survive, and he liked that.

Bepy and company were now first-class citizens. They had money behind them. So they all wore sharp suits and topcoats from the best haberdashery in Brooklyn.

"It's time to spend a little money and sharpen up my people," Bepy had told them, and it was music to their ears. They went and bought suits and really played their parts as young hoods. They smiled at each other as they were being fitted by the tailor—a good feeling for the men. The women in the neighborhood were drawn to them like magnets to steel. And the men enjoyed the feeling of respect for them that was growing rapidly among the neighborhood people.

Bephino had finally bought his own new car, a black Oldsmobile. It was a beauty! He was so happy about having his own car that he couldn't sleep that first night. He kept looking out the window to see if it was all right.

The very next evening he picked up Dana and drove over to her aunt's house to show her aunts and uncles their new car. All the little cousins asked to go for a ride. So, following the family new-car tradition, Bepy took them all over to Coney Island for hot dogs. As Bepy finished ordering the hot dogs, out of the corner of his eye he caught a glimpse of a red-headed man shaking his head and laughing. Walking through the crowd carrying plates loaded with dogs, he looked closer and saw it was Red and his secretary and another tough-looking guy, drinking beer and eating. He wondered why Red seemed so happy? He was laughing like hell. He watched them for a few moments, then headed for his car to feed the kids.

The whole next day Red kept coming into his mind. He was never sure if he could trust Red, especially now that he knew he was a poor, sloppy crook. But maybe not such a poor one at that! Red had always been a funny kid, a great charmer and a good pipe man. But he had changed from the old days, Bepy thought. Now he was an enemy. But the time was not right for vengeance. Red still had a share in the hero stores, but Little Pauli was now handling the loan-shark and gambling business. Bepy had taken Red off those operations as a first step out the door.

Paul "Little Pauli" Sigura was his name but not his frame. He was husky, handsome, six feet two—a real ladies' man. He never gave anyone reason to dislike him. He was so pleasingly honest and sincere that when a few men in the neighborhood caught him pulling up his pants and climbing out their bedroom windows, they believed he was there to use the toilet. Pauli was smooth as silk. He was a good worker and a good friend. His pleasant manner seemed to give him a personality of nonimportance. His fear of Bephino Menesiero was his most valued asset. The Sigura Family was from Ramina, Sicily.

As Bepy walked to his office, he got cold sweats thinking about Red, and it was annoying him. Who was that guy with him? he asked himself. Tomorrow morning I'll call Red for a meeting. I gotta talk to that bum. I think the time has come for me to leave this Wall Street stuff and take over the stores.

Early the next day, Bepy and Red had coffee in the office of Downtown Hot Foods, their sandwich-shop company. The secretary gave Bephino a half smile, as if to say, "See, I'm still here, and you're paying for me."

Bepy looked at her with an expression that made her nervous. But she still kept looking at him with curiosity.

"How ya doing with our business these days?" Bepy asked Red.

"I'm doing good, Bepy. Why?"

"Well, I had a little nightmare about you last night. I even got a cold sweat thinking of you, and you know, Red, I wasn't even sleeping. I was walking in the street. How could a guy have a nightmare awake? And how could I get a cold sweat, huh, Red?"

"How the hell do I know?" Red asked, laughing.

"I dreamed I saw you with an ugly guy, and you were discussing very ugly things. Are you telling me everything, Red? Is there anything going on I don't know about or should know about? If I find out you're sneaking around at my expense, I gotta reconsider my decision and my agreement."

Red's face was getting bright as a tomato, as it usually did when he got nervous.

"You know, Red," Bepy continued, "for some reason you always light up like a pinball machine when you're hiding something." He turned to look at Red's secretary. Raising his voice he said, "and while I like Milanese women to fuck, I think I'm gonna hate Milanese men all my life. So tell me, Red, what's up? I don't cold-sweat for no reason. Tell me what the fuck are you up to. I wanna know who you shit with. You have a smell about you today. What is it?"

"Nothing's wrong," Red said, thinking that Bepy must have heard something. He started talking nervously. "Maybe you mean my new business venture?"

"What new business venture?"

"I'm opening some new stores with Johnny Mac."

"You mean Johnny Mac from downtown? Johnny Macaroni?"

"Yeah."

"So that's the ugly man in my dreams. I thought he looked familiar. What kind of stores?"

"Oh, just some more hero shops."

"Oh, just some more hero shops," Bepy mimicked Red sarcastically. "You know, Red, you're really testing me. You know that, huh?"

"Johnny Macaroni wants me to go partners with him."

"You know, Red, you're bringing me to the end of your line. That's it, Red, the end of your line."

"It's only a few stores. What's it to you?"

"What's it to me? You got a partner: me. Right? First you robbed me for two years and got off cheap. Now you insult me to my face by going in with a terrible guy from downtown."

"Look, Bepy. You know Mac is connected on Mott Street. He's a big guy. He's strong, Bepy. He's the best hit man in New York City. How could I say no? The guy's a heavy. He wanted me to invest with him."

"Whatta ya got, some kind of thing for hit men? What the fuck you wanna be close with a guy like that for? He'll swallow you up later on," Bepy said, shaking his head. "So Johnny Mac is the best hit man, and you're impressed with that bullshit! If he's so big, why does he want to sell sandwiches like us, huh? Fuck it, it's none of my business what he does anyway. OK, Red, let's just talk about our business, not Mac's business."

Red looked at Bepy's eyes and knew he had said the wrong thing.

"How much salary are you taking from our hero company? Refresh me."

"I take three hundred fifty dollars a week. You already know that. All the betting profits go in our kitty, and you know that, too. You got Pauli handling that."

"I like to be refreshed on things. You may have given yourself a raise since then. I have to watch you, friend. Ah, so you take three fifty a week? Nice, huh? Tell me, Red, what did you eat last night for supper? A nice fat steak? And maybe Big Tits over there had a big steak, too?"

"We had macaroni and meatballs, with beef and pork in the sauce, over at her house, and then we went to Coney Island later for clams and beer. Why d'ya wanna know what I ate? You gettin' personal now?"

"Because I heard you got a load of steaks stashed in the freezer of store number three. Who paid for 'em, Red? The company? Or is that too personal for you to answer, too?"

"Why ya askin' me what I ate last night for? That's an insult." Red did not answer the steak questions.

"Insult! Oh, yeah!" Bepy snapped. "Who paid for that pile of beef? I wanna know, so stop avoiding the answer."

Red bowed his head, then looked over at his girl friend.

"It's a nice world, Red. You eat and my company pays for it. Am I right or wrong?" Bepy shouted.

"Yeah, it's our company," Red pointed out. "You're right. So what? What the fuck's a few steaks?"

"Is Johnny Mac eating steaks on me, too?"

"Only once. What's the big deal?" Red asked.

"You got it so nice: three fifty a week and you eat so well at my expense. People earn one fifty and they think they're kings. You take three fifty like it's coming to you. Your shoes are imported from Italy. I wear Thom McAns. Do you wanna continue to eat so well? Answer me, Red, do you wanna keep eating steak?"

"Of course, Bephino. Come on, cut the bullshit. Whatta you giving me a sermon for? It was my idea to open this business in the first place. You're bullshitting me today, and you know it. I had all the ideas about this thing."

The secretary looked up with a grin. Bepy noticed.

136

"Your ideas? Bullshit? I bullshit you, Red? You're fuckin' that cunt over there. Look at her grinning at me. She looks like she's hiding behind her tits. She's spending two hundred bucks a week of my money. You fuck her, and my money pays for it. I think the story of Red the Milanese is coming to a historic end. *Finito.*

"I tell you what, Red. You got two hours to get your shit together. Either cancel your business with Johnny Mac or have Big Tits over there prepare you your last supper—manicotti and sausage, or whatever the fuck you want. It's on me, because I'm gonna put you in a concrete kimono and make you suck mud under the Hudson River."

"Look, Bepy, I can't cancel nothin' with Johnny Mac. He'll hit me in a minute if I try to cancel the deal."

"Look, Red, I'm still your friend, believe me," Bepy whispered. "We'll hit Mac first together. We'll put two slugs in his head before he hurts you. OK? You can start fresh with me. Don't worry about Mac. The guy's no good. Remember he killed a seventy-four-year-old man for a roll of dimes. Get away from him. He's bad news. We'll wax him together this week. OK, Red? We'll give him a good send-off. Don't make this blunder, Red. We go back a long way together." Red stared at him blankly and didn't reply.

"He killed a seventy-four-year-old man who sold newspapers," Bepy said, pleading with him. "None of us ever did that kinda thing. We're bad, but we got respect for all the old people in the neighborhood."

"So what? The guy was a Jew anyway," Red replied in disgust.

Looking into his friend's eyes, Bepy saw that everything was over between them. He realized there was no possible way for the business or the friendship to continue. It was dead. *Finito.* "Take your choice," he whispered in a thick voice. "Either Mac hits you or I hit you. You got some future, Red. It ain't worth shit."

After a few silent moments, Bepy said, "OK, Red. You made a decision for yourself. I see that. You want Johnny Mac. I give him to you, or you to him. Meet me at four this afternoon at store number one. I want everyone there, including Little Pauli. Make sure you're at the meeting, Red. This concerns your future with our organization."

Leaving the office and realizing that a decade of close friendship was ending, Bepy turned back to his old friend. "It's a shame, Red," he said in a voice swollen with emotion. "I really didn't want it this way. We go back such a long way together that, in spite of everything, I almost could say I loved you."

All of the summoned men were at store number one right on time. They waited quietly for Bepy to speak.

"Pauli, from now on you report only to Alley or me. No more to Red, understand?" Bepy yelled across a long table.

The men seemed suprised at the sudden order. They looked at each other, wondering what was going on.

"Do you understand me, Pauli? Red is *finito;* he's through." Bepy looked at each person, gauging their reactions.

"Sure, Bep," Pauli answered, looking quickly over at Red.

"All our gambling and loan-shark money goes only to Alley or me," Bepy repeated. "That's the new deal, Pauli. Like Roosevelt, we make a new deal for ourselves." He turned to Monkey. "Monkey, you are now the regional manager of all the stores. You wear a suit, not an apron. Don't ever let me see you wearing a fuckin' apron again. You've been loyal. So you're a boss now." Bepy reached over to touch his arm. "Go buy six suits and charge them to this bastard. He'll pay for them. Right, Red?"

Red sat with an angry look on his face and didn't answer.

"From now on, Red's office is your office, Monkey. And that includes that big-tit secretary, if you want her. You make all company deposits, handle all cash, sign all company checks, and you hold all the checkbooks and cash deposit slips for me. If you have any problem, see me, only me. Understand?" Monkey nodded. "I changed all of the bank accounts this afternoon. Red signs nothing at all. Not even a fuckin' free lunch. I also told the bank that Red is out and you are in as of today. Understand?"

"Yes, Bephino, I understand," Monkey answered, his face glowing with excitement.

"Go see Mrs. Steinberg. She's expecting you. You gotta put your signature on the account cards."

Red still said nothing, while Bepy continued his verbal whip-lashing.

"Red, how much did you say you took for salary? Three fifty a week? Well, my salary at Julius Hart and Company is only one hundred fifteen dollars. I give you the same from now on, and you don't even have to show up anymore. You can stay home or open new stores for this guy Johnny Mac. You better get yourself married and stop jerking off. It's affecting your brain. You've made some very bad decisions these last days."

Bepy stepped closer to Red, "Now you're better off than me. I gotta work every day, for one hundred fifteen dollars, so I look like a nice fellow. I can't afford to blow my cover. But today, you blew yours. You are my enemy. Do you know that? You made a habit of fuckin' me,

Red—me, your old childhood friend!" He was getting angrier and angrier, yet Red just stared defiantly. "Red, you fat-assed bastard, for some unknown reason, you show no emotion. You act proud, but I see a poor, miserable person without courage." Bepy turned away. "In other words, you ain't shit in my eyes!

"Monkey, sign your first check and give Red one hundred fifteen dollars, minus his taxes, and get his and Big Tit's keys today. When I get a raise, he gets a raise. Red, you get no business profits. It's all over. I'm officially and openly making my move against you. *Ah finito.* You're finished with me. And make sure you don't get caught eating in any of my stores. *Ah, capeesh,* Milanese?" Bepy looked around at everyone in the room and then dismissed him. "Give my regards to your big hit man. Now get the fuck out of my sight!"

Red got up and looked at Bepy face to face, his eyes filled with hate. Bepy turned away first and then quickly looked back at Red. "Did it really have to be like this?" he asked. "It's even hard for me to accept. We always were all together. We all started this together. Why did you forget about us so quickly—about *our thing?*"

Everyone there knew that it hurt Bepy to have to move against Red. They had never seen him so emotional or angry before. There was a long heavy silence after Red walked out.

Finally, Bepy turned to his men. "Now we organize. We have competition moving in, and they're rotten killers out to hurt us. They want our business. I want daily reports on everything. The first guy who gets lazy or gets friendly with our competition is out! So don't fuck up. Anybody has troubles or complaints, see me. Nobody has to steal steak like Red did. Nobody has to worry. Everyone will eat. You're all paid well for your services. Christmas, of course, you all get your bonus, if you do the right thing. If I need you on other work, I give you extra pay. I eat, you eat. We're one family and we don't ever destroy one another. Loyalty is our most valued asset. It's our strength. Now I go take a bottle of aspirins to get rid of this fuckin' headache."

"Speaking of headaches, I'm hungry," Joey D yelled. "Let's eat."

Everyone tried to give him a smile. Monkey yelled, "What a clear head Sabu's got. We're sittin' in the middle of a funeral, and he's hungry."

"How come you're still paying Red a hundred fifteen bucks a week?" Alley Oop ventured to ask. "Why didn't you just throw him out? The guy's no good. He's a traitor to our family. He stole from you. Why do you still pay him?"

"Because he still owns forty percent of the company, on paper. If I was to throw him out without anything, a rat like that will someday be turning state's evidence against all the guys he dealt with. It could be a problem that just killing him wouldn't even solve. I could smell it all over him. He's a potential witness for the police or the FBI. He's gonna get swallowed up by Mac. He'll have to run for cover somewhere, probably to the feds. If I didn't continue to pay him, it could be considered extortion. So I changed the records today. His hours were cut and so was his salary, so there's no extortion. And there'll be no profits at the end of the year. I'll see to that. But I got plans for him, Alley. I won't forget him, don't worry. He's gonna disappear someday, sure enough."

Bephino's men saw Red constantly with Johnny Mac. Bepy knew that he probably would have to deal with both Red and Mac someday, but he figured it would be a few months off. It would be a while before Mac could make a move against him on Red's behalf, so he let the problem drop for the time being and got ready for his wedding day. He felt secure and sure of his "family" situation.

Bepy went to Monkey's new office late on a Friday evening to check on a few things. "Wait for me in the car," he said to Alley Oop. "I'll be out in about twenty minutes. I gotta look over the week's sales."

"OK. I'll take a nap," Alley Oop answered, turning down the radio.

Bepy walked up to the second floor and was about to put his key in the lock when he realized the door was unlocked. He entered slowly and heard someone moving in the next room. Cautiously, he peeked in. He was surprised to see Big Tits filling her pocketbook with papers and other items. He ran in and grabbed her. She was frightened.

"What the hell are you doing up here?" he demanded.

"I came to pick up my personal things I left behind."

"I thought you turned in your keys?"

She smiled. "I had an extra set."

"Is that right? An extra set, huh? Why, you bitch!" he said. Clenching his jaws, he tightened his grip on her arm. "What are you stealing. Empty your bag out." he yelled.

"I'm not stealin' nothin'. These are my personal papers. See, look at them."

He quickly grabbed them from her and looked them over. "You're a real cunt, you know that? You got balls coming up here on a Friday night when nobody's around! Where's your boyfriend, Red?"

"He's up my ass!" she snapped. "How do I know where he is! What d'ya think, I see him twenty-four hours a day?"

"Up your ass? What kinda answer is that? Up my ass," Bepy said, tightening his grip in frustration.

"He's probably sleepin' with Norma tonight. I really don't know and couldn't care less!"

"And who are you sleepin' with tonight? Johnny Mac?" Bepy taunted.

"How'd you know that?" she answered, grinning.

Bepy looked at her with surprise, then slowly glanced around the room. "Who brought you up here tonight?"

"No one. I'm alone. I came here all alone."

He stared at her. "You know, Big Tits, I really should slap the shit out of you for coming back after I told you to scram. You're a nervy cunt."

She smiled at him again.

"What the fuck are you smiling at?"

"You, Bephino Menesiero. You make me laugh."

"I make you laugh? I oughta make you cry, you fat bitch."

"Yeah, you make me laugh. You're always so serious. That's why I'm smiling at you. Because you're always so serious. I've been looking at you for weeks now. Didn't you realize that?"

Bepy listened as she continued. "I've been looking at you and thinking about you, but you've been romping and raging at Red over business and never appreciated me." She pulled her sweater tight over her large bust.

"Is that right, Big Tits? You've been thinking about me?" Bepy focused on her breasts as she pulled the sweater down and her nipples stiffened.

"Yes, I have." She pretended to brush something off her sweater, rubbing herself casually. "Even when I'm alone I think of you."

"No shit?" His eyes were looking her up and down. "Do you play with yourself while you think of me?"

"No," she answered sarcastically. "Of course not. I don't play with myself. I don't do those things. That's not my style." She giggled. "But I do other things." She burst out giggling again.

"Oh, yeah? What kind of other things?"

She hesitated for a brief moment, and her voice thickened when she answered. "I'll show you if you just unleash me. You're hurting my arm."

Releasing her, he backed away a foot or two and leaned against a file cabinet. She turned off the lights and moved toward him slowly, smiling. With her right hand, she reached out and petted his crotch. Then, taking two fingers, she lowered his zipper, reached into his pants, and began to fondle him. "Ahhhhh, you're a big boy, aren't you?" she whispered, licking her lips. Then, lowering his pants and fully unleashing his large cock and balls, she dropped to her knees and began to lick him. Her lips were like two feathers teasing the head of Bepy's prick. She was a head specialist, all right, and he liked her technique immediately. She bobbed and weaved up and down, licking the sides of his thick pipe, making sounds of love. Bepy was surprised at her velvet touch and her eagerness to blow him. She had an oral technique that only a man could appreciate. She sucked on him harder and harder, until he grunted and moaned in anticipation of his climax. As he began dumping it into her mouth, she eagerly consumed him. Her eyes widened and stared up at him, watching his facial expressions as he shuddered to her licking.

His body suddenly squirmed to Nero's delight and became limp from the vacuum pressure of her large lungs pumping on him. Gently, he began to push her away. He couldn't take anymore of her vacuum. "That's enough," he said. But she continued passionately. "Stop, I'm finished," he whispered, petting her head. "I'm emptied out," he said softly. "I can't take no more."

What a fantastic blow job, Bephino thought. No wonder Red's going nuts. She's sucking his brains loose.

"Two hundred a week for you was cheap," he said, smiling weakly at her. "You're unbelievable, you know that? You give some head."

"And you were complaining, weren't you, Bephino?" She smiled. "You never knew what you were missing."

Suddenly the sound of heavy footsteps was heard, and Alley Oop, tired of waiting downstairs, walked in. In the dim light, he saw Bepy tucking his shirt in his pants and the girl straightening herself up.

She saw Alley and began to giggle. "Who's that?" she asked.

Bepy looked at her and shook his head. "She's still giggling. Would you believe it, Alley? I just filled her head with dick, and the broad is still giggling. She needs more dick, Alley. Go ahead and fill her jowls again. See if she's still giggling when you jam your stump down her throat. After you finish, get her fuckin' keys. I'll be waiting in the car.

"I just gave you the appetizer," he said, smiling at her. "Now comes the main course, sweetheart. And don't forget to tell Johnny Mac you sucked our cocks, when he kisses you tonight."

Alley Oop quickly unbuckled his belt and dropped his pants to the floor, exposing his large testicles and enormous penis. This time Alley was the one grinning and smiling. She stared at him nervously as Bepy left the room.

Walking to the next office to get the sales records, he heard Alley Oop giggle. Then he heard Big Tits. "What do you want?"

Alley just giggled again in response.

"No, no. Don't do that," she said, sounding upset. "It's too big. It looks so ugly. What are you, a freak? Please let me go. It's too big. I said it's ugly. I don't want..."

As Bepy slowly walked down the steps to the first floor he heard a harsh choking sound. He had to smile at the thought of Alley Oop jamming his large genitals down Big Tits' throat.

9

Bepy and Dana were married on May 7. More than three hundred people attended. Violin and guitar strings gracefully echoed Italian music through the brightly decorated Brooklyn ballroom.

The two tables Emilio Morrano had ordered were filled with Mafia Dons from New Jersey, Philadelphia, and parts of upstate New York. They were invited by Morrano as if Bephino were his own son. His guests proudly presented the bride with envelopes containing hundred-dollar gifts; Don Emilio gave the couple one thousand dollars. Bepy was greeted like a man of importance. For some of the Dons, attending this wedding was partially business. They had heard the whispers about Bephino Menesiero and came to see the man for themselves.

Bepy's and Dana's parents could not understand why all these big Mafia figures were there to pay respect to such a young fellow. How did he know them?

The music played, and some of the guests danced; others enjoyed the abundant food and wine. Dana's mother, excited and nervously hoping that everything would be perfect for her youngest daughter's wedding day, smiled and blinked as she heard the whispers of the guests, who constantly were trying to be nonchalant about the hierarchy of the underworld sitting at special tables. Pasquale didn't know whether to smile and be proud of his son or to be embarrassed. He looked at Bephino, his mind jumping from one emotion to the other.

For their honeymoon, Bepy and Dana flew to Florida for two weeks. Dana was purring. They did the usual tourist things and the usual honeymoon things. It seemed liked paradise to them.

When Bepy called to check on business, Monkey asked, "How's your honeymoon?"

"We've been to Parrot World and Monkey World—you know, all kinds of bullshit like that. Dana likes to sightsee. So I take my new bride on tours all day. That's what you do on a honeymoon, Monk. You visit zoos."

"I thought you're supposed to screw on honeymoons."

"You do. In between the visits to zoos, that's when you screw!"

The young couple stayed at the newest hotel in Miami Beach. Don Emilio had connections all over the country and used his power to make their honeymoon extra special. The hotel was informed that Bephino was his friend, so VIP treatment was extended. Dana and Bephino were surprised when the manager greeted them upon arrival with complimentary champagne and a box of cigars. Bepy knew that only the Don could be responsible for such special treatment. Pat Zoopeli, also known as Pasquale the Great, was entertaining there. Dana and Bepy loved Pat Zoopeli, because his jokes were Italian and Jewish.

"You really love the good life, don't you?" Bepy asked Dana one quiet afternoon in their room. He had watched her moving around their suite as if she had always been in such elegant surroundings. "You really love fine hotels, good food, and beautiful rented cars." He smiled at her. "You really lap this shit up, huh, Dana?"

"Why not? Don't you?" she asked, rubbing his chest slowly. "That's why I married you, Bephino Menesiero, the Sciacchitano. Why do they call you that?"

Releasing her, he turned toward the balcony, "Ah, it's from the Old Country, from my grandfather's time. The old guys like to call the younger Italians things like that to keep them in line and thinking like loyal Italian men, not like children. It doesn't mean anything. Forget it."

"I don't believe you, Bep. I saw the way those important men greeted you at our wedding. They greeted you like you were really a big shot. But you're so young. I can't figure out why they treated you so fine."

Bepy, looking out at the ocean from the balcony, said nothing.

"I asked my brother, Armando," Dana continued. "And he told me he doesn't know how true it is, but that you're known to be a hit man for the mob. They say you're with the top man, and that the Don makes it known he likes you. I told my brother he was crazy. That you would never..."

"Dana, what the fuck? Are you and your brother news reporters or what? Hit man? Your brother doesn't know what the hell he's saying. He's probably joking. I work on Wall Street. You know that. We take bets for the Mob guys. That's how I know some of them. And I got sandwich shops, right? So what's with the hit man bullshit?" He walked over to her and gently put his arms around her waist. "Let's get laid or something. We're supposed to be on a honeymoon, not an interview of my life. Would you marry a hit man, you schmuck?" he said, trying to get her to smile. "Those guys are killers. Come on, let's screw."

"How can we make love if you talk to me like that?" Dana pouted. "It turns me off. 'Let's screw.' It sounds so ugh."

"Turns you off? Is that so? Well how do you think I felt on my beautiful honeymoon night when I put on my nice new terry-cloth robe for you, open the champagne, and you came prancing out in a beautiful negligee and your hair set in rollers?"

"But I screwed you anyway. I didn't make a scene, did I? I figured it's your first time at bat, so I didn't want to upset you and mention the rollers in your hair. The damn things kept hitting me in my eye. If you weren't my wife, I would have jumped out the window and run. Didn't your mother tell you how you're supposed to act on a honeymoon?"

Dana's eyes were dancing and she was smiling.

"So that's it!" Bepy said, realization dawning. "She told you to wear rollers in bed with me, huh? To slow me down? Am I right?

"That's it! She got even with me. And I thought she was a meatball! I'll be a son of a bitch. All the time, I thought she really was stupid! The woman blinked her way right into my honeymoon bed!"

"My mother, stupid? Your mother's stupid, not my mother," Dana declared. "And don't call her a meatball, understand?"

Bepy laughed at Dana sprawled out on the couch. She looked like she was getting ready for war. "Come on, my little Napoletana, get off your belly and come to bed for a matinee," he said. "But first, take off your armor—I mean those rollers."

"No, Bepy. I need to keep my hair set for tonight. You'll have to take me as is if you want me!" She opened her robe, exposing her nude young body to him. Bepy's eyes widened with pleasurable thoughts.

Dana slid into bed, and they began wrestling and kissing. After a few hours of good love-making and a nap, Bepy woke and yelled, "Hurry! We're late for the dinner show. Let's shower together, Dana? We'll save time."

She gave him a look and said, "We're late and you wanna start playing again." She hesitated. "If I know you, we'll never get to the dinner show."

"Don't tell me your mother even warned you about the GI-shower-and-soap-story." He stepped into the shower leaving the glass door open for Dana.

"Are you kidding? My mother doesn't know those things. My mother's a saint. And stop talking about her, will ya? Move over!"

Dinner was excellent and the show was fantastic, with Pat Zoopeli in rare form. After the show, he came to their table and shook hands. "The hotel manager is sitting over there," he said. "And he asked me to come over and say hello to you and your pretty bride. Why? Why do I have to say hello to such a young fellow?" he asked jokingly. "Then I said to myself, 'Maybe this kid's a don or the son of a don?' So I better drop over and say hello."

Awkwardly and uninvited, Pat sat down. Bepy and Dana laughed at his attempts at small talk and jokes.

He invited them to go sailing on his boat the next morning. He had a crew of three, who were well-trained to take care of guests.

Bepy thought, This is a far cry from Brooklyn. And Dana quietly asked Bepy, "Isn't this the life?"

Pat and Bepy found they had a lot in common and liked each other. They talked about getting together in New York.

The next day Dana and Bepy flew back to New York. Dana's brother picked them up at the airport and took them over to their newly remodeled apartment. It was cozy and smelled of new furniture.

Aunt Anna had found it. "Take that apartment! It's a bargain!" she had screamed. "Only forty-two dollars a month." Everyone kept quiet. They figured they'd better take it or else. Bepy's Aunt Anna threw punches when people didn't listen to her. But it was a very nice apartment.

That night back home in their Brooklyn apartment, while Bepy and Dana were lying on the couch watching television, the phone rang. Bepy took the call in the bedroom. It was Alley Oop checking in.

"Who called, Bepy?" Dana asked, when he returned.

"Alley Oop."

She began to laugh. "Why do you call him Alley Oop?"

Bepy explained. "His real name is Alfredo Opolito. When he was a kid, he stuttered a little when he talked. He used to say, 'My name is Alley Oop-Oop-Oop' and couldn't say the rest. But he's not stupid, Dana. Let's just say he's loyal."

At the age of twenty-three, Bephino Menesiero was about to become a father. It was confirmed that Dana was pregnant.

"Dana, don't do this. Don't do that. That's too heavy. Let Bephino lift it." These words echoed through their parents' apartments in Brooklyn.

It was beautiful to watch the little acts of love and affection a pregnant woman could bring to grandparents. And it was amazing how lazy the future grandparents could make a young pregnant woman. But it was only temporary, of course. Because after the baby was born, they would be visiting every weekend to see it. And the daughter-in-law was watched very carefully by the proud grandparents to make sure she did her job well.

November 12, 1952, was the date for a big heavyweight fight between Morrani and Bobby Louis. Ringside tickets were seventy-five dollars apiece. Don Emilio bought twenty tickets and gave four tickets to Bephino, who took, as his special guests, Alley Oop, Monkey, and Crazy Mikey. They felt like big shots, being invited by the Don himself.

When they arrived at Madison Square Garden, Alley and Mikey smiled broadly. "Man, these are ringside seats. We're big time now. We can see everything from here!" Mikey kept saying.

Don Emilio, with three beautiful women, and his soldier troop were seated next to them. The Don was in high spirits, caught up in the excitement of the fight arena. He gave Bepy a hug and a punch on the shoulder, and then invited Bepy and his men to a wedding on the twenty-second. One of his Capos, Big Pat Aniello, was getting married. The guy was fifty-six and he was marrying the woman he had lived with for eight years. Important people from all over the country would be at that wedding. Big Pat was well known to all families, and all families would honor the invitation to his wedding. Bepy felt honored to be included.

It was a great fight! Afterward, Morrano invited the group to Mott Street for a *scungilli* and *calamari* dinner.

Saturday, ten days later, was the night of Big Pat's wedding. Bepy and his group ate, drank, and had a good time. At one point, Bepy walked over to pay respect to Don Emilio and spoke to him in Italian. They laughed and joked. It was strange to see the Don laugh and joke so much, because that wasn't his style. Bepy had never seen him in this kind of mood.

Morrano told Rocco Borrelli to take Bepy from table to table and introduce him. They stopped to say a special hello to Nick, the Don from Queens, and the other bosses and top mob capos, soldiers, and button men who were in town for Big Pat's wedding.

Back at his table after making his rounds, Bepy's eyes focused on a man and woman talking to the people at the next table. "Don't look, but I see Sally DeMatteo here, with the Spanish fly on his arm," Bepy told Alley Oop and Monkey. "And I think he's coming over to our table.

That's the guy who wanted to kill me for fucking his girl when I was a kid."

"What does DeMatteo mean in Italian?" Monkey asked, taking another swallow of his drink. "You know, all of our names mean something in Italian."

"Look in your Italian dictionary. It must mean demented bastard," Bepy answered curtly. It had been a long time since he had seen Sally and Anita, and he was not too comfortable.

Sally, making the rounds of all the important people, also made a point of stopping at Bepy's table. He stretched out his hand. Bepy, perfectly still, considered the outstretched hand for a moment, then shook it. Sally was smiling to beat the band and acted like they were old and good friends. He knew, through the family, that Bephino Menesiero was now a preferred person, on his way up.

Bepy greeted Sally cordially, but gave him no added confidence. Sally quickly turned to his wife and said, "Anita, you remember Bepy Menesiero? He was only a kid when we met him."

What a fuckin' rabbit Sally turned out to be, Bephino thought.

Anita was smiling brightly and had a sexy look on her face. Sure she remembered Bepy, and how he had fucked her into near oblivion. She, too, reached out to shake Bepy's hand. When their hands met, Bepy knew immediately that she was once again turning on her internal charm. Her hand was clammy. She rolled her palm over his in such a way that Bepy's thoughts were flashbacks of this woman fondling her large firm breasts in erotic pleasure. Her eyes were still telling him of her desire, and he understood it clearly. She looked radiant, and Sally looked like shit—balding, blemished, flakey-faced, nervous and unsure of himself. The man has changed, Bepy thought. I wonder what's happened to him.

"We just bought a house in Red Hook. Come see us," Anita murmured to Bepy. "Come see us," she repeated, trying to keep her voice nonchalant and not too eager.

"Hey, yeah," Sally agreed, a bit reluctantly, "come and visit us." He watched his oversexed wife unconsciously flexing her breasts in a wiggle of excitement. Anita was not through with Bephino Menesiero yet. She wanted more; he could sense it.

With a frozen smile, Sally gently touched Anita's arm and said, "Come on, honey. We gotta say hello to the others." But even as she strolled from table to table, Anita's eyes returned to Bephino.

"Now there's a woman who really enjoys Italian sausage," Bepy said, turning to his friends with a laugh. "She could really devour a man of the sword."

Monkey, encouraged by Bepy's joke, began to tell one of his little supposedly funny jokes. "Take a guy like Bephino Menesiero. He has no enemies—no enemies at all. Why? Because they're all dead!" He yelled, "Get it? They're dead!" Only he cracked up with laughter.

Bepy gave Monkey a chilling look, then looked at Alley Oop. "He's drinking too much. Dry him out. Now."

Bepy had to be careful about loose talk, especially in front of high-ranking Mob people.

After the party, Bepy headed home to his mother's in his old neighborhood, because Dana was staying there that night while Bepy attended Big Pat's wedding.

As he walked into the dimly lit vestibule of the building, he heard weeping coming from a dark corner behind the stairwell. He approached the sound slowly and discovered Jesse, the old black man who washed the floors and shined the brass mailboxes in the entrance lobby.

Bepy crouched down to talk. "Why are you crying, old friend?"

Jesse looked at Bepy and began to wipe his eyes with a filthy polishing rag.

"Mr. Bepy, I haven't seen you in a dog's age. How is you? I heard you're a married man now. Where are you living now, Mr. Bepy?"

"Near Fort Hamilton Parkway. I've been married a while now. Why are you weeping, Jesse? What's wrong?"

"Mr. Bepy, I'm so unhappy I could die," the old man started to explain. "Do you remember I always washed the floors in the afternoons and I would play my harmonica for you? I loves them days. Well, now all the landlords in this neighborhood make me wash the floors only at night—from midnight to seven in the morning. Well, because I's not home at night anymore, my family is being hurt."

"Hurt? What do you mean hurt?" Bepy asked.

"My wife is seventy years old. I's seventy-two. My baby grand-daughter is only thirteen years old. Her mother died, and we tooks the little girl for our own. After I leaves for work, two no-good fellas who live upstairs in the same building comes into our apartment and takes my little grandgirl into their apartment, and they hurt the little girl. They force her into sex acts, and she's only a babe. They even gives her drugs. She's becoming a drug addict.

"One night they kicked my wife in her stomach three times. She about died. My wife is sick. She's so very sick. I's told them never to do that again, and they said they'd kill us all if I opens my mouth to the police. I can't tell the police. I can't talk. All I can do is cry.

"Yesterday, my grandchild was bleeding bad. They fucks such a young child—even in her backside. And them needles hurt her arms.

'Granddaddy, them boys hurts me,' she said." The old man began to cry into his polish-stained rag again.

"I can't believe they do that stuff to a young kid! This is making me sick! And very upset!" Bepy said. "Tell me, Jess. Are these guys kids? White? Black? What are they? How old are the guys?"

"They ain't no kids, and they is black as my ass. They about twenty-five years old. They's pimps, Mr. Bepy. That's what they is. Pimps." he answered. "And they calls me Uncle Tom because I work for white folk. There ain't no colored folk to work for, is there?"

Bepy looked at Jesse, thinking. "Give me your apartment number, old friend. I may know a fellow who can help you," he said slowly. "Give me the pimps' apartment number, too. Do you have a pencil?"

"I sure do. The point is busted, but you can use it, can't you?"

"Sure enough," Bepy said. "I'll just file it down on this cement floor until enough lead comes."

"It's sure good to see you again, Mr. Bepy. I misses you." Then he asked hopefully, "Who's this fellow, Mr. Bepy? Who's this man that's gonna help me?"

"His name is Pete. He may be able to use those two pimps."

"Is he Italiano like you?"

"Nah. If anybody asks, you tell 'em he's Jewish. I think he comes from Temple City. Good night, old buddy. I don't think you'll have to cry much longer."

The next evening Bepy, Alley Oop, and Monkey were shooting pool together. "Around midnight, we have something to do for an old friend of mine," Bepy told them. He then told Monkey to get a car and be ready to go at midnight.

"Ok, Bepy. Can we go to Mulberry Street to eat when we finish this job?" Monkey asked.

"Yeah, why not? Good idea. I'm in the mood for *scungilli* tonight."

"Did I hear *scungelli*?" Joey D, shooting pool at the next table, yelled.

"It's *scungilli*, ya mutt, not *scungelli*," Monkey chided him.

"Yeah, you wanna come?" Bepy asked him.

"Yeah, I'm hungry for the *linguini a fini* and clam sauce, with a little side order of *scungelli* salad, *al bianco* with plenty of *aglio* on it." He smiled. "Did I say it right?"

"You like *aglio*, huh, Sabu?"

"Yeah. It's good for you. Garlic is healthy, don't you know that? But I can't take that hot sauce. The last time I had it my asshole fell out—and stayed out for two weeks."

"Ok, we leave at twelve sharp. Be ready," Bepy said.

Later that night, they went to Jesse's. "What the hell are we doing in this smelly neighborhood?" Joey D asked. "It smells like raw broccoli around here."

"Quiet. We got work to do," Alley told him.

"I'm losing my appetite from this smell," Joey D again complained. "We're supposed to go out to eat. Why are we creeping around this nigger neighborhood?"

"Joey D, don't let me hear you until this work is done," Bepy said. "Understand? Alley, take Joey D in with us. I want him to see his first hit. He's still a cherry. We can't afford to have cherries in our family."

"Whata you guys up to? Your criminal antics again?" Joey D asked.

"Shut up, Sabu. Tonight you lose your cherry," Bepy said, silencing him. "Come with us and keep your fuckin' mouth shut."

They entered the building and waited in a dark corner near Jesse's apartment door. Monkey stayed with the car. About twenty-five minutes later, the two pimps came down from the floor above and walked straight to Jesse's apartment. They used their own key to let themselves in. They were tall and lean and appeared to be under the influence of something other than warm milk.

A few minutes later they came out of the apartment with a mahogany-colored child. She was wearing a pink nightgown that was torn in the rear. She had a real Kewpie doll face and seemed still half asleep as she was led to the stairwell. Bepy was almost sick to his stomach. He wanted to blast them right there, but didn't want to frighten the girl.

The three of them moved in orderly fashion very much like a ritual.

Bepy shook his head in disgust, motioned for Alley Oop to follow him, and walked up to the pimps. He flashed a laundry ticket and his gun. "Excuse me, gentlemen. We're from the Treasury Department. We wanna talk to you. It's nothing serious, so don't try anything or make me shoot you for no reason. Let's stay calm."

The pimps were in another world. Their eyes were glazed and their pupils dilated.

"Where the hell did you guys come from," one asked, startled.

"Please walk upstairs quietly. It'll only take a minute. We think you have some welfare money coming to you. Have you applied for assistance lately? We're from the Treasury Department," Bepy repeated to keep them calm.

"Treasury Department?" the other asked. "We never apply for any financial assistance. Ok, what the fuck do you wanna know about our financial status? We ain't no damn fools, so get on it."

"Let's just go to your apartment and talk about it. We have a couple of checks signed by you."

"Ok, let's talk about it. How much money is involved?"

Bepy, in Italian, told Joey D to take the girl back to her apartment. "Get her out of the way, in case I start shooting," he said.

Joey D quickly took the girl from the pimps and walked her back down to her door. "Now you go back to bed, OK? Be a nice girl. Good night."

When the pimps heard Bepy speaking fluently in Italian, they looked at each other, but said nothing. As they watched Joey D take the girl, they started mechanically up the stairs.

Bepy and Alley Oop followed them to their apartment, holding automatics to their backs. The lights in the apartment were all red, like a whorehouse.

"Hey, you got some pad. It's beautiful in here. I like it. I really do," Bepy said, casting an icy smile around the room.

Suddenly, he saw another person, moving around in the back, near the bedrooms. It was a girl who looked like a guy. She seemed very nervous. She was white, shorthaired, and blond.

Shit, Bepy thought. I was hoping no one else would have to get hit. Then the idea began to take shape in his mind that they were bringing the mahogany child for the white butch client to play with. Slowly, his blood turned to vinegar.

The pimps were talking in low voices, but Bepy heard them clearly. "These mother-fuckers are pigs," one said. "They're holding their guns to our heads. They ain't got no welfare money for us. They bullshitted us."

"OK, man. What's these questions you wanna ask us?" one asked, impatiently.

Bepy directed the lesbian and the men to sit down on the couch. "All three of you together. Is anyone else here?"

"No, just the three of us."

Bepy quickly checked all around. He had been forced to devise a new plan of action, because there were three to kill, not two. He had planned on using a knife, to keep the noise down, but now there were three of them. Should he use the gun instead? He had to think fast.

"Keep the door locked and don't touch anything," Bepy told Joey D in Italian. Joey D, standing with his back holding the door closed behind him, listened but was too frightened to answer.

"What are you guys talking about?" one of the men asked. "I don't understand that jive." Spreading his nostrils, he asked, "Why you got

152

them guns in our faces? These motherfuckers are talking shit!" he said turning to his friend and the butch.

Bepy decided to go with the knife. Speaking to Alley in Italian, he pointed his finger at one of the pimps. "Take this *tutzone* in the other room, lay him on the bed, and use the stiletto. Stab him in the stomach, one time, good and hard. Then let him bleed until he's dead. But keep him quiet. Alley, use only one plunge. Hold him firm until *morte*. Let him bleed to death like a suicide. Don't bruise his body and be careful he don't kill you. These guys are fast, very fast. Come back into the living room after he's dead." This was spoken quickly in Sicilian dialect.

"Don't worry. My gun will be stuck in his ear," Alley answered in Italian. "He won't move."

The blacks didn't understand what was happening. The butch's eyes seemed to spread wide with fear.

From behind, Alley grabbed his man off the couch by the neck and shoved him toward the bedroom. With his gun in one hand, he got his stiletto out of his pocket with the other. As they got near the bed, Alley very quickly and unexpectedly plunged the long blade into the man's stomach. One strong, twisting plunge. The pimp's eyes rolled white in his head. He had been watching the gun, so he didn't expect the knife. Alley laid him on the bed before the blood hit the rug and held him down firmly until he bled out.

In the living room, Bepy ordered the butch to the floor, face down, and ordered his man to lie on the couch, but the man refused.

"I ain't gonna do shit, man. Shoot me if you gonna. Go ahead, shoot."

Bepy took aim at his head, and the man's eyes bulged in terror.

"OK, I'm on the couch. See! Here I am on the couch!" He lay flat on his back.

Bepy got up close, pointed the gun to the man's face, and quickly plunged his knife deep into the man's chest. He aimed for the heart and twisted his knife with the special style of a fisherman, trying to tear the ventricles apart. Then he stabbed the man repeatedly in his stomach and up at the shoulders, leaving the appearance that a savage murder had taken place. He cut the dead man's hands and chopped lightly at his face. It had to appear that a brawl had resulted in the deaths, a fight between the pimps. He needed hours before the bodies were discovered. Time was essential to this hit.

The lesbian was still face down on the floor alongside the couch. Bepy stood over her with the gun pointing at her head. She tried not to see the butchering that had taken place, but she couldn't help hearing the bubbly sound of the man's liver and other organs popping in his thin body. She felt faint as she heard the final gargle through the dying man's vocal cords. Her bowels began to acknowledge her fears; shit ran loosely down her legs, uncontrollably. She yelped, as if to vomit.

She lifted her body and begged Bepy for mercy. "Oh, my God, oh, my God," she moaned. "Why did you do that to him?"

"Was it right for him to fuck that little nigger kid downstairs until she bled from her ass? Was it right to pump her full of drugs?" Bepy asked her grimly, in a low voice. "He was gonna kill the grandparents. Did you know that?" Then he raised his voice, "What were you doing to that little kid, huh? Why were you here? She's only thirteen. What the fuck is wrong with you people, anyway? She's only a kid. That's why I killed those rotten bastards; that's why. They're fuckin' dirt!"

Suddenly, he lowered his voice as he continued. "Because you're a white girl, we won't hurt you. So stop shittin'. Don't worry," he said, reassuring her so she wouldn't panic further. Her body was now numb with fear; she was unable to function.

Alley entered the room briskly. "The fuckin' yam is *morte.*" Then he asked, in Italian, "Whatta we gonna do with the butch?"

"She's gotta go, too, of course," Bepy told Alley speaking in his Sicilian dialect. "She'll open her fuckin' mouth. It's too dangerous for us. Twist the dyke's neck," he ordered Alley. "Snap it fast. Don't let her suffer."

"OK, I do it," Alley answered without hesitation.

Suddenly the lesbian propped herself up and began to beg loudly in fluent Italian for her life. Bepy and Alley were stunned by the shocking realization that she was Italian and had been able to understand every word they said.

Bepy remained silent, staring at her. Alley Oop's mouth gaped open, he growled, "Holy Shit!"

Confusion covered Bepy's face as he looked at Alley and wondered what to do next. Unable to speak without the girl understanding, he looked at Alley and signaled the *bocca la morte,* using his eyes like a mute. Alley understood and moved in for the kill, breaking her neck with one twist of his powerful hands. He then kissed her once on the side of her mouth, giving her the sympathetic send-off of *bocca la morte.*

"Why did she have to be here tonight?" Bepy asked. "I only wanted to kill the jigs. I feel bad for her. But what choice did we have?"

"We had absolutely no choice," Alley agreed sympathetically, while still leaning over her and making the sign of the cross.

Bepy went into the kitchen and found a butcher knife. Handling it with extreme care, using a handkerchief, he dipped it in the blood of the man on the couch, repunching the holes in his stomach and chest. After making sure it had plenty of blood on it, he went to the bedroom and placed it in the knife hole gaping in the stomach of the man on the bed. He wrapped the man's fingers and hands around the handle. By putting both bloods on the murder weapon, he made it look like a killing fiasco and then a suicide. It would look like the man lying in the bedroom had twisted the lesbian's neck, then, in an argument over her, murdered his friend by chopping at his heart, and took his own life, using the murder weapon. His prints were the only ones on it, and both blood types would be significant to the case. The drugs they probably had taken could also have contributed to the deaths.

Before leaving, Bepy walked over to the far side of the bed where a candle was resting in a tray. He lit the candle.

"Should we take their cash?" Alley asked as he watched Bepy blow at the match. There was a roll of twenties on the dresser.

"Take only half their money. I don't want this to appear like a robbery. It must look like an internal situation." Walking out of the bedroom, thinking again, he turned to Alley. "Rip a button off that guy's shirt in the bedroom and bring it to me."

Busy wiping everything in sight, he looked up at the door. Joey D was frozen solid, the color of a jade goddess. The only things moving were his eyes. Bepy had completely forgotten about Joey D.

Alley returned with the button, which Bepy wiped and placed in the lesbian's hand, to prove the man in the bedroom was her murderer. It seemed to be a perfect crime to take place among pimps, lesbians, and drug users.

Joey D was totally exhausted from the horror he'd played doorman to.

Bepy walked up to him and slapped his face lightly. "Wake up, kid. It's time to go eat."

"I thought this thing was never gonna end," Joey D replied. "You really take your time. You guys got some clear heads. How could you do all that on an empty stomach? I feel sick, Bep. I feel strange."

"Bep, why'd you bring him with us?" Alley complained. "Look at him. He's shaking like a leaf." He pinched Joey D's face. "Cut it out, ya rubber. You're making me seasick."

They walked down the steps wiping handrails and anything else they might have touched. They had been careful, but tonight they had broken a company rule: they had not worn gloves. Handkerchief in hand, Bepy opened the still-unlocked door of Jesse's apartment and tossed in the roll of bills they had collected from the pimps. Then they left the building and got into their waiting car.

"Holy shit! What the hell were you guys doin' up there so long?" Monkey said as they drove off. "I spend my whole life waiting in cars. I was getting worried. I moved the car four times. Christ, I was worried! What happened? You took so long."

"Please don't ask us," Joey D answered. "I don't wanna relive that scene. I'm sick to my stomach. These two guys are nuts. I can't believe them. They make eyes at each other, they snap necks, and then make the sign of the cross after they're finished. They're like two monsters!"

"How come you threw that cash in that apartment?" Alley asked.

"I figured the old man could use the money. Christmas is coming. He's an old friend of mine."

"Now he's Santa Claus," Monkey said. "A few years ago he was a rabbi. Next year he'll be Robin Hood. I wanna see who the hell pays the check tonight."

Bepy, collecting the stilettos from Alley Oop, said, "Remind me to boil them tonight. I wanna get all the blood off."

Joey D gagged.

"They had a fuckin' drugstore up there," Bepy told Monkey. "I saw a table full of morphine and bags of white powder, maybe heroin. I hope the little kid didn't get hooked bad on that shit."

Alley Oop nudged Bepy, trying to get his attention, and whispered to him, "The big joke of the day was that lesbian being Italian. I never knew there was Italian lesbians. I feel bad for her."

"There's all kinds of suckers from all over the world," Bepy said. "I feel kinda bad, too, Alley. But we had no other choice. We had no choice, really. It was her fate."

Alley laughed. "Maybe she was really French and just spoke some Italian. There ain't no Italian lesbians. I never heard of them in Italy."

"Ya wanna bet, Alley?" Monkey laughed.

The next morning Jesse arrived home from work to see police and ambulance attendants carry three bodies out. A crowd of people around the front of the house told him the pimps were dead. "Drugs made them kill each other. Drugs drove them crazy," people in the crowd were whispering excitedly. They heard there was a girl dead, too. The bodies were discovered by one of the pimps' whores.

Jesse, thinking the dead girl could be his grandchild, pushed his way through the crowd. He rushed into his apartment wildly and found his wife and granddaughter sitting at the kitchen table counting the cash. There were hundreds of dollars. "Where you get that money, child?" the old man asked in a deep voice.

"We found it on the floor, right over there, Pappy."

Jesse gathered the money quickly, before the police started going from apartment to apartment asking questions. Humming a tune, he put it away.

The child told him that the pimps were taking her again last night and that some white men brought her back and told her to go to sleep.

Jesse abruptly turned to her and touched her shoulder. She looked at him as he spoke in a strong but loving voice. "Look, child. Them was not white mens. They was angels. Do you understand, child? They was angels. Tell no one of them. No one."

The child hugged her granddaddy, confirming that she understood what he meant.

10

"Is it true? Tell me, is it true?" Bepy asked Dana, without taking his eyes off the road. He just looked straight ahead at the traffic and grinned.

"What the heck are you talking about, Bepy? Is what true?" Dana asked lazily, leaning back in her seat.

"Did your mother really wrestle Mrs. Fontano for that last mozzarella at Orellio's market? I heard they were all over the floor wrestling, pulling the mozzarella back and forth in front of people— right in the store."

Dana grabbed at Bepy's shoulder, causing the steering wheel to swerve the car to the left. "*Ma tu si pazzo.* My mother would never do a thing like that. Where do you get these stories from—the poolroom?"

"Watch it! The car is swaying. Careful where you hit!" Bepy warned, playfully. "The poolroom? You know, if I got it there, it would have to be true. You know that, don't you?"

"Cut the baloney, Bepy. I'm not in the mood tonight. You're always teasing about my mother. And she treats you so good. Tonight she made you tripe. She's always trying to please you."

Suddenly Bepy stopped the car.

"What now?" Dana asked. "Why are you stopping?"

"I gotta get some hot bagels. We'll have coffee and fresh bagels when we get home. They're baking early tonight. I smell them. Hm-m-m! God bless them Jews. They make such good bagels. Have we got any butter at home, Dana?"

"Yes, I just bought a pound of whipped sweet a coupla days ago."

"Good. We'll have a cup of coffee and hot bagels. It's cold out tonight."

"Sounds good," she agreed. "I feel like noshing while we watch the late show."

As he walked toward the store, Dana yelled out the window, "Get some with the seeds!"

He entered the store. "One dozen bagels, sir. Half with seeds, half without," he told the man cleaning out a bread bin. He whiffed in the freshly baked aroma. "Boy they smell good," he said with a smile.

"We don't have any with seeds yet. It's too early," the baker replied. He leaned over the counter with his long banana nose hanging and waited for Bepy's next move.

Dana's request for seeds was a big problem. She was pregnant and Bepy knew that if she didn't get the seeds, the baby might be born with skin seeds on his face. The Old Italians call the craving a *woolei*. They also said that if you dream of strawberries, the baby might wind up with a berry on his face.

Why did I stop here for the fuckin' bagels? he thought. My life never runs smoothly. My kid better not have seeds on his face.

The baker asked, "Well, do you want bagels or not?"

"Sir, my wife is pregnant and she has a *woolei* for them bagels with seeds. Please make me some. I'll pay you extra for them." He smiled again. "It's important that she gets the seeds. She's pregnant seven months now. You can understand that, huh, sir?"

"Look, fellow. We're running a bakery here, not a hospital. We don't make the bagels with the seeds till 5:00 A.M. I'm sorry. Either come after five or try us again next year."

"Come on, mister. Jews and Italians got the same ideals and mystiques about their kids being born right."

"Not really."

"Look, mister. Don't get smart. I'm a customer, so have some respect. When the bagels go in the oven, throw some seeds on—just a few, huh? My uncle Antonio is a baker and he always throws a handful of seeds on the bread at the last minute. It's no problem for him. I used to watch him when he makes Italian bread. Do me a favor. My wife is like a balloon out there. I gotta get some seeds in her. It's important. We're Italian, and she's got a *woolei.*"

"Is that so? Well, go see your uncle what's-his-name. See if he can make a bagel with a *woolei.*" The baker walked towards the back.

Bepy called out to him, "Come on, mister. Do me a favor. Make a few of them with seeds. How about it?"

"No, thank you."

"OK, then, just make one with seeds, just one," Bephino yelled.

"I told you, 5:00 A.M. Set your alarm clock and come back."

"Look at this shit," Bepy thought to himself. "This fuckin' Jew wants to start a war over a bagel. The guy is a real wise guy—'your uncle, what's-his-name,' and all that bullshit—'Set your alarm clock.'"

Looking around, Bepy saw another guy, in the back working the ovens.

"How many bakers you got here?" he asked the first one who was coming back to the front with a tray of egg bagels.

"We're two brothers. Anything else you should know?"

"Yeah. You gotta telephone here?"

"No, we have no phone. What else do you want that we don't have?" The baker grinned at his own wit.

Bepy grinned, too. "I'll be right back." He ran out to his car. "Hey, Dana, how bad do you want those damn seeds?"

"What's wrong with you? You know I like seeds sometimes, and tonight I feel a *woolei* for those seeds. Get half and half."

"That's what I thought." He reached under his seat, took his gun, and slipped it in his pocket. "Dana, stay in the car. I'll be right back. The guys are baking them, so sit tight." Dana hadn't seen him grab his gun.

Bepy walked back into the bagel shop, locked the door behind him, and went directly into the rear. He found the wall switch and shut the front lights off so the store looked closed. In the rear the two brothers were busy making bagels on the table.

"Oh, look who's back," the first one remarked. "What's-his-name, the Italian baker's nephew." The two men began to laugh in harmony.

"You guys look like the Schmuck Brothers," Bepy yelled out to them. "Remember the Smith Brothers?" he asked. "Well, you guys are the Schmuck Brothers." He pulled out his gun. "OK, schmucks. I've killed a lot of guys in my day, but this is the first time I kill two nozzle-nosed rabbis over a fuckin' seeded bagel. Now make me a thousand bagels, all with seeds. Right now. Fast or we're gonna see if you Jews really can walk on water." He paused, then added, "With your fuckin' heads blown off. Now make them bagels fast, you smart-mouthed bastards." He cocked the hammer.

Seeds were soon flying all over the place. The first tray came out. Bepy filled a bag with a dozen and dropped one dollar on the table.

"This is for my original order. Now I want the rest of the thousand bagels—all with seeds; make sure they all got seeds now—delivered at seven to Saint Rosalie Church—breakfast for the kids. Make sure you have them there at seven sharp. The kids like bagels with their eggs in the morning. You make a nice donation to the Catholic church. And if you don't show, I'll come back and kill both you guys. So start baking. You got a lot of bagels to make, and don't forget the seeds."

The brothers stood there with their twin noses hanging sad and confused. At the door Bepy turned around, winked, and said, "OK, fellas. Cancel the order."

"Thank you, thank you!" they repeated, bobbing their heads and with their hands clasped in front of them.

Bepy got in the car and drove off.

"Boy, those bagels smell so good. Huh, Bepy?" Dana said as she peeked into the bag.

"Yeah, those guys can really bake. They were nice people; they understood how important *woolei* is to us."

"That's nice. I'm glad there's still some considerate people left in this world."

"Yeah! Me, too!" He looked up at the sky and frowned.

Trading was hectic on Monday. Bepy had become Mr. Gustini's personal trader, and he was buying thousands of shares of Paso Del Nova, a gas company. In the excitement of the bustling trading room, Mr. Gustini didn't say much to Bepy. He was too busy pumping orders as he talked on the phone. "Yes. OK, Julius. I'll put your orders in right now." He peered over his glasses and yelled his instructions without hanging up on Julius, "Buy! I repeat, buy! Buy ten thousand at the market. Buy ten thousand at five. Buy twenty thousand at four and seven-eighths. Make it an open order at four and seven-eighths." He listened and continued his instructions to Bepy. "Hurry! Give me an execution on my ten thousand at market."

Bepy phoned the orders to the floor of the exchange. For a few moments they waited for the reply from the floor. Bepy saw his opening and asked, "Mr. Gustini, what's up with Paso Del Nova?"

"Julius heard that a very good report is about to be made to the public on Wednesday. That will move the stock. Right now there are a lot of outstanding shares. My group is buying heavy. There's still a large block offered at six and a half. It will go to ten, Bephino; you can buy any amount for yourself, any amount. I like the stock for quick profits. But short term only." Mr. Gustini's phone rang again, and he waved Bephino to get on with his business. "Keep me posted. I'll be in conference with Julius. Oh, and I'll be leaving for Rome tomorrow morning. I'll be gone a couple of weeks."

Despite his hectic day, that afternoon, when Mr. Gustini's orders stopped coming, Bepy took the time to buy twenty thousand shares for his own account. He paid five and an eighth. Mr. Gustini had purchased a total of two hundred thousand shares, at an average price of five. Other brokerage houses were buying heavily also, and the stock closed on the California OTC Exchange at six and a quarter. Bepy had made almost twenty thousand dollars on paper. He figured that when Mr. Gustini sold, he would sell, too.

Ever since the wedding, Bepy and Dana's sister, Gina, and her husband, Phil, had become close. He knew that she was always looking for a good deal and spent a lot of time getting her fortune told. So he called her and told her about the stock.

"Buy me one thousand shares," Gina said excitedly. "I want it. I have a good feeling about it. I like the name."

"What do you mean, good feeling, you like the name? It's a tip, Gina. The name doesn't mean anything."

"Don't tell me!" she countered. "Yesterday I went to a fortune teller on DeKalb Avenue and she said I'm gonna make a good hit. I got minerals coming. That's what she said, Bepy."

"You really believe in that bullshit?" Bepy asked. "Remember when the fortune teller broke the egg you slept with all night and ink came out and you believed it was cursed. She wanted a thousand bucks to take the curse off you, and you were gonna go for that bullshit? Remember, Gina, I stopped you. Now you're gonna tell me about fortune tellers again. The only minerals you got coming, Gina, are gas in your stomach. You ruined my excitement. Now I feel like selling my shares."

Bepy hung up. "I hate them gypsies. They're full of shit. If this stock moves a little, I'm selling. Hers and mine. I don't believe in fortune tellers." He finished his conversation with Gina without her.

Two weeks later the stock jumped to eight and a quarter, and Bepy called Gina. "Hey, sister baby, I'm selling my shares. The hell with you and your fortune teller. I'm taking my profit."

"Let's hold, Bepy. I told you I feel good about it."

"Bullshit. I'm getting out now. Before the stock falls to three bucks. And don't you go back to that damn gypsy."

He sold his entire block of stock at eight and five-eighths. Then he sold Gina's thousand shares at eight and seven-eighths. It went up to nine and one-eighth. He called her up. "Hey, sis, I just sold your stock for you at eight and seven-eighths. You made a nice profit. Are you happy?"

"I didn't tell you to sell my shares. Why did you sell? How much did you get for yours?"

"Eight and five-eighths. What the hell do you want? We made money in two weeks doing nothing."

"But I feel the stock will go much higher. The fortune teller said my ship will arrive."

"Hey, Gina, cut the baloney. Your ship will arrive. And when it does, I'll be the damn captain, and don't you forget that."

"The stock will go higher. I feel it, Bepy."

"Holy shit! I don't believe this! I was trying to protect you. I was trying to look out for you."

"I can look out for myself. I'm a big girl," she stated.

Forty minutes later Mr. Gustini called from Rome and asked for the market price and size of Paso Del Nova.

"Eight and five-eighths to eight and seven-eighths. Ninety thousand by four hundred thousand," Bepy told him. "The high was nine and an eighth. The stock got a little softer. There was some profit-taking this afternoon. A California broker has placed a large block for sale at eight and seven-eighths—four hundred thousand shares."

"OK," Mr. Gustini bellowed into the telephone "Bephino, sell two hundred thousand shares for my special account, you know the number. Credit the commissions to the Rome office. Keep selling, but don't let the floor know how many you have to sell. Handle the order carefully. Try not to let them know we're unloading." Excitement filled his voice. "Be sure to stay in front of that large block by an eighth of a point. And sell, sell—very carefully."

"OK, Mr. Gustini, I'll handle it carefully. I'll wire your executions." He began entering sell orders and watched the number of buys and sells closely. He sold one hundred sixty thousand shares, from eight and three-quarters down to eight and one-eighth, and forty thousand shares at eight. The stock dropped quickly as more sellers entered the market. Paso Del Nova was soon selling at seven and one-quarter in brisk trading.

The next day, Mr. Melvin, while checking all trades for the previous day, saw that Bepy had sold, for his personal account, twenty thousand shares at eight and five-eighths and that Fontano had sold one thousand shares at eight and seven-eighths.

"How did you acquire the money to buy over one hundred thousand dollars' worth of stock?" he asked Bepy.

"I come from a rich family. We own olive trees in Sicily."

"Is that so? And who is this Fontano?"

"That's my sister-in-law. She's a good client of Jules Hart and Company. Why you wanna know about Fontano?"

"I'll let you know," Mr. Melvin said, and turned and left the office.

He was back in thirty minutes. "I want to talk to you in private, Mr. Bephino Menesiero." They went into the conference room, and Mr. Melvin sat looking up at the ceiling. "You broke the rules of the Stock Exchange, and that's a very serious offense. In fact, you could cause our firm to lose its license. You broke a very important SEC rule, Mr. Menesiero."

"No, I didn't."

"Certainly you did. You received a call from Mr. Gustini in Rome. He said to sell two hundred thousand shares, but you sold your stock first, to protect your own price. You broke company rules and SEC rules."

"Bullshit. I sold my shares forty minutes before he called. Check the time on my orders. I stamped them with the order clerk's time clock, which is normal office procedure! Mr. Gustini called forty minutes later and gave me instructions to sell. I had already sold my shares. Check with the floor. They've got clocked orders, too. In fact, I had no idea Mr. Gustini was going to call and start selling his shares. What d'ya think I got, a gypsy with a crystal ball?" Bepy was becoming irritated.

"Well, what made you decide to sell your stock when it was moving up? You sold it on an uptick, almost at the high of the day."

"The high was nine and an eighth. So what? Maybe I figured it right. Maybe I'm a good broker. Didn't you see the mark I got on my exam? Ninety-seven. That's not bad for a kid from Brooklyn. Anyway, it was my right to sell. I didn't take precedence over any customers' orders."

"That remains to be seen, my boy. I'm going to check with the phone company for the actual time you received the call from Rome."

"Hey, why are you always trying to nail me, Mr. Melvin? Don't I do my job? You've been sneaking around looking down my shirt ever since I've been working here. All the other executives like me but you. Why? Are you trying to upset my life?"

"I'm not trying anything, and that's not the issue here, anyway. I have to check these things. If there's something improper, I must report it—no matter who it is. I am in charge of these things."

"Ever since I met you I've had the feeling that you hate my guts. What did I ever do to you? Huh, Mr. Melvin?" Bephino continued.

"Not a thing," Mr. Melvin answered, and walked away.

Bepy stood and stared after him. "See what I mean," he said. "He hates me."

He had earned sixty thousand dollars on those transactions and was fast becoming financially comfortable. But he still continued his old lifestyle, so as not to be conspicuous. He and Dana had a beautiful apartment, the best of clothes, and a new car, but they kept their spending under control.

The hero shops were making big money. But Red and Johnny Mac were opening up posh new shops, with beautiful decor and fancy booths near Bepy's stores. The people in the area liked the new shops. So business dropped off, and this concerned Bepy. Red was smart. He had capitalized on Bepy's weak spots to improve his own company.

"I think the time has come for Red," Bepy told Alley Oop one day. "He's defying me again. He's testing my heritage. He opened another store right across the street from our number four store."

"Let's hit the mother," Alley said impatiently.

"I gotta think about this, Alley. It's not that easy. People know I have bad blood with him. I gotta think about this real good. It's gonna be tough. I waited too long. I fucked up. If I knock him off, I'll be a suspect for sure. So far my life has been clean. No one believes I'm a capable person. If Red bites the dust, I'll be looked at closely, and I don't want that, Alley. I can't take that chance."

"I'll kill him for you," Alley replied.

A few days later Bepy got word that Don Emilio wanted to see him.

"I'm giving you that big hit we talked about. Remember? Big bucks?" the Don said when they met. "We need you to go to New Orleans."

"New Orleans?"

"Yes. We're sending another guy with you. His name is Benny, and he's experienced in out-of-town hits. He's from Staten Island. You and he will split the contract. It pays a hundred grand each, plus expenses.

"Benny is one of the best. He's like a snake. He gets in and out fast. He's an independent worker, like you. He don't belong to anyone. You two should get along fine. You're on the same team. Don't forget that.

"And, Bepy, don't try to fuck this guy's wife, like you did to Sally. This guy is trigger happy. He'll hurt you, understand? When he kills, he kills quick. He's bad news. So be careful. Sometimes you don't mix too well with others. I remember how Sally wanted to hit you for what you did. I think this Benny's a funeral director by trade, so be alert."

Bepy understood the joke. But he didn't like the idea of going away from New York City to make a hit.

The Don continued. "Benny can do anything. He's also a bomb man. I believe *you* are the best, Bepy, in exotic hits. You seem to make a hit very confusing for the police. I like your style. You use your brains. You don't shoot 'em and run; you shoot 'em with a story. That's nice. Imagination, you got imagination. It's clean *and* confusing." He patted Bepy on the shoulder.

"So you and Benny work together on this and make a deal on how this work gets done. The hit must be high quality. It's very important to my good friend Angelo, in New Orleans; he has a big problem, very big. That's why the contract price is so large. He can go to prison for many years if you fail. I believe you are my man for this, Bephino Menesiero. This hit needs a man with brains, not a guy like some we got, who trip over their own feet. They shoot with shotguns and miss their targets. There's a lot of bums out there looking for work. I can't use 'em; they're morons. I remember when we were young. The pay for a hit was only five dollars, and, believe me, we were happy to get the work. And we did it right, like you Bephino. Every hit man has his own style."

"Am I working for this Benny?"

"No, Bephino. He's working for you. Brooklyn boys don't work for Staten Islanders; they're farmers over there. It's all farmland. There's hardly anybody there, but it's our territory, so we use it. We dump bodies from time to time on Staten Island. The Staten Island guys are a vein in our family, and they take our orders.

"But you must respect Benny because he's very experienced. He's Sicilian and a real pro. He's been making hits for us for twelve years. We recruited him by accident. He hit one of our guys by mistake. He's a little *pazzo*. He used to kill guys for no reason. One of our people saw him make a hit. When we questioned him about it, he just laughed. So we use him from time to time for special hits."

Morrano shook his head, remembering Benny's actions. "You go see Benny. Make your arrangements with him."

Bepy listened quietly and waited to see if Morrano was going to tell him more about Benny or give him the details of the situation.

"We pay you after the hit this time. And your expenses. But don't get no bills, huh, kid? Just tell me what it cost, and I'll get it from New

Orleans. They pay three hundred thousand plus, so we pay you and Benny one hundred thousand each plus, and I get one hundred thousand net for my people.

"This is a very big one, kid. It's a political hit. That's why we get this nice fee. The boys in New Orleans can't figure out how to do this one, and we only have a few days left. You must come through. Make it confusing. Something nice, OK? Like an accident, maybe, a car accident. They always work. I use you, my young friend, because I trust your judgment and imagination."

"How do I get in touch with this Benny?"

"Here's his phone number. Call his office and make an appointment. Leave for New Orleans as soon as possible. Benny already knows what I just told you. We had him over here earlier today and gave him all the info on the important man we represent in New Orleans. We also told him that you're young, but that we have the utmost confidence in you. Don't let us down, Bephino." The Don smiled and grabbed him by both shoulders.

"Did you tell Ben that I've been young all my life?" Bepy asked drily.

Morrano grinned.

"OK, Mr. Morrano. I'll call you when I get back to New York. I'll do my best."

The Don embraced Bephino. "*Buona fortuna,* Bephino. Have a safe journey."

Bepy went home and called the phone number for Benny. A husky voice answered and told him to call another number in fifteen minutes. Bepy waited, called the new number, and a different guy answered.

"Hello, is this Benny?"

"No. Whatta ya want?" a deep voice said sharply.

"I want an appointment for lunch—with Benny."

"Your lunch is on for one tomorrow at Fishermen's Wharf on Staten Island. Table fourteen," the man replied and hung up. Bepy understood the reason for the abrupt conversation—telephones are dangerous and can be tapped—but why such deep voices?

He took a hot shower. Dana's cooking smelled good! So he sneaked into the kitchen to peek. He saw mashed potatoes and veal cutlets. He loved veal cutlets.

He moved behind Dana, patted her ass, and kissed her. "I love you, honey," he whispered.

166

"I love you, too, honey," she said, mimicking a husky mysterious voice.

"What the fuck's with the voices today?" he snapped.

"Can't you take a joke? I was just playing."

He held her tight for a moment as he thought of what was ahead of him. "Umm, that smells good."

"Yeah," Dana replied. "They better smell good. Do you know how much these cutlets cost me a pound?"

"No, and I don't care. Don't tell me prices, Dana. Just buy the best for us, OK? I give you plenty of money to shop, so keep up the good work. Live up to your mother's reputation. She's so proud of her cooking, and you're just like her. A little old lady."

Dana grabbed for her magic wand, the wooden spoon that every Italian cook has.

Halfway through dinner, he teased Dana again. "The veal and the wine are great, but the mashed potatoes are a little lumpy. What happened to your magic wand tonight?"

"Lumpy? Your head is lumpy." Dana got insulted immediately. "They were not lumpy. I mixed them for twenty minutes. If that's the way you feel, next time I'll make French fries from them frozen bags. OK?"

"No, it's not OK. Get your wand fixed." After dinner he asked, "Is the coffee ready?"

Dana poured the black espresso and sat down again at the table. "Here, try this," she said, cutting up a cheesecake. "The German baker made it. See if you like his cooking."

"Honey, let's get serious for a minute. I have to leave on a trip for a few days. Don't tell anyone I'm gone, and don't talk on the phone about me to anyone—not even my mother or father. It's important that the world thinks I'm still in Brooklyn. OK, Dana? So don't even talk to anyone for a few days. Stay off the phone."

"Where are you going, Bepy?" she asked suspiciously. "Sounds real important. Whatta you doing, robbing a bank? Or are you going to Vegas with Margie?"

"Margie?"

"Yeah, Margie. Your mother told me you were plowing around with her for years."

"Is that what you and my mother talk about? I haven't seen Margie in years. I was just a kid. I guess I'll have to tell my mother to stop bragging," he said irritably. "I'm going on a fishing trip, and don't ask me any questions, understand?"

"How do I know you're not cheating on me?" she pouted.

"You're so beautiful. You're like a movie star. And we're having a baby soon. Who's got time to fool around?"

"What kind of fishing you gonna do?"

"I'm gonna fish for Moby Dick. When I was a kid I promised myself I would catch Moby Dick. Now I'm going to get him."

"Moby Dick?" she yelled. "Tell me a better story, so I won't worry. I don't like that one." She stared at him with her cat eyes and sad oval face, then rubbed her belly to remind him she was carrying his baby.

"You wanna better story? OK. I'm a fuckin' Boy Scout and I gotta go on a two-day hike. Hey, Dana, you wanna break my balls now, huh? Look, I got business. Don't ask questions and don't talk to me anymore about these things. What I gotta do, I gotta do. And you know this. So shut up and go buy a nice sexy nightgown for my return. I wanna plow around with you." He laughed.

"I gotta buy a sexy nightgown with this belly? Thanks a lot, sport." She laughed with him. "That's exactly what it would be—plowing around. Look at me. I'm like a bulldozer."

At one the next day, Bepy and Monkey arrived at Fishermen's Wharf on Staten Island. They walked to table fourteen and found it totally covered with snow. It was January twentieth and twenty-one degrees.

"Hey, Bepy," Monkey joked. "What are you having a sit-down with, an Eskimo? It's freezing out here!"

"I don't know. This is weird, huh, Monk? They said table fourteen and this is it. I don't understand this." They looked all around.

A door opened, and a tough-looking guy came out. "Are you Bephino from Brooklyn?" he asked in a sweet, high-pitched voice. His face and voice did not match.

"No, sweetheart," Monk said. "We're a couple of Eskimos from Alaska. Where the fuck's the heat around here?"

The guy laughed. "Come on, follow me."

Monkey whispered, "This guy sounds like a canary."

"Yeah! And another one, on the phone, sounded like a bullfrog."

They followed him to the wine cellar, where Benny was waiting at a table. The men shook hands, and Benny told his bodyguard to go upstairs and take "the unkeymay" with him. "You guys eat upstairs. We have to talk," he said. "OK with you, Bephino?"

168

Monkey didn't like what Benny called him in Pig Latin, and he looked at Bepy in confusion. How did Benny know his nickname was Monkey?

Bepy nodded to him. "It's OK," he said. "Go eat with the canary. I'll have lunch with Benny the bullfrog."

"Whoa, whoa," Benny said, jumping from his seat, "Look, Bepy, or whatever your name is, don't ever call me Benny. You call me Ben. *Ah capeesh?*"

Bepy was surprised by Benny's sudden move. Why this little rubber, he thought, he's starting that bullshit already.

"OK, Benny. You want me to call you Ben, so I'll call you Ben. And you call me Bephino, not Bepy. My friend's name is Aldo, not unkeymay. Don't forget that! And tell me, Ben, is this introduction over or do you want me to know your middle name, too?"

"Yeah, it's over," Ben said, realizing that Bephino was his kind of man. The waiter came just then and they ordered fish and wine.

While they ate tender *calamari,* they talked about their trip to New Orleans. Bepy said that when he was a kid his grandfather talked about New Orleans a lot. *"New Orleansa duta Siciliano et New Orleansa,"* he had said, meaning a lot of Sicilians in New Orleans. "They settled there for the good fishing."

"Yeah," Ben said. "Your grandfather's right. They're first and second generation, like us. They were born there. It's funny though. They look Italian, like us, but they speak like Rebels. Their voices don't seem right, coming from those faces. Don't start laughing when you meet them. We don't need to upset anyone."

"You mean—like your bodyguard upstairs?"

"Yeah! Like him. You're on the ball, Bepy."

"Don't call me Bepy. I said call me Bephino." They broke out laughing together.

"Boy, I can see we're gonna get into a lotta trouble on this trip," Benny said. "You are fuckin' nuts!"

"And don't forget that," Bepy said with a sly grin. "Now, tell me about the plane, hotel, and all that stuff."

"Our plane tickets are only one-way, because we don't know when we'll finish our work. We decide how to get home after we make the hit. Oh, yeah, take a few grand in case we need cash."

"Yeah, that's *real* smart," Bepy said sarcastically. "When all the confusion starts, we try to hitch a ride home. It doesn't sound too good, but go ahead, Ben, continue."

"We leave tonight at eleven-thirty. Our tickets are in different names. And we don't travel together. You're in the front of the plane; I'm in the rear."

Bephino grinned. "Yeah, I know the niggers ride in the rear down South, and we're headed South, so you better stay in the rear, Benny."

Ben laughed, but a bit weaker as he sensed Bephino moving gracefully toward assuming control. Nevertheless, he continued. "Let's talk seriously. We gotta get it right, because after today, we never talk to each other until we arrive in New Orleans. We fly to Chicago, where we have other reservations for New Orleans, in other names. We pick them tickets up at the counter in Chicago. There will be a guy waiting for us in New Orleans. He'll be wearing a gray hat with a press card in the hatband."

"Gray hat, press card?" Bepy laughed. "What the fuck, are we making a movie?"

"This is the way these things are done. But remember, don't speak to me until we're in the car. We're still solo. We singly follow Gray Hat to his car, and he takes us to a mattress and a meeting with this Italian Rebel, Don Santoro."

"Oh, is that his name, Santoro? I don't remember Morrano mentioning his last name to me," Bepy said.

"Santoro's one of the most powerful bosses in the country and he's got plenty of dough. He was smart. He took over his father's shrimp boats in Louisiana, and then he took over everyone else's, too. He was a real Bayou Pete, a real pirate. People had no choice. He just put the arm on them. But he gave them all jobs. And now he's really liked. He looks out for the shrimpers. He keeps New Orleans in line. Believe me, this guy is big.

"But he's also in big trouble with the feds, and the Congress boys, and the Senate Rackets Committee. That's why he needs Morrano's help quick. And that's why we got the contract. You and me are not known to the FBI, so we can move around without being spotted. Morrano's smart, too. He's always got a good reason when he gives out a contract. He knows that if he sends his regular goons, they'll get spotted before they leave Brooklyn."

Benny paused. "OK. Let's get going. I'll see you on the plane tonight." They shook hands and left.

At three in the morning the connecting plane landed in New Orleans, and the two men, carrying only small overnight bags, reported to the pick-up area, where they spotted Gray Hat. Separately, they followed him through the dark, foggy airport parking lot, got into his car, and were driven to an old garage. There were just two small rolled-out mattresses on the floor, with blankets. None of the three men spoke a word; business was now in progress. The atmosphere was lonely and grim. The two New Yorkers were exhausted from the trip, and rest was essential for the job confronting them. They hit the dirty, stained mattresses.

The next morning, about nine-thirty, they were awakened by a knock on the door. "Good morning, gentlemen," a man said. "It's time to go."

Ben crawled slowly out of the sack, looking like a dazed cobra coming out of his hole. "Where can we wash up?" he asked.

"There's a hose downstairs in the garage."

"Are you kidding? A hose? We wanna wash our faces, not our car. Ya got any hot water? And where do we piss? Out the window?"

"Come on, fellas," the man said. "The big man is waiting to have breakfast with you out at his ranch. We gotta hurry. It takes at least an hour and a half to get there. Next time you guys come to New Orleans, we'll put you up at the best hotel in town. OK?"

Bepy went down to the garage, holding his toothbrush and his toothpaste. He managed by holding the hose in one hand and brushing his teeth with the other.

Ben said, watching, "Gee, I shoulda brought my toothbrush, too."

"You forgot your toothbrush?" Bepy asked, with a mouth full of toothpaste. "That's a sign of carelessness." He spit the toothpaste on the garage floor and rinsed out his mouth. "I gotta teach you farmers from Staten Island how to travel. I hope I don't have to teach you how to do this job we gotta do."

Putting the cap back on the tube, he asked, "You wanna suck on the tube and rinse your mouth, Mr. Pro?"

Ben laughed confidently, as if to confirm he really was a pro. Then he said, "Slow down, kid. Slow down."

They collected their things and left to meet with Don Angelo Santoro out at his ranch. The place had a traditional Southern house and thoroughbred horses grazing in large paddocks fenced with black oak. Thick, rich grass sprawled over the rolling hills. It was something they had seen only in the movies.

"What a place. This ranch is beautiful," Bepy said admiringly. "I think I'd love this life in the country." Then, in a low voice, he added, "I gotta have one of these someday."

The Don was anxiously waiting as the men unloaded themselves from the car. He greeted Ben first, kissing him on both cheeks, which made Ben feel very important. He then turned to embrace Bepy with the

171

same welcome and suddenly remembered him from Big Pat's wedding. "Ahh! I remember you. We met at Pat's wedding in Brooklyn," he said, smiling.

"Yes. It was a beautiful wedding!" Bepy replied.

"I heard nothing but good things about you, Bephino," the Don said. "You are an up-and-coming man, and I'm glad you're here. I heard about your previous work—very fine and expertly done. Come, you must be hungry. We have Eggs Benedict, New Orleans style."

The men were served breakfast in a flower-filled glass room overlooking a training track for race horses, a few of which were working out. Bepy and Ben were impressed with Santoro's spread. Being there made them feel important.

"The eggs are very good," Bepy said.

When breakfast was finished and the last cup of coffee drunk, Santoro got down to business.

"Why don't we walk and talk outside?" Bepy interrupted to ask.

"Why?" Santoro asked.

"I see a lot of movies in Brooklyn," Bepy explained. "And the plants always have microphones in them. You never know; you can't be too sure even in your own home these days." Smiling, he added, "And you got a lotta plants in this room." He motioned with his eyebrows in the direction of the door.

The Don, surprised at this young man's decision to call the talks outdoors, agreed quickly. Ben patted Bepy on the back. He now realized that Bepy was a real sharpshooter and that Don Morrano's praise of him seemed to be justified.

Outside, Santoro lit up a long cigar and offered one to each of them. Ben accepted.

As the three men walked the race track, Bepy and Ben received their orders. But they still didn't know the identity of the hit, who was obviously a very important man. Don Santoro repeated twice that no mistakes would be accepted. No stories could be told. They had to be exact on every move. Excuses would not be tolerated.

"This is a do-or-die hit," he told them with a firm look. "I'm paying three hundred thousand dollars for this job and I expect it to be done with style and confusion for the police. I also expect it not to lead back to me. That's very important; it must not look like I was involved. Do you understand?"

Ben's and Bepy's eyes met briefly. They realized how much was at stake in this job.

Don Santoro explained that on Wednesday there would be a hearing in Washington. Three Southern congressmen were heading an investigation against him for racketeering. "If I knocked them off, it would completely destroy my position and my image of innocence," he said. "The repercussions would be devastating for my entire family. But time is closing in. I must act. The committee has me cold turkey and I know it. I must take drastic steps or face twenty-five years in a goddamn federal boys camp. One congressman on the committee must be dead by Wednesday." He paused to let the impact set in fully.

"The others will weaken fast if one is nicely dead. In fact, one congressman's almost bought off. He just needs a little more coaxing, and I believe he would drop his campaign against me.

"I'll put them in mourning for a while," he said raising his voice, "Then they'll realize they have to keep peace with me. The one I want dead is Congressman McDonald." He looked both men directly in the eyes. "He's the goddamn leader in this campaign against me. This is his home address. He eats at no special restaurant and he doesn't belong to any club in town. But he does play golf at the local country club once in a while. He's a Louisiana-born blueblood. The creep isn't even married. He lives with his brother. He has no bad habits that we know of. I can't put any of my men near him. It's too risky. If they were to goof up, the repercussions would be too much for me to handle."

Ben looked a little doubtful. "He's gotta have some bad habits. Everyone does. He's not married, lives with his brother? Is the fuck gay?"

"I really don't know. I've never heard anything like that about him. But he does have a Louisiana pistol permit. I know that. So he might carry one—a small-caliber handgun, most likely. I can't tell you how important it is for me to get this fellow out of Congress. He's a menace to our country."

Ben's and Bepy's eyes met again when Santoro said "menace to our country." They had to control themselves. Now was not the time to see the *irony* of it.

"He hates Italians," the Don said, his voice higher and more Southern. "I mean to settle up with this man for good."

Ben smiled at Bephino as if to say, "See what I mean? They're Italians like us, but they talk different."

"What kind of heating system does he have in his house? Is it natural gas?" Bepy asked.

"I really don't know these things. We can't get close to the man. All we have for you is his office and home addresses, nothing else. I'm sorry, fellas," Santoro said, letting the weight of his problem show on his face. He scrutinized the two men who were going to decide his fate, two Brooklyn characters who were asking questions that were unanswerable. "It's a touchy contract. I know it," he said, rubbing his chin.

"Let us think about this the rest of the day," Bepy said. "It's Saturday, and everyone will be out on the town tonight. It might be a good time to make a hit, provided we can make contact with your man. If he's in town, we'll try to do it tonight."

"Does he eat at any special place on Saturdays?" Ben asked.

"I told you, he never eats at a special restaurant. This bum has no habits, except that he's a real son of a bitch. The only habit he's got is church on Sunday. Every Sunday he stands outside with the pastor and shakes hands with everybody. How can you hit a man in church?"

"Even the saints would walk off the job," Ben interjected.

"Yeah, I guess the saints are in a different union," Bepy said.

"Here's a recent newspaper clipping on him. This was in last week's paper. It looks just like him." Santoro handed it to Bepy. Ben looked over Bepy's shoulder.

"Does his brother look like him?" Bepy asked. "I don't want the wrong guy."

"No, but that's a good question, Bephino," Santoro remarked. "You're smart. I never thought of telling you that. Don't worry, though. His brother is very dark, not like him at all. Their mother must have fucked around in bayou towns. The brother looks Creole."

"Well, if he goes to church every Sunday, he may be religious, he may be covering up something, or he may be just creating an image for his voters. Everybody does something they don't talk about. Maybe we gotta see to it that he does something wrong. Real wrong." Bepy suggested.

"Maybe the bastard's gay, and no one knows it yet," Ben added. "Maybe he's a pervert. He could be a closet queen. Maybe we gotta take him out of the closet."

"You could be on to something. But I'm not quite sure if those things work out well," Santoro commented.

"Mr. Santoro, can we have two long-barrel .38 specials, with shoulder holsters. We need throwaways, with silencers, if you got them. Mr. Morrano said you got anything we need. We also need a driver—one you don't need—because after the hit, we must hit him, too," Bepy stated flatly.

Santoro rolled his eyes. "Look, fella. I can understand what you're saying, but I don't want my driver hit. The guy who'll be with you is not known by anyone in town. He's clean and safe. He has four kids, and he won't talk with four kids and a wife. And he doesn't know either of you guys or where you're from. He does know the New Orleans area well—which you need—and he'll drive you wherever you want to go. I've used him on hits before. He's a good man, and I trust him. OK? Just McDonald. You make it clean and confusing—like suicide or something—and you'll have a big bonus on this one. I don't like the idea of killing the driver, too. Too many bodies raise too many questions."

"Whatever you say, Mr. Santoro," Bepy said. Then, turning to Ben, "Come on, let's go to town. We have a lot of work to do." Santoro gave them the guns and the driver, and they left for the city.

"This one ain't gonna be too easy, huh, Bep?" Ben whispered in the back seat. As the car reached the main gates, the guard waved them through. "I can feel the pressure already," Ben mumbled. "I tell ya, these out-of-town hits pay good, but they're a pain in the ass. I hadda make a lot of out-of-town hits for Morrano. He always gives me all the shit jobs. One time . . ."

Bepy interrupted, speaking in a very low voice. "Let's get our heads together and figure a nice funeral for this guy. I'd like to be back at my job on Wall Street Monday morning, so no one will know I was gone."

"You work on Wall Street?"

"Yeah. That's how I make my living."

Ben looked at him wide-eyed, but said nothing.

"Stop at the corner," Bepy told the driver as they reached the New Orleans city limits. "I'll be right back. I gotta make a call."

He walked into a phone booth at a drugstore and called an airline. He made a reservation for a Mr. Alvarez on the eleven o'clock flight to Chicago. Then he called another airline and made a reservation for a Mr. Sanchez from Chicago to New York City. He also made reservations for Ben, using different names and reversing the airlines, but leaving at approximately the same time. If they were lucky and the hit was complete, they could be out of New Orleans tonight. He returned to the car.

"Where'd you go, Bep?"

"Don't call me Bep! Call me anything, but don't call me by my name!" he hissed into Ben's ear, nodding toward the driver.

"You're a fuckin' nut." Ben laughed.

Bepy again signaled that they shouldn't use names in front of their driver, just to be on the safe side. Then, whispering, he told Ben about the plane reservations. Ben smiled and patted Bepy's knee. "You're a real thinker," he told him.

Bepy then asked the driver to show them the red-light district in town.

"Do you want the first-class or second-class?" the driver asked.

"I want the dirtiest cunts in this town. I want a real fuckin' pig. Take me to the fourth-class district."

The driver looked up into the rear-view mirror, his eyes betraying his confusion.

"I guess you're gonna call the shots on this one, huh?" Ben asked.

"Yeah. If it's OK with you, I'll take a shot at it."

"I know it's your first out-of-town hit, but you seem confident, and I'm not. This is the first time I've ever been even a little confused for some reason. I don't feel so comfortable. This isn't my normal-type hit. I like to whack 'em and blow town. This one is real deep shit, and I just don't feel comfortable," Ben repeated.

"Yeah, I wish we could whack him and blow town, too, but this takes thinking, not wishing. But I kind of like this deep shit," Bepy reassured him. "I'm at my best when they're kinda hairy."

They had toured New Orleans' red-light district for about an hour when Bepy asked the driver, "Where's all the whores?"

"They come out later in the day," he answered.

"What time do the pigs walk the streets?" Bepy asked.

"They come crawling outta the sack around seven."

"OK. Let's stop some place and have some lunch."

They went to a little Creole seafood house, and the driver, thinking he was going to sit with them, began to introduce himself. Ben stopped him. "Go find yourself a table, OK? Bring us your check. We'll take care of it."

The driver was surprised, but he got the message fast and moved to a corner table.

"I hope you got something good in mind," Ben remarked. "Because if we fuck up, Santoro will put a contract out on us."

"Listen to me good," Bepy replied. "You're considered a pro by Morrano, so you should be telling me this. But, OK, I'll tell you and you listen, Ben, because I have my own style, and I like my style. It keeps me alive, and I have no intention of letting anyone fuck up my life. If something should go wrong for some reason and we only wound the hit or we fuck up and things get out of control, we double back to Santoro's ranch and we kill him and everyone there. We're the only outsiders the guards will let enter his ranch, so we know we can get to him. Then we kill the guards, the driver, and Santoro. Even the fuckin' butler if he's there. *Tu capeesh,* Ben?"

"You wanna hit Santoro?" Ben said, shocked. "Are you nuts or what? You're talkin' treason."

"No, I'm talking sense."

Ben stared intently into Bepy's eyes. "What about Morrano? What about him?"

"If we have to hit Santoro, we'll throw Morrano out of a fuckin' window with his pajamas on, like he was walking in his sleep. Look, Morrano comes later; so we can think about it. We have time in that case, right?"

Ben, stunned by Bepy's cold-blooded plan, leaned over close to him and groaned, "You're nuts, kid. I'm tellin' ya, you're nuts."

"Yeah, I'm nuts ... about saving my life."

Ben thought about the idea for a while, his face showing that he was obviously nervous about it. But then he smiled in agreement. "Yeah, Santoro said 'do-or-die.' Well, if we can't do, he dies. OK, Bepy, you gotta deal. It will look like, while we were doing our job, another gang wiped out Santoro and his people. Then maybe we won't have to bother with Morrano. We can let him be. You know, Bepy, I really respect your ways. You got balls."

"I respect you, too, Benny," Bepy said, smiling, "for going along with such a drastic, crazy proposition. But that's only as a last resort. I don't plan for this to go wrong. I plan for it to go smoothly."

"Yeah. It's a survival plan," Ben said as he looked at the menu then back at Bepy with admiration and confidence. He knew he was dealing with a strong guy. He really believed Bephino would knock off Santoro and Morrano, the Boss of Bosses, if he had to.

After lunch they drove to the congressman's house, where they parked across the street and watched and waited for about an hour. Around three o'clock, two men arrived dressed in sports clothes.

"That's him. I'm sure," the driver said. "The one with the blue shirt. That's McDonald. They look like they were playing golf or something."

The two men entered the large white mansion. About fifty minutes later, the other man came out. After a while Bepy ordered the driver to take them back to the mattress over the garage. "I need a nap. I'm too groggy to watch anymore."

"How can you sleep with this thing in front of us?" Ben asked.

"You watch me. I need this nap. I gotta be sharp for this hit, and a nap will make me sharp. It's too important to Santoro. I figure the congressman is doing the same thing—taking a short nap. And if he's a single guy, he's probably going out for dinner later tonight—probably has a date or something. We'll be back in time for dinner. If I'm right, it could be perfect. Right now, I got a rough plan in mind."

"What plan?" Ben asked.

"I make a plan in my mind to fit the day. The hit, the day—everything has a style. I try to combine things, and it works well for me. Don't worry, Ben, leave it to me. *Ah capeesh?*"

"I never make a hit staying in the dark," Ben replied. "And you got me totally in the dark about this plan. I don't think I like it."

"You got a better idea, Benny? You wanna call the shots? I'll sit in the dark. I don't mind. Just say the word, friend."

Ben, looking confused, didn't answer.

"OK, then. Wake me up in one hour—no later. Don't forget, five-thirty. I'll need to clear away my cobwebs before the plan can really come together."

"I won't forget," Ben grumbled. "I don't believe this. Now I gotta baby-sit for this guy."

An hour later, Ben woke Bepy, who went down and rinsed his face from the hose once again.

"OK. Let's hurry and get back to the house," he ordered the driver while wiping his face with a paper towel.

The driver started going too fast. Bepy told him sharply, "I said hurry, but I didn't mean speed. We can't afford to get stopped."

"Did you enjoy your nap?" Ben asked wisely.

"Yeah," Bepy answered, not looking at him.

They arrived at the big white house shortly before six. It looked like a mansion that might have been used in the movies about the South, but it was set in a busy residential area. They parked up the street, not too close to the house, and waited for McDonald to appear.

Bepy stared at the old mansion as if in deep thought. Finally, after about twenty minutes, he broke the silence.

"It's Saturday night," he said to Ben. "If my hunch is right, he'll come out in the next few hours."

"Suppose he don't? Suppose he stays home tonight. Then what?"

"Then I'll go in alone and do a job on him. I got a back-up plan in mind that will also keep the heat off Santoro. If McDonald doesn't come out by eleven or twelve, I'm going in to do what I gotta do. But we'll wait till eleven to decide that. He'll come out. I feel sure of it."

"I hope so," Ben answered.

The hours passed slowly for Ben, quickly for Bepy, who was running through the plan over and over in his mind. At last the front door opened, and Congressman McDonald walked down the long steps to a car in his driveway. He was dressed in a light tan suit and a bright blue shirt, with a tie that matched his light tan shoes. He got in his car and quickly drove off.

"Hey, fellas, look!" The driver pointed excitedly. "He's driving off!"

"Relax. Don't get so excited. Get on his tail gradually. Not too soon," Bepy ordered. "Follow him and don't lose him. Stay behind about three cars' distance. He'll never dream he's being followed."

As they tailed McDonald, Bepy gave the driver further instructions. "When he stops for a traffic light, or when I tell you to, pull right alongside him. We'll jump out and get in his car with him."

Pulling his gloves on, he pointed to Ben. "Put your gloves on. When we get in, you take the hit's wheel. Get ready. It's almost time to go."

"Suppose he parks his car before we make our move?" the driver asked.

"If that happens, the minute he attempts to park, pull up right next to him, and we'll unpark him real quick. Remember, we don't know New Orleans. So you gotta be lead car for us. Make sure you don't lose us. We'll follow you in his car to that red-light district. When we get there, you get us a whore, a real pig. Something smelly looking. Offer her any amount of money. Just get her in your car fast, OK? We'll park right behind you or nearby. After you pick up the hooker, drive to a dead area, the waterfront maybe, or a secluded parking lot closed for the weekend. Something like that, OK? Make sure it's remote and shut-down." Bepy was talking fast, to give the driver a clear idea of what he wanted. "There must be a lot of factories that are shut down at eight-thirty on a Saturday night?"

"Yeah. I know just the spot," the driver answered. "Don't worry. Leave it to me."

"But no matter what happens," Bepy ordered, "you don't leave us. Understand, buddy? You're our quick exit out of New Orleans."

"Don't worry. I also got my instructions from Don Santoro. I'm your taxi out of here and I stick with you like glue until you tell me my job is *finito*."

"Get the whore real quick. Speed is very important to this plan. You're doing fine so far. And it's important she be alone, not with other hookers. Talk to one that's all alone." Bepy continued to pump instructions as they followed McDonald's car.

After tailing him another ten minutes, the Congressman's car headed north. He stopped for a light at a boulevard crossing.

"Let's get him, now!" Bepy said, urgently pushing Ben. "I'll keep him under control. You drive the car."

They jumped out and walked quickly to the car, Ben on the driver's side, Bepy on the other side. They pulled open both doors, and Ben placed his gun to McDonald's temple, roughly forcing him to move over. They slid in from both sides, trapping him in the middle.

"What the hell's going on here?" McDonald demanded.

Bepy jabbed the tip of his silencer in McDonald's ribs.

"Shut up!" he demanded. "Make a foolish move and I'll kill you, Mac. Keep calm and you'll live. We just gotta talk to you. So don't panic. We only wanna talk. It could mean your life if you fuck up. Don't make me pull the trigger." Bepy had his own style. He liked to keep things calm, to avoid struggles and possible mishaps.

"It's your birthday party tonight, and your gift is a beautiful lady for the evening," Ben told him, trying to be just as cool.

"Is this a joke or something? I'm a United States congressman. My name is McDonald."

"No shit?" Ben mocked him. "Thanks for the confirmation. If you open your mouth one more time, we'll fill your ass with so much lead, the navy can use you for an anchor. So shut up. Someone has to talk to you, and it won't take long. So keep quiet. Don't talk to us, and you'll be all right." Ben now talked to show Bepy he was confident.

They followed the driver's car to the red-light area. A prostitute was walking along, waving at cars. She was a real flashy black with a blond wig.

Great! Bepy thought. She's perfect—a black broad with a blond wig! This hit could be so perfect it might even go down in history. She was exactly what he'd had in mind.

The driver negotiated with her, and after the usual dialogue about his not being a cop, she agreed. She got into his car, and the driver led them to a spot that was shut down for the weekend. It was dark and very remote, a good location. Ben parked behind the driver's car. So far, things were going smoothly.

The Congressman didn't know what was going on. Bepy was thinking ahead. He had to keep the hit moving fast. He got out and went over to the other car and leaned in the front window.

"Hi, honey," he said to the hooker, shaking her hand. "How much do you charge?"

"Twenty for a complete treat, ten for a head job, fifteen for half and half," she answered, smiling.

"Look, we wanna have some fun. I got a guy in my car and I'll pay you two hundred bucks just to rub your pussy all over his face. I wanna teach him a lesson, because he's still a cherry and never saw a pussy before. But you gotta do it fast, because I'm in a hurry. OK, sweetheart? And I tell you what—if you shit on him, I'll give you another two hundred as a bonus."

"Do I hear you right, mister? You want me to rub my pussy on his face for two hundred, and then you want me to shit on him? Are you all right, man? I never had a request like this," she answered, shaking her blond head. "You mother-fuckers are crazy! Take me back."

"Look, honey. This is business. I have money to spend. And I just want you to rub your cunt all over his face. I want him to smell of pussy. That's all. He's a fag, and we wanna teach him what cunt is like. I'll give you two hundred and two hundred more for any extras you can do. I want this guy to smell bad, understand?"

The hooker stared at him, then asked smoothly, "What makes you think my pussy smells, honey? They calls me Sugar around town."

"OK, then rub your sugar all over him. Make him smell sweet. I don't care; just rub his face real good." He held the money up to her face and said, "Come on, Sugar. We're in a hurry now."

"OK. Who's the lucky dude?" she asked, rolling her eyes.

"Forget who he is. He's just some creep from Baton Rouge. No matter what he says, you do what *I* say, understand? I'm paying the bill. Don't forget that, and we'll be OK together."

She agreed, nodding her head. "You're payin' and that means you're sayin'—that makes you the man, Sam."

Bepy handed her the first two hundred bucks, and she was feeling so right, she almost shit right then. As she walked to the Congressman's car, she asked Bepy, "Hey, mister, suppose I piss on this dude? How much will I get?"

"One hundred bucks for that," he replied. "I'll tell you what, Sugar—I'll even make it two hundred for the water sports. OK?"

The hooker, becoming serious about the work, tried to act like a businesswoman. "That's cool. That's cool," she replied. "I'll piss all over this mother fucker for openers. I gotta go bad. Maybe I'll even give him the cherry jubilee. That's worth the whole six hundred."

She hopped into the back of the car and said to the Congressman, "So you're daddy?"

Bepy ordered McDonald to get in the rear of the car with her. "Climb over the seat," he said. Searching him first, Ben found his pistol, a .25-caliber automatic.

"Get next to the young lady," Bepy ordered. Then, speaking in Italian, he told Ben, "Hold his gun and his wallet ready. I'll need them soon."

Ben was amazed at the style and skill with which Bepy was handling the entire job. He kept silent.

The Congressman was ordered, with guns to his head, to get his pants down and to get them down fast. But he balked. "What! I'm not gonna fuck that nigger," he yelled.

"Why not? She's a beauty," Bepy yelled back. "OK, McDonald, you got ten seconds to eat her cunt, and you better eat it good or we're gonna kill you. We'll kill you so fast you'll never know what her pussy looked like. Your brains will be all over your car."

The hooker quickly got herself into position and said, "You better be hungry, mister. There's a lot to eat here."

"Maybe I'm better off dying than having to touch this black bitch," McDonald replied defiantly. "I think I'd rather die."

Bepy pulled back the hammer on the gun and again pointed it to McDonald's head. "Whatever you say, Mac."

McDonald quickly dropped his pants and underwear and lay back on the seat, showing his lifeless possessions.

"Don't be prejudiced and get moving, ya little twerp. Eat the broad," Bepy commanded.

The hooker had sucked him a little trying to be friendly. Bepy stopped her roughly. "That's enough of that shit. Put your ass on his face. Rub your smelly box all over him real good now. And be quick about it. Make him smell like pussy. I want this creep to stink."

The hooker put her head down to the seat and her ass up high, aiming for her man, as Bepy's harsh words rang through her ears.

Ben stared as the whore climbed over the poor congressman, rubbing her ass up and down on his face, smearing it with her juices.

"How's this, man?" she asked.

He nodded in satisfaction. Her heavily perfumed ass was like a sewer, he thought. He was pleased with their choice, but he had to turn away for a moment to get some fresh air. Ben was holding his nose.

"Damn you, nigger!" McDonald yelled. "You stink! Kill me! I'd rather die!"

"Hey, mister, get that two-hundred-buck bonus ready," she yelled. "Here it comes." And she pissed a heavy stream all over McDonald's face and clothes. It was the most incredible sight. Ben's eyes were so big he looked like a raccoon peeping through the darkness.

The Congressman started to choke and squirmed around on the seat gasping for breath. The hooker held firmly to the seat and the side door.

Her head was slipping almost to the floor in order to keep her ass in the air aiming at McDonald. Bepy held him down at gunpoint so he would be well soaked.

"Stay down, Mac, you fuck. Don't make me shoot you," Bepy whispered to him. "Stay down." But McDonald desperately tried to escape the gush of urine.

Bepy took out his stiletto and handed it to the hooker.

"What's this for?" she asked, holding it in her hand. "What's this for, man?" Her head was still down on the floor and her ass was flying high and still dripping-wet.

"Open it for me, sweetheart," Bepy ordered, ignoring her question. "I wanna cut his leather upholstery up. I hate this bastard, with this fancy car."

She opened it, and Bepy, wearing gloves, took the blade and quickly plunged it into the Congressman's chest, aiming for the heart. He must have hit the vital spot, because the Congressman died instantly. His tongue hung out. Bepy left the knife in the chest and quickly took the Congressman's gun from Ben. The whore panicked when she heard the knife enter McDonald's chest and the gargled sound of death arriving and life leaving. She tried to get up and open the back door. But before she could get out, she caught two slugs in the back from less than two feet away. Bepy had shot from almost the same angle McDonald was lying. He quickly put the pistol into McDonald's hand, to get some of the powder residue on his hand.

Taking the dead man's wallet, he put it in the girl's coat pocket, but not before he added an additional two hundred bucks in new bills. He took three more crisp new bills and put them in the side of McDonald's shoe, as most guys do to hide his money from a hooker. Then he emptied McDonald's pockets of his regular cash, cleaning him out, and put some of that loose money in the hooker's coat pocket.

It was vital to the success of the hit that the police clearly see that McDonald shot the hooker after she had stabbed him. They must think that he was able to get two shots off before he died. They would see that the hooker had pissed on him—whether it was his idea or not—then stabbed the poor man, took his wallet and cash, and tried to leave the car. It looked perfect to Bepy.

"Check them," he told Ben. "Make sure they're both dead. We can't find out that one of them lived through this thing. Make sure they're both dead, Ben. This is the final scene. We're almost home."

Ben checked both for a pulse and looked into their eyes. While looking at the hooker's eyes he said, "Believe me, when you see tongues hanging out like that, they're already in heaven."

Suddenly the woman's face turned upward and a deep groan left her body. Her eyes opened wide at Ben.

"What was that?" Bepy asked excitedly. "She's still alive!"

"No, she's just left us. That was her death groan. She's dead; they're both dead," Ben replied.

"OK, let's get the fuck outa here!"

They walked away from the car, leaving the terrible odor behind. They ordered their driver to head for the airport.

"Don't speed," Bepy said as he sat back in his seat. They put their gloves in their overnight bags and slid the .38 revolvers under the seat.

"Give these guns back to your boss," Bepy said. "They're clean. We put them under the seat." The driver nodded. They didn't talk much.

At the airport, they said a brief good-bye to the driver and left him with his mouth open. Ben and Bepy then split up, picked up their tickets, and met again in New York City, at the airport coffee shop, as planned. Bepy wanted to avoid having a taxi driver see his face, and Ben had a car in the parking lot. They felt safe now. They knew they had been successful.

"I can't believe you masterminded such a hit in only a few hours," Ben told Bepy while driving back to Brooklyn. "If I hadn't seen it, I wouldn't believe it."

"That's why Morrano sent us," Bepy said. "We were the right team for the job."

"Yeah, but I didn't do much. I feel bad," Ben replied.

"You did fine, Ben. You didn't crowd me, and that's what I like. You had confidence in me."

11

"How good are you with those bombs?" Bepy asked as he put down his menu, having decided on veal parmigiana with fettucini on the side.

"Why?" Ben asked.

"I need one. I know a Red bastard that's gotta go. He's long overdue; his time has come. Last month, when Morrano told me about you, he said you were a good bomb man."

"Morrano's right." Ben smiled. "How can I help you?"

"Make me a bomb—one that works on a car. Make me a powerful bomb, OK, Ben? See if you can make a special one for me."

"I have just the thing. Don't worry, it'll be powerful—car and all goes to heaven."

After the waiter took their orders, they continued their discussion.

"By the way, what kind of business are you in?" Bepy asked Ben. "You never told me."

"I thought you knew. I own a funeral home on Staten Island."

"Are you kidding? Come on, don't con me. You're a funeral director?"

"I really am," Ben said seriously. "I own a funeral home. I'm not bullshittin'. I got it from my father when he died years ago." Ben's eyes watered for a moment. "My father liked that kind of business."

"Don Morrano mentioned that you were a funeral director, but I thought he was kidding me. How'd you come to make hits for the family?"

"Well, about twelve years ago, when I was twenty-one, business for my father was very slow. He would curse in Italian, 'Nobody dies anymore! Now they get penicillin. We better close the doors!' and bullshit like that. He cursed the moon. I heard him complain everyday. Then I read in the newspapers that there was bad blood among the Mob on Staten Island. But nobody was getting bumped off. They were a bunch of second-class hoods: all bullshit, no action. They looked like a bunch of fat old guys, like farmers from Italy.

"So, I went out one night and made a hit on a Mob guy in front of his club. I knocked him off and, because Staten Island was so small, my father got the job. He had the only Italian funeral home."

Ben continued after the waiter had brought their food. "Then one family blamed the other family for the killing, and they hit one of their guys, and it went back and forth, back and forth. My father wound up having a good year." Ben laughed. "Now these guys found their balls to fight. 'Thatsa good,' my father would say. So, from then on, whenever business got slow, I sneaked out and made a hit. I'd start a new war every once in a while, just to keep business coming in. I had to bite my tongue to keep from laughing when my father would say the good words over the coffin. If my father had only known I was getting him all his business!

"Then my father died, may he rest in peace, and I wound up with the joint. I got careless one time years back, and some guy saw me make a hit and told Don Morrano, and Morrano grabbed me for some contracts. He couldn't believe it when I told him this story. I laughed in his face. Even Morrano laughed about what I was doing. Since then, he's been using me. So now I work for him on the side. The money is good, and I'm used to the work. But now there's three Italian funeral homes on Staten Island, and the bastards got my last two jobs. So I stopped making hits for business."

By this time, Bepy was laughing so hard, he almost choked. "I can't believe it. The pay is good, and you're used to the work. You gotta be joking. What a story! You should write a funny book," he said, laughing. "I can't eat any more—my stomach hurts from laughing. Benny, underneath it all, you're really a sick bastard." Trying to regain his composure, he repeated, "A funeral director who provides his own clients. Unbelievable!"

The nine months finally came to an end, and Dana went to the hospital, at eleven o'clock in the morning. When Bepy got there, Dana had already been delivered. He was overwhelmed with joy at the sight of two babies in his beautiful wife's arms. They had been blessed with a little girl and a little boy.

"Look, Mr. Menesiero," the nurse said, "the boy has hands like Jack Dempsey. And your daughter ought to be in pictures."

Bepy felt very proud to be the father of such beautiful twins and became very protective of them. He made a rule that everyone holding them had to wear a surgical mask. It was funny to see their apartment full of people dressed like surgeons. Even the grandparents had to wear masks when they went near the babies. Dana's mother complained, but nevertheless did as Bepy asked.

After several weeks of this, they all started to give Bepy a hard time. And he reluctantly agreed that surgical masks were no longer needed. He watched everything that went on, however. He called home every hour, he rocked the cribs in his dreams, and he called the doctor if they spit up.

"I'm surprised he's such a concerned papa," his mother said. "He fooled us, huh, Pasquale? He was always such a crazy boy. Now he's a good husband and papa."

One day when the twins were a month or so old, Dana got up to answer the doorbell. Standing there were Bepy's father and his two uncles. The three of them were red-faced from the brisk winds outside, but they had big smiles plastered across their faces.

"Oh, Papa, this is a surprise. What are you doing in this neighborhood? Come on in," Dana invited, opening the door wider and stepping aside. She spoke in her high sweet voice, trying to sound happy about this surprise visit. As they came in, she couldn't help noticing how they were dressed. They were wearing terribly drab long overcoats and pea caps. She purposely hurried them into the apartment so the neighbors wouldn't spot them.

The men were oblivious to her thoughts as they entered, smiling from ear to ear.

"Come on in, Papa. Take your coats off. It's so nice to see you," Dana said. "Bephino is sleeping. Make yourselves comfortable while I get him up."

When she returned a few moments later, the three brothers were still standing in their overcoats, holding their pea caps in their hands.

"Bepy will be right out. Take your coats off. Nobody's gonna steal them," she added with a grin as she walked toward the kitchen. "I'll fix you something to warm you up."

Bepy entered the room, also smiling over the surprise visit. "Hey, come on, you guys are still standing?" he said, embracing them. "Sit down, have a glass of wine. Make yourselves comfortable." Then he looked them up and down. "Where'd you get the snazzy coats? You can take them off. Nobody's gonna steal them here." He grinned, not knowing Dana had just made the same remark.

The men looked at each other, smiling at the similarity of the comments, and slowly began removing their overcoats. Bepy poured wine. Dana yelled from the kitchen, "I'm bringing you some cheese and biscuits, to have with your wine. Then I'll make a pot of coffee."

"We eat later," Pasquale whispered to Bepy. "We have some business to discuss. After our business, then we eat."

Bepy looked at his father, this time without the smile. Casually, he glanced at each uncle. Suddenly, everyone seemed serious.

"Business to discuss? What kinda business we got, Papa?"

Pasquale leaned closer. "We come to see little Pasquale, my grandson," he whispered. "Your son."

Dana overheard this, and the kitchen suddenly became a quiet zone. Putting down her coffeepot, she tiptoed quietly to the doorway. Bepy sensed she was listening and glanced toward the doorway. Looking back at his father, he asked, "What kinda business you got with the baby? You come to see Patsy boy for business, Papa? How come?" Then he smiled. "Sounds like small business to me."

Pasquale stared into Bepy's bewildered eyes. "Look, *figlio mio*," he said, speaking seriously. "We are Sicilian people. The honor of our heritage must be obeyed. And when we have the joy to have a baby boy like your son, my grandson, we must welcome him to our family with honor. The time has come for your bambino to be tested as a true Sicilian."

"True Sicilian? Tested?" Bepy screeched harshly. "For what? What test are you talking about, Papa? The kid's like a bull. He's perfect. He's twenty pounds already. He's gotta co . . . he's even been circumcised, like me. What kind of test you gonna give to an infant? Whata you guys, *pazzo* today or what?"

"It's our test," Pasquale replied in a low but firm voice. "It's the test of our people, and we must test your son's spirit today. It's been done for hundreds of years by all grandfathers of our villages. It's my privilege to do this simple thing to our boy," he said, and paused for Bepy's response. "Trust me, Bephino, you *stupido!*" he yelled in embarrassment, as the uncles shook their heads over Bephino's reluctance to approve his father's request.

Not wanting to embarrass his father any further, Bepy tried to explain. "Hey, come on. I trust you, Papa. I was just wondering how come I never heard of this test before. How come you never told me about this? You spring this on me. You wanna test my son? At least if you'd warned me, I could've made the baby practice for it."

"No practice," Pasquale said, smiling. "It's a one-shot deal, a surprise—especially for the baby. You almost failed your part of the test already, son. It's something we never speak of until we are ready to act. It's an honor for the grandfather and not for the father," he growled. "He will decide the time. He will reap the toil if the baby is strong and he will cry in sorrow if the baby is weak."

"Oh, yeah? How come Grandpa Gustavo never told me about this?" Bepy asked nervously.

"Our people can't talk about this. Grandpa always kept this silent. We don't talk about this after today. Remember, never talk after today," Pasquale replied. "My father tested you as an infant, too. But we never talked about it. *Ah capeesh?*"

"*Si, io capeesh.*" Bephino began to realize the seriousness of the matter.

"Someday," his father said, "you will carry on this proud moment to your grandson, and you will see in his courage what others will never see in him. It's important to test the strength of the young ones." His brothers nodded their heads in agreement.

"This sounds crazy to me," Bepy said in a low voice. "Does it hurt?"

"No hurt. It could make the baby cry, but it no hurt."

"Patsy boy never cries. Renee doesn't either. You'll see, Papa. They laugh. Ok, do what you gotta do."

"We'll see if they cry," Pasquale told him.

Bepy led them into the room where the twins were sleeping. The four men were gazing down at the infants when the door swung open.

"What are you people doing?" Dana demanded unceremoniously, pointing at her father-in-law. "I know it's your grandson and his son," she mimicked sarcastically, "but I don't want this test. I heard you talking. I don't think I want this test, Bepy. Why should we do it? He's only a baby; let him sleep. Why disturb his sleep?"

"We gotta test little Pasquale," Bepy whispered. "Go wait outside. It'll only take a minute."

"No," she replied. "I don't want you to . . ."

Before she could finish, Bepy grabbed her arm and escorted her, gracefully but firmly, to the kitchen. "Look, Dana, this is a Sicilian custom. The baby's gotta have this test. It's important to my father and uncles. It's our custom. It's a matter of respect. *Ah capeesh?*"

In the bedroom, the uncles were talking about Dana.

"That Bephino's wife is full of spirit herself," Bruno said. "She's a strong, salty woman. She stands up for her children even to the father and grandfather."

"Yes," Pasquale agreed, looking up at the ceiling. "She's a fine girl. We love her for her affectionate ways."

Bepy and Dana were still battling in the kitchen.

"Why don't you test your creepy uncles?" Dana yelled. "Test them! Maybe they're screwballs. Did you see the way they're dressed? They look like the Three Stooges came to Brooklyn. Did you ever see such shabby coats?"

Bepy laughed and grabbed her again. "Hold it. That's enough now," he yelled. "You're talking too much and you were pointing at my father before, so be quiet or I gotta break your finger."

"But Patsy boy is only half Sicilian," she yelled back. "He's half Naples, remember?"

"How could I forget?" he replied angrily, losing his patience. "Now stay in the kitchen and don't move until this is over. You stay right here," he ordered and walked away. She began to follow. "Don't push me, Dana," he said sternly.

"Don't push me either, you stooge," she yelled back.

He turned around, trying to keep a straight face, but then burst out laughing at the way she was holding her ground. "Hey, come on, don't worry," he told her. "It ain't gonna hurt the baby. Stop worrying."

"It better not hurt," she yelled.

He returned to the babies' room, apologizing for Dana's behavior. "Mothers, hah! They always worry about their children."

The men smiled at Bepy as Pasquale began his act. With eyes full of love and concern, he stared deeply at the sleeping infant.

"This child is the continuance of my life," he said looking at the men.

The room was silent as he again concentrated on the sleeping infant.

"Will he be strong-hearted? Will he act swiftly when attacked? Will he bring honor to our people?"

He began to touch the baby's body with different annoying movements. He touched him harder and harder, as if he were being attacked. The baby's eyes opened wide, and he began to squirm and grunt. He thrust his little arms forward in fighting fashion, pushing forward and waving them above his face. Pasquale kept up his annoying tactics and then began to make harsh, ugly sounds at the infant. The baby moved his arms and grunted harder. He didn't cry, as most babies would have done when aroused out of sleep. Pasquale kept it up, but the baby didn't cry.

Bepy looked back and forth from the baby to his father and his uncles, like he was watching a tennis match. Pasquale was getting rougher, but not a whimper came from the baby.

The uncles began to smile, confirming the success of the test. Pasquale was smiling with tears of joy.

"Get me the olive oil," he ordered. "We must reward this courageous child with the treasure of our people."

Bepy's face lit up, and he ran to the kitchen. "Where's the olive oil?" he asked Dana.

"What happened? What's wrong?" she began yelling.

"Nothing's wrong," he replied. "Just give me the olive oil."

"What's wrong? Tell me," she insisted.

"Everything's fine, Dana. Just give me the damn oil, will you?" he went back into the bedroom with the oil bottle in hand.

Pasquale, intent on his work, spoke again. "We must anoint his lips with the sap of the Old Country." He rubbed the baby's lips over and over. "We have a fine boy, Bephino."

"I told you, Papa. The kid's a terror. He never cries; he loves to fight. He's strong." Then suddenly he said, "Hey, let's test Renee. She's got guts for a girl. I'm tellin' you, she's a . . ."

The door swung open. "No, you don't, Pasquale," Dana said, grabbing the oil bottle. "Don't you wake up your granddaughter." Pointing at Bepy and his daughter, she smiled at all the men. "Renee doesn't need any testing. She's just fine."

The men burst out laughing.

Business was going on as usual. One day Bepy had an appointment to see a possible new store location on Canal Street, at the edge of

Chinatown. It was a perfect location, right next door to a large bank and the New York Telephone Company. The Diamond Exchange, where thousands of people shopped each day, was across the street. There was also a gigantic Chinese laundry that employed about two thousand people, twenty-four hours a day. It was just off Canal Street around the corner on a side street. After visiting the vacant store twice, Bepy made a verbal agreement with the landlord, who was a wealthy Chinese, and decided to open a hero shop there the following month.

The landlord's name was Sid Choy. He was a spunky little guy from Hong Kong. He was the three-hundred-dollar-suit kind, with diamonds on four fingers, and he drove expensive cars. He always had a beautiful Chinese babe sitting nearby with her leg hanging out up to her thigh. This landlord had the best of everything, and Bepy admired this enormously.

Bephino Menesiero and Sid Choy agreed on rent of eight hundred dollars per month. Bepy requested a contract or lease and offered his company's check for one month's rent in advance to bind the deal.

"My handshake is a contract," Choy said, holding his head erect like a man of honor. "Don't worry. The store is yours, my friend. You send me a check at the end of the month, and I'll give you a key then."

"OK, sir," Bepy said. "As you say, a handshake. We gotta deal." Their hands met in a firm grasp. Bepy said he would start the remodelling in a few weeks. He liked the little, rich man's style—a deal's a deal. He had always believed in that style: a man's word meaning more than a contract.

Three weeks later Bepy went to Mr. Choy's office to give him a check for the first month's rent and security deposit. His carpenters were coming the next day, and he needed the key.

As he walked past, he peeked at the future hero shop number six and thought he saw carpenters already working in the rear. It couldn't be. He looked closely, and saw Red and Johnny Mac standing with the foreman of the crew looking at plans. Bepy broke out in a cold sweat. He couldn't believe his eyes. What the hell are Red and Mac doing in my store? he asked himself. He stepped back into the street to see if it was the same store. He thought that maybe he was on the wrong block. But he wasn't. This was his store. How could this have happened? He had made a deal with Mr. Choy! We made a fucking Chinese handshake, he thought.

He went to a phone booth and called Choy.

"Mr. Choy's away in Los Angeles," the secretary said.

He felt frustrated. "Please, miss. Can I have his phone number in L.A.? It's very, very important." He wanted that location bad. It was perfect. The secretary was very hesitant.

"He's at the Hollywood Hills Hotel, suite 1210," she finally said. "But call in a few hours. It's only 8:00 A.M. there."

Bepy was so furious he immediately called California. He was so nervous he couldn't get the dimes in the slots and was dropping coins on the floor of the phone booth and banging the receiver around. The operator wanted more money. Finally he convinced her to charge the call to his business number.

The suite phone rang six times before a low foreign voice finally said, "Hellooo?"

She sounded like a fucked-out chick who had spent the entire night in a hot tub sucking on the plumbing.

"May I please speak to Mr. Sid Choy."

"Mr. Choy is sleeping. He sleeping," the woman said. "It's early."

"I'm sorry to disturb you, but I didn't realize the time difference. I'm calling long distance from New York."

Reluctantly she got Choy to the phone. "Hello. Who is this?" he asked in a groggy tone.

"This is Bephino Menesiero from New York City!"

"Who gave you my number?" Choy complained. "And why you call me so early?"

"Mr. Choy, that was my store on Canal Street. We shook hands, remember? I was counting on that location."

"Oh, the store. Yah, yah. I gave it to Johnny Mac," Choy replied. "Very sorry. Very sorry. Too late now."

"But you shook my hand! You gave me your word!"

"I shake a lot of hands. So?" Choy answered firmly. "I never heard of you, Bephino. Johnny Mac is a big guy. It's his neighborhood. I gave him the store. It's his now. If you don't like it, take it up with him. Very sorry. Good-bye, my friend." He hung up.

Bepy looked at the dead phone in disbelief and anger. He began cursing. "He called me his friend, the little yellow rat," he mumbled, struggling to get out of the phone booth. "Johnny Mac a big guy? It's his neighborhood? Why, that Chinese bastard. I'll put him and Johnny Mac in the same coffin. I'll fix them. I'll bury them together." Bepy was walking in a daze. "So he shakes a lot of hands, huh? I'll make him shake hands. I'll fix that fuckin' Chink good."

Suddenly he looked up and saw Red and Johnny Mac laughing and watching him from the front of the store. He looked them up and down slowly. Momentarily confused, he dodged to the right and wound up in the side street entrance of the Chinese laundry. He entered the building to get off the street and to calm down.

In the vestibule, he leaned on a wall to think about his next move. Unconsciously, he began mumbling out loud, "Handshake," he repeated. "Handshake, my ass. Them Jap Chinks shook hands with Roosevelt and then bombed Pearl Harbor. Now the Chinese are doing the same thing to me."

"Can I help you?" a screeching, awkward voice interrupted his thoughts, startling him. A big, fat Oriental in a T-shirt was watching him.

Bepy jumped. He had thought he was alone.

"I'm a friend of Mr. Sid Choy," he said, trying to think of an excuse for being there. "He sent me to look around the place."

"Ah," the man smiled. "Yes. He's the landlord." Suddenly his smile vanished, and the huge man, who looked like a wrestler, banged his hands on a table and yelled, "I despise Choy! He no good Chink man. He little cockroach. Where is he?"

Bepy, hearing this outburst, thought, Holy Shit! Now what am I getting into? This Chink is calling the other Chink a Chink. What a day this is turning out to be! Whatta fuckin' day I'm having! I don't believe my bad luck.

The silence worked to calm them both.

"Mr. Fat," Bepy asked him, "how about showing me around this laundry? I never saw a real laundry before. What d'ya say? I gotta kill some time."

"You wanna see my laundry?"

"Yeah, I really would."

"Why you call me Mr. Fat?" the huge man said with a grin.

"Mr. Fat means good person with plenty of dough in Italian. Show me how you launder your dough through this joint," Bepy said, trying to be humorous. "My head is all fucked up today. The truth is, I need help, Mr. Fat. There's a couple guys outside I'd rather not see at the moment."

The man seemed to like Bepy calling him Mr. Fat; Bepy guessed that it must have meant something important in Chinese. Peeking out the window, he saw Johnny Mac and Red standing on the corner talking and eating apples from a pushcart peddler. They knew Bepy had been surprised to lose the location. As he watched from the window, Bepy's tongue felt like a hunk of cotton in his mouth. He knew then he had no choice but to act on this insult with all his power.

Look at the rat bastards! They're laughing at my expense, Bepy thought. I've been kicked, robbed, even pissed on by Red over the years, but now I'm being laughed at by him and his friends. My grandfather was right; I should have listened to him. I fucked up. I trusted the Milanese. I opened my heart to him. Now I gotta bury him. Red doesn't respect me. He thought I would yield to Johnny Mac because of his reputation, but he's wrong. He made a bad decision. So now I'm gonna kill them both—right away. I hate them both. They fucked me over and laughed about it!

He had been in a deep trance when the high-pitched voice again caused him to jump. "OK. Me, Fat, I show you the laundry," Mr. Fat said.

The laundry was a really big place, with Chinese workers all over the building, moving laundry bins from section to section very quickly and quietly.

After about half an hour, they wound up in the basement, where all the chemicals were stored. Vapors were rising from a large rectangular vat in the center of the floor.

"Please, no smoking," Mr. Fat said. "No matches, OK?"

"What's that?" Bepy asked.

"Acid. White acid. Chinese call it *sinei*. We dip machine parts in vat once a month. After we dip stainless-steel machine parts, they become very, very clean, and then we pull plug and it goes down and cleans city sewer," Mr. Fat whispered. "But don't tell anyone. We not supposed to have open tank like this, but we pay off city inspector. He likes money; he see nothing."

"Don't worry. I didn't see nothing either. I got more fuckin' *sinei* than that in my stomach right now. Us Italians, we call it *acido*."

Bepy was thinking about the vat and looking around the basement. Slowly a smile crept across his face. "Hey, Mr. Fat, what would happen if a person fell in the *sinei?*"

"Fall in *sinei?* Ha, ha!" Mr. Fat laughed. Then his expression changed and he became serious. He answered in perfect English. "He would completely melt to shit. Only his belt buckle or rings would remain at the bottom. Only metal remains. The acid doesn't affect metal, but everything else turns to liquid—leather, hair." Mr. Fat rubbed his fingers together holding up one hand. "Liquid."

Slowly, a cat came creeping around the corner of the tank. "Ah, cat—he catches rats." Mr. Fat picked up the gray-and-white cat and dropped him in the tank. "See, see? No more cat," he said, laughing. The cat tried to swim, but in two seconds it had almost melted away. Only his head was still afloat. The cat didn't even have a chance to scream, and a few seconds later the head disappeared, too.

Bephino's face showed emotion for the little cat. "Did you have to kill it?" he asked. Quickly regaining his composure, he remarked, "I really like that vat. You've got something there."

"Ah, vat. Very good, huh?"

Bepy and Mr. Fat chuckled together like two good buddies. What luck, Bepy thought, to run into this unusual Oriental.

"Who's the boss of this company?" he asked.

"I am. Who you think?" Mr. Fat answered, reaching behind his head and touching his ponytail in a very awkward fashion.

Bepy's eyes glittered at the sight of this obese male acting the feminine cow. "I mean who owns this big business?" he asked.

"Oh, owner, owner. My brother-in-law is a very, very rich man. He lives in San Francisco and runs another big company there." Mr. Fat explained that he was top man in New York City and that he had managed the business for nine years. He repeated that he and his brother-in-law hated Mr. Choy. Sid Choy, it turned out, had beat them out of the purchase of the building when they were negotiating to buy it from the last owner. Then he had doubled their rent.

"Sid Choy no good man. We hate him," Mr. Fat mumbled.

Bepy nodded in agreement, then asked, "How come some times you speak good English and sometimes you mumble broken English?"

"That's my shit," he said, smiling. "I speak both ways. I think it's clever, don't you?"

Bepy didn't reply to the question right away. Instead, he smiled at him and asked, "Hey, Mr. Fat, how about letting me put a sandwich concession on the main floor of this laundry? I'll pay you rent. We got real good food." Both of them stopped smiling as Bepy continued his pitch. "That's my profession. I own sandwich places."

"What kind of sandwich places?"

"Italian. Good hot Italian sandwiches."

"You got good food?" Mr. Fat asked with a twinkle in his eye. "Can I eat for free? Every day?" Bepy nodded. "Then we make deal. I eat no charge!"

"Of course you eat no charge. You're a VIP. Eat all you want; no charge for you. How much rent for the concession area?"

"One hundred dollars per month. Very cheap. OK?"

Bepy quickly nodded his head, and they shook hands. "OK, you got a deal. Show me our space. Tomorrow we start."

What a steal, he thought. A hundred bucks a month. What a bargain I got. Then he thought, Oh, shit. Another fuckin' Chinese handshake.

Back at the company office, he told Monkey, "Call the boys. We're working late tonight. And get coffee urns, sandwich and steam table equipment ready to roll. We're setting up another shop, fast—in a laundry."

"What laundry? I thought we had a store."

"We *had* a store! Red and his hit-man friend got it now. All we got is a hallway in a laundry next door to them."

They worked all night putting together a sharp-looking cafe-style food shop on the first floor of the laundry. They even used an umbrella for sidewalk atmosphere.

During the next few days, all the Chinese in the building, on their lunch break, passed the stand, looked, and kept walking. Monkey reported that Red and Mac had stopped by to check it out and left laughing at the unsuccessful operation Bepy had.

Two weeks went by, and business was still terrible. The Chinese didn't go for spit, except for Mr. Fat, who was fatter. Bepy couldn't figure it out.

"These Chinese don't drink coffee; they don't even chew gum. Nothing, *neinte,*" Bepy complained to Little Pauli and Alley Oop. "Red and Mac, them two cocksuckers, open their new place and it's doing great! I can't understand what the hell's wrong. We're open twenty-four hours a day, and no business. We're dumping so much food in the garbage, it's crazy."

As he ranted, a thought entered his mind. I wonder if these people can read English? Holy shit! No wonder they aren't buying anything. They can't read the damn menu. He was frantic. He went to see Mr. Fat. "How come you didn't tell me they can't read English?" he asked.

Mr. Fat just smiled at Bephino's anger.

Bepy went back to his Wall Street office and asked a Hong Kong associate to translate the menu into Chinese. Then he and Alley Oop had five thousand fliers printed in Chinese and handed them out to all the laundry workers. They were reading it and yelling, "Ha yah, yah! Ah, ah, good, good."

The problem was solved, business was unbelievable, and the Chinatown location became a winner.

"Boy, I was worried about this spot," Monkey confided to Bepy. "I'm glad you figured out the problem. I thought Red and Mac had given us the *malucais.* I saw Mac make the horns at me one day."

"Mac gave you the horns?"

"Yeah. He zeroed right in on me with his fingers like this," Monkey said, making the sign of harm with his index and little finger.

"No shit? That bastard gave us the *malucais?*"

"Yeah," Monkey answered, once again.

"All right, don't worry about Red and Mac," Bepy said. "If Ben doesn't come through with that bomb, I got a nice hot bath coming up for them, Monk. I have to take you out of the office for a while. I need you to run this place until it's established. I need you here to keep an eye on Red and Mac, because very soon I'm gonna scrub those bastards clean. We're gonna baptize them with sewer water. I'll see you later, Monk."

"OK, Bep. Call me tonight, and I'll give you the figures on today's business."

"OK. Come on Alley. Let's go."

"What the fuck does he want?" Alley asked, pointing at Mr. Fat.

"I think he likes you, Alley."

"Yeah, well I don't think I like him," Alley said, glaring back at Mr. Fat. "He always stares at me with them fuckin' eyes."

"Stare back at him, Alley. Your eyes look like his."

Alley turned to Bepy and grinned.

12

When the twins were baptized, Bepy and Dana threw a fitting party at their new farm in upstate New York. Bepy had wanted to have a farm since New Orleans, and now that big money was coming in, he had decided to buy one.

All the relatives from both sides of the family came to help prepare for such an important occasion. Special foods were cooked, and the aunts and cousins worked like clockwork, carrying on the traditions of the Old Country.

The house was an old resort, with about twenty large bedrooms, so sleeping arrangements were no problem. The uncles and other guests looked over the house and grounds while the women cooked. Three uncles sat under the large oak tree and played their instruments, making for a romantic Italian atmosphere. As the mandolins and guitars played, the wine flowed. People moved about laughing and enjoying one another—until the Sunday-afternoon barbecue, when Bepy's great-aunt Nina called his father over.

"Patsy, looka, there'sa well over there. Getta me a nice glass of *acqua fresca*. The frankaforta they too salty."

Pasquale went to the well and began to pump. "Hey, look at this *acqua*," he yelled to everyone. "It's so cold and clear. *La bella acqua*."

He handed his aging aunt the glass. "Here, *Zia, stabuona questa acqua*." Everyone had been so busy drinking wine that this was the first they knew there was a well on the farm. They all lined up and started to pump water, drinking and laughing.

"You can't beat Catskill Mountains water. You know that?" Bepy's Uncle Jim said. "Look, it's so clear and cold. We love wine, but you need good water to live. Right, Pasquale?"

"You ain't kidding," Pasquale replied. "You gotta have good water like this in your body. It's a must!"

The next day, *gagazula* arrived, more commonly called diarrhea. It was a sight to see, with everyone on the run. "What happened?" they asked, holding their stomachs. "It couldn't have been the wine. It must have been the lousy water," more than one remarked.

"Hey, Pasquale! *Acqua fresca,* my ass!" Aunt Mary yelled to her brother as she, too, ran for the nearest available toilet.

Everyone was suffering from cramps. "Call the Health Department. Something's wrong with your water. What kinda farm did you buy?" Pasquale asked his son sarcastically.

"What kind of question is that?" Bepy turned to his mother for help. "Listen to this guy. He makes me laugh. Yesterday he offers everybody water from the pump, this big shot. Now he blames me. I never even knew we had a well. Blame Aunt Nina. She found it. Maybe the well hasn't been used in years. Maybe there's some dirt in there."

The next morning an inspector from the Health Department came to test the well and found the water to be contaminated. That's all everyone had to hear. They loaded their cars and headed for Brooklyn, where the water was pure and fresh. A few uncles stayed behind to help with the problem, or perhaps to finish the wine. They loved the idea of staying and sending their wives home. They argued all night, in Italian. They also played a game of brisco, then argued about the well some more. The best part was that they couldn't drink the water; so they drank wine all week.

They finally decided it was the septic system's cracked pipes seeping into the well. It had to be dug up to find the leaks, one of the uncles declared. With unanimous agreement, they began to dig. They ripped out sewer lines all around the house and dug up the tank. The place looked like a bombed area. The lawn was no longer beautifully landscaped. After the day of digging, they sat down to brisco again. The wine barrels seemed to have no bottom.

After another week of conferences and observation of the open system, they decided to put everything back together, but a totally new system, new pipes, new tanks, charged to Bephino at the local plumbing firm. They chlorinated the well, and it was ready to be retested. The inspector felt sure it was going to be all right, but said he'd be over shortly. It was always best to test again, just to be sure. This time the water showed a higher contamination level. They all yelled at the inspector, "*Ba von quolo!* You stupida. You said it would be better."

They sat and talked a few more days. Like Columbus, Italians never give up, so the next plan was to check the entire countryside. The very next day, the uncles took a walk through the woods and up the mountain. One uncle carried the wine, another carried a roll of toilet paper. Toward late afternoon, they came across a smelly stream and followed it up the hill to a neighboring farm, which raised guinea pigs.

There were hundreds of guinea pigs in crates, and their waste was being discharged in a stream that ran down the hill to Bephino's property. They began yelling in Italian and waving their arms, pointing at the guinea pigs. "This is the reason we're all sick and got cramps! This guy ruined Bephino's beautiful farm."

The owner, hearing the commotion, ran out of his house with his shotgun. He couldn't understand what they were saying or why they were there. They continued to wave their arms and then switch to holding their heads and stomachs.

The farmer ran back into the house and called his brother, "Look out there, Elmer. Get your shotgun. We gonna get us some Mexicans."

Bepy was in Brooklyn and unaware of what was taking place on his farm. He had a lot of laughs when he heard how the two guinea pig farmers came out shooting, until they saw Uncle Jim hold up a bottle of wine. Then they all sat down to share it and discuss the water situation. When the wine was gone, the two brothers agreed to move the pens to the other side, away from the stream. It was the kind of problem that only his uncles could solve, he told Dana.

One Sunday Ben called Bepy. "Hey, Bep, what's new? When can I see you? I got something for you."

"Why don't you come over today. We'll have dinner together. Dana's making lasagne and roast beef. Do you like lasagne?"

"Does a nigger like watermelon? Of course I like lasagne. What time do you want us over?"

"Whatever time you want; just come on."

Ben and his wife, Peggy, arrived carrying a big cake box. For dessert, they had brought a dozen Italian pastries from the only Italian baker on Staten Island.

Table conversation touched on every subject except the reason Ben had wanted to come over. After dessert the women automatically retreated to the kitchen chores, and Ben and Bepy went downstairs to Ben's car to see what he had for Bepy. He had the bomb Bepy had requested.

"I made this special. It's almost an atom bomb. Them guys will blow far away when this goes off. You better be sure you want to use this on them, because when it blows up, you can kiss them guys good-bye. You ain't gonna see them no more."

"It took you long enough to make it. The war coulda ended by now." Bepy studied the bomb seriously. "OK. I want you to connect it in their car Wednesday morning. They eat breakfast together every Wednesday. I've been clocking them. You put it under their hood. OK? I want them bastards to reach the moon."

"Yeah! What's left of them," Ben assured him. "I'll wear my mechanic's outfit, in case someone sees me. They'll think I'm a repairman working on their car. And I'll pack a rod in case Red and Mac catch me in the act. Either way, I'll melt both of them."

"Good. It's time for these creeps to part company with me. They gave me a lot of *acido*. I'm sick over Red. We grew up together. They took my location for my new store and they both laughed about it. That was a very bad scene for me. Did they think I'd let them get away with that? The balls on Red! He knows better. Do it, Ben. Set the fuckin' bomb Wednesday. I'll get you the information you need about the car. Make it good. If they spot you in the act, shoot them both—slaughter them."

Wednesday morning Ben worked fast. He set the bomb in the car and quickly headed back to Staten Island. On the ferry, he sat in a men's room booth, so no one would notice his returning from Manhattan so early in the day.

At nine-forty-five, after finishing their breakfast, Red and Mac got into the car and started it. BOOM! The blast was heard seven blocks away. The car's wheels blew across the street, the hood flew one hundred feet into the air, the engine was gone, and the two doors blew off. Red

200

and Mac got out and walked away, a little shaky, but without a scratch. It looked just like a circus-clown act as they dusted themselves off and walked away.

When Bepy heard the news, he couldn't believe it. He called Ben at his funeral home.

"You're a bomber? Ya little bastard! Them mother fuckers are still walking. You make atom bombs, huh? You make shit! Those guys have probably hit the mattresses already, so now I got real trouble. I gotta find out where they are and go in shooting like a fuckin' cowboy, or they'll blow me and my family away. You made a fuckin' mess now. They'll know it was me. What the hell happened?" Bepy was screaming, in a low voice.

"Bep, this is the first time this ever happened to me," Ben replied. "I don't understand it. I put enough stuff in that thing to flatten a tank. Maybe the sticks were facing north instead of south. The sticks gotta face south to blast the passengers. Otherwise the blast only gets the motor."

"North, south, who gives a fuck? The next thing I know, I'll be getting squeezed into one of your fake tuxedos in a pine box. You'll be looking at me bare-assed on a marble slab. Which way you gonna face me? North or south, you little rubber. They gotta know it was me," he said. "So now I gotta play cowboys and Indians. I had it made until you blew it. I had the jump on them. Now they'll be shooting at anything that moves. I missed the boat; this is very bad for me."

"I'm sorry, Bep. Sleep over at my house till we get them. Bring your family over now. We'll make a plan to bring them out to a table, huh? Then we blow up the table."

"Blow up my ass! Don't do me any favors with those fuckin' bombs!" Bepy screamed into the phone. "I don't know! I gotta think about this one. Mac is such a no-hearted bastard that they might get sloppy and hurt my wife and kids. Believe me, Ben, he could get rough and blow up my house with the kids in it. And this guy moves fast. He's bad news. He's got about thirty notches on his belt. He's the guy that killed that seventy-four-year-old newsstand man. The murder made front-page news for weeks."

After hours of thinking, Bepy decided what he had to do. He left his office and visited Norma, now Red's wife.

"I heard about the bomb in Red's car," he told her. "I came over to get the word to you and let Red know it wasn't me. I wouldn't do that to Red. I think it must have been somebody who was after Johnny Mac. So get the word to them that it's not me. OK, Norma? It's very important they know it wasn't me. Things like this can get very confused, very fast. A war sometimes starts for nothing. So tell them right away."

"OK, Bepy. I'm glad it wasn't you. I'll tell him. I'm having a baby next month and I need my husband to raise my child." She kissed Bepy on the cheek. "We go back a long way, since we were kids, and you know how horny I am, so don't kill my man. I need him."

"You know I would never kill Red; you know that, Norma," Bepy assured her. "We grew up together."

"Look, Bepy, I know the story, and you're right about Red and the business. But you do owe Red. Remember when he saved your life from those niggers at school? I called him. Right, Bep? I called him for you."

"Yeah, he saved my life. You're right, Norma. He did come and get me out. I remember that." Kissing her cheek and patting her belly, he said, "Just get word to him that it wasn't me. He should know bombs are not my style, anyway, but tell him just in case. We have no bad blood anymore. Tell him to get in touch with me. Maybe we'll join forces."

"OK, Bepy. Thank you. God bless."

Two days later Bepy got a call at the office from Red.

"How are you?" Bepy asked. "Are you all right? What the fuck happened? I want you to know I don't deal in bombs. You know that. Right, Red?"

"Yeah. I told Johnny Mac I didn't think you would use a bomb. It's not your style. If you wanted to hit us, it would be bullets. Mac is really on the warpath. He wants to hit everybody and anybody. He even wanted to bust into your home shooting."

"My home? What for?"

"He thought it was you," Red explained. "And, frankly, so did I."

"Look, Red, I heard a story you and Mac should hear. I think I know who wants Mac dead. It's not you they're after, Red. *He's* the target. Don't mention we talked about this. I'll tell you more when I see you. We go back a long way, Red, and I want you to know that I'm not out to hurt you. Understand?"

Red hesitated, then asked, "Do you know who it is?"

"Meet me in Chinatown tomorrow at three. We can't talk over the phone. You know that. Tell Mac maybe I can help out. Maybe we team up, huh? We'll be stronger if we join forces. Talk to him about that. But until tomorrow, stay out of sight. Sometimes things happen for the best."

"OK, Bepy. We'll talk about it."

"And tell Mac to stay cool. He better not come near my home. . . . I'll be waiting next door in the laundry. I'll send someone over for you at three. Don't tell anyone we're meeting. I don't wanna get a bomb thrown at me while I'm with you two. You guys are very hot at the moment."

Red laughed.

"I'm not joking, Red. I heard a story, and if it's true, Mac's got problems."

"No shit? It's that bad?"

"Well, you almost got your balls blown off. Sounds pretty bad to me. Don't talk about our meeting tomorrow to anyone."

"OK. Three tomorrow. I'll be there with Mac. Good-bye . . . and thanks, Bep."

Bepy called Ben. "I want you to see how it's done in Brooklyn, ya little rubber. OK?"

"What are you gonna do, one of those shit scenes like the thing we did in New Orleans? Tell me, so I can bring a gas mask."

"Don't be funny, you fuckin' dwarf. You're talking on the phone like you were in a pasture. Whatta you mentioning cities for. What happened to the old Ben who was always careful on phones, table fourteen, and all that bullshit. Just be at the Chinatown store at two tomorrow."

"You mean that hot-dog stand? You call that a store?"

"Come on, Ben. Stop breakin' balls. I got problems. Just be there. We got work to do. You got me into this damn mess and don't forget it."

"I'll be there, don't worry."

At two the next day, Alley Oop and Bepy were eating and talking with Mr. Fat. Bepy smiled and asked him, "Vat, ah good, huh?"

"Ah vat, ah *sinei.* Ya, good. Strong *sinei,* good."

"*Sinei,* ah full? Huh? Tank full?" Bepy asked seriously.

Mr. Fat now knew something was on Bepy's mind.

"What is your brain thinking about, my friend? You want to dunk someone?" he asked in clear English.

Bepy leaned closer. "Yeah. How much you charge?"

"Two hundred dollars a head. Very cheap, very reasonable."

"Two hundred bucks, you gotta deal." Bepy quickly put out his hand to lock in the deal. And they shook hands.

"When?"

"In about an hour," Bepy replied.

"I go check downstairs. Make sure tank full."

Bepy then turned to Alley Oop. "This guy is unbelievable! I didn't expect him to go for it so quick. The fat guy is a little *pazzo.* He must dump guys in there from time to time too. He didn't even blink when I asked him how much. I kinda like him; he keeps his word."

"He really understands English good, doesn't he?" Alley Oop said.

"Yeah, and he understands money, too. But I must say, his prices are reasonable. But he gets us good on the chow line! Have you ever seen his plate at lunch time? It's like a Saint Bernard's dish—deep and round. It's his own dish. He loads it up with sausage and peppers."

"How's everything, Bep?" Ben said as he entered.

"Fine, but you're late. I said two, and it's two-ten. You'd better eat. You're gonna need your strength for this one."

"I couldn't find a place to park. That's why I'm late."

"Hey, undertaker," Alley said, laughing, "you almost missed the funeral."

Earlier that day, Bepy had called Sid Choy. He told his secretary that Johnny Mac wanted him at the hero shop at three-fifteen sharp. It was very important that he be there.

At three, Bepy told Alley Oop to go next door and get Red and Mac.

"Bring them here for the meeting. Tell them it's safe, that no one can see us in the laundry. Tell them their store is too risky for all of us, but that no bombs will land in our building. There's a lot of people around here. Make them feel safe, Alley."

Alley went next door and came back in five minutes with Red and Johnny Mac. They were led to Mr. Fat's office. This was the first meeting between Mac and Bepy. They had never met face to face, eye to eye, but knew a lot about each other.

Mac was a big husky fellow, tough-looking, with tattoos on both arms and hands. It was well known that he didn't give a damn about anyone. It was said he had killed instantly and without good reason. Now he shook hands with Ben and Bepy—two other reasonably well-known hit men.

Bepy smiled and acted hospitable, moving Red and Mac to the soft sofa. It would keep them deep and low. He wanted to prevent them from moving around fast. Red and Mac looked at each other after sitting down, realizing too late that they had allowed themselves to be put in a vulnerable position.

"This place smells like piss," Red remarked with a scowl.

Everybody laughed. Togetherness at last, Bepy thought. "Go get the Chink," he whispered to Alley Oop. "It's three-fifteen. We'll be waiting right here. Take Mr. Fat with you. He knows them well."

Mr. Fat went with Alley Oop to make sure he brought back the right guy. They saw Choy arriving, walking fast down the street.

"Mr. Choy?" Alley Oop asked. "Johnny Mac is over here." Choy followed them to the laundry office, taking short, fast steps and keeping his head down.

Red and Mac were surprised to see Mr. Choy enter the office. "Hey, uh, what are you doing here?" Mac asked awkwardly.

Choy reached out to shake hands as Bepy watched. They love to shake hands, these double-crossing bastards, Bepy thought.

"What the hell are we all doing in this small, smelly office?" Bepy said. "Let's go downstairs, where we have more room to talk."

Red and Mac hesitated; Mac looked at Red and nudged him. Alley, Bepy, and Ben saw the nudge. Each pulled out a gun. "Be cool. Don't get jumpy. We wanna show you a few things," Bepy, giving the orders as usual, said. "If you guys move, you're all dead. Red, you can tell Mac my life story, so he knows I mean what I say. If he moves, or even farts, I'll kill him instantly."

"Mac, be cool," Red said. "He means it."

"Do I have any other choice?" Mac replied, the muscles in his jaw tightening.

Alley quickly relieved Red and Mac of their guns.

"What were you guys expecting?" he asked. "A war?"

Sid Choy, angry and nervous, started toward the door.

"I don't stay for this. I leave," he said.

"Where the fuck is he goin'?" Alley asked.

Ben quickly grabbed Choy by the shoulder and smacked him across the face so hard his mouth began to bleed. Choy stopped in his tracks.

They herded the men down into the cellar. Ben, now trying to be smart, said, "Hey, Bep, what are you going to do, crush grapes? Is this your wine cellar?" There was no response from Bephino as he led them down the steps to the tomblike basement.

"Whatta ya, *pazzo?* Foolin' around at a time like this?" Alley whispered to Ben. "He's gonna get pissed off at you."

"Take all their metal," Bepy told Alley. "Belt buckles, rings, everything."

Alley quickly began stripping them and found rolls of bills in their pockets. "Hey, Bep," he said, waving the cash. "These guys are loaded. It looks like thousands here."

"Nothing's changed, Alley. Take all the cash they got, even the fuckin' coins ... especially the coins. Strip these bastards clean. Where they're going they don't need nothin'. Get those diamond rings from Mac and the Chink. I'll have them reset for Dana. She loves diamonds." Bepy smiled, then laughed outright at Choy. "So your friend Mac's a big guy in your neighborhood, huh? Ya fuckin' Chink bastard. Take a good look at him—him with tattoos on his arms and fingers. Take a good look. This is what you're gonna be sleeping with."

Mr. Fat went up the stairs to lock the cellar door and returned silently, wiping his brow as he watched. He knew there was no turning back. He saw that these men were professionals. His face became wet and shiny, and his smile was going on and off like a blinking light.

"Being that you're the biggest guy in the neighborhood," Bepy sneered at Johnny Mac, then glared hard at Red, "and the best hit man and the dirtiest bastard, you're gonna take the first bath."

"Come on! What are you fuckin' guys, crazy?" Mac pleaded. "We're all Italians here. Give me a break, will ya? What'd I ever do to you, Bephino? What the fuck did I ever do to you? I don't even know you. I never did nothin' to you. Why you wanna knock me off?"

"It's not what you already did to me, Macaroni; it's what you could do to me if I let you go. You're a fuckin' animal from way back. I heard of you when I was only a kid. And you're too close for comfort with my partner. You knew I wouldn't like it, but you didn't give a shit. You moved right in. So now you can move in with St. Peter!"

Looking coldly at Mac, he continued. "Remember the newsstand guy, Mac? This is for him."

"Don't do it, Bephino." Mac was beginning to panic. "He was..."

"Yeah, I know. He was a Jew. And he also had a family that loved him, ya rotten bastard!" Bepy said slowly, raising his gun. He squeezed the trigger and shot Mac in the face. The bullet hit the center of his forehead and dropped him hard on the floor.

The shot echoed through the cellar. "See, Red. He was the biggest and the best hit man in New York, huh? Watch how small I make him now. Watch this bastard disappear. You watch him, Red, and don't turn away. I want your brain to curl before you die. If you turn away, Milanese, you go next, before the Chink."

Red trembled with fear, staring into the vat in disbelief as Alley and Mr. Fat picked up Mac's heavy body. "Bephino! What are you doing?!" he cried out, turning away.

Mr. Fat and Alley Oop dropped Mac slowly into the vat. He began to melt instantly. His flesh and hair began to lift away from his skull, floating to the surface. The acid bubbled as his body sunk.

"You stole my money and got away with it," Bepy said. "You guys were stealing my business; then you were even laughing at me. You went too deep into my heart, Red. I gotta baptize you for that. Those laughs really cost you, Red. I hope they were worth it. I gotta melt you like a candle." With the gun, he turned Red's head toward the acid. "Say good-bye to your friend."

"Yeah, we're gonna wax you, too, ya fuckin' Red pumpkin," Ben added.

"You're gonna kill me because I had a couple of laughs on you? What's wrong with you?" Red pleaded. "Please don't kill me, Bepy. I feel so sick, Bepy. Please, dear God, help me." He was trembling and shitting in his pants and begging. He was a pathetic sight.

"Ah, here we go again. Even this bastard's scouring now. Jesus Christ, he smells bad," Ben said. "You're a real organic bastard. You know that, Red?"

Red just stared at Ben as he nervously bit his fingernails and mumbled a prayer.

Bepy was in no mood for Ben's ridiculous remarks. "Grab that Chink," he told Alley. "He's next at bat."

Alley grabbed Choy, who was near passing out.

"Where's your long-legged lady friend today?" Bepy asked him mockingly. "Soaking her ass in a hot tub? Well, this is your hot tub, you little snail."

"Ya. Ya, my lady in my apartment hot tub," Choy replied. "You like her?" He motioned with his arms, offering her to them.

"Yeah, we like her, and we'll take her after you're in the sewer, you yellow rat. Mr. Fat will fuck her tomorrow. He loves skinny chinks with long legs. Right, Mr. Fat?"

Mr. Fat forced a smile and wiped his forehead and neck again.

"Ok, fine, fine," Choy said. "He can have her." He felt better. He hoped his offer might be accepted in exchange for his life. "And very clever, very clever. Fine, fine. He can fucky her. Shake hands," he said, putting his hand out and smiling, as if a deal had been made. "Shake hands," he said again, looking at them despairingly when no one took his offer.

Bepy looked at the little man who always liked to shake.

"Drop him in head first, Alley. I can't stand this guy," he said in Italian.

Alley picked him up by the legs as Choy fought, punching, struggling, and screaming for his life. Alley dropped him in head first, then jumped back quickly to avoid splashing acid on his black patent-leather shoes.

Sid Choy swam half a breaststroke trying to get out. He managed to raise himself up and stared toward Mr. Fat. His face, grossly distorted and with the eyeballs completely gone, he looked like something from a horror movie. Slowly, he sunk back into the acid.

Everyone remained silent but Ben. "Boy, these Chinks are ugly when they're dying, ain't they?"

Mr. Fat was emotionally unbound. He was sweating and laughing, then whimpering, and then laughing again. This scene was obviously too much for him.

"Red, you're next. Get ready," Bepy said. "And don't be a coward. Be a man. Don't make me shoot you first. Let me see you go like a real Milanese, huh? You can swim a little, but don't scream. Be a man. OK, *paesano?* Be a man." Bepy's voice was thick and strange.

"Bephino, Bephino," Red screamed instantly. "Please, for old time's sake! We were kids together. Please have mercy on me." Moving slowly closer to Bepy, he said, "We were always friends, Bep. Don't do this to me."

Ben stepped in between to block him, pointing his gun at Red's head.

Red looked so pathetic. "Bepy!" he pleaded. "My wife's having a baby. Please let me be a father. I never was a father, Bepy. Please let me live. Have mercy. I love you, Bephino Menesiero. I always loved you. I was wrong. Have mercy on me." Tears mixed with mucous ran over his lips.

Alley Oop moved toward him, grabbed him in a bear hug, and dragged him to the vat. "You betrayed us, Red," he whispered in his ear. "We have no choice. I'll try to numb you, *paesano,* so you don't feel it." He punched him a few times in the neck to relax him, and Red went limp.

Red looked into Bepy's eyes. As he held himself up he smiled. "My mother and father always loved ya and I always loved ya," he whispered. "We grew up together, Bepy."

Alley looked at Bepy for the final OK, but Bepy waited because Sid Choy wasn't completely gone.

"He's still floating around, like scum with jet-black hair," Ben said.

The men looked at Choy's still-floating remains. It seemed as if the acid had gotten weaker from all that blood and flesh.

"These Chinks got tough skin," Ben said. "It takes longer for them to melt. Look at that black wig still floating around. Let's dump Red in now. He'll mix with Sid nicely."

Bepy looked into Red's eyes, and he remembered him in their schooldays, the laughs they'd had when they stole nickels and dimes from other kids, how they bought their first pea caps together and felt so fine wearing them up and down the neighborhood. He remembered how they swore to be friends forever . . .

"Bephino, please don't kill me," Red moaned pitifully. "Don't kill me," he repeated over and over like a child.

Alley Oop, expecting to get the nod any second, was squeezing Red and watching Bepy's face. Ben and Mr. Fat stood in complete silence. Suddenly, Red stopped begging, and there was a deep silent pause. Everyone waited for Bepy. Even Red watched for the nod. He knew nothing more would work; a decision had been made. Alley began to lift Red.

"Wait a minute," Bepy said. "Put him down. Let him live. I don't wanna kill him."

"What! Are you fuckin' nuts?" Ben yelled. "He's gotta go. He saw too much down here today. I say he goes."

"And I say he lives," Bepy quietly stated. "We'll let him live. He's been through enough. His wife will have a baby next month, and the baby's gonna need a father." He continued to try to justify himself, so they wouldn't think he had made a bad decision. "Besides, he'll be a useless man the rest of his life anyway. His mind will never be the same after this. He'll never be a man again. Have Joey D fuck his wife once a month after her baby. Why should she suffer from this bum?" Bepy rubbed his face in a gesture of fatigue.

"Look at him!" Ben yelled. "I say *morte*. He's like an imbecile already. I say *morte*."

"Let him go, Alley. You'll get that smell on you. He's got that yellow shit all over your new shoes," Bepy said.

Alley released him and looked at his shoes. "Damn it! Look what he's done!" He stomped his foot.

Looking at Red, Bepy warned him. "You charmed me on your deathbed. OK. I reversed my decision for once in my life. You'll be a father. I hope I did right, Red. If you ever see me around, you had better disappear quick. And get out of the business, too. This could be the biggest mistake of my life, Red, but I'm gonna let you walk. You charmed me once again. You won me over again."

Red thanked all the men humbly and tried to kiss Bepy's hand, but Bepy refused to be touched by him. "Just get your life together and keep away from me."

"Yeah! You'd better go in the corner and wipe your ass," Ben told him. "You're a mess."

Mr. Fat saw that Choy was gone. He quickly turned the valve to release the acid into the sewer. Alley collected all the metal objects.

Bepy told Mr. Fat he wanted the slug that came out of Johnny Mac's head in the bottom of the vat. Everyone else had forgotten about the bullet. "We leave nothing behind," he said. "Hose everything down." Then he told Red, who was still standing there. "Go home and go to church. Pray. Thank God you're alive. It was the most difficult decision of my life."

As they left the building, Bepy handed Mr. Fat four hundred bucks. Mr. Fat thanked him, then returned two hundred dollars, saying, "Choy is on the house. I'm so happy; I can't charge you for him."

"Ya got balls, ya know that, Mr. Fat?" Alley Oop told him. Mr. Fat smiled proudly.

"I wanted Sid Choy and Johnny Mac in the same coffin," Bepy whispered to Ben. "I made them that promise and I kept it."

"How come you chickened out with Red?" Ben asked.

"Chickened out? Ben? What am I, ten years old? Chicken out! Listen to this shit. I just melted two guys, and he calls me a chicken. I must be going nuts, hanging around with you."

Then, serious, he said, "I did it for old times' sake, Benny. I knew him as a kid. It was a tough decision for me. He helped me once, and I owed him for that. He's been hurt enough for a lifetime. We go back a long way, him and me." He paused and smiled. "I gotta give him credit."

"Give who credit?"

"Red. He was smart right down to the wire. He asked me to let him live to see his unborn son, knowing a Sicilian couldn't deny him that privilege. A request to see the unborn is sacred. I don't want to be a rotten killer right down to the core. I'm glad I let him live. I feel good about it. Deep down in my heart I know he loves me, and I love him."

"I think you're nuts. You should have melted him, too. He conned you and got away with it. A Milanese used a sacred Sicilian belief to save his life. You fucked up, Bep. He's gonna kill you someday. You wait and see. He's gonna fuck you someday," Ben repeated.

"I hope you're wrong, Ben. Any moron can make a decision to kill. It takes a real fuckin' man to spare the life of an enemy. Don't you agree, Ben? I made a tough decision. I let my enemy live because he was once my friend. I can't believe it myself, but I feel good about it."

"Nah, I don't agree. I think you're nuts. He's out there alive. If he can hurt you someday, he will. You made a wrong decision, Bephino, and you know it. I just hope I'm not sitting next to you when he hits you."

"Ah, the fuckin' acid was gettin' too weak anyway," Bepy murmured.

Leaving the building, they waved to Monkey, behind the sandwich stand. Alley Oop reached over the counter and grabbed a hot meatball from the steam table. Then they all walked out onto the streets of Chinatown.

All in all, business was good at the Chinatown location.

A few months had passed quietly when four Oriental men in their mid-twenties showed up and asked for the owner. They all had toothpicks in their mouths, and they wore white turtleneck sweaters, leather karate gloves, and white sneakers.

Monkey was tempted to break out laughing, but he knew better. "What'll ya have, fellas?" he asked as he stirred his tomato sauce.

They moved closer to the stand, spreading out very quietly. One asked, "You own this business?"

"Who wants to know?" Monkey replied.

"Me, Jimmy Lee. I want to know," he replied.

"Your name don't ring a bell to me," Monkey answered. "Are you selling something?"

Jimmy Lee smirked and then motioned to his friends to move around the counter.

Monkey noticed the positioning and spoke quickly. "I'm not the owner, I only work this stand. Some guys from Elizabeth Street own it. Whatta you, a salesman?" he asked again, nervously, trying to keep the dialogue going.

"No. Me no salesman, but I offer you insurance policy for protection. I offer you protection from annoyance in Chinatown," Jimmy Lee said.

"Protection? We don't need any protection," Monkey replied. "But I'll mention it to the owner. OK? He calls in every day. I'll tell him you were here."

"Yes, you tell him you need protection from annoyance in Chinatown. You pay one hundred dollars a week; we make sure nobody annoyance to you."

"A hundred a week? The rent here is only a hundred a month. Boy, you really got your wires crossed. You're kinda high, ain't ya?" Then Monkey smiled and said, "Ah, see, you *are* a salesman. You're selling annoyance, and I gotta buy a protection policy or else, right?"

"No. I offer you protection. I no sell annoyance. Annoyance is free. No charge for that."

The four Chinese started laughing.

Monkey prepared for combat by placing a long, two-pronged fork closer. He stared at Jimmy Lee eye to eye, waiting for the next move.

"What you say about that?" Jimmy Lee asked, smiling.

"I say take a fucking walk, Tojo. Amscray! Go suck ya fuckin' wontons, and take these other rabbits with you."

Jimmy Lee's face fell and he began to squeal angrily in Chinese. Suddenly Mr. Fat, hearing the noise, came running out of his office. He saw it was Jimmy Lee yelling and retreated four giant steps back into his office. Monkey did not notice his entry or disappearance.

Jimmy Lee was known in Chinatown as the boss of the Sunga gang from Hong Kong. He ran a protection scam and was draining all the poor Chinese merchants. He had a reputation as a deadly killer, without an ounce of mercy. Rumors said he had even decapitated children in China. If he decided you were dead, you were iced instantly. But Monkey didn't know any of this.

The four Chinese went into action, dragging Monkey over the counter. They began drop-kicking him, then chop, chop with their fists. Monkey lost the long fork but fought back, landing a swift haymaker to one guy's head, then dropping another with a powerful punch to his temple. When the guy hit the floor, the remaining three let out a howl and went to work on Monkey. They hit him with everything they had. Blood was soon gushing out of Monkey's ears and nostrils.

He was hurt badly, but, surprisingly, still conscious and aware of the beating he was getting. Suddenly, he reached out and caught one assailant by the leg. He hung on as they both crashed to the floor. Absorbing furious punches and kicks from the other three, he began collecting his strength. He grabbed, scratched, and bit, still taking punches and karate chops and kicks to his head. Raw welts were opening.

With one final desperate lunge, he tried to bite the chin of the guy under him, but in the struggle wound up with his ear instead. He clamped his teeth down with his last ounce of strength, and the man screamed in pain. Monkey had it all now, the whole ear in his mouth. Near unconsciousness, he knew he'd got a break. He had the ear good. The other three were now picking Monkey up off the floor and trying to separate the two men. When the final destruction of Monkey came, the man's ear was ripped off his head and hung out of Monkey's mouth.

Too weak to fight anymore, Monkey lay with the ear in his mouth, like a fighter's mouthpiece. They continued to beat him to a bloody pulp. Unconscious, with the ear still clutched between his teeth, and his body limp, Monkey looked dead. The four men left quickly, Jimmy Lee grabbing a towel from the counter to cover his friend's bloody head, from which blood was gushing as though from an open faucet.

Mr. Fat peeked through his office door, and after seeing the Sunga boys leave, he came out and removed the ear from Monkey's mouth so he could breathe. Monkey was still unconscious when he arrived at the hospital.

Mr. Fat called Bephino and played dumb about the entire incident. He was deathly afraid of the Jimmy Lee gang.

Two days later, Monkey was out of intensive care and awake and talking. During the questioning by police investigators, he insisted that he had fallen off a mozzarella truck. They cursed him and left in disgust. The doctors told Monkey he would be all right, his broken ribs would heal and he would recover from his concussion.

All the Bay Ridge boys visited Monkey and were very upset about the Chinese hoods.

"They got no respect. We gotta straighten this shit out," dapper Little Pauli said as he walked back and forth in the hospital room, his heels clicking on the hard floor. "Those fuckin' Chinks are outta line. We gotta do a job on them," he shouted.

When Bepy asked Monkey what the hell happened, Monkey explained the whole story.

"Protect who from annoyance?" Bepy asked. "Protect us?"

"Yeah, you, me, our people? They wanna protect us. *Ah capeesh?*"

"What the fuck! Are these Chinks going nuts? Didn't you tell them we're with the people from Elizabeth Street?"

"Yeah, but it didn't mean shit. They acted like they never heard of Elizabeth Street. They didn't even blink when I mentioned it, so I didn't bother to tell them we're Sicilians. They probably don't give a fuck who we are. They're only interested in Chinatown and think we've trespassed. That's it."

"I've heard of this guy Jimmy Lee. He's the boss from Singapore or Hong Kong. He's a bad guy, very bad. But I never dreamed he would fuck with us. I thought he only kept the Chinks under his control," Bepy said.

"It's OK. You get well, Monkey," he added. "In a few weeks we'll settle the score with Jimmy Lee. We'll make chop suey out of those bastards. We'll be back to see you tomorrow. I'll bring you a bowl of ziti with sausage from Mott Street."

"Oh, yeah, Bep! One more thing," Monkey said. "Them guys all dressed the same—white turtleneck sweaters, sneakers, and they all had toothpicks hanging out their mouths. Why the toothpicks?"

"Maybe they just ate? How the fuck do I know about those Chinese guys," Bepy said, turning toward the door.

"Hey, Bep," Monkey called out. "I bit one Chink's ear off. I remember it ripping away from his head. The whole fuckin' ear came off in my mouth."

Bepy looked back, and thought shadowed his face. "Good. I'm glad you told me that, Monkey. Very good."

Early that evening Bepy went to see Mr. Fat, to find out Jimmy Lee's address.

Mr. Fat was very cool. "Look, my friend, I don't go against my own people. You understand that? It would not be healthy for you to seek out Jimmy Lee. You will have severe consequences in your future if you do. Jimmy Lee is a very important man in Chinatown." Mr. Fat glared at him. "It would become a very unhealthy presence in my laundry."

"I understand and I fully respect you for that, Mr. Fat," Bepy told him. "I realize it's a matter of respect and loyalty to your people. It's important for a man to be loyal. But I have a very good friend who's been hurt real bad by Jimmy Lee. And, like you, I must be loyal to my people. If you don't tell me what I must know, I'm gonna make arrangements for your trip, Mr. Fat. Do you understand what I'm saying? You must tell me, or suck mud under the Hudson River. I'm gonna settle the score with Jimmy Lee with you or without you. I have made my decision. Your loyalty must be to me first. Otherwise I'll have to dress you in a concrete kimono before your boat leaves."

Mr. Fat finally said, reluctantly, "Today I played the number 129B. If I win, I'll be able to buy that house on Mulberry Street."

Bepy realized immediately that Mr. Fat had told him a Chinese proverb without the fortune cookie. Jimmy Lee's club was at 129B Mulberry Street. That had to be his hangout. B was for basement.

Mr. Fat grimly bowed his head twice to Bepy and walked to his office with his head down, as if in shame.

Bepy watched him and then walked over to the sandwich stand to check on Monkey's replacements, Augie and Frankie Boy.

"How's business?"

"Everything's fine, so far. How's Monkey doing?"

"He's feelin' OK. He'll be out in a week." Bepy looked around casually and then leaned over the counter, "Both you guys got heaters?"

"Yeah, we're both packin'."

"Good. Don't get hurt. These Chinks play rough. If you need me, call me at home. I'll be there all night."

Five weeks later, when Monkey was much better, Bepy called a meeting with Alley Oop, Crazy Mikey, and Monkey. "Tonight we take care of the Chinaman," Bepy told them at the start of the meeting.

"You're gonna hit Mr. Fat?" Crazy Mikey asked.

"No, not Fat. Jimmy Lee."

"Good. I like Mr. Fat. He's a funny guy."

"Cut the shit, Mike," Bepy said sternly. "Who gives a fuck if those Chinks are funny or not. They'll shit on us in a minute if they can. Monkey got ruined over there, and Mr. Fat was nowhere in sight. Even to stop them. He's always around that laundry. I got a bad feeling about him.

"Mike, you're gonna drive tonight. I got DeFilippo from downtown to steal us a taxicab. It's waiting for us in a truck garage near Delancey Street and the Bowery. All we gotta do is pick it up. We'll tour Chinatown like tourists in a cab. Wear a cap with a button, to look like a cabby, Mike. Then, when we get to Lee's club, us three"—pointing to Alley Oop and Monkey—"we'll hit the club with all we got. Monkey, you use these two .45-caliber army automatics. Each has ten shots. Try to put a few in Jimmy Lee's head. You know him; we don't. The guy with one ear should be easy to spot; hit him, too. You know what they look like. So pick your men carefully. Alley and I'll have these two sawed-off double-barrel shotguns with magnum loads, so we should be able to blow the whole club away if we have to. We'll surprise them Chinks. They're always in their den after hours, so we're gonna surprise them. Don't get too close to them, remember. These Chinks can fly. They're like them karate experts."

"I know," Monkey said, "I've been there."

"Hey, remember reading about the Valentine's Day Massacre?" Crazy Mikey said. "In Chicago. Al Capone and them guys?"

"Yeah, I remember," Bepy replied. "So what?"

"Well, this is gonna be the Chinatown Massacre. I wish Monkey would drive, because I wanna come inside. It's important to me. I'm a historian at heart. This could be important history, right?"

"Yeah, you're right; it could be. But you drive anyway, Mike, so we can be around to read the history books when they're printed. OK? Leave the history-making to us." Bepy patted Mikey's head. "I'm really only interested in Jimmy Lee and One Ear. If we can just knock those two guys off, I'll be satisfied. We can spare the rest, and we've settled the score."

Alley Oop looked at Bepy, "These guys are Chinks. They're gonna hit us back at the laundry, and next time, Monkey gets killed or somethin'. Let's throw a bomb in and run. Fuck 'em!"

"Come on, Alley, why should we kill 'em all just to kill? There's gonna be a lot of old guys in the club that have nothing to do with this thing. This is business, and it's Jimmy Lee that's gotta be taken care of. He's the troublemaker. I'm not looking to blast the whole joint. If we have to, we will. Let's play it by ear. Let's see what it looks like in there."

"OK, let's play it by ear," Alley replied.

"The good part about this is the police don't know we have a vendetta with Lee. They'll think the Chinks are at war with each other in Chinatown," Bepy explained.

"Come on, let someone else drive," Mikey complained. "I wanna be in on this. People tell me I look like Capone; ya know that?"

"Forget it, Mike," Bepy yelled. "Cut the bullshit with the Capone stuff. We've got problems ahead of us."

Later that evening they collected the stolen taxi and drove to 129B Mulberry Street. It was about midnight, and the streets were not too busy. That was the reason Bepy had picked a Thursday: not too many tourists and cars to hamper their getaway. They parked the cab a few parking spaces from the club.

"Mike, be ready to roll when we come out."

"I'll be ready, don't worry. Just make it good."

"Remember, these guys can fly, so don't get too close," Bepy reminded the others. "They'll kick our teeth out. OK, let's go do it."

They entered the club wearing nylon stockings over their faces. The room was dimly lit and heavy with pot smoke, making it difficult to see faces. About twenty-five men were huddled in one room talking and laughing.

"They all look the same," Alley whispered.

Suddenly, a few spotted the three masked men in their midst holding weapons. Startled, they began to jump up and howl and point. Monkey and Alley held firm, to see what Bepy was going to do, to see how he was going to select his targets and spare lives, as he had talked about earlier. It seemed impossible to spare a roach's life in this crowded smoky room.

Bepy knew he had only a second to make a decision. "Fuck 'em," he yelled. "Hit 'em all!"

They blasted away at the crowd at close range. Four blasts from the sawed-off shotguns downed a large portion of the men there, but some were still staggering around.

"Reload," Bepy told Alley. "Let's hit these bastards again."

They quickly reloaded and blasted them again. The noise was like bombs going off in the small room, and plaster fell from the ceiling like snow. The wounded Chinese were screaming and moving in slow-motion. Blood was shooting out of the pellet holes in their bodies. Monkey stood patiently, pinpointing his bullets, hitting the already wounded who were crawling around trying to evade more of the blast.

"Jesus Christ," Alley Oop yelled, "they look like snakes crawling around. Look at 'em." His stomach was directing his brain, and that was bad business.

Bepy gave him a quick sharp look. It was taboo to speak on this type of hit. A survivor could confirm to the police that it was an English-speaking man with an Italian accent. Anything was possible. Alley Oop had showed emotion for the first time ever. Monkey was still hitting heads with the automatic, blasting away at his targets.

"OK, let's go," Bepy grunted. "Come on, move out."

They ran wildly out to the waiting cab and it pulled away.

"Holy shit. What noise! I heard it up the street. I was watching to see if anyone was calling the police. It sounded like bombs going off," Crazy Mikey said.

The men remained silent, trying to get themselves back to sanity.

"Dump the cab on Elizabeth Street in the old school yard," Bepy ordered, looking back to see if they were being followed.

They dumped the taxi, removed their gloves, and put the weapons in a potato sack. Then they walked up the street to their own car, parked in the lot of an Italian restaurant, and put the sack in the trunk. They knew the owner of the restaurant, and he would testify that they had been eating and playing cards all night if need be. It was a *capuzzella* restaurant, where they only cook the head of a sheep, a special Italian meal that older Italians enjoyed.

"Boy, does that *capuzzella* smell good!" Alley Oop exclaimed as they approached the steps of the restaurant.

"Who the fuck's got the stomach to eat after that mess?" Monkey answered.

Alley replied, "Me, and Mikey, we got the stomach. Right, Mikey?"

"OK, let's be cool," Bepy said. "We eat and enjoy the rest of the evening. Let's try to be normal people again. It's nice and quiet in here tonight, and it's too early to cross the Brooklyn Bridge. It's only 1:00 A.M. We gotta kill some time. So let's eat."

"Yeah, let's kill time for a change," Crazy Mikey said, laughing.

Bepy didn't acknowledge his attempt at humor, but went straight to a corner table in the rear.

"Hold the eyeball on mine, OK, buddy?" Monkey told the waiter when they ordered.

The waiter gave Monkey a look with his own blue eye.

"Yeah, hold the eyes on all of them *capuzzelle,*" Mikey said. "We don't like to see the eyeballs staring at us."

"What d'ya mean? I like the eye," Alley protested. "It's good for you. It gives you brains."

"Alley, it's fish that gives you brains—not the fuckin' eye of a sheep."

"How come you talked, Alley?" Bepy asked, sipping a glass of red wine."

"What d'ya mean, talked? To who?"

"Yeah, how come you opened your big mouth during the festivities?" Monkey said.

"What did I say?" Alley asked.

"You said, 'Jesus Christ, they look like snakes crawling around.' Clear as day. I heard you. You know it's taboo to talk on a hit. If there's a survivor, he could give information to the police."

"I got a lousy feeling watching them Chinks crawl all over each other," Alley said. "I didn't realize I spoke."

All the men were quiet.

Then Alley asked Bepy, "How come you talked on that one?"

Bepy looked surprised. "I didn't talk."

"Oh, yeah? That's what you think. You yelled out, 'Fuck 'em. Hit 'em all' and started shooting."

"Did I say that?"

"Yeah, you did," Monkey reluctantly agreed. "And you also said, 'Reload. Let's hit those bastards again.'"

"See? Nobody's perfect," Alley said, smiling and showing his large ivories.

"That's what I told my father when I was a kid," Crazy Mikey said. "Nobody's perfect, Pop. But he still kicked the shit out of me."

Bepy burst out laughing. "Come on, bring on those heads," he yelled. "I'm getting hungry listening to these unconstructive, miscalculated, superficial, out-of-context remarks by these three distorted-looking bastards."

"See! When he's wrong and he knows it, he starts to say them big words that he don't even understand what they mean," Alley yelled.

Book IV

1960–1965

13

In the balmy spring of 1960, Mr. Gustini retired from Wall Street and went to his villa in Rome to enjoy life. At the same time, Bephino, now thirty-one and wealthy, also retired. He did not show off his wealth. He lived high, but not as high as he could have.

He now had a beautiful ocean-front home next door to Ben on Staten Island. It was like a small estate, worth about half a million dollars. The property was surrounded by eight-foot-high walls, because he loved privacy.

The twins were getting big now. Dana loved to spoil them, but they were taught the meaning of *respect* almost from birth. It was very apparent, when an adult met the children, that respect was what a Sicilian child had to offer.

Don Morrano's amorous life had begun to change, too. His Hollywood-doll life style had had its affect on him. But his friendship with Bephino had become stronger, and he was impressed by the tranquil, secluded world Bephino had built for his family. He loved to visit him, just to sit with him on his private beach. They were both very private people who had very private things to talk about. They would crunch their cigars, smile, and watch the waves. The secrets of their past were locked tightly in their hearts. *Omerta.* The Don smiled secretly as he thought about Bephino.

Morrano's wife would whisper to Dana that Emilio really loved Bephino and trusted him very much. Although the women did not approve of their husbands' business, as usual in these Italian families, they had nothing to say about it. They were not allowed to ask questions or discuss the men's business. But when it came to spending money, they had no difficulties. They would go shopping and buy the best of everything, and the men would laugh with pleasure when they came home and showed off their purchases.

One Saturday afternoon, the Don called to say that he and his wife were coming to stay overnight. He only invited himself overnight when he had some important business to talk about. While the women and children were on the beach, Bephino and Morrano played cards by the pool. And the Don told Bephino what he had on his mind.

"I need you to take a trip for me," he grumbled, crunching his cigar between his teeth.

"I was wondering when you'd talk about it," Bepy asked with a grin. "Where to?"

"Los Angeles. I want you to represent my family."

"Why me? Why don't you send Big Pat Aniello or Rocco Borrelli? They're your Capos."

"Because you're the one I want to represent me, not Aniello or Borrelli. And because you're the one I want to handle this. This will involve you later on in years."

"OK. If that's what you want, I'll take care of it. When do you want me to leave, and what do I have to do?"

"A man by the name of Alan Stone, from Las Vegas, will be your rabbi from now on. He already has been assigned as your permanent adviser, and he'll meet you in L.A."

"A rabbi as my adviser? I never had an adviser. And I sure don't need a Jewish adviser. I got *you,* don't I? This Alan Stone sounds Jewish."

"That's right, he's Jewish. So what?"

"I don't know. But you said rabbi. Who needs a rabbi? I don't wanna hang around with a rabbi. They give me the creeps. When I was a kid in school, they hated me, those Jews."

Morrano laughed. "Why should they hate a nice innocent boy like you? And anyway, every important Italian man has a rabbi behind him."

"A real rabbi? You mean with the fur hats?" he laughed.

The Don laughed, too, remembering the rabbi Bepy had in mind. "No, it's a term we use. Rabbi means a 'good-luck charm.' He's just a Jewish man with brains. He'll bring you good luck.

"He's yours. He'll be available to you whenever you want him. He knows all the answers, and if he doesn't know, he'll find out for you. This is what we mean by a rabbi. He keeps you informed. He does what you want."

"Sounds like some kind of a genie. Everybody gets good gifts. Me? I get a Jew." Bepy laughed. "I can't believe this. You could have bought me a race horse. Instead, you give me an Israeli."

"You will like this man, trust me," Morrano said, smiling. "Listen to me, Bepy. It's important that you trust me. This is a good gift. In return for his loyalty, friendship, and advice, you will protect him. He will also front for you in any big deals. He will represent you to other Jewish people."

"More Jewish people. Sounds great."

"But in return, you must keep him safe from outsiders."

"*Speta,* I even gotta keep him safe? Beautiful. I love the gift. I'll lock this guy in the closet."

Despite the seriousness of his intentions, Don Morrano had to laugh at Bepy. "Seriously now, Bephino," he said, "this Jew owns a hotel in Las Vegas. The hotel will be like yours." Bepy's eyes widened. "Sometimes he has problems collecting from other families and tough guys around the country. You will collect it. It's easy for you. You can handle the tough guys. If you need me, I'm always available to you. You're to keep half of all collections you handle. Stone gets the other half. OK, Bephino? I want this friendship for you. I know you need a man like this, even though you may not think so. I have one; all don's have one. You must have a Jew like this behind you."

Bepy was puzzled. "All dons have one? I'm not a don. I'll never be a don. I got you if I need advice. That's enough, isn't it?"

"No, it's not enough. I'm getting old. You must be prepared to be on record throughout our world," Morrano replied. "You must get in the records now, while I'm strong enough to control our people."

Then he changed the subject and began briefing Bepy on the real reason for the West Coast trip: a meeting in L.A. with the Grimaldi brothers.

"You have to be very careful with these brothers. They are terrible people and, even worse, they're stupid people. They make wrong decisions. Don't trust any of them. They're three *carfoni* from Sicily.

"They loaned Alan Stone two million last year for his hotel, a large, beautiful hotel on the strip, called the El Banco. And now they've refused the two million plus interest that was originally agreed upon; they want a piece of the hotel. Alan has the money ready for them, but they've refused it. And while he's trying to pay without giving them a cut, they're charging him thirty percent interest. So you are going to represent me and negotiate with them.

"All decisions must be made by you. Handle it with care and try not to make trouble. If they try to hurt you, then do what you think is necessary. Once you leave here, you are not to contact me until after the deal is closed and you return. Don't even call me on the phone to say hello. My phones are tapped, and it's easy to slip into the wrong conversation while we're talking, so you make the decisions. But try to keep it nice. Negotiate.

"Now do you understand why you must go to L.A.? Why you are to handle this? I need a man with style and class. A man who can outsmart them, like a good salesman. These guys are my enemies from way back. Big Pat is too old to handle these guys; his brain has slowed up, and he'll lose his patience to negotiate. He'll hit them. I know Pat. They're very bad people, with no heart. And very hard to deal with. Big Pat will turn thumbs down at the first sit-down, but I know you'll negotiate. Be careful, Bephino. You'll be in their camp, and they have no respect for no one. Not even me."

Bepy puffed on his cigar in silence, and Morrano added, "Try your best to negotiate, as I said. That's always the best way."

Two days later Bepy arrived in Los Angeles. Alley Oop and Crazy Mikey were with him. Stone had a beautiful suite waiting for them. It had two bedrooms, a living room, and two baths. A chauffeur-driven limo picked them up at the airport and was to remain with them for the duration of their stay. All this was paid for by El Banco Resort, Inc.

Alan Stone was waiting at the hotel suite for a private meeting with Bephino Menesiero. Over hors d'oeuvres, cocktails, and small talk, Bepy appraised his new Jewish friend. He was a richly tanned man of medium build, with manicured fingernails. His short, curly gray hair and eyebrows were neatly groomed. Heavy-rimmed, thick-lensed sunglasses sat on his slightly hooked nose. He had a square chin and pearly white teeth, and looked like an attractive, mature businessman trying his best to look young. His clothes were flashy but casual, and he wore heavy gold chains around his neck. He puffed a large Teamo, secured in a holder, which seemed more for style than for pleasure. His lingo was humorous, and he spoke with a smile. Bepy liked what he saw in Alan Stone.

"The first thing I want you to do is get rid of the chauffeur," he said.

"How come?" Stone asked.

"I don't want anyone around who doesn't have a personal interest in this thing. Go downstairs, Mike, and send him home."

While Bepy and Stone talked, Alley Oop peeked in once in a while, but never entered the room.

After Stone had left, Bepy took a book out of his attaché case and began to read. He was trying to learn more English words. It kept him calm before a battle. Pronouncing the words in a low voice, he whispered, "Cre-a-tiv-i-ty, pro-duc-tiv-i-ty, ob-jec-tiv-i-ty. Cred-i-bil-i-ty, cred-i-bil-ity..." The word seemed to hang on his tongue.

"What ya readin', Chinese again, Bep?" Alley Oop asked, walking into the room. He lifted it slightly to see the cover. *How to Speak Proper English,* by Professor William C. Sherwood. "Why d'ya wanna learn English? You already know it. You speak it every day."

"Yeah, but not properly enough to keep up with these slick California guys, Alley. This book teaches me a lot more than I know. It also calms me down, because at the moment I'm pretty worked up over this fuckin', crummy trip to California to listen to some paranoid guy tell me he ain't paranoid. *Ah capeesh*, Alley?"

"*Si, io capeesh*," Alley answered.

"Alley, I gotta do a lotta thinking about this guy. I'll make a decision for him. He's gotta realize we're for real. He may confuse my kindness with his weakness, and that's bad for our friendship." Looking back at his book, Bepy said, "It's a good book, Alley. It's gonna help me learn to speak better. You should read it, too."

"Nah. I don't need to learn English. I already speak it good."

"Hey, Alley, what time is it?" Bepy asked. "My watch is on the table."

Alley, looking at his watch, replied, "It's two minutes before ten till nine."

"Whatta ya mean, two minutes before ten till nine? What is it, twelve minutes to nine?"

"Yeah, yeah, twelve to nine. That's what I said."

"Maybe you should get a book on how to tell time." Bepy suggested.

"Come on. I can tell time. I just get confused with that little handle moving around all the time," Alley said, defending himself.

Bepy smiled and began reading his book again.

Alley Oop returned almost immediately. "Hey, Bep. You know that guy you're just talking about, Alan Stone? Me and Mikey think that guy's Jewish."

Bepy smiled at his faithful friend. "Alley, our life now is beginning to change. The negative now becomes the positive for us. It'll be all right, Alley. Don't be concerned."

"Yeah, that's what I thought," he walked back into his bedroom and closed the door, to give Bephino his privacy.

Alan Stone arranged a meeting with the Grimaldi brothers for the next day at an exclusive Beverly Hills Italian restaurant off Rodeo Drive that was frequented by starlets and movie people.

Pete, who was the oldest of the three brothers, set the pace, speaking first. "We get a piece of the El Banco hotel. That's what we decided, so there's really nothing to talk about. You flew here from Brooklyn for nothing."

"Mr. Morrano says different." Bepy replied. "You're entitled to interest on your money at the same rate that all families charge—not thirty percent compounded daily, like I understand you're asking. You must be reasonable. Trust is important in this business of ours. Loans would be out of the question if you required properties and businesses as payment in lieu of cash. The interest rate here sounds like a vendetta against Mr. Stone. Mr. Morrano wants this settled fairly for all concerned."

"If Mr. Morrano wanted this deal, why didn't he lend Stone the two million in lieu of cash that he didn't have?" Pete replied with a grin. "He turned his back on Stone, didn't he?"

"I don't think Mr. Morrano would ever turn his back on Alan Stone," Bepy responded coolly, "That's why I'm here."

"Yeah?" Sam, the youngest brother interrupted loudly. "Well who the hell are you, Bephino Menesiero? We never heard of you. Who the hell are you supposed to be? You're a nobody. We shouldn't even be at a table with you. It's an insult to my brother Pete."

Bepy smiled, then wiped his lips as the waiter, bringing the drinks, interrupted their talk.

A good-looking girl came to the table and hugged Sam. She was introduced as Christy McBride, a dancer in a show in town. Her eyes focused on Bephino.

Bepy smiled at the woman, casually glanced at Sam, then returned his gaze to the woman. He saw collusion on their faces. Christy charmingly, but obviously, focused on Bepy. She was a big, sexy thing—a tall, light brunette with big tits and a rounded ass like the perfect counterweight. Her thighs were protruding through her skimpy skirt. Yes, she looks like she was born to be fucked, Bepy thought.

"Christy, have a seat and stay a while," Sam invited.

She sat down next to Bephino, asking him to slide over in the booth. Very casually, she occasionally brushed against him. He never looked at her. Instead, he watched Pete's expression change as the conversation dwindled.

After a while, Sam flicked his hand, and Christy almost instantly said she had to go.

"Gentlemen," Bepy said when she was gone, "let's try to settle this in a mutually agreeable manner. You are entitled to full payment of the principal plus a fair interest rate on your loan. I have the authority to make an especially good deal with you, something that should be satisfactory to you."

"Who the hell gave you authority to get involved in this thing?" John Grimaldi, a very hard, square-faced giant, asked angrily. "What the hell are we doing sitting with this guy anyway?" he asked, turning to Pete.

226

"I told you gentlemen that I represent Mr. Morrano and that I'm here to close the case. Mr. Stone has now been assigned to Morrano's group for his duration."

Stone swallowed at the word *duration* and puffed his cigar to conceal his nervousness, which only made him appear more nervous.

"Stone assigned to a New York group? Who the fuck did the assigning?" Sam asked. "Suppose we don't wanna do business with you, Menesiero? Suppose we escort you out of L.A. in a fuckin' sack?"

The table became silent as Sam carelessly lost control of his tongue.

Bepy was trying to keep from spitting in Sam's face for talking like a moron. He decided, instead, to soften the tone of the conversation.

"Now why would you wanna talk like that, Sam? I thought I was your guest. We haven't even finished our pasta and already you're escorting me out of town in a sack."

He stared hard at all three with a disgusted look. "Here I am trying to talk serious business with you gentlemen, and you're talking sacks. Let's be businesslike and not *cafoni*, OK? Have some respect, Sammy. I'm not a soldier. I'm here to negotiate. *Ah capeesh?* I'm in California only to help out and discuss business, not to provoke you fellows into a war. Business is business, war is war, and I'm a businessman. You don't have to threaten me. I'm nobody important. And nobody will even look for me if you hit me. So save your sack, OK? You don't have to accept my offer, but I expect you at least to hear it out. I expect some courteous treatment while I'm in L.A." He was trying hard to convince them he was not capable of ripping their gizzards out or plucking their eyeballs from their sockets.

"Don't call me Sammy; call me Sam," Sam murmured.

Bepy looked up in surprise as he heard familiar words.

"Hold it Sam. He's right," Pete said. "He's our guest. We talk business. We don't have to agree on nothin'. We can listen to him."

Then Pete leaned over close to his brothers and whispered, "He's a nobody. Don't scare him anymore. Let him enjoy his dinner and let him talk. Then later we chase him back to Brooklyn."

The brothers nodded. Bepy heard Pete's words and he smiled meekly. Stone opened his eyes in disbelief at Menesiero's acquiescence.

"Let's have our dinner. We'll talk business later," Pete suggested.

When they resumed the discussion, Bepy said, "Mr. Stone is prepared to pay you one million above the principal loan of two million. You'll get a total of three million—cash—which is not a bad deal. That's fifty-percent interest on your investment, twenty percent more than you're charging to close this deal. But the compound stuff is out. That's an insult. High interest, OK. Compounded is a word bankers use. This way we all go home happy. I'll arrange for immediate payment upon your acceptance of my offer."

The men puffed cigars and sipped coffee as they listened to Bepy trying to settle the deal peacefully. "I think that's the fairest way for all, one million profit. You were talking thirty percent," he reminded them. "I'm offering fifty-percent interest only for the term of the loan, not for the time you took refusing payment. If you people agree, we'll close the case right now. Emilio Morrano would like to see this settled with both sides satisfied, for old times' sake."

John threw his napkin carelessly on the table. "I still can't accept the idea of you guys from New York getting involved in this. My answer is no. I wouldn't settle this deal for four million. What d'ya think of that, Bephino, or whatever your name is? And you can tell Morrano he can keep his men in New York and out of L.A. This is our deal with Stone. We put up the cash, not him."

"Yeah. I ain't goin' for the deal either," Sam said in support. Pete remained silent.

"You say you won't take four million?" Bepy replied sarcastically. "OK, what about five million? I'll give you five million to settle this thing right now. I'm in a spending mood at the moment, gentlemen. Will you close it for five million? But you must promise never to go into El Banco. You and Stone are *finito*." Bepy was losing his patience.

The three Grimaldis were thinking and nodding their heads. It was obvious the five million sounded good to them. "How come you're so interested in us closing this case fast? You jumped to five million in two seconds," Pete asked. "How come? Ya think that you guys are gonna take the hotel? Go tell Morrano to stay in Brooklyn, and in them poolrooms, and leave hotels to us. OK?"

The other two laughed in support of Pete's message to Morrano. "My answer is still no," he said as he flicked ashes in a plate.

Bepy grinned, "Look, fellows, I tell you what. Not to be disrespectful to you or to rush you people, I'll stay here a few days. You think about it, and we'll talk again. OK? Alan will call you tomorrow at three. Why rush your answer? I'm sure you want to be reasonable and respectful to Mr. Morrano. He expects this from you, for old times' sake," he added.

The three brothers laughed again. "Is that what he expects? *Ah respecto?*"

"Yeah, that's what he expects—*ah respecto!*" Bepy replied. "So please give this some serious thought. We're talkin' five million to end this."

That night, back at his hotel suite, Bepy watched television. Alley and Crazy Mikey were snoring like two gorillas in their room. At ten the telephone rang. It was Alan Stone.

"I just finished dinner over at Charlie Wongs," Alan told him.

"How was it?"

"Terrible. When I bit into my egg roll, there was a fuckin' note in it."

"A note? From who?"

"It said, 'Bang—you're dead.' It has to be from Sam. I know it. What d'ya think of that? Are they nuts or are they nuts?" Stone asked.

"Boy, these guys really are stupid. They don't even know the difference between an egg roll and a fortune cookie," Bepy joked.

"Yeah. My date thought it was a joke, also, but I ate the rest of the meal with a lump in my throat. I'm sick. These guys are too strong. They even prepare my Chinese food now. I'm finished. I've even been thinking about killing myself," he groaned. "How could you offer them five million? I don't have five million dollars to give them. I may as well shoot myself now. Who could raise five million? I'll have to borrow again. The most I've got is three million, and that puts me in bad shape. I can't go along with that deal, Bephino. I don't think you're handling this problem in my best interest; we look weak. I'll go out on a limb and make it easy for everyone. I'm buying a rope tomorrow. You people can fight over my will. I know a big tree that's got a good, stout limb. I think this deal will cost me my hotel—and maybe my life. We're up to one hundred an' fifty percent. Whose interest is this anyway? Whose best interest is this? Tell me. We're dealing from weakness."

"On the contrary," Bepy said, trying to calm him. "Your best interest is why I'm here. These fellows seem like radical men. They threatened me, then fed me. Usually they're supposed to charm you, feed you, then kill you. These guys work opposite to the rule. They make you sick before you eat. It's gonna be tough to make a deal with them. They're wild. And this is their territory. But I've seen this before, Alan. So I play with them a while, and now they fed you a note in your egg roll to make you scared and try to weaken you. Remember, they refused four million on their own. I offered five million to feel them out. I just met them today. Don't expect a miracle in one sit-down. I'm making myself appear weak. It's better for my final decision; it gives me more room. They'll trust me because I appear soft and scared. Everyone trusts a weak person. I'm watching their moves, and though they seem strong, they're being stupid. Let me do this my way, Alan. I believe they'll get nothing. Zero."

"What d'ya mean, zero?" Alan replied. "These guys will make chowder out of us. They're crazy. You know that, don't you? Next, the soup blows up in my face.'

"Yeah, I know, but I see the handwriting on the wall. We probably can't deal with these guys, but we can try. I know they're bad."

"Bad?" Alan exclaimed loudly. "These guys killed half of L.A. last year. Do you know who you're dealing with, Bephino?"

"Yeah, I know. That's why at the table today I decided to give them nothing. I'll talk to you tomorrow. Don't worry. I can handle this. Right now, I'm watching Peter Lorre on television, and I'm missing the best part, Alan. He's sticking a knife in Sidney Greenstreet's back, and I don't wanna miss it. See you tomorrow. Don't worry, OK? It's my problem, not yours."

"Who's worried? I'm sick already."

Bepy laughed. "Relax, will ya? You're playing into their hands. That's what they want."

"Well that's what they got," Alan mumbled. "A scared Jew who can't stand egg rolls anymore."

"Call me in the morning. We'll have breakfast together."

About an hour later, there was a knock at the door. Bepy opened it slightly and saw the tall brunette from the restaurant, smiling.

"Good evening, Bephino," she said. "Can I come in?"

He was surprised, but he unlatched the chain. "Yeah. What's up?

"I thought I'd come over and tuck you in."

"How come? And how'd you know my room number?"

"Let's just say I like guys with curly hair from New York, so I tipped the desk clerk."

Bepy knew that the room was registered in the name of Alan's hotel, not his name. She had blown it already. Now he knew she was Grimaldi's pawn for sure. She'd been sent by the brothers to keep him off guard in case they decided to hit him. He looked her up and down and thought he'd like to throw her out the window, but he couldn't cause problems.

"Will you pour me a drink?' she asked.

"Help yourself. There's the bar."

Christy moved toward the bar and helped herself. After a short time, she asked, "May I use your bathroom, Bephino? I gotta tinkle."

"Go ahead, but make it snappy. I'm gonna hit the hay soon."

About ten minutes later, she came out wearing only panties, bra, and garter belt. She looked unbelievably sexy in her high-heeled shoes, which forced her plump buttocks to become more rounded and fill her panties. Her breasts bulged out of a too-small bra, and her nipples were visible through the sheer fabric.

She strolled up to Bephino as if walking in a Miss America pageant, snapped his suspenders, and dug her fingernails into his white-on-white shirt. She began to breathe on him and lick his lips, acting like a hot cat in heat. Then she kissed him passionately.

"Do you always act like this after a tinkle?" he whispered to her.

"Sometimes," she said, with her eyes open wide. She smiled and began rubbing herself against his pin-striped pants.

"I bet you could fuck all night tonight," he said.

"You know it," she sighed. "And all day tomorrow. I'd love to suck you, Bephino," she said dropping slowly to her knees.

He pulled her up off the floor and guided her to the couch. "Look, miss, you just got here, and already you're giving me head. What's with you, huh?"

As she reclined on the couch, she spread her long legs wide. "I got the hots for you. Can't you see that?" she said. "Come on, darling, play with me," she invited, pulling her panties to one side.

"Whatta ya gonna do, play with it?" he asked bluntly.

"Yes. Is that what you like?" she asked.

"Yeah, that's what I like. Work on it. I'll be right back. Get it ready, real ready," he told her. He knew she was sent from the Grimaldi camp to do a job on him, and she was making a good attempt, but he was not going to fuck her.

He stopped and looked back at her. She smiled sexily at him and began to caress herself with stroking fingers, licking them between strokes. Oddly enough, she really was horny; she wasn't faking it. She wanted him badly. Her eyes were dilating. She was really enjoying herself solo, her tongue licking at the darkened room as she waited for him to return.

Suddenly, she sat up stiffly, arching her back, moaning and gasping in pleasure. Prematurely and unintentionally, she had brought herself to a climax.

Bepy returned with Alley and Mikey and saw her straining her loins in pleasure. He told them to take her to their room and take turns fucking her until the next afternoon. They were almost in shock. "Holy Christ," Alley said. "Where'd you get her?"

"She climbed in the window," Bepy said. "I want you to fuck her brains out, and when she can't walk, call Sam Grimaldi and have him pick her up. But fuck her good, Alley. Do a job on her. I don't want her to forget this important moment of her life."

Alley was standing there in his extra-large black-and-white polka-dot boxer shorts, looking like a half-dressed panda. He bent over and grabbed her, trying to be gentle. Christy was still experiencing waves of aftershock and still trembling. Alley Oop stopped and looked back at Bepy. "She's still comin'," he said.

Crazy Mikey, glaring at this beauty climaxing before his eyes, thought he had died and gone to heaven. He began to scratch his head nervously, eagerly anticipating their return to the bedroom.

Christy, still intimately involved with herself, looked over at Bephino and, in a gasping, harsh voice, mumbled, "You bastard, you."

"What did you say your name was, honey?" Bepy asked her.

Alley Oop echoed the question. "Yeah, what's her name? If we're gonna fuck her, we'd like to know her name. Right, Mikey?"

"Yeah, names are important when it comes to sex," Mikey answered, scratching his rump. "Look at her," he said. "She can't turn off."

Staring at the men and listening to their conversation, she swore at Bephino again. "You son of a bitch. I'm not going with those two morons. Listen to them. They're stupid."

"It's bad manners to talk while coming," Bepy said. "As you said, you have all day tomorrow. So take your time. Be nice to my friends. Don't call them terrible names. They're very nice guys, once you get to know them."

She was led away. She would never forget Bephino Menesiero from New York, who had turned down a beautiful woman in heat. It took great courage on his part, he thought.

The next morning, Bepy met Stone for breakfast. He told him about Christy McBride. They laughed as he described the look on her face when she saw Alley Oop and Crazy Mikey standing in a daze in their large, loud-colored undershorts.

"Alan, I gave your problem a lot of thought last night. First, we offered these bums three million, and they responded with a refusal of four million. You're only willing to pay three, right?"

"Right."

"But now they think they can get five million."

"You're right," Alan replied. "They figure five million is in the bag. We shouldn't have mentioned five. Now they've got the figure five on the brain."

Bepy was quick to catch Alan's use of the word *we* and responded just as politely and with the same emphasis.

"We didn't mention five, Alan. I did. I will deal with these men my way, and the day they live to collect the five million from El Banco, you will have a beard down to your balls like Rip Van Winkle. OK, Alan?"

Alan did not respond.

232

"So the way I see it," Bepy continued, "these guys will be real trouble for us. There's no satisfying them unless you give up a piece of your hotel. And this, Morrano said, is out of the question. And the offer of five million was a joke, in case you didn't catch it."

"Thank God," Alan remarked, fumbling with a gold chain hanging around his neck. "Strength at last. These brothers work very diligently at their jobs, you know. For fuckin' morons, they persevere."

"They persevere? The only way for the Grimaldi brothers to persevere in peace is for me to kill all three of them. They will persevere peacefully in their graves. These men are disturbed, Alan. And I will be instrumental in seeing that they achieve their peacefulness. So I made a decision. I'm gonna dispose of all three, like removing rubbish from society. Only their mother will miss guys like that."

"I was hoping it wouldn't get that far," Alan mumbled. "With my luck, I'll probably have to deal with their mother. She'll probably show up with black high-heeled shoes, trying to collect for her boys. How you gonna do all this without a war?"

"There's not gonna be a war, Alan. There's only gonna be a funeral. There's a difference. A funeral is always much easier and much quieter than a war. We have on our hands three important underworld figures in L.A. They all gotta go at the same time, so it's gotta be something special. You know, like a big accident—plane crash or something."

Alan looked into Bepy's eyes. "You mean like flying the three of them somewhere in a small plane, then having the pilot bail out, leaving the three brothers staring at each other?"

"Yeah, something like that. But in a small plane the guy can't get the privacy to put on a parachute. And the route planning and that stuff make it very difficult to do. It's gotta be something more simple, but realistic. Do you know any stuntmen?"

"I know a guy who used to be a stuntman."

"What's he doing now?"

"Nothing. In fact, he'd be perfect; he's out of work. He's a gambler, and he owes the hotel at least fifty grand the last I heard. And I'm sure his markers are still outstanding."

"That's my man," Bepy said. "Get him for me. Tell him I'll pay him fifty grand and clean up his markers in your hotel. That'll get him interested."

"OK. I'll call him tomorrow."

"No, call him today and call him direct. Don't go through other people. I don't want anyone to know we're in contact with him. Where does this guy live?"

"Vegas. The schmuck's a bad gambler. He loves Vegas. They say he also was a bad stuntman. I understand he got hurt a few times."

"That's good. He sounds like a born loser. You contact him, and tell him we meet in Vegas. Make the appointment for late tonight. Call the Grimaldi brothers to a meeting sometime today."

That afternoon Bepy sat across a table looking at Pete Grimaldi. "How about it? What did you fellas decide?" he asked. "Can we make a deal or not?"

"Yeah, we all agreed to take the five million and keep peace," Pete replied.

"That's it, though. That's the deal; five million or nothin'," Sam said. "All in cash."

"I was gonna pay you by check," Bepy told Sam.

"Are you nuts or what?" Sam screeched across the table. "We gave this Jew cash; we want cash back."

Bepy smiled; that was just what he wanted to hear. "OK, Alan. Pay them five million in cash. That's their price for peace, and we all want peace. These men have their price," he repeated. "I'll tell Morrano we did our best for you. I got to head back to New York in a few days. Let's all leave for Vegas this evening. I'd like all three of you to come as our guests for some fun and a few laughs and to pick up your money. I will not risk transporting that kind of cash. You guys can handle it.

"We'll all meet tomorrow at El Banco Hotel about three for the count-up. I want all three of you to get the cash so there's no stories, OK? I will witness the money being paid to you and I will report back to Morrano when the deal is completed. But remember that will be the last time you set foot into the hotel!"

The Grimaldis agreed to go to Vegas and get the cash.

"And, Sam," Bepy suggested, "don't forget to stop at my hotel and pick up your girl friend. My friends fucked her so much, the kid probably can't walk. She's gotta be bow-legged by now."

"What girl friend?" Sam asked, playing dumb.

When Bepy returned to his suite later that day, much to his surprise Christy was still there. She was fully dressed and waiting. Alley Oop was watching TV with her. Bepy looked her over. The sexually spirited girl of the night before had been reduced to a useless pawn. She looked docile and pale. It was apparent she was totally fucked out by her guardians.

"Didn't those bastards claim her?" he asked Alley.

"Nah. Nobody called for her."

"Did you feed her?"

"Yeah. We fed her, we fucked her, and we gave her a bath. She's all powdered up and ready to be sent back to them," he murmured exhaustedly. "Can I sleep now? I'm beat from all this action."

"Yeah, go to sleep. I'll wake you later. We leave for Vegas at six o'clock."

"Can I go now?" Christy asked softly.

Bepy stared right into her eyes, a silent smirk crossing his face, trying to reduce her further.

"What the hell are you lookin' at, Bephino?" she screamed suddenly, glaring at him angrily. "You could've had it all for yourself last night. No way! You gave it to those fuckin' morons. And now you're staring at me with those horny eyes! I wanna go home. OK?" she whimpered. "Just let me leave."

"I'm sorry if you think my eyes are horny, because I didn't want you, honey. I just felt sorry for you. They were eyes of pity. Actually, I wouldn't even piss on you. You're a hustler pig spy for a worse bunch of morons. You're a dumb cunt that's being fucked by morons back to back. From New York to L.A., you hump them all. Are you proud of yourself? You begin to masturbate at the drop of a hat. It don't take much to turn you on, does it? You started off with a tinkle," he reminded her. "Then the next thing, you had your hand up your ass, in public no less. Doesn't that bother you?"

"No, it doesn't. One word from Sam Grimaldi and I whip it out. Do you want me to warm it up for you so you can eat it hot? Or are you afraid of getting dirty and messing up your fancy suit?" she asked him sarcastically.

"You're a very pretty girl, but a very disrespectful person. And a very bad spy. For your information, Sam doesn't have the smarts to keep you from getting hurt. He's a fuckin' wart, without an ounce of class. Last night I thought I gave my friends a classy piece of ass. Nice thighs, long legs, big tits, and a pretty face, but you just devalued my gift. You're just a nothin' broad, and they'll probably be unlucky and end up in some veterinarian clinic trying to get rid of some strange strain of clap."

She jumped up, tossing her long silky hair back. "Veterinarian hospital?" she asked him chokingly.

"I said clinic."

"Do you want me to masturbate for you or not? I know you loved it, you pervert! You're a pervert. Why don't you admit it? I know people like you. I saw it in your horny eyes." She began to fight back. "You picked a fine time to be celibate, Mr. Stripe Suit. What ya gonna do, your communion or confirmation today?"

"Get the fuck out of here, you little douche bag," he replied angrily. "Be thankful you're still breathing. I must admit, you're beautiful even when you're angry. You look tempting, but you have the heart of a fuckin' mutt. I can look at you, honey, and as a man admire you for being such a cunt, but thank God I don't desire you."

"You don't desire me? Then there's something wrong with you," she said, flaring up. "Every man desires me. Look at me!" she said, raising her skirt to show her naked bottom. "Look at my pussy. Tell me you don't want me. You know you want me bad, unless there's something wrong with you. You're the mutt, not me." Then suddenly she began to laugh, pointing at him. "You're a queer; that's it. You're a fuckin' queen. Stripe Suit is a queer. That's why you don't take me. Wait till I tell Sam. Your men had to do the job for you..."

Bepy hit her open-handed, a hard wallop, bringing tears to her eyes. He stared into her face, looking at the red handprint, "You wear my hand so gracefully," he said. "Don't let me enlarge your rectum to the size of your mouth, honey. Be nice. You've said enough today. Now go back to Grimaldi and talk that shit to those sick bastards."

Her pride was gone. She flipped her hair away from her face and smiled at him honestly for the first time. He opened the door for her and smiled honestly back at her. She seemed to admire his strength and defiance of her sexual advances. She reached out and covered his hand affectionately with hers and whispered, "It could have been something special for both of us to remember. I'm sorry, Mr. Menesiero. This wasn't my idea."

He looked at her with understanding. "I know that and I understand. Don't worry. It'll be taken care of. Stay well...Christy."

Later that night in Las Vegas, Bepy met with the stuntman, who agreed to take the job. The guy was fat and out of shape but said he was able to do it. The stuntman asked for five thousand in advance, and Bepy agreed to give it to him the morning of the job, the balance after it was complete.

The men talked for a few hours before they decided on a plan: the stuntman was to drive the Grimaldis to the airport. On the way, he'd dump the car over a cliff, jumping out just before.

"The car ends up at the bottom of the ravine, and the three brothers become three angels. Simple. It's a simple plan," Bepy said. "It's so fuckin' simple, it'll work. When the police come, they'll believe it was an accident. Alan, you and I follow in our car. The stuntman can go down to get the cashbox, with the five million, while we wait. Make sure the box can take the fall or a hot fire without busting open."

"Don't worry. It'll be built like a safe," Alan answered.

"The plan is an old-time procedure. It's the only way we can hit all three, and better than fuckin' around with guns. Try to booze them up before they leave," Bepy said.

"Sometimes the old ways are best. A cliff-hanger always looks real," Alan agreed.

"I don't want this to look like a phony movie," Bepy said, looking directly at the stuntman, and then at Alan. "Where all the money flies away, and the movie ends."

"Don't worry, Bephino. I'll handle that," Alan said. "Believe me. I gotta clean out the cage to raise that much cash. The box will be the best money can buy...."

"When the Grimaldis see the weight and size of the box, though, maybe they'll decide to get driven to L.A. instead of flying."

"Yeah, you're right. That's possible. We gotta be ready for anything. They might have their own driver standing by. So let's expect the unexpected. I'm sure they're not gonna walk out with five million under their arm without a plan. Unless, they really are stupid guys."

"They won't check that box in at the airport like luggage. So maybe they'll ask *us* to drive them back to L.A. Then we can have more time to play with these bastards," Alan suggested. "That would be great. But with five mil, they probably made arrangements already to rent a golden limo. They don't need us."

"Well, we'll follow behind their car, far behind. When it stops for a piss break, we can move into action and get the box. We'll hit them with all we got and then get the hell out as fast as possible. *Voi capite?*" Bepy asked, winking at Alan.

"*Sì, sì, señor,*" Alan answered, not knowing the Italian.

"OK, let's call it a day. I'm beat. We gotta rest and clear our heads. I can't think good when I'm tired."

Alan was still talking and worrying. "Don't forget, five million is one big pile of cash. These guys are strong. They may have an army hanging around in Vegas to escort them out. Don't you think so?"

"Maybe and maybe not. We'll see soon enough. This is something that's hard to plan. We gotta wait and see. If we have to scrap this plan, I have something else in mind," Bepy said.

"Suppose they refuse our assistance and take the cash and blow town with their own escort? What'll we do then? This could turn out to be a fiasco."

"Don't you think I got them tailed," Bepy said curtly. "I know everybody they're talking to in this hotel. If I feel their people have arrived, my decision will be to nail them in their rooms and bring them out in suitcases, nice and quiet. You got three large trunks available, Alan? Have 'em ready.

"Look, if I have to, I'll even hit 'em in your bed. Make sure your sheets are clean. The only reason they're still alive is I'm trying to make it clever and clean, and that takes considerable planning. Otherwise all it takes is a machine gun. Come, let's forget this for a while."

Later that evening, when Alan and Bepy were alone, Alan asked, "How about the stuntman?" He peeked over his respectable spectacles waiting for Bepy's reply.

"Can he fly?" Bepy asked. "When he comes up with the box, we take it, then Alley Oop throws him back down to his grave. If he can't fly, he's fucked."

"Yeah, can he fly. That sounds good," Alan said without laughing. "I made sure to tell him to use the first open-pit mine that's closed. It's right after a sharp right-hand curve."

"We need a real ghost town for this thing, so nobody will see this happen," Bepy told him.

"Don't worry. I know most of the mines in this area. I used to buy shares for tax shelters. I know them all. This one's only about fourteen miles out of Vegas. It's a deserted spot. The only question is: Do you think they'll get wise, driving fourteen miles out of the way? The airport's only three miles out."

"Maybe not, if the stuntman drives fast and keeps talking. Maybe they won't realize how far they went. What are they going to do? Shoot him? They'll probably be busy planning what to do with the money. It's gotta work. We have no choice.

"Why don't you take a ride with him and Alley Oop to case the area. Check the ravine and make sure the state didn't fill in the fuckin' hole, OK? I want a few-hundred-foot drop, at least. I want a dry run before the hit. The area must be well known to the stuntman. Let him practice his moves. He's gotta be right on target. And don't drive out there with a limo. Limos in the desert are eyecatchers."

The next day, about three, the Grimaldis were suddenly in a great hurry to leave Vegas, they told Alan Stone. They wanted the money the following day and no later, and were going to the airport with the box and flying back to L.A. They had 2:00 P.M. reservations, and asked to be taken to the airport at one. "We only need a ride to the airport," Sam said.

Alan told them his limousine would be made available to them.

The next morning the counting and inspection of the money took place, and the Grimaldis were soon ready for their departure.

At the last moment, they made their move. Sam, having second thoughts, refused a limo from Alan and insisted on taking a cab to the airport instead. "It's OK, fellas," he said, shaking hands with Bephino and Alan. "If you're ever in L.A. again, stop over and say hello."

"Whatta ya mean, take a cab? Alan got his limo ready for you. Go ahead and take it to the airport. Have a good trip. The car is in front waiting for you," Bepy insisted. He knew now they would never take the limo, so he kept forcing it, making them feel safe and happy that they were taking a cab. They now believed they had outsmarted him.

"No, we're taking a cab. Don't worry. We'll be all right," Sam insisted. "We'll be less conspicuous in a cab."

Look at this prick, Bepy thought. He thinks he's one step ahead of me all the way, huh? They really are stupid guys.

He had anticipated this move, so a stolen cab was ready.

Alan ran into his office, saying "I'll call for a cab." He called downstairs to the stuntman and told him to take the cab, not the limo, and pull up in front. "They'll be down in a minute. Make sure they get in your cab. Be alert." Talking to himself, he muttered, "These guys like cabs, so we give them a cab."

The Grimaldis took the box and walked to the front of the hotel like three soldiers going AWOL. They were in a hurry, and climbed quickly into the waiting cab. "To the airport," they told the driver.

The stuntman pretended he was reporting his trip to the dispatcher. He was actually talking to Bepy in the car pulling out behind them. He asked, "What airline?"

"TWA. We're in a hurry, so get going," Sam said.

The phone setup had been rigged by Crazy Mikey to a plain-looking sedan for Bepy, Alan, and the boys.

"Yellow cab twelve," the stuntman said. "Three passengers to TWA, Vegas air terminal, leaving El Banco Hotel at 1:05 over and out." Following orders, the stuntman left his radio on, so Bepy could hear the Grimaldis conversation. He was a little surprised when he heard a reply from Mikey ordering cab twelve to report to Muddy Creek shopping center after his drop. "There's three Indians that just hit the jackpot, could be a good tip in it for you." The stuntman held back his smile.

The three brothers started to relax as the stuntman sped toward the ravine. They were talking so much they didn't realize they had passed the airport three miles back.

"Did you see their faces when I told them to forget the limo, we're taking a cab? That fuckin' Bephino's mustache dropped to his chin. And how about the Jew? He nearly shit. They think we're stupid. I seen movies. They close the window in those limos and pump gas on the guys in the back seat. They probably had that all ready for us." Sam laughed at his own words.

"I got four boys waiting for us in L.A.," John told his brothers. "If these guys try anything, that's where they'll do it—in L.A., not Vegas. So our boys are at the airport waiting. We gotta get the box home fast. Those jerks back there don't know we've got a private plane waiting. They think we're dragging this box on a commercial airline."

"Bephino asked me what airline we're takin'," Pete said, laughing. "What a fuckin' schmuck he is. I told him Alaskan, and he believed me!"

Bepy smiled as he listened, thinking, "The schmucks rented a plane but forgot to rent a car."

"Boy, those guys were scared. That Bephino don't know his ass from his elbow." Sam laughed again. "We scared 'em good with that sack story. He couldn't eat; he couldn't even fuck Christy. Nobody in their right mind turns down Beverly Hills' highest-paid piece of ass! Did you see how fast he came up with the five mil?"

"Yeah. He didn't care about the money. He was so scared, he was happy to give away the Jew's money, just to make a deal," Pete said. "Morrano sends a guy like that to settle a deal like this. He must be getting senile. He's lucky we didn't hurt that kid.

"I thought ol' Alan was goin' to choke on his cigar when he heard five million," Pete added. "Little did they know we would've taken four."

"I can't get over that fuckin' Bephino didn't even fuck the broad," Sam remarked. "He's just a punk. The broad said he was strong and refused her outright. She admired him for that, she said. I say he was fucked up in his mind and couldn't get a hard dick."

"I think he's a punk fag," John remarked. "He acted like one. Mr. Morrano this and Mr. Morrano that. . . . The guy's a fag. I'm sure. Nobody refuses Christy."

In the midst of all the laughing and joking, Pete looked up in surprise.

"Hey, shouldn't we be at the airport by now? Wasn't that road back there the way to the airport?"

"I'm going around the back of the airport. To avoid the construction jam," the driver said.

"Don't you know these Nevada drivers are just like the ones in New York?" Sam said. "They fuck you on the clock. They're goin' to take the longest way. Don't worry, we can afford it." He patted the box.

"We gotta come in from the rear of the airport. The front is being paved today, so I gotta go around," the driver explained. "I'll turn the flag off if you want me to. They announced it on the radio today that the road would be closed."

The cab began to climb up a hill.

"You're going up a fuckin' hill, friend. The airport is down there," Pete stated.

They were almost there. Just a little bit more. The driver peered in his rear-view mirror and saw their eyes look all around.

The cab reached the ravine and the stuntman drove right up to it doing sixty miles an hour, just as they had rehearsed. With his left hand, he swung his door open at the last second and rolled awkwardly onto the sandy ground, almost rolling the remaining twenty feet to the edge of the cliff. He'd misjudged the speed and distance and was hanging on the edge, head first, but he managed to avoid going over.

Alan and Bepy were watching anxiously from their car. "What a schmuck!" Alan yelled. "He almost went over himself. Look at that shit. He almost went with them. We could have lost him before we got the box back. The fuckin' guy's a bad tumbler."

Bepy's face was like ice, and he didn't answer Alan. He was listening to the Grimaldis, still talking over the speaker.

"Hey, where'd that driver go?" Sam yelled. "Oh, my God. What the hell? That fuckin' Bephinooo . . ."

Bepy smiled and said, "If I could've only seen their faces, it would've made my day complete."

The cab had flown over the edge, crashing onto the rocks at the base of the cliff, then bursting into flames.

"Get the box," Alan screamed to the stuntman, running to the edge and looking at the flaming wreckage, waving his arms, his gold neck chains flopping around. "Get the fuckin' box before it melts." He was a nervous wreck.

The stuntman quickly climbed down into the ravine, slipping on loose rocks and sliding most of the way on his ass, to retrieve the box. The cab was still in flames.

"I can't get it! It's too hot!" His voice echoed off the ravine walls as he looked up at the four men.

"Get the fuckin' box!" Alan screamed hysterically, his voice also echoing. "Get the fuckin' box!"

Horrified to see the box wedged between the melting springs of the seats and the dead Grimaldis, who were seemingly trying to grasp it even in death, the stuntman reached in and tried to grab the charred handle. He recoiled in pain as his fingers adhered to the hot metal. Struggling and in pain, he managed to get the box half out of the wreckage, hindered by the charred body of Pete Grimaldi, who seemed to be clinging to the box.

Seeing the body, hair still smoldering and flesh melting, he screamed in terror, waving his burned hands at the men above. "It's too hot! I can't get it! My hands are burned!"

"Get the fuckin' box!" Alan kept screaming. "Don't give me no shit! Hurry up, before it melts!"

The stuntman looked around, picked up a heavy branch, and returned to the wreckage. Pushing the smoldering skeleton of Pete back into the cab, he managed to free the box and drag it away. He took off his belt, tied it to the handle, and began to drag it back up the side of the cliff.

When he reached the top, Crazy Mikey helped him with the box, pulling it up the rest of the way. Alley Oop shook his burned hand and warmly congratulated him on a job well done.

The stuntman, totally exhausted and breathing hard, indicated that Alley's firm grip was hurting his hand. When he tried to break the handshake, Alley held on tighter. Then he picked him up and threw him back down the steep ravine.

Earlier that morning, Alan had given the stuntman an envelope with five thousand in cash. It was marked "Thanks" and signed by Pete Grimaldi. It would look as though the stuntman had business of his own with the fried Grimaldis.

"It really seems so funny that those fellas fell for such an old trick, switching cars and falling off cliffs," Bepy said while riding back to the hotel. "It's on TV every day. But it still works. Unbelievable how it still works."

The job had gone smoothly. The Grimaldi brothers flew to Los Angeles by way of the four-hundred-foot cliff. Alan got his money back, and everything was kosher. He was happy, but his nerves were shot, so he stayed in his penthouse suite for the rest of the day.

Two days later the men were back in New York. "What happened over there?" Don Morrano asked Bephino. "How come you had to whack four guys to settle this thing? I asked you to negotiate. Is that what you call negotiating? Whacking four guys? Compromise?"

"I tried to make a deal," Bepy explained. "I tried very hard. But they acted stupid, like *cafoni*. At one point they offered to put me in a sack. You said negotiate, and I did. I tried to compromise, but it was impossible. They were very unreasonable people. They made the decision for me. It was

242

the only way to settle it. They were outlaws. They wanted five million, or the hotel, in return for two million. Those guys were crazy and, you were right, stupid to boot.

"From the start of our talks, they had no respect for me or the Morrano family, and they told me this bluntly." Bepy spoke seriously, then smiled. "How you gonna negotiate? Those guys had no respect, none at all. They sent you a message. Stay in your poolrooms in Brooklyn and keep out of the hotel business. So they had a dreadful accident on the way to L.A. Did you read the papers? They even stole a cab. Wasn't that stupid of them?"

"Yes, we read the papers, and we were worried about you in Hollywood. We thought you were making a movie there," Don Emilio said, squeezing Bepy's shoulder. "They were never reasonable men. I know this. I just hoped it could be settled easier." He chewed his cigar and drank his black coffee, whispering to himself. *"Sta beni,"* he said. "Now you know why I sent you, Bephino. It's a shame, but even in Sciacca them boys never had *ah respecto*, not even in the Old Country. I remember that when Pete was a boy he stole my bike. He was always *pazzo*, even then. *Morte e uno topo*. Death to a rat."

Bepy grinned, but really wanted to laugh at the bike story. Morrano remembering about Pete's stealing his bike after all these years! What a thing to remember! But he knew the Don was satisfied with his decision to end all discussions with the Grimaldi family.

"Alan Stone asked how much he owed for these services. I told him to contact you for that answer. I thought maybe you would like to decide the price. Because he's ahead three million now."

Don Morrano puffed again on his cigar and looked at Bephino, his friend who never once forgot the meaning of *rispetto*.

14

Home with his family a few weeks later, Bepy woke early one morning and went to the kitchen for a glass of orange juice. There he found the twins, eating from a large bowl. They were now plump eight-year-olds.

"What are you kids eating?" he asked.

"Pasta lendica," the children answered.

"At seven-thirty in the morning?" he asked. "You eat cold *pasta lendica,* and out of the same *piatto.*"

The twins giggled. "It was left over from last night, and we were dreaming about it. And, Daddy, Patsy ate my mozzarella yesterday. He didn't save me none," Renee called out to her father.

Trying to keep from laughing, Bepy walked back upstairs and said, "Hey Dana get up and check on your kids. They're down in the kitchen! They take after my brother, Mario, eating cold pasta for breakfast. They dream about *pasta lendica* instead of cornflakes or ham and eggs. And go buy a case of mozzarella. I just got a complaint from your daughter."

Dana staggered sleepily to the kitchen to retrieve her cubs.

Later that day, Bepy met with his men to discuss future business plans. Alley Oop and Crazy Mikey bragged to Monkey, Joey D, and Little Pauli in great detail about their trip to the West Coast and the beautiful, sexy girl they fucked for sixteen straight hours.

"Boy! Her legs were so long, she was like a giant squid," Alley said. "She wrapped them around me twice. She was like a real animal—am I right, Mikey?"

Mikey grinned and his eyes lit up. "Yeah, she was a real giant *calamara.* Would you believe she sucked two pricks at one time and stuck all her fingers up both our asses all at the same time. I still can't believe it happened. Alley's right; she was like an octopus."

Bepy listened and then asked, "Are you guys through telling your octopus stories? I suppose you were like two dancing daisies while her fingers were up your asses. We'll talk about sucking cunts later, OK?"

"Who said anything about sucking cunts?" Alley answered abruptly. "We didn't suck her. She sucked us. Right, Mikey?"

"OK. But take the fingers out of your asses and let's talk a little business. And, yeah, if you guys start to drip, go to a vet, not an MD. I think she was a . . ." Then, remembering how Christy had stood up to him he said, "Nah, she wasn't a bad kid, after all. She had guts for a broad."

"Yeah, she had some cunt, too," Alley said. "You should've saw it, Bep. Just like fur. It was like mink. You really missed out on something!"

Bepy cut the kidding off by saying, "I'm glad you guys enjoyed her." Then he informed them that they were expanding their business into Mexico, through a new importing and exporting company that he and Alan Stone had recently been working on. The headquarters would be in Mexico City.

244

"I've had this idea for a long time. I mentioned it to Alan, and he said, 'Let's do it.' So an overnight decision was made. Alan's already been talking to some large stores. They seem interested in handling our products."

"What products? We ain't got no products," Alley said.

"Yes, we do. Pottery and furniture, to start. It's all made in Mexico! They already sell it on the West Coast. We're gonna flood the East Coast, Canada, and Europe."

Then he turned to Joey D and laughingly said, "Since you look almost like a Mexican, you will have to head up the office and warehouse operations in Mexico, and we gotta find you a new apartment."

"Apartment? Me?" Joey D asked in surprise. "I don't look Mexican. Why me? You're joshing me, right, Bep?" He looked at Bepy's eyes, then excitedly yelled, "Why don't you send Alley Oop? He looks like a . . ." He stopped after glancing over at Alley Oop.

"Nope. You're a Mexican, all right, and you're going to Mexico," Bepy told him. "You're our man, Joey D, and you're going with me and Mikey. So get yourself adjusted to the idea."

"Why do I get all these shit jobs?" Joey D complained. "Now you guys are putting me in exile. I got a lotta obligations. I got responsibilities. I got commitments in this country. How can I leave America? People will miss me. I can't go to Mexico. I don't know anybody there. Who'll I talk to?"

"Who's gonna miss you?" Bepy asked. "Only your mother, that's all. You're gonna have a beautiful life, fuckin' all those hot tamales. You'll have wall-to-wall pussy! Our company will rent you a villa. You'll live like an ambassador, ya schmuck. You'll have it good there."

"But look, Bepy, I got broads in Brooklyn. You know what I mean. How am I gonna leave them? I got commitments. You guys don't understand," Joey D protested.

"Yeah," Monkey cut in. "He's got broads, all right. He screws all the retards' wives. He makes the rounds once a week to all their houses. You know, like he fucks Norma twice a month, and this one, and that one. He even fucks Vera—you know, her husband's the guy who sells shoelaces on the subway."

"Vera gives good head," Joey D yelled at Monkey. "She's a terrific blowsky. Whatta you know about broads, ya fuckin' ape?"

"Maybe she's a good blowsky, but she's also about eighty-two years old, ya fuckin' mutt. Go to Mexico and do us a favor. You're an embarrassment to our neighborhood." Monkey laughed.

"Which Norma is he fuckin'?" Bepy asked.

"You know, Norma, Red's wife," Joey D answered. "She ain't bad. She's a little fat but she's young."

"Yeah. Alley told me a few years ago I had to hump her at least every month, because Red was through as a man. And you gave the order she was to be screwed every month by me."

Bepy glanced at Alley questioningly. Alley looked back at him with his oriental smile and large ivories.

"Yeah, Bep, at Mr. Fat's tomb," Alley Oop explained. "You said, 'Have Joey D fuck Norma, why should she suffer, Red's finished as a man.' So I told the schmuck, and he ran right over."

Bepy had completely forgotten about this unimportant remark. He began to laugh heartily as Alley Oop continued.

"So when Joey D goes over there he brings a bag of shopping for her and the kids. He makes his rounds. Nicea nice. He does the right thing. Joey's a sport."

"Yeah, nicea nice. He fucks the whole neighborhood with his plastic shopping bag," Monkey yelled. "The guy's got an imagination like a fuckin' whale. He takes home the empty shopping bag for the next trip. I seen him on the subway with the bag folded under his arm. I mean this guy is an embarrassment to us!"

"Joey D, what did Norma say about this?" Bepy, still laughing, asked.

"I told her you gave the order, so she had to do the right thing. And she's fuckin' my brains out. She's afraid, Bep. The broad is scared. The minute I walk in the house, she starts giving me head. I give it to her a few times a month, just to keep up the commitment."

Bepy felt a jolt of remorse for Norma. He abruptly changed the subject.

"We leave for Mexico City Monday morning. Be ready. Tell all your broads you're leaving. Wind up all your commitments, because you are leaving on Monday. Understand, Joey?"

"I should've bought that newspaper stand that was up for sale at Madison Square Garden. I coulda made a good living without losing my citizenship," Joey D yelled. "What the hell's next for me—China?"

Alley butted in. "He's talking like a bimbo—newspapers his ass. He's got it made with us. Whatta ya wanna be a bimbo selling newspapers for? And freezing your balls off behind them stands, huh?"

"Yeah, so I'll go to Mexico and sweat my balls off in the heat with diarrhea. Is that better? No sports. No Yankees. Only diarrhea. That's all."

Bepy looked at Joey D and whispered, "You're less than competent and you're very sports-minded, ain't ya? How ya feel about parades? Do you like parades with horses?"

"Don't worry, I'll be ready," Joey D mumbled. "I'll be ready."

That evening, they all went to the Italian-American Club for dinner and a little gambling. Ben came in from Staten Island. Even Alan Stone was in from Vegas. He fell in love with the Italian food at the club.

Alley Oop got in a dice game in the back room. They could hear him yelling and cursing in Italian. He was calling his numbers out. When he didn't make his point, he cursed the devil; if he made it, he praised the saints. "Seven, seven I need...Ohh, no, not snake eyes! I'm dead. That's the eyes of the devil! I hate you."

While they were having coffee, smoking cigars, and relaxing, Alley Oop entered the dining room, smiling and counting money. "Hey, fellas, I just won twenty-one hundred dollars from them stupid guys in there."

"No shit, Alley, ya won?" Monkey yelled. "Beautiful! Now you can pay the check."

"I knew I could beat them, I knew it." Alley grinned triumphantly.

"How did you know you could beat them?" Ben asked.

"Their eyes told me the story. Their eyes were half open; they were tired men, like guys that were jerkin' off too much. I seen it in their eyes. The weakness gave them away." He smiled and strutted across the floor to the men's room.

"Look at Alley," Monkey pointed. "He feels so good, he's quoting Shakespeare."

"Shakespeare?" Ben asked.

Bepy, Joey D and Crazy Mikey left for Mexico on Monday as scheduled. They stayed for two months, organizing the new Mexican corporation, though Bepy spent a lot of time flying back and forth from Mexico to New York. Much work went into starting up the new company. Joey D revived his dormant talent for figures and became an impressive businessman. He also surprised everyone when he showed he could handle the Mexican people smoothly.

Trucks rolled out of Mexico, crossing the border at El Paso. Twenty trucks a day were soon heading for their New Jersey warehouse. From the warehouse the products were shipped to four hundred clients Alan and Bepy had lined up. They had convinced the retailers to have special "Mexican Handcraft" sections.

The Mexicans were by then working seven days a week, sixteen hours a day to keep up with the orders. Joey D was like an American ambassador to them. He was a changed man, and ran International Amex Corporation like it was his own.

Bepy knew that Don Emilio continued to praise Bephino Menesiero, the Schiacchitano, to other families, like he was grooming him for bigger things. But Bepy was interested in business, not in being talked about by the Mob. He had got in it for the money, not the glory, and now he wished he was out of it. Although he never said it, he really wasn't interested in making any more hits. He'd been lucky the police had never thought of him as a hit man.

For the new enterprise he met with the big buyers, and planned the advertising strategy, using business magazines and newspapers in the U.S. and Europe. Spanish products had become popular, and low-cost Mexican crafts filled the demand. The discount department stores were his largest clients. Bepy was incredibly pleased and satisfied with the results of the new venture.

Bepy then shifted his attention to his Las Vegas interests. He spent more time with Alan Stone. He was getting along very well with his rabbi. He had learned to respect Jewish brains and Mr. Stone, so they became very close. Dana couldn't believe Bepy could ever feel that way about a Jew, but he made it known that Alan would be treated as family. Everyone liked Alan very much; they thought him a beautiful person.

Bephino Menesiero had become well known in Los Angeles and Las Vegas after the dismantling of the Grimaldi family. The new L.A. boss became a great ally of the Emilio Morrano family, and Bephino's name was whispered at parties as the man to know.

Christy McBride, who was doing a lot of her own whispering after seeing how quickly the Grimaldi's had disappeared, had only kind words and praise for him throughout the jet set. She claimed to be a personal friend. Privately, she shivered at the thought of her near sexual encounter with Bephino Menesiero.

In February 1962, Bepy and Alan went, with Alley Oop and Ben, to a villa in Puerto Vallarta owned by a leading movie star and good friend of Alan's. This was a vacation, but Joey D had seven meetings set up for them in Mexico City. There they had a hectic schedule.

They were now shipping from Mexico directly to Europe, not via the United States. The Mexican export fees were significantly lower for European buyers. A fantastic deal for both buyers and sellers, and the reason for several of the meetings. The last meeting was with two gentlemen from the Netherlands, who entered the executive offices of

International Amex Corporation like foreign diplomats, smiling. One man introduced himself as Baron Dirk Van Steir, of an Amsterdam firm; the other was Jean Chaval, of the Paris and Brussels branches of the same firm.

Bepy felt he recognized the latter, but did not say so. He was careful not to show any sign of recognition. As they began to discuss business, he studied the man. He had to be sure.

After ten minutes of foreplay, Chaval made an unexpected request. "Gentlemen, I'd like a private meeting with just the immediate heads of International Amex." A familiar sound rang through Bepy's ears as he spoke. "Can we clear the room for a while? I have something very private to discuss," Chaval said, waving smoke away.

Bepy was reluctant but wanted to hear what Chaval had to say, so he nodded to Alley, Ben, and Joey D. Only Alan remained, puffing on his Teamo cigar.

"Open the window before you leave, Joey," Bepy said.

The two Europeans seemed more comfortable as the smoke cleared, and Chaval began slowly talking.

"I hope you understand that the atmosphere, from all of the men smoking in here, was not very desirable. I hope we did not offend anyone."

"No, you didn't. It's the end of our day. We all began to relax too soon. Go ahead with what you have in mind. We are listening," Bepy replied.

"Mr. Menesiero, you have been recommended by important people in New York as the person who can handle any type of deal."

Alan choked on his cigar; he could tell what was coming next.

Bepy also knew what was coming. He looked with distaste at the two men and asked, "Who in New York told you about me?"

"I'm not at liberty to say," Chaval replied.

"Did you ever live near a U.S. Army base in France?" Bepy asked.

Chaval stared at him as recognition, then fear slowly spread over his face. He remembered the court-martial.

"What the hell's going on, Bep?" Alan asked impatiently, but, looking at Bepy's eyes, fell silent.

"You want us to move drugs for you?" Bepy asked coldly.

Chaval could only nod his head in the affirmative.

"Ahh, Monsieur Cocksuckoor," Bepy said softly. "You're back in my life; a million-to-one shot and we meet again. First you want to put me in a French prison. Now you insult me with a drug deal. You really are a little cocksucker, aren't you?

"What a small world, Alan. I can't believe what a small world it really is. The only man I hate in Europe shows up here in Mexico to insult me for the second time in my life. This has gotta be fate."

Alan got up to shut the window as Bepy got louder.

Chaval, who had turned white, nervously declared, "I don't know what to say. I didn't come to insult you, sir. We were hoping to make a deal with you. I just don't know what to say. You can understand my . . . reasons?"

"What's wrong?" a confused Van Steir asked. "What's going on, Jean?"

Bephino, enjoying his confusion, smiled at the Frenchman.

Chaval, seeing his smile, misunderstood and began to feel better. He started to speak like he had in France, his tongue flickering with self-esteem. "It was a very long time ago, Mr. Menesiero. I'm sure you can understand, can't you?" Then he smiled at Alan and explained. "Many years ago, this man hurt a French boy. I had no choice but to speak the truth."

"Yeah, it's true," Bepy said, interrupting. "It was a long time ago, and I did hurt a French soldier. It was a barroom brawl. Anybody could've gotten hurt. We all were drunk." Bepy's memories ignited his emotions. "How about you, ya little shit? You sell drugs. How many boys do you hurt each year? How many, ya fuckin' little creep?"

He walked to the door, opened it, and asked Joey D, "Do you have a rope anywhere?"

"No, but I can get some electrical wire." He took from a closet a coil of about sixty feet of thin rubber-insulated wiring.

"Yeah. That's fine."

Bepy tossed it to Alley Oop, who was sprawled out on the couch in the front office. Speaking in Italian, he said, "Tie this little cocksucker by his ankles and hang him out the window. I hate this sharp-tougued bastard. He's a fuckin' crook—worse than us—and he plays the fuckin' good guy."

Chaval, who understood Italian well, made a sudden lunge for the door. Alley Oop stopped him with a bear hug. Ben tied his feet.

"Please don't, sir! Please, sir, don't do this!" Chaval screamed, grabbing for something to hold on to.

Ben opened the window, and Alley Oop picked him up and dumped him out like an unwound yo-yo, holding him by the wire. Chaval screamed as he dangled, fourteen floors up, from an office building in Mexico City.

Meanwhile, Van Steir was having a nervous breakdown.

"Vot are you doing? Vot, are you people crazy?"

Bepy told him to hold the wire or he was next. As soon as he grabbed it, Alley and Ben let go.

"Are you crazy?" he yelled, struggling with the wire. "Help me, please! I can't hold him alone!" The weight dragged him closer and closer to the window. With the wire slipping through his hands, it looked as though he would drop Chaval.

Alan nervously took a look out the window, then motioned to everyone to stop. "Come on, pull him up. That's enough already. The guy looks dead. My stomach's turning. This is crazy."

Van Steir collapsed, and the wire slid quickly across the floor, uncoiling itself like along snake. Chaval was on his way to meet St. Pete.

Everyone grabbed for the wire as it slithered out the window and began pulling Chaval back up. They weren't too gentle as they pulled him in, banging his head against the building and scrubbing his face against the brick and the window sill. When they pulled him in, his face was bruised and cut. They put him on the floor and removed the wire from his ankles.

Joey D quietly rolled the wire back up very neatly and stored it back in the closet.

Chaval had turned blue but was still breathing, but after about twenty minutes his color was much better and he was breathing normally. He was obviously very shaken by his ordeal. If he ever spoke at all about it, it would be softly, not sharply. He had seen Death.

Bepy told Van Steir to take him back to Europe as soon as possible. "Get out of the drug business. You guys are hurting youth all over the world. Kids in Europe and all over are getting fucked up from drugs, and you are responsible for it. Now leave our office, and don't ever contact any of my people about drugs, because the next time it will be the end of both of you."

After the two Europeans left the office quietly, Alan asked, "Did you do all that to the guy because of something that happened many years ago?"

"Of course not, Alan," Bepy answered bluntly. "I did it because when I think of my little twins, I wonder what they're gonna find when they get out into the world. The dope people are destroying our society. And it's those miserable bastards in France and Holland we fought for and died for that now sell drugs to our children. And, believe me, Alan, someday you'll see them fuck America good. They really hate us, the jealous bastards. They won't even give us credit for saving them in the war.

251

"Look, Alan, I'm not a barbarous man, and I don't consider myself a religious man either. I'm a businessman. A barbarous man would've dropped the bastard out the window. I let him live, and the funny thing about it is that I'm not sure I did the right thing.

"Someday our country will ask Europeans for help, and they'll refuse us. I'll bet you anything on that. Maybe I should've dropped him. I hate drug dealers. They're shit."

Then he smiled ruefully at his men. "It's four o'clock. I've had enough of this bullshit. Let's go to Joey D's villa and have a drink. Tonight we have dinner with the Mayor of Mexico City. And tomorrow we leave for the ocean."

"Yeah," Ben agreed. "I love that place, Puerto Vallarta. It makes Staten Island's ocean look like a garbage dump." Then he moved up beside Bepy and whispered, "You should've dropped that French bastard out the window. You're getting soft, Bep. You're getting soft. Now ya got two guys to worry about—him and Red."

"Leave him alone, Ben. Don't get him crazy. He's crazy enough already with this business. Let him be soft. It's better he be soft," Alan yelled over, waving his cigar.

Bepy agreed. "I know you're right, Ben. I should've let the twerp fly." Then jokingly, he said, "Mr. Ben Delponte, you're a real Merry Undertaker. You're never happy unless you get a body, huh, Ben?"

Ben smiled like a cobra as Alan remarked, "You guys make some team. You chop 'em, he buries 'em."

Near the end of their stay in Puerto Vallarta, Alan asked Bephino, "Is it OK to host a gala party at the villa this weekend? Your wife and Ben's will be arriving Thursday. We'll throw a big party for them."

"What do you mean, gala? What the fuck is 'gala'? You wanna have a party, have one. Don't talk Jewish. Sure, go ahead. Have a gala party. Charge all expenses to International Amex. Ben, call Joey D. Have him fly in for the gala weekend. He loves *gala* parties. And, Alan, make sure all the Jews from Acapulco come to our gala party, OK?"

Alan laughed as Bephino rubbed it in.

Dana and Peggy arrived at the villa. They fell in love with Puerto Vallarta; it was paradise to them. They had a ball shopping.

That afternoon, everyone sat around the pool drinking, relaxing in the sun, and listening to a three-piece Mexican band.

"Boy, you live some life, Bep?" Dana said. "Who owns this house? It's beautiful."

"We rented it."

"That's nice. You rented a house. I'm home in the snow washing clothes and you're here humming like a bird and listening to your own band."

"Sometimes it's good, sometimes it's bad. You only see the good times, Dana," he said, rubbing lotion on his body.

"I think I only see part of the good times," she replied, pulling the tube from his hand.

"You know, Dana, you really got a clear head. You think I got the world by the balls because you hear a little music, but you're wrong. It takes a lot of hard work to get to the top. And, believe me, I've been through a fuckin' nightmare and I was awake all the time."

She smiled and hugged him. "Sure, I know, darling. You work so hard."

"That's why I never invite you to my good times, Dana. You're full of shitty remarks. Enjoy the place; you may never return."

"Oh, yeah? That's what you think."

Saturday's party was indeed a gala affair, one that everyone would remember. There were personalities from Hollywood, Acapulco, Mexico City, and Puerto Vallarta at the villa. When the word got out, all kinds of people showed up. The place was crawling with jet setters. Everyone was loaded; drinks were being poured over the rocks, and even over some of the wild large-breasted women. All kinds of exotic things were happening. Dana approached her husband. "I thought you said this house was rented."

"What's the difference? Have a good time. Does it matter who's house it is?"

"Yes it does. There're pictures in the game room of all kinds of movie stars, and I see your face smiling in one of them."

Bepy smiled. "Be nice, will you?" He squeezed her with affection as he kissed her face. She kissed him back.

One young girl, Sheila Diamond, was feeling so good she began to dance and strip for the crowd. The music had gotten to her blood and the wine to her head. She was a short, honey blond with hefty tits. She danced and shook her ass all over the villa, and before anyone knew it, she was born again, stark naked, with high heels, a gold chain around her neck, and wearing a suede watch band. That was her costume while she performed an unbelievably erotic dance.

Alan watched her dancing and then searched the crowd for Bepy.

"What should I do with this broad?" he asked. "She's a Jew kid from the Bronx. She's been dancing balls naked for the last half hour. She's starting a commotion with all the wives. We gotta do something."

"Where's Dana?" Bephino asked, glancing around. "I'm surprised I haven't heard from her about this."

"She's in the game room playing the nickel slot machines with Peggy."

"Good. They'll be there for the night then. Let's go see this broad. Maybe we'll let Joey D cast her for a movie. He can sign her to a one-night contract. He's probably tired of Mexican meat, anyway, so we'll treat him to a kosher belly dancer."

"Good idea." Alan laughed. "I'll put her with him. Two schmucks. They'll be all right together."

Ben leaned over to Bepy and whispered, "Letting our wives come to this place was like taking a ham sandwich to a smorgasbord. Am I right, Bep?"

Peggy, coming up behind him, heard the remark and replied, "Yeah? Being married to you is like eating a jelly sandwich instead of steak."

Sunday afternoon the wives left for New York and the men went to Las Vegas for business. Sheila hooked up with Joey D and left for Mexico City to stay at his villa. She moved in with her male Great Dane and two cats.

When the four men arrived in Vegas that evening, problems were waiting. The casino manager reported to Alan that a couple of guys from Dallas had received credit for half a million bucks and had gone back to Dallas without paying their markers. After a number of telegrams and many phone calls, the two men had finally sent word that they were connected with Pete Falcone.

"I guess that means we can't collect," the manager said.

"Who's this guy, Falcone?" Alan asked Bepy.

"He's a boss in Dallas," Bepy said. "I'll look into it. Put all the details and markers in my office. Tomorrow I'll look them over and decide what to do. Now I gotta sleep; call me for breakfast."

"OK, Bep. You want breakfast in your suite or mine?"

"Let's have it in the coffee shop. Good night, gentlemen."

The next morning, Alan, Bephino, Ben, and Alley Oop were around the table. Ben was trying his best to down a poached egg. Alley Oop had a double stack of pancakes, with eggs and steak on the side, a milk shake, and bananas with whipped cream waiting on hold. The other two just had coffee and English muffins.

Alley Oop flagged down the waitress for more rolls.

"He eats like he's going to the electric chair," Bepy said, grinning. "He loves food."

"The way he orders, I'm sorry I own the hotel," Alan said. "I get stomach pains thinking about supporting a gorilla like him."

Everyone began to laugh, because they knew Alan was only kidding. He threw money around like water, and he really enjoyed seeing Alley Oop eat.

"You're lucky, Alan," Bepy replied. "Ben and I are leaving for Dallas tonight. We leave Alley Oop in your custody. Feed him well."

"Yeah, I know. One hundred pounds of raw beef daily, right? Why are you leaving for Dallas?"

"Well, I looked over the Falcone markers this morning. One-half-million collection—of which I get half if I collect. Right?"

"Right," Alan agreed.

"Well, I'm in the mood to earn a quarter-million. Do you want me to work on it, or do you want to let your collection department try again?"

"My collection department is my *dreck* department. They already tried for a month. This looks like a scam. It's yours, Bep. You handle it."

"I've heard of this Falcone. He's a tough guy, who talks real sweet, with a nice drawl, but he'll kill you while he's feeding you and smile all the way through dinner. I heard about him from Morrano. He's an Italian cowboy. He was born in Dallas, his mother and father came from Italy. The guy controls from Texas to Georgia and is connected with Santoro in New Orleans."

"Oh, he's like those Italian Rebels in New Orleans? They look like us, but talk different," Ben recalled.

"Yeah, something like that. We gotta be careful with this guy. He's bad news. He'll try to hurt us just to set an example, to show he doesn't take any shit. Besides Santoro, he's friendly with that Rebel group from Savannah. He has strength. I know that for sure, but I know we can handle him if we get to him."

That night, in Dallas, Bepy called Falcone from a street phone and, after receiving the run-around from his answering service, finally managed to set up a meeting for the next night at the Mustang Club, one of Falcone's cowboy nightclubs. During the telephone conversation, the service tried to find out where Bepy was calling from, but was unsuccessful.

"She asked where we're staying," Bepy told Ben. "I'd never give a guy like that our hotel number. He'd be on us in a minute; we'd be sleeping and he'd be all over us. The guy's a cowboy, with all his broads and whorehouses. I'm not taking any chances with this one."

"How you gonna collect from a guy like that?" Ben asked. "This guy's a knock-around guy. It ain't gonna be easy."

"Maybe I won't collect—but if I don't, he won't live to spend it," Bepy vowed menacingly. "I'll give him one chance at the table. After that, I'll kill him to set an example for guys that think they can scam El Banco Hotel. If he doesn't pay, we'll hit him before the month is up. They gotta have respect; they know this hotel is with me. The word went out after the Grimaldi hit. All the Mob guys know this. That's why I'm acting quick on this thing."

"I was wondering why you jumped on this so fast. I knew you must have a reason. Are you gonna make it exotic?" Ben joked as usual.

"No, Ben. If I have to hit this guy, it won't be done by me. And I won't give him the compliment of an exotic hit. It'll be just a plain old rub-out—Mob style. I do want publicity on this one. Maybe a machine-gun job, like the old Chicago days. But I'll have to be in England or some place so the FBI can't prove I was involved. I gotta stay clean; that's real important. I'll get the fame, but not the blame. We're enjoying the absence of scrutiny. That's been an important factor in our lives. Do you agree, Ben?"

"Yeah. I agree with you. But I never really thought about it before."

"We'll probably have our hit guys piss on Falcone's coffin or something, just to make it exotic."

"I thought so." Ben laughed. "You're always with them exotics. Where'd you learn that word *exotic*? But you're right, Bep. You can't let them walk in your hotel and take the credit and think they don't have to pay it back. If we hit this guy, the word will spread all over that he didn't get away with it. But do you think any of his people will try and get back at us?"

"I really don't think so, but that's the chance we gotta take. In these Southern gangs, the number-two man is usually a Southern preacher. He'll go for the money first and the broads second. He's gonna be too busy taking control to worry about us."

The next evening Bepy and Ben arrived at the club at nine o'clock to meet with Falcone, but he wasn't there yet. Two goons seated them at a table.

"All the drinks are on Mr. Falcone," they were told.

A cowboy was singing on stage, with a band playing a beautiful Western ballad, about cool water.

"Is he coming?" Bepy asked.

"He'll be here later. Ya wanna wait or leave? It's up to you," one guy said flatly.

Bepy smelled that Falcone was up to some shit, letting them drink on the house and get drunk and tired so he could deal with sloppy people. He must have realized they were in Dallas for a reason, so he was going to act strong and let them wait and get drunk.

"Do you think he'll try anything here?" Ben asked.

"No. He owns the club. It's the first sit-down. He'll wanna hear what we have to say. If he doesn't like what we say, he'll try to lure us with some pussy. Then, in the early-morning hours, he'll try to blow us away."

"You really think so?"

"Well, that's what I would do if I were him. So that's the way I gotta think."

Finally, near midnight, Bepy went to the men's room to enjoy that overdue piss he had been holding for Falcone. Ben followed him quickly.

"Bepy, I think he's here. Some guys just walked in with two beautiful chicks. He had the goons jumping around when he talked, so it must be Falcone." Then Ben began to laugh and talk at the same time. "The fuckin' guy's dressed like a cowboy. I don't believe it. Like a cowboy in the movies."

"Is he wearing his six-shooters? Come on, let's go meet this guy."

He led the way to Falcone's table, where they introduced themselves and shook hands.

Falcone, speaking in a drawl, motioned to empty chairs. "Sit down, boys, have a drink. I'm sorry I'm late. I was detained by these two young heifers."

The two women were large-breasted Texas cowgirls, wearing vests partially opened to entice the world.

Ben whispered to Bepy, "Did you hear his voice?" Then he had to look away to keep from laughing. Bepy kicked him under the table. But Ben continued. "Look at them tits. They're like melons, and they're making me crazy."

Bepy asked Falcone if he could get rid of the dolls for a while. "We have important business to talk about."

Falcone, reluctant to release the girls, said, "You can talk in front of them. They're with me."

"Are you kidding? Talk in front of them? They're broads. Whatta ya mean, they're with you? We got business to discuss. Get rid of them a while."

"No," Falcone answered coldly. "I'm not kidding."

"Well, this is a first for me, a sit-down with girls present; but I guess every day is a new experience. OK, Don Falcone, you want to do business in front of broads, it's OK with me. You people scammed a half million from a hotel in Vegas," he said, careful not to mention names. "You know of it because you approved it. Your people say it was your idea.

"Now, Vegas knows you're the type of cowboy who would rather die than pay back the money, so these hotel people have decided to have you hit. They've already put a contract on you, effective next Tuesday at 6:00 A.M.

"The contract was accepted by six bad niggers, money-hungry mothers who can't wait for the checkered flag to fall. If the first six coons fail, six more will be coming for you, and if they fail, six more will come. The contract runs until you're dead, which, considering the way you dress, shouldn't take too long," Bepy said, jokingly. "You're not exactly inconspicuous. But, regardless, you'll be hunted from six Tuesday morning until you're dead.

"If you wanna live, Falcone, make sure the cash is paid back by Monday noon. That gives you the rest of this week to get your cash up to Vegas. I was paid twenty thousand just to give you this message. I'm only carrying a message of importance, so I'm sure you can understand the interest they have in your future—however brief it might be. The hit men are getting much more than twenty grand. By the way, the reason the contract doesn't start for a week is that you have a friend—I can't mention his name—who requested that you get a chance to square this before the contract was put out. Your friend hates to see you dead. He said you always fix him up with nice broads when he's in Dallas.

"So, seeing that you're Italian, like us, I figured I'd pick up twenty grand, and possibly save your life. But this will be my last contact with you. I drink to your health, Don Falcone." He raised his glass.

Don Falcone tried not to look worried in front of the women. He laughed and said, "I guess it's Blue Monday or Black Tuesday for me, ain't it, girls?" In fact, he was sick to his stomach, and everyone at the table knew it. "That was some speech, son," he said, trying to be cool. "Who wrote it for you?"

Bepy got up and started to leave without saying a word. Ben followed suit.

"Hey, I thought you were staying at the Manor Inn?" Falcone called after them. "I checked all four in Dallas, and you're not at any of them."

"Why? Did you want to take us to one of your famous dinners?"

"No, no. I wanted you boys to have these lovely bed warmers this evening." He indicated the women seated at his table. "You know, Bephino, I think I've heard of you from one of my friends in the South. I'm gonna check you out. Understand? I'm gonna find out all about you. The Big Cowboy in the sky watches over me.... Ya know that, fellas?"

"Go ahead and check me out. Then you'll know the seriousness of this meeting, Mr. Falcone. Take my advice," Bepy said coolly, "there're other hotels you can rob. You just picked the wrong one this time. Oh, and give my regards to the Big Cowboy, because if you decide not to pay what you owe, you'll be seeing him real soon. Good night, my friend. *Ciao.*"

Ben and Bepy left, got into their rented car, and lost themselves in the city.

"Boy, that was really some speech you made," Ben said, grinning at Bepy. "Six bad niggers on contract? And that he had a friend trying to keep him alive? How did you come up with that story? Tell me. I gotta hear this one."

"OK, Ben, another free lesson for you. I knew I couldn't scare him on his own turf. He really doesn't know the name Bephino Menesiero that well. He probably never heard of me, so he could think I'm a real nobody. But he's gonna check me out. Right?"

"Right."

"I took the gamble his blood wasn't red, like New York Italians' blood. So, I had to come up with a story that a fancy cowboy would believe. He knows he robbed the half million. Now he has to decide if it's worth it to have six *tutzones*—he doesn't know—out on a contract. That's a rough contract to know about, especially when it's on yourself. All them jigs look the same to him. Every time he sees one washing a floor, cleaning a toilet bowl, or driving a cab, he's gonna think, Is he my hit man?

"Falcone will worry himself to death with that story. Every guy who walks by he'll have to watch. So I gave him a few days to think. And the more he thinks, the more he won't be able to get the monkey off his back. The cash will be there by Monday noon; I'll bet on it. He can't afford to call our bluff.

"He was a fancy guy, so I gave him a fancy story. Sometimes you just have to play it as it lays. If he knew we were behind the whole deal, we would never get out of Dallas. He'd hit us, believe me. Like Jesse James, he'd blast us cold turkey.

"The part about a friend, well, he must have a lot of friends he gets laid while in Dallas, so that had to fit into my message. He can also think about that for a while. He'll convince himself; you'll see. He'll scare himself to death. He'll think and think. Then he'll realize his life is worth more than the cash."

"Are we going back to the hotel?"

"Hell, no. Are you kidding? Don't sell that cowboy short. After a few drinks, he'll be ready to knock us off, and he could still pay Vegas to get his account square.

"We'll drive to Fort Worth, dump the car, and fly out as soon as possible. Boy, was he a gaudy-looking bastard! That mustache and long curly hair! He looked more like Buffalo Bill than an Italian."

"Yeah. You said his blood wasn't red. If his blood's not red, what color is it?"

"A gaudy guy like Falcone? Probably lavender," Bepy said and grinned.

"And I thought I was a clever hit man," Ben commented. "You're the best, Bephino. You even took his blood type—lavender. That's some shit. But I'll tell you one thing: you're not a lover. I would've banged those chicks for him. Did you see the tits on those broads?"

"Yeah, like two pumpkins," Bepy said. "When I was a kid, I used to go nuts for big tits like that. But now I think I go for more of a medium-built broad."

"I would've stayed to hump them two. They looked so good sittin' there smilin'." Ben looked over at Bepy.

"You mean you would've stayed around tonight to bang those cowgirls? It would've been your last hump, Ben. Falcone would've killed us while we were in the saddle. The guy's bad. Don't let that sparkling suit fool you. Benny, I love you. You're my friend, but you're crazy. That's why he brought those broads there: to tie us up so he could make a decision.

"You know, Ben, I've never seen you shoot even a BB gun. You haven't made an actual hit yet with me. You made me an atom bomb once that didn't work, but that's it. You're really a fuckin' nut. Now you wanna bang cowgirls. That's the real joke of the trip. You wanna stay and fuck under these conditions. I can't believe you. You never wanna do the right thing. What are you, a real sickie?"

"Yeah, I'm a real sickie. And I've made a lot of hits. Morrano likes me," Ben defended himself as he pulled away from an intersection and headed west to Fort Worth.

"Oh? Morrano likes you? But I don't like you, Benny. You're chicken-hearted. You relax. I'll make the hits. Don't worry. I'll look out for you." He laughed as he mocked Ben.

"You know what I'm thinking, Bep?"

"What now?"

"He said he's gonna check you out. Imagine if he asks Don Santoro if he ever heard of you. Santoro will tell him a story that will make him shit his pants."

"Yeah. Santoro will tell him to be very careful before he gets pissed on by a hooker before he gets waxed."

"When we get back to Vegas, let's get two tall, long-legged broads from the show. I really feel in the mood to get laid. But they won't have pumpkins like those two had. They were nice."

"I know they were really sweet, but deadly. Believe me, Ben. Look, there's two new broads in the Arabian show we can grab. They're nice and tall. Alan introduced them to me and they're ready to go. I saw it in their eyes. Maybe I'll take both of them to bed with me at one time. I'll let them eat each other; then I'll bang the shit out of them."

"What about me?" Ben asked.

"Fuck you, Ben."

Back in Vegas, Bepy slept late, and was awakened by the house operator for brunch. While he was in the shower, Alan and Ben entered his suite, and Alan, moving toward the glass door of the shower, called out, "It's me, Alan, so don't get worried."

Bepy looked out the door, soap covering his face and body.

"Hello, Alan. What's up?"

"I called out to you so you shouldn't worry," Alan said, smiling. "I got good news for you. We didn't want to wake you up, so we waited till now."

"Stop talkin' Jewish. I shouldn't worry. Now I'm worried."

"You can pick up your quarter million whenever you're ready. Falcone sent a suitcase full of cash to Vegas, and we already returned his markers to his bag man. You must've really scared him."

"Well, what d'ya know! Falcone, I had you figured right. I just told him a scary bedtime story, so he'd shit his brains loose. He was a fuckin' mutt anyway. The 'Big Cowboy in the sky' and all that bullshit," Bepy said, getting out of the shower and onto the blower ramp.

Ben laughed. "He must of checked you out with Santoro. Hey, Bep. Should I cancel those six niggers?"

261

"Yeah, Cancel them."

"What six niggers?" Alan asked.

"Let's go eat. It's already after twelve. I'm starving," Ben said impatiently.

While they were having brunch, an old comedian came to their table to speak to Stone. Alan greeted the man, calling him Pasquale. Bepy looked at him closely, and remembered him from Miami Beach, many years ago. He waited to see if Pat Zoopeli would recognize him after all these years.

Pat asked Alan for a chance to play the hotel's main room, and Alan referred him to his show director, Sid Feinbloom.

"I've seen Sid eight times in two years," Zoopeli said. "He tells me he'll call and never does. Things are bad. I need a job, Mr. Stone. If I can play Vegas it'll give my career a shot in the arm."

"Look, Pat, I'm having lunch now with my associates. I'm not giving shots in the arms today. Please talk to Sid Feinbloom," Alan said, dismissing him. "That's why I pay him."

"You know, Mr. Stone, I hate to interrupt your lunch, but I really believe Sid hates Italians. He never gives me a break, and he always acts cold to me, like I'm a nobody. And I got a good act. All the East Coast gamblers, the Italians and Jews from New York, love my act."

Ben leaned over to Bepy. "You know who he is? That's Pasquale the Great. He's from Brooklyn. The guy's terrific! Pat does some act. These fuckin' Jews, they always give him a hard time," he whispered.

"That's nonsense, Pat," Alan replied to Pat's remark. "Sid grew up with Italians. He's from an all-Italian neighborhood in Philadelphia. He loves Italians. And please, Pat, you're interrupting our lunch."

Bepy decided that this was the point to enter the conversation. "Nonsense, my ass, Alan. I know a lot of Jews that hate Italians."

Alan was surprised to hear Bepy interfering in his business conversation.

"I worked for a guy named Bernie Melvin," Bepy told him. "He hated me because I'm Italian."

Alan started to laugh; he thought Bepy was joking.

Pat slowly realized that this was the kid he had met many years ago in Florida. They hadn't seen each other since.

It was a nice time to meet again, especially since Bepy felt he was in a position to help Pat.

"What is it that you want to do?"

"I'd like to play the main room with the superstars. I can come out, warm the crowd up for an hour, and then the main show can start after my act," Pat answered. "I can do the job. They love me in this town!"

"He wants to play with the superstars direct from Miami Beach," Alan blurted out sarcastically. He looked up at the ceiling, flicking his unlit cigar.

"Believe me," Pat said, seeing Alan's reluctance. "I can do the job."

"I know you can," Bepy agreed. "You're a great comedian. I agree."

Ben grunted, "Good boy."

"Give him a contract for six months, with an option to renew," Bepy told Alan. "If we like Pat's show, we can renew it every six months. Have Sid draw up a contract today. Pat, you fill in your fee. I'm sure it will be OK with Mr. Stone."

Alan's expression changed from plain surprise to astonishment. His still unlit cigar wobbled nervously in his fingers.

Pat couldn't believe what he was hearing. "Thank you, Bephino. Thank you."

"Don't thank me, Pat. You got a terrific act. You're top-notch, and don't let anybody tell you different, either—especially a Jew. You're Pasquale the Great. You're Italian. And you belong in Vegas." Then, looking sternly at Alan, he said, smiling, "And you belong in the main room, not the fuckin' basement."

Pat again left the table, thanking both men humbly.

Turning again to Alan, Bepy said, "Tell Sid Feinbloom I want to speak to him. If I smell that the Jew really doesn't like Italians, I'm sending him back to Philadelphia, or wherever he came from. Maybe he'll learn to love Italians the second time around, 'cause he's gonna work in an Italian bakery mixing flour on the night shift. And you can tell him I said that."

Alan knew Bepy was upset about Sid, so he agreed coldly. "Whatever you say."

"And make sure all the big stars know who Pat Zoopeli is. They better treat him with respect," Bepy added.

Alan, speaking in a somber, icy tone, then told Bepy, "We have another problem more serious than Zoopeli's."

"What is it?" Bepy, steamed up, asked.

Alan, peeking over the top of his eyeglasses, smiled. "Our corned beef is ice cold, thanks to your Zoopeli," he said, and the men burst out laughing. Alan was coughing and laughing at the same time.

The waitress came over. "Are you all right, Mr. Stone?"

"Bring us new orders. This is cold," Alan said. Then, turning to Bepy, he said, seriously, "We have a dinner appointment with those two Arabs tonight. Is that OK with you? These guys are important to the hotel. They're heavy rollers. I told you about them last week, remember?"

"Ben, you eat with Alley Oop tonight. I'll be with Alan and his clients. I'll see you later in the evening."

After eating, Ben said, "OK, I'll see you guys later."

"Alan, what's with the Arabs?" Bepy asked.

"I don't really know. These guys are filthy rich. They play dice a ton a roll, and tonight they want to talk to me. I want you there. It could be interesting."

That evening the Arabs mentioned that they needed information on how to obtain a hundred American-made automobiles. The United States government had banned all shipments of automobiles intended for use by foreign governments. The Arabs wanted the cars, but no one could help them.

"What can we do for them?" Alan asked Bepy. "How can we sneak a hundred cars out for these guys?"

"First, we check the restrictions on cars leaving the U.S. If there's a loophole, we'll find it, and they will get their cars legally. But how much will you pay for the cars?" Bepy asked.

"It makes no difference. We have the dollars right here in Las Vegas, Mr. Menesiero, and we need the cars badly."

Alan peered over his glasses at Bepy and gave a look. Bepy liked the answer. "OK, one way or another you'll get your cars. I'll let you know in a few weeks."

"Allah be with you, Mr. Menesiero."

"Thank you. I'll need him"

Everyone bowed to seal the agreement.

The next day, Alan and Bepy were sucking down raw oysters and clams at the casino's oyster bar.

"You know, Alan, when those Arabs said to me 'Allah be with you,' it gave me a certain feeling. When I was a kid in Bay Ridge I saw a movie about a sheik, and they always said, 'Allah be with you.' And they rode off into the desert on those beautiful white horses. It impressed me so much as a kid. And now an Arab really said that to me. That's somethin', for a guy from Brooklyn!"

Ben and Alley Oop came walking in, and both were smiling. "Ah, we found you two guys having clams without us," Alley Oop said.

"Come on, sit down," Bepy said, grinning at his loyal friends. "Have a drink and eat with us. These littlenecks are good."

"Tell Bepy about Lake Tahoe," Alley Oop prompted Ben.

Ben nodded and smiled, "Abe Rothman invited us to Tahoe for two weeks as his guests at his hotel. Everything's on him."

"Honey," Alan said, stopping the waitress, "bring us a platter of pearls of the sea. The large one—the hundred-fifty-dollar size."

"See?" Ben yelled. "He had to mention the price. 'The hundred-fifty-dollar size.' A fuckin' Jew is a Jew. He always does it, the same shit. Now I can't eat the pearls of the sea. He spoiled my appetite."

"So starve ya schmuck," Alan replied. "Whose asking you to eat? The hundred-fifty-dollar platter is for three—Alley, Bep and me. You were out from the start. It's fifty bucks a head."

"And bring me four dozen littlenecks," Alley added. "I love them raw littlenecks."

"That's good, Alley. With all that humping you've been doin', you'll need them," Bepy teased, patting Alley on his shoulder. "You go ahead and go to Tahoe. I'll be here for at least two weeks. When you get back, we'll all head for Brooklyn. You guys go and have a good time. Abe Rothman will treat you right."

15

Pat Zoopeli, working under his new contract for the hotel, came on stage one hour before Jerry Laney. Jerry Laney was a very popular country-and-western singer. It was Pat's job to warm up the audience. He did great on his first night; he had them bursting their sides.

Alan insisted that Bepy see the opening of the show, and though Bepy didn't care for Jerry Laney, he went, to keep Alan company and to see Pat's opening night.

They sat in Alan's booth, first upper tier of the middle section. In the booth to the right of theirs were Jerry Laney's guests; to the left were Pat's. To Alan's way of thinking Jerry was paid more than he was worth as an entertainer, but he was a smash at any club or hotel he worked, so Alan enjoyed a sellout crowd. Jerry was a cocky guy. If he wanted to say something insulting, he would say it on stage or off. He had just signed to do a movie, so his head was as big as his ass that evening.

Sitting in Jerry's booth was his wife, Tova, a flame-haired beauty from Sweden. Sitting with her were Felix and Elkie Powsner, the German movie magnate and his very attractive wife, from Hamburg.

The audience applauded like mad after each song, except for Alan and Bephino, who never applauded entertainers. It's company policy in Vegas that owners don't applaud; they just sit and puff their cigars.

"What's wrong with you two guys over there," he yelled from the stage. "Are you depressed or something?"

The audience laughed at his remark. The singer didn't know he was talking to the largest stockholder and owner of the hotel and a prominent man in the New York Syndicate. Although he'd sung in many hotels in Vegas and was fully aware that the center booth areas were usually reserved for VIP's, Jerry Laney did not show proper respect. And to make things worse, he continued to needle them. People in the audience were stretching their necks and leaning over their seats to see who Jerry was talking about. Still Bepy and Alan didn't respond; they just sat there sipping their drinks and puffing their cigars quietly.

Then Jerry, after a joke and a jingle, said, "Yeah, I know what's going on with you two guys sitting together, you're tired from your housework. I understand, fellows."

By this time Bepy was fuming and Alan was infuriated.

"What a schmuck, what a fuckin' schmuck!" Alan, his Teamo clinched between his teeth, whispered to Bepy. "He's pressing his luck."

"Doesn't he know you?" Bepy asked.

"No," Alan replied. "He deals through Feinbloom's office. I never get involved with the entertainment; these people are too temperamental for me. But he should know who sits in this booth."

"I wanna see this bum after the show, when the crowd leaves," Bepy told Alan. "Bring him to my office. Don't let him change his clothes. Bring him to me hot and sweaty, even if you have to drag the little bastard. I wanna see him tonight while he's still feeling so self-important. Look at him shake his ass up there. When I get through with him, he'll be a totally different person. I'll fix his ass real good tonight, the little rubber."

"OK, I'll take care of it," Alan said, smiling. He picked up his phone and called Feinbloom at home.

"Sid, come to the main room now, right now. Come straight to my booth. I want you here yesterday already."

Less than two songs later, Sid rushed in, wearing shoes without socks. He sat down and ordered a drink. When he realized no one was talking to him, he knew something was terribly wrong. Cautious, he remained silent.

Over at Jerry Laney's booth, Pat Zoopeli was casually trying to smooth things out by dropping Alan's and Bephino's names to Jerry's wife. Like a barracuda, Tova was swallowing the stories Pat was telling her. She kept looking over at Bephino, who was directly facing her.

"He's a real handsome guy," she said, as Bepy read her lips. "Is he Italian?"

"Is he Italian?" Pat asked. "Is the King of England English? Of course he's Italian. He's a very important man."

"Is he in the Mafia?" she asked naïvely, her eyes opening wide.

"No, he's in the Sons of Norway," Pat said sarcastically. "Look, Tova, this guy could have you flushed down the toilet, and Mr. Tidy Clean would swear he never saw you go by. This ain't Sweden. This guy is a Sicilian from Brooklyn; and that means your husband *used* to be Jerry Laney, the Las Vegas singer."

"What do you mean, 'used to be'?" she asked sharply.

"What I mean, Tova," Pat said, imitating her accent, "is this guy is a heavy, and your husband is breaking his balls in front of two thousand people. Jerry really went crazy tonight. Instead of singing his golden record, he'd better start singing his own eulogy. He had no reason to attack these men in public like this... *especially* these men."

But the women, laughing, were not taking Pat seriously.

"I'll *bet* he's got big ones," Elkie said to Tova and her husband. "He looks good, don't you think, Tova? I love his mustache, so black and sexy. Felix, you should grow a red mustache. I like a mustache," she said, touching his upper lip.

"Ja, perhaps I grow mustache," Felix mumbled to his wife's teasing.

"Yes, he does look good," Tova said, eying Bephino. "He reminds me of an Italian I used to go with in Sweden. He had a thick black sexy mustache like that, too. I couldn't stand to look at him, he turned me on so."

Pat's eyes were going to Tova, then to Elkie. "Well, be careful dealing with this Italian, Tova, because Jerry may wind up singing 'God Bless America' in dog kennels around the country," Pat warned her.

"Would you introduce me to this man Bephino. I'd like to meet him," Tova asked.

"Sure, be my guest," Pat said, reaching for her hand.

She got up and walked with Pat to Alan's booth. It was a clever move by Pat to show Laney that his wife was now in the booth of the men he was insulting.

Tova had a perfect body. Her breasts, shaped like two large pears, were almost bursting through her form-fitting pink gown. It was obvious she wore no bra. Her buttocks were round and firm and made the gown move in sexy waves to the rhythm of her buttocks. Tova's red hair framed a fine-featured face.

The men made room for Tova and Pat while Jerry, watching from the stage, began singing a bit off key. Pat introduced Tova to the men, and her eyes immediately settled on Bephino. She didn't waste a minute.

She said, smiling, "I had a boyfriend years ago that looked like you Mr. Menesiero. He was Italian also; his name was Tony."

Bepy was too upset to enjoy this beautiful woman's flirting, but he tried to be charming. He looked right in her big cat eyes, smiled, and said, "That's funny. I had a woman when I was a boy, and she looked just like you. Her name was Margie."

"Oh, then you had her?" Tova replied sharply. "Was she worth it, Mr. Menesiero?"

"Yes, as a matter of fact, she was," Bepy answered coolly. "Will you be, Mrs. Laney?"

Hesitating for a moment, her eyes glittering at his direct reply, she said, "Perhaps," smiling, then excused herself and returned to her table.

"She's only a kid, about twenty-one years old," Feinbloom confided, speaking for the first time. "Jerry met her on the French Riviera. It was in all the papers. It's a real shame she's with a guy like Jerry Laney. The guy's a real asshole. Last year he took a fourteen-year-old black girl into his employ. He got caught sucking her cunt in his dressing room, but the owner of the club swept it under the carpet. Jerry has his moods—sometimes white, sometimes black. I think the creep even likes guys once in a while. He's a real cuckoo."

"I suppose he likes black guys also," Alan said, laughing. "If so, I'll have to cancel out Big Nathan. Big Nathan was to be his security escort to your office later. I decided to use hotel security in case of a lawsuit. The hotel policy covers entertainers for ten million."

"He ain't gonna like guys black or white after tonight," Bepy said firmly. "I want Nathan to rip out his fuckin' tonsils. Look at him up there, shakin' his ass. He turns my stomach."

Sid's eyes dropped.

"Too bad Alley Oop has already left for Tahoe. You could've had Nathan and Alley tear him apart," Alan joked. "You could've had half and I could've had the other half."

"I wouldn't want half," Bepy said.

"Oh, no?" Alan answered, turning his head around to look over at

Tova in the next booth. "How would you like that half?" he asked.

Bepy glanced over at Tova for a second or two.

When the show was over, and the crowd began to drift out of the room, Bepy left through the kitchen and went to his office. Alan sent Nathan backstage to get Jerry. After some fifteen minutes of convincing, Jerry went quietly. He had refused at first, trying to disclaim any knowledge of whose booth it was. Humiliated, he tried to apologize to Big Nathan as they walked along.

"Shit! Don't apologize to me, honky. Save that shit for the man. The way I hears it, you in big trouble."

At Bepy's office, Alan and Sid opened the door for Big Nathan and Jerry. Tova was following a few steps behind them, but Alan closed the door in her face, telling her to stay outside.

Bepy saw the door slam on Tova and said, "She's part of this congregation. Let her in also."

"Are you sure?" Alan asked. "You want her to see this?"

"Yeah, I'm sure. Let her in." Tova entered the office and was offered a seat by Sid.

Bepy confronted Jerry. "What was that all about tonight, Jerry? Do you have an explanation for your disrespectful remarks to Mr. Stone and myself?"

"I was only kidding around," Jerry replied. "I didn't know who you were. I'm sorry for my stupid remarks. I apologize to you both." He was shaking badly. "Please accept my apologies," he pleaded.

Bepy liked the tone of his voice as he apologized. He thought the guy was sincere, and it took the anger out of him. He really didn't want to make a mess of an entertainer, but he wanted something special for him so he would never forget this night.

"Change his shirt; he's soaking wet," he told Big Nathan. "But don't hurt him. I just don't want him to catch cold. I accept his apology," Bepy said.

Everyone watched in silence. Tova watched in despair, but at the same time she was amused at the way Bepy was toying with her ding-a-ling star husband. Big Nathan grabbed Jerry and shook him right out of his shirt; he ripped the shirt right off his body. The guy was standing there half nude, not a hair on his body. He remained silent and humiliated, trying to hold back his tears. Nathan threw the two-hundred-dollar ruffled shirt on the floor like a rag.

"Next time you sing for me let me enjoy the show," Bepy told Jerry. "Don't make me upset. I accept your apology this time. Be a nice boy. OK, Jerry?"

Jerry, too frightened to speak, nodded his head in agreement. He walked back to his dressing room covered by Sid's jacket. His wife remained.

Tova, realizing what a fool her husband had made of himself, stared quietly at Bepy. She had been interested in him. And now she was more interested than ever. She was drawn by his power and his smoothness. She knew he was ruthless, but he was also sympathetic. He hadn't harmed Jerry. She also liked tanned Italian men.

Alan politely escorted her to the door, and she left smiling slightly, confident that she had made a friend.

"You acted magnanimously, my friend. I like that," Alan said. "Yes, I like that very much. You didn't exploit your power. Let's go have a drink. I'm buying."

The next day, about two-thirty, Bepy entered the poolside elevator and met Tova, dressed in her tennis clothes.

"Hi. How are you?" she said.

"Fine. It's nice to see that you're enjoying yourself," he commented.

"Yes, I had a nice time playing tennis today; now I'm ready for a bath and a drink."

"That's just what I'm going to do," Bepy said. "Have a nice martini and relax in my whirlpool."

"Whirlpool? You have a whirlpool?"

"Yes, I have one in my suite. Don't you?"

"No. All we have is Hollywood tub," she explained. "No whirlpool. I'd like to see your whirlpool. Can you arrange that, Mr. Menesiero? I'm curious to see what you have."

"You're a very married person for such a curious lady."

"Yes, I am. Either way, I'm still curious, Mr. Menesiero," she said, smiling smoothly.

"To see what I have?"

"Exactly. To see what you have."

"In that case, call me Bephino, OK, Tova?"

"I like that name. Bephino. It sounds so Italian," she said, slipping her arm through his.

He escorted her into the foyer of his suite and opened wide the French doors that led to a large white-and-gold living room. While she twirled around looking at the elegance and exclaiming about "how beautiful" everything was, Bepy went directly to the bathroom. He opened the faucets to fill the tub and added some bubble bath, then walked over to the bar to make some drinks. She crossed to the bathroom.

"Well, there's the whirlpool. How do you like it?"

"I love it! It's twice the size of ours at home. You can put six people in that tub," she said. "It's fantastic."

"I only like two in my tub. Six is not my style." He smiled into her eyes, handing her a drink.

"You're right; six is too many. It's not fun—too many. I tried it in Sweden. You know, I feel very comfortable with you, Bephino. You have a style I like. I feel I met you before."

"Maybe in the other world." He laughed. "But I'm glad you feel that way, because the feeling is mutual. You certainly have a *unique* figure, Tova. I find myself admiring you."

"Oh, my figure? What about my figure?"

"Well, like I say, it's unique and interesting to me."

"Tell me, tell me more. I like to hear nice things about my body. What do you mean by interesting?"

"I never spoke to a woman like this before, but you have me thinking different today. Well, your body is full and kinda wickedly shaped. Your bust is large, your waist is small, your bottom is plump— you really have it all, like a poem."

"Very unique." She smiled. "Yes, that is unique...a poem for me."

"You know, Tova, you bring out a side of me that seems strange even to me. I haven't thought about a poem since I was nine years old and had to recite in front of the class."

"That's sweet."

"Well, I told you how I feel about your body. It's beautiful and you're beautiful. It's not that easy to meet people and hit it off from the start. And it's not easy for a guy like me to compliment a woman so quickly," Bepy explained. "I'm usually kind of different."

"I know. It's not easy to meet people, but I knew when I saw you last night I'd like to be with you. So please accept my compliments also. Did you feel the same?" she asked as she moved up close to him, her breasts brushing against the front of his shirt.

"No, I didn't, Tova. I was too upset last night. But today is another story. When I saw you on the elevator, the fibers in my body began to expand. I felt that uncomfortable feeling run through me. That's when I..."

Tova rolled her lips, wet them, and kissed him. After a while, she spoke softly to him. "Those fibers must be catching, because I feel them expanding and running through my body right now. They are uncomfortable; you're right. I feel so strange in your arms all of a sudden." She kissed his jaw and let her soft lips glide down the side of his neck.

He whispered, "You mean the fibers running through your unique body? You have a unique body."

"Oh, yes, I forgot—my unique body." She began to swallow, very seductively, using her tongue to meet his. She was thrusting deep into his mouth.

"Bephino, hold me, squeeze me. I feel so good so fast. This is strange. I just met you. How could I...darling," she whispered in a thick voice, "I believe the spirit is moving me already."

She began to tremble in his arms. Her lips opened wider, with a slight tilt of her mouth, which Bepy understood as a climax.

"Is it time for your bath, darling?" she asked, trying to catch her breath and regain her composure.

Bepy walked to the bathroom and casually removed his clothes, dropping them to the floor. She watched his every move, and he knew her eyes were on him as he slowly lowered himself into the whirling hot water.

Tova liked what she saw. Her face became a mirror of her thoughts. "May I?" she asked.

"Yes, you may." He looked at her and tried to be cool and charming, but he was hot and horny, and very uncomfortable. He wanted her so badly he could taste it.

She undressed in seconds. Her breasts were indeed large and pear shaped, and her thighs and legs complemented her round ass. She was a beauty, no doubt about it. Bepy was delighted at what he saw approaching him. He was accustomed to beautiful women, but this was a very special one. He sensed that Tova was suffering as he was. He wanted to escape into an oblivion of sexual enjoyment and not think about his anguish for Tova's husband, Jerry, or the guilt now making itself felt. As thoughts of Dana and the twins kept flashing in his mind, Bepy needed to escape from reality, if only for a few hours.

Tova entered his bath and slid her body right between his deeply tanned thighs and began kissing him eagerly, her left hand around his neck and her right hand underwater, probing.

"You made me an irresistible offer, darling," she whispered. She had spotted his endowment as he undressed and was well aware of what was waiting for her. She slid her hands eagerly down his flat stomach and moaned with pleasure.

"Oh, God, it's so big." He knew she was a great admirer of abundance by the flushed look on her face as she had watched him undress. She had proved his thoughts to be correct by quickly grabbing at him underwater, securing him as if to confirm her first glance at his nude body.

Suddenly she was wild with passion, kissing him hard, feverishly, like a woman who needed love desperately. She began to lick his lips, murmuring softly in Swedish, as they rolled around in the hot whirlpool kissing and exploring each other's bodies as if it was the first time they had seen the opposite sex.

She performed exquisitely, fondling his genitals in the soapy water. There was something special about the way she lathered his body and stroked his large organ, as if it had a special importance to her. She seemed to protect it in greedy, selfish gestures. She continued to slide her hands and fingers up his buttocks, as if to grasp all he had to offer. His body felt the urge to climax, but he fought it off to keep strong for her. His balls began to swell with pain, but he still refused to come. Tova whimpered. She was a loving little thing, and there was no doubt that her heart was wide open.

Experiencing increasing pain from holding back his climax, Bepy stood up. His huge penis was standing erect and throbbing almost to the point of explosion. He pressed a button, and a hot shower began to rinse him off.

"What are you doing? Where are you going?" she asked.

"I want to fuck you. Let's get out of this tub. I'm hurtin' bad for you."

"You're hurting?"

"Yes. Come to the bed. My balls are too full, I need you now."

Tova couldn't take her beautiful eyes off him. Gradually she lifted herself up and began to rub herself between her thighs, as her eyes reflected her satisfaction with this man standing before her. He stepped out of the hot tub onto a ramp, pressed another button, and hot air began to dry him completely.

Tova rinsed herself quickly and hurriedly stepped onto the ramp, where he was still standing. She began to dry off with him, the warm air blowing on both of them. It was a feeling both would remember always.

"I want you, too," she murmured.

Bepy pulled her toward him and kissed her wildly. She was so delighted and aroused, she couldn't wait to be fucked. Kissing him and running her mouth over his dark, hairy chest, she slowly dropped to her knees and tried desperately to devour him. She sucked and licked him with growing lust. She held on to his hurting balls and ran her fingers up the crack of his buttocks. She was a nymph at play.

What a remarkable lover! Bepy thought. He had had many women in his life, but Tova was a winner. They dried off together, but she remained on her knees sucking him without stopping. Although she was breath-takingly beautiful and sucked with enthusiasm, her teeth suddenly touched his cock. It felt like razor blades. In pain, he desperately tried to come to rid himself of the pressure in his testicles. But her teeth further deferred his climax.

Before she blistered his prick with her ivories, Bepy pulled out of her mouth and walked away from her, stepping up to his Egyptian raised bed. Tova followed him and lay beside him on the bed, touching his body.

"Please fuck me, darling. I need you, too," she implored, teasing him with her fingertips. He looked down at his penis and noticed the deep redness that her hunger had caused. Hoping he could finish what he had started and relieve the ache in his loins, he crawled over her body and kissed her passionately. He looked down at her as she raised her thighs to the fulfillment of a man's dreams. Then, with a thrust he knew she was ready for, he rammed his large shaft directly into her. First came a slight moan, then the feel of her hot sweet breath on his shoulder. A look of relief crossed her face as he slid deeper into her, further than she had ever experienced before.

"Oh, darling! Hurt me, darling, treat me beastly," she moaned. "Treat me beastly."

He manhandled her to let her feel what she was yearning for, but at the same time his touch was soft and caressing. He kissed her breasts passionately.

"Harder, ram me harder. I love it that way. I'm coming," she whispered. "I'm...Oh, Bephino! Please touch my...please touch it. I love that, darling." She scratched at him, putting his hand on her ass. "Touch me, darling, touch me there."

Another wonder of the world, he thought, laughing softly in his throat. "But so beautiful, so very beautiful."

She spread her body wide, trying to absorb all of him. She needed depth, and he knew it. He raised her up with his hands and pushed deeply into her body as she moaned and groaned to his manly thrust. He reached down with his right hand, his fingers caressing her sexy buttocks. When she felt his touch, she moaned loudly in appreciation and kissed him feverishly. Her moans then became screams, which echoed through the large suite.

Suddenly the expression on her face showed she was beginning the full climax that was harboring in her body. He was also ready to relieve his balls, so hard and swollen from holding back. "Darling, I'm arriving," she moaned, slipping into her European version of coming. "Oh, oh, Bephino, I'm coming. It's so beautiful." Apparently she liked to talk while making love. She was completely out of control, and he was ramming harder, pushing as far as he could go. For a small woman, she had no trouble absorbing every bit of him.

They clung together violently, she digging her fingernails into the tensed muscles of his back. He emptied his passions into her body completely, and pain dispersed with his spectacular climax. He had never experienced such an explosive climax.

They lay together peacefully in the silent suite until sleep fell over them. When they awoke, Bepy got out of bed and began to mix drinks.

Lying on her side, her face still in her pillow, Tova asked, "Is it supposed to be this good? It was so wonderful, darling," she said turning over, then sitting up to accept her drink.

"Yeah, you were fantastic, Tova. I enjoyed it, too. For a while there I was kinda worried, but then it all came together."

"Ja," she smiled, while sipping her white wine on the rocks. "We come together. So wonderful."

Over the next ten days, they made love every chance they had. Tova followed Bepy all over the hotel, pretending to bump into him by accident. She wrote notes, like "I want to fuck you now! now! now!" on napkins and slipped them to him. He would read them and laugh, but she was getting emotionally involved. She was acting like a schoolgirl falling in love while on vacation.

Bepy enjoyed fucking her. Tova was a very fine lady and a great lover, but it was old now, and he was bored and fucked out.

Jerry Laney had four more days to play at the hotel before he was to start a movie in Spain. Tova was getting nervous; she didn't want the beautiful fling with Bephino to end.

"Will I ever see you again, darling?" she would ask him.

"Of course. I'll call you in Spain. I'll fly there to see you."

And she believed him.

One day, Tova called Elkie to her suite and explained her secret to her. They were both Swedes and equally beautiful, but Elkie seemed a bit stronger and more confident, maybe because she was a few years older and wiser. Tova explained that she was wild about Bephino, and that she was confused and needed to talk to someone.

"Does he know how you feel?" Elkie asked.

"I don't think so," she answered. "I tell him I love him, but he never replies to love talk. He fucks me dizzy, but says very little," Tova explained. "I can't get enough of this man. He said ve'll see each other in Spain, and I hope he really means it."

Elkie smiled. "These Italians are very strange people. They usually have a wife at home baking bread, and they go out and fuck everybody else's wife. Don't you know that, Tova? Italian men are famous for that," she said. "They are known fuckers. If you really want to keep a man like this, you must drive him wild with excitement. You must give him something no one woman can offer him."

"Like what?" Tova asked. "We make love like no one could ever dream of," she explained. "I need a large man to fill me, and he fits me so fine." Elkie's eyes widened, as Tova continued to speak. "A small man, like Jerry, does nothing for me. I think Bephino loves me; he's always ready for me; he's always hard—even on the elevator."

"You think so?" Elkie laughed. "Italians are always hard, but that means nothing. They live for love; they were born with a hard on. If you give him two beautiful women at one time, you'll win the game. You'll own him forever. Then he'll really love you, and fill your body with endless joy. Do that and he'll be ready for you whenever you desire him. That's the secret—two women at one time. He'll be hard even in his coffin." Elkie chuckled.

Tova smiled. "Two women? What do you mean, Elkie?"

Elkie looked deeply into Tova's eyes, and said softly, "Offer him you and me together."

"What? You too want him, Elkie? You want to make love to him?"

"No, no, Tova darling. Not for me, for you. I don't care to make love to him. I don't even let Felix enter me. That's how I keep my body tight. I think this man of yours is beautiful, but he's yours. I will just complement the affair. I can pay attention to you, Tova. He'll like that. As a matter of fact, he'll love it. Make it a threesome, darling. Don't you know men love such affairs. It gets in their blood, and then you'll own him."

Tova was thinking about what Elkie had said. Pay attention to me? What does she mean? A trio? She walked over to the bar and nervously began to mix drinks. She looked back over her shoulder and asked if Elkie wanted hers on the rocks.

"Yes, and make mine a double, darling," Elkie replied.

As they sat sipping their strong drinks, they looked into each other's eyes. Tova's smile wavered; she was confused, unsure of herself and uncertain of Elkie's true intentions. Elkie smiled at Tova, but the smile was different; it was false.

"You must trust me. Trust me, darling," Elkie whispered softly, casually reaching out and slowly running her hands over Tova's thighs, exposed by her very short shorts. "Such smooth skin you have, darling," she murmured, caressing her. "And such a beautiful suntan."

Elkie moved closer. Tova, too startled to move, sat stone still. Elkie's face was inches from Tova, and her breath gently fanned her cheek as she whispered into her ear, then kissed the side of her lips gently, without lust. "You know I love you and I would only give you the best advice. That's why you called me, isn't it? Is it true or not, darling?"

Tova was even more startled by the strong vibrations she was receiving from Elkie. They did not move for a few moments. Then Elkie kissed Tova full on the lips. Tova liked the feel of Elkie's lips, even though they felt strange—she had never been kissed by a woman before. But she didn't move away.

Elkie sensed the positive response to her advances and made another move: this time a more passionate kiss, using her tongue, urging a response from Tova. The kissing was tender and beautiful and hot. Tova responded to the love offering and began to move her body and soul toward Elkie for another kiss.

Elkie's eyes lit up when Tova responded with passion. They kissed tenderly, Tova's tongue returning the hot flicks of Elkie's advances, their hands touching each other with soft caresses. Elkie, in a deep, excited voice, said, "Take your panties off, darling. I will make you feel something fantastic!" Tova stood up as Elkie began to unzip her shorts.

Suddenly the door opened in the other room, and Jerry Laney walked in, humming like a bird. The women separated quickly and moved to different parts of the room.

"Hi, girls, I guess it's my lucky day. I get two ladies for the price of one, right? Two beautiful sexy ladies in my bed at one time," Jerry said, "How about it girls? Sound good?"

"Sounds like *Scheissen*," Tova answered, using the German word so he wouldn't understand. "You can't even handle me, Jerry, and you want to try to handle both of us? What's up with you today? Do you want to have a heart attack? Or did you take your E vitamins with your breakfast cereal? It's been a month since you even touched me."

Elkie laughed at the way Tova took out her frustration on Jerry.

"Well, I'm gonna take a nap anyway," Jerry said quickly. "I was only kidding. You Swedes take sex too seriously. Already you're talking about vitamins and breakfast cereal."

"I'll walk you down to the casino," Tova told Elkie. "We'll let Jerry rest before his show."

On the way down she said, "He's always home at the wrong moments. But maybe you're right, Elkie. I never thought of that triple approach with Bephino; it sounds very sexy. Let's try it tomorrow afternoon. I'm supposed to meet him in his suite at two. You arrive at two-thirty, and I'll answer the door. Be patient, because we'll probably be in the whirlpool. I'll get out of the tub to let you in, and you act pleasant—just watch us play a while and then ask if you can join in. I'm sure Bephino will love this idea. He's a very sexy man and loves erotic ladies."

"I'm glad you realize that," Elkie said, grinning. "I'll be at his suite at two-thirty sharp. Shall I wear my waterproof watch, darling?"

That evening at dinner Alan asked Bepy, "Hey, lova boy, are you still shtupin' Tova? Or is it over with Tova, Rova?"

"Rova is almost *finito,*" Bepy replied. "He's got about a half a fuck left in him and then it's up for grabs. I'm all fucked out from her. She leaves for Spain in a few days, and then I can get back to my normal sex life. This girl is too much. She has such a large cunt for a little lady that I can't believe it. I'm getting a small-dick complex. She tells me I'm huge, but I feel small in her, and she never seems to get enough. It's like screwing a volcano! Big and hot, with plenty of eruptions. Every day she pages me and begs for it. I feel sorry for the kid, but I think she knows I'm getting tired of her. Tomorrow, I'm gonna tell her not to call me anymore, that I'll call her if I want her. I need a rest from her. I'm getting pains in my chest. I hope it's just gas."

"I didn't think you would screw her this long," Alan said. "You never stayed with any of the girls more than a day or two."

"Yeah, but this one is really hard to discard. Every day she's got a different trick. She knows the sweetest ways to have sex, and she practices them on me. Each time it's a surprise. Alan, you wouldn't believe this broad. So I hang in there for the next surprise and the next. I'm living on raw eggs and clams."

"I know. I heard the clam-bar guy wants to quit, but he's afraid of Alley Oop," Alan said. "I hope you don't hang in for any of the reruns. My hotel's clam bar is low, and even the chickens are starting to get weak. Try eating egg bagels; they work also." Alan laughed at his own jokes. "You like that? Oh, well, forget it. You're getting like a zombie already. You can't even laugh anymore. Tell me some of the things she does Bep. I'd like to hear about some of these kinky tricks."

"Ahh, you know. One day she sucks toes, the next she's like an animal licking me all over my ass. Then she's gotta be banged in her ass, in front of a mirror. She's got a million tricks, and loves every one of them. I can't keep up with her. Then, remember, I told you about that first day we met, and how I got blue balls? I couldn't come because I held it back to be a good stud, and my balls blew up and hurt so bad. Then, when she sucked my dick, the feel of her teeth held me back further so my nuts got swollen. Later, I was hurtin' and comin' at the same time. Now, that's an experience in itself, Alan. You can't believe the feeling."

"It must be like giving birth to twins and coming at the same time." Alan laughed.

"Yeah, yeah, somethin' like that," Bepy said and joined in the laughter.

The next afternoon at two, Bepy let Tova into his suite. She had her hair in braids, a new twist: big tits, unbelievable body, and now braids like a little girl. She was nude under a tight jersey dress. The dress was so tight he could see the dimples in her ass through it. But she was looking and acting like a young schoolgirl. It was crazy, he thought, not knowing if he liked it or not. But then he decided that he did like it, after all. No man would turn away from this.

"How do you like me, darling?" she said, snuggling up to him.

She's done it again. She's got my balls feeling crazy again. This broad is born to be fucked, he thought. She knows a million tricks. This time the little girl with braids is gonna drive me wild.

Tova began undressing without speaking. She pulled her dress over her head, exposing her entire body. She stood there smiling, like she had another surprise for him. Then she began to fondle her own body casually.

"What's up, Tova?" Bepy asked.

"What do you mean, 'what's up'? You're up, I see," she said. "I'm getting ready to play, darling." Smiling, she put her hand inside his robe and touched his crotch.

"You're smiling like you've got a vibrator up your ass. What's up, Tova?" he asked her again.

Slowly and sexily she slipped into the hot tub. Looking like a beautiful doll, she beckoned to him. "Come in the tub, darling. Let me suck your enormous prick. Stand in the tub for me in front of the mirrors, so I can look at you as I lick you."

"Are you going underwater this time or staying afloat?"

"I'm staying afloat today. I can't get my braids wet."

Bepy dropped his robe to the carpeted floor and moved toward the tub. "Easy on the teeth this time, Tova, honey. Use your tongue more. OK?"

"Yes, darling. I'll be careful." She began to suck him. Her face on him and her braids were too much to look at. He almost had to turn away.

Tova stopped sucking him for a minute and looked at her watch.

279

"Darling, my girl friend may stop over to say hello. She wants to meet you before we leave for Spain. I told her it was all right."

"Well, if she's coming here, what the hell are we doing in the tub?"

"Oh, don't worry. She's such a lovely girl; she'll love to watch us make love."

"You gotta be kidding!" Bepy exclaimed. "What the fuck is this gonna turn out to be—a side show or something? I'm getting dressed."

"No, Bepy. She's my best friend. This is the very first time we are meeting like this. I'm crazy about you, darling, and I want you to enjoy every moment of sex with me. Let my friend watch us. She wants to very much. I want her to also. You will love this romance with me. This is my gift to you."

"You gotta be kidding," he repeated. "Damn if I don't get the strangest gifts."

While Bepy stared at her, the door buzzer sounded. Tova ran, pulling a towel around her, to let Elkie in. Bepy, still standing, reached for a towel, then thought better of it and sat deep in the tub. Waiting to see what Tova was up to, he mumbled, "First I get a Jew for a gift and now she gives me a . . . Christ, a twin! Wow, what a broad! A duplicate of Tova."

"This is my best friend, Elkie," Tova said. Then she dropped her towel and slid back into the tub, cuddling up to Bepy, establishing her ownership. But Elkie sat on the velvet bench, acting elegant and charming—very much the visitor.

Tova began to kiss Bepy and stroke him. Acting foolish, she began showing Elkie his large endowment. Bepy had no choice but to enjoy the attention. Elkie watched with conspicuous interest, and it was obvious how quickly she became aroused. She was turning different shades right in front of them.

It was a side show and he was the star—another erotic surprise, he thought, but this one was the final scene. He played their game and began to return Tova's affection, kissing her and probing her body underneath the churning water.

Tova seemed to enjoy the audience. She turned on quicker knowing that Elkie was watching them. After a while she stood up in the tub, exhibiting herself, then slowly but enticingly spread her buttocks to tease Elkie. Elkie's eyes were almost falling out of her head. Her face seemed to change from that of a little doll to a bulging-eyed frog. Her lust overwhelmed her, and the blood rushing to her face made it look badly sunburned. Bepy was watching both women now. Gradually Elkie began to regain her beautiful smile, seeming to have already climaxed in secret sitting on the bench. Her tits were pointed and hard in her white low-cut dress.

"May I?" Elkie asked, standing up.

Tova, totally in command, replied, "Yes, you may."

Bepy was amused by this interchange. It was as though they were playing giant steps, a game from his Brooklyn childhood.

Elkie quickly removed her dress by pulling on a string around her waist. Completely nude and standing in her high-heeled shoes, she looked extravagant, another Swedish classic, Bepy thought, only without the braids. She strolled over to the tub and exhibited herself for the other two by way of the fully mirrored walls and ceiling, turning around like a model, so they could view her from all angles. Bepy and Tova gaped as she removed her shoes and slid into the hot tub.

The two women began to kiss Bepy, grabbing and sharing him with loving care, kissing and touching the dark hair on his chest. After the three had whirled around for about twenty minutes, caressing one another, Bepy was ready to get out. He rinsed and stepped out onto the blower ramp, still watching the two lovelies, who were now feeling each other's breasts, reaching under the water to touch each other's pussies, and kissing and tonguing each other. Their faces were expressing what was building up in their bodies.

This was Bepy's big scene. He stood on the ramp, set the blower control on medium, and stood balls naked, like a Roman warrior. He had the largest erection of his life, and testicles to match.

What else could a man ask for? he thought. Two women so beautiful and sexy, kissing and hugging each other. It was the most exotic and erotic scene he had ever had a part in. Then, as he watched the women play with each other, he began experiencing waves of hatred, fear, paranoia, anxiety, and lust. His extremely swollen balls hurt again from not being allowed to come. He felt now that, if he came, he might die from the delightful feeling he would experience. Yet his thoughts strayed back to Brooklyn. A voice sounded in his ears, telling him to clean up his act; his infidelities were becoming his stupidity; he should remember his wife and kids.

Suddenly his body was brushed by the girls as they got out of the tub onto the ramp. He reached out and pulled both up close to him. He decided to forget Brooklyn for a while longer. Elkie went wild with passion, and tried to mount him standing. All three played with feverish passion and were completely blown dry together. They moved to his large bed.

Elkie exhibited herself, exposing her true ambitions. "Fuck me with your big prick, Bephino. Fuck me first. I must have it. You don't mind, darling?" she asked, looking over at Tova. "You've had him so often."

Tova wondered about Elkie's promise to be there just to complement her, but she yielded to Elkie's dominance.

Bepy looked at Elkie spread out on the bed begging for him and decided to take her. He mounted her, but as he attempted to slip himself in her, he realized she was too tight for him. Tova, the kid, was too big, and this one was too small. She was so tight her womb felt like a rubber band fastened tightly around his prick.

Elkie now was begging for Tova. "Kiss me, Tova, kiss me. He's hurting me, he's hurting me, darling," she gasped with pleasurable pain.

Tova rolled closer, to kiss Elkie, and caressed her like a child. Elkie began lubricating and soon was dripping wet. Bepy was ramming at half power, so as not to hurt her, and she was just as passionate as Tova had been all week. Elkie and Tova were kissing each other wildly. Soon Elkie had all of Bepy in her and was in full control.

"Never in my life have I been fucked like this," Elkie murmured. "Never. Oh, Tova, oh, he's so fantastic. I love it, Bephino. Don't stop, please."

But he did stop. He needed a little break. The excitement had drained him, and he needed to recoup. He was getting limp, and she felt it.

As he lay back to rest, both women immediately began to devour his genitals. Both beautiful faces were on the head of his cock, bobbing and weaving, licking him up and down lavishly. They also began kissing each other between long lavish licks of his testicles. He watched their tongues meet.

That was it. That was all he could take. He began to come. He came so hard and so thick, it ripped through him like an erupting volcano; wave after wave, hot lava rippled through his body as he weakened. In wild ecstasy, the women absorbed him recklessly. He moaned with pleasure as he fell into a state of total depletion. Life was completely sucked out of Bephino Menesiero. The hurting in his testicles was gone. Such agonizing relief, he thought. Why do I get this pain, this enjoyable pain? It's these women. They make me crazy.

As he fell asleep, the women continued loving each other. He awoke later to the murmuring and moaning sounds of Tova, who was being delightfully tortured by a piercing tongue. She was on her back, with two pillows under her buttocks, and Elkie was between her thighs devouring her. The women were really into it. Elkie was pleasing Tova and doing a fine job of it. Tova seemed to be in a trance, in a long climax that would never end.

Bepy, still groggy, watched quietly, and realized that no man can satisfy a woman as well as another woman can. They have such patience with each other, he thought, and such respect for each other's orgasms.

As Tova lifted her buttocks from the pillows beneath her to get more of Elkie, she began to tremble passionately. Elkie briskly bobbed and weaved to help her with long flickering affections of her tongue. Tova began moaning louder and louder.

The phone rang, startling Bepy. He quickly answered, and a strange voice announced, "There's a fag down here looking for his wife. Ya want to give her back or not?"

"Who's this?" Bepy asked, still groggy from his trance.

"This is house security, you big fuck," Alan said, bursting out laughing. "Get rid of her already. The guy's in the coffee shop looking under tables."

"OK, OK." Bepy laughed and hung up. He allowed both women to reach their passionate pleasure. Then he told them about Jerry.

They got dressed, fixed their faces to hide their fucked-out appearance, and kissed Bepy good-bye.

"So, what's new?" Alan asked Bepy that evening at dinner. "How's your love life?"

"I'm getting a claustrophobic feeling in my own bathtub," Bepy replied. "It's all over, Alan. I've reached the outer limits of sex. There's nothing left for me. Now she's cloning new broads that look just like her. I try to get rid of her, and she clones me another. I can't even handle one, and now I'm fucking two."

"Who's next, Jerry Laney?" Alan asked, laughing.

"I think that's what's comin', but I quit—*finito*. Fuck Sweden."

"After a couple of weeks' rest, you'll be looking to make those two broads again. I know you won't let them get away that easy. Maybe we'll go to Spain when they're filming and see them, huh, Bep? Am I right or wrong?" Alan asked, imitating Alley Oop.

"I believe you're wrong, friend. I got my wife coming up on my menu. She gives me a tough exam—checks my blood count and pulse rate! All kinds of shit. Anyway, I've had enough of them. I got the feeling these girls are just warming up. They've got big plans for me. I heard

Tova tell Elkie she'd love this to be a real *ménage à trois*. These Swedes are serious about their sex. The next time, they'll be at it with the toys and vibrators. A guy could get hooked on this shit."

"Stop it! Stop talking!" Alan screamed. "You're making me crazy. I love broads like that. It's my weakness."

"Alan, I'm surprised at you. I never knew you had a weakness for the ladies."

"It's the fuckin' toys that get me!" Alan screamed. "The toys!"

The next morning Alan, Bepy, Alley Oop, and Ben had breakfast together. Ben told stories about Lake Tahoe. Then Alan asked again about Tova.

"I can't believe the story you told me last night, Bep. She is really something, a real fuckin' maniac. Am I right or wrong?"

"Hey, don't use my line, Mr. Stone," Alley interrupted. "That's my format."

"Format?" Alan asked smiling. "You gotta format now? Just as long as you don't start handing out business cards, Alley. Format, OK, but business cards would be too much for me to handle."

Alley Oop, still making the turn on the rail, asked, "Who's got a business card? I ain't got no business card."

"Who's this maniac?" Ben asked. "This fuckin' Alan's got us all confused this morning."

Their horsing around, after Bepy told them about Jerry Laney's wife, was interrupted by a page for Mr. Menesiero. It was the hotel operator, who screened all of his phone calls.

"It's Dana, Mr. Menesiero."

"OK, put her through."

"Look," Ben whispered to the others. "Notice the tan as it leaves his face. A hundred bucks to a doughnut it's his wife. I know him like a book. Look at him. He's sick already."

"Hi, honey, what's up?" Bepy said. "Is everything all right? How're the kids?"

"Everything is fine and the kids are OK. They send their love. When are you coming home?"

"Next week," he replied.

"Why so long? You've been away for such a long time this trip."

"I got business to take care of."

"You stay too long in Vegas. Peggy called this morning and said, 'Let's surprise the boys. Let's fly to Las Vegas.' But I wasn't sure if we should."

"Dana, forget it. I don't need any more surprises in my life," he said, looking over at Ben. "So tell Ben's wife that for me, OK? And tell her to join a gym or something and lose some weight. Take her to Brooklyn and surprise your mother. She could use a good surprise. Bake a cake and be nice, Dana. I'll be finished with my business next week and then I'll be home."

Bepy hung up and looked at Ben. "Your wife wanted to surprise 'the boys' and fly out to Vegas to see how we fuck. What do you think of that? Suppose she found you balls-deep in your show girl one night?"

"Then Benny would become a little evangelist or an escapilist, or a pistcapilist, or even worse, a Zionist," Alan said, jumping at the opportunity to swallow Ben up. "The little schmuck would have become a big schmuck."

"Just as long as I don't become a matzo creep like you, Alan," Ben answered, and everyone laughed.

"I could just picture little Benny climbing off that six-foot-four broad he's humpin' and his wife catching him. That would be a real cartoon, huh, Bepy? Am I right or wrong?" Alley Oop said.

"You're right, Alley. It would be a real cartoon if his wife saw his little ass climbing off that giant, because he's really a little animated bastard anyway. See the way he moves his face back and forth, back and forth?"

"Yeah, I see," Alley Oop said, staring at Ben.

"He does look like a cartoon character," Alan said.

"You guys are pickin' on the wrong guy today—all three of you."

Later that month, back in Brooklyn, Bepy called his attorney to investigate the regulations on the exporting of automobiles to the Middle East. As soon as he knew what they were up against, he called Ben early one morning.

"Hello, Benny."

"Don't call me Benny."

"Yeah. I know. Hey, Ben, how come it's always short people that got a hang-up—don't call me this, call me that? It ain't gonna make you look taller by my calling you Ben, Benny."

"Holy shit. You call me eight o'clock in the morning to tell me that I'm short? You got some clear head, friend."

"Meet me at the Greek diner for breakfast in one hour. We gotta talk. OK?"

"I don't eat in Greek restaurants. I hate the fuckin' Greeks—especially in the morning!"

"Cut the shit, Ben. Where do you wanna have breakfast then?" Bepy asked, getting a little irritated.

"How about the Back Street Coffee Shop?"

"OK, Back Street. In one hour."

At breakfast, Bepy told Ben he needed a car dealer who handled large new cars.

"Yeah. I remember. For Alan Stone and his Arabs."

"I need a big car dealer and a banker who lends money to the dealer," Bepy explained. "I gotta squeeze one hundred cars out of them. First we gotta see the banker. He's the key to this one. You got a guy we could squeeze?"

"Yeah, in the Bronx. He's OK, but I don't know how easy he'll squeeze. The guy's a little *pazzo*. He shoots back."

"Never mind. Does he lend to dealerships?"

"That's his racket. He likes to lend to car dealers; he holds car transfers as collateral for the loans. He controls all the collateral now, because the bank got burned one time for a million bucks."

"OK, call him right now—there's a phone on the wall over there—and make an appointment for lunch."

"I'll be right back." A few moments later Ben returned. "OK, we're expected at his office at noon."

"What's this guy's name?" Bepy asked on the drive to the Bronx.

"Fat Arty," Ben replied.

"What d'ya mean, Fat Arty? The guy's a banker. What's his real name?"

"Oh, it's Arty Argento. He lives in Westchester and is the bank president. I buried his brother-in-law for him years ago. We gave him a nice funeral."

"Is that one of your back and forth, your father-had-a-good-year deals?"

Ben burst out laughing.

They arrived at the bank on time, but Arty was in conference. As they sat outside the banker's office, the door suddenly opened. A man in a dark blue suit came out and hurried off. In his haste, he didn't pull the door closed hard enough, and it slowly swung open about three inches. They could see a man sitting in a chair and a fat man bending over him, punching the shit out of him and yelling obscenities. The guy was bleeding from nose and mouth.

"What the fuck is going on in there?" Bepy asked Ben.

"Ah, probably nothin'. Just a collection, maybe."

"What d'ya mean nothin'? Somebody's getting killed in there! I can see a guy getting hit. Take a look, Ben. Is this a bank or not?"

"I told you Arty is a little *pazzo*. He's a real crazy bastard. If you get a loan from him and don't pay your note on time, he invites you to his office for lunch. When he gets you here, he makes his chauffeur hold you and he beats the shit out of you. He's three hundred and forty pounds of mean *cappicola*. You'll see soon enough. This guy's an unusual banker."

Arty Argento, also known as "The Bank," was short and fat, and had dark brown hair. His cherub cheeks were rosy, and his round chin sagged evenly between his massive shoulders and arms, which were like two sides of beef. His fists, resembling pork butts, were scarred from hosting his "collection" luncheons. When he moved, his body swayed like he was winding up for a punch. He'd grab a guy's shirt during a conversation, perhaps just a habit or maybe to get a better punch at you. Suddenly realizing it, he'd hastily begin to dust away his fingerprints. He'd use foul language, but in such a tone that even the Pope wouldn't mind hearing it. He was an immigrant Italian, but an educated banker, from Naples. Arturo Garibaldi Argento was the picture of a tough, sweet-talking cherub.

"How the hell did he get to be president of the bank?" Bepy asked.

"He probably beat the shit out of the board of directors. I don't know for sure, but he's been president for eight years now. He's got a lot of influence in New York politics. This guy is good to know, believe me," Ben said.

"I hope so. I hope he cooperates with us. I need those cars. I've committed myself."

The door opened wide, and two guys half-carried, half-dragged a man out of the office. One was holding a towel to his head, soaking up blood. They dragged him down the hall and out the side exit to a car.

Ben and Bepy stared in amazement, then entered Arty's office.

Ben embraced him, and they kissed on both cheeks. Then Ben smiled, rubbing Arty's stomach. *"Banco bello,* you look good. This is my partner, Bephino Menesiero. He's from Brooklyn." Arty shook hands with Bepy.

"What happened to that guy? Was he late with a payment?" Ben asked, grinning.

"You know, Ben. I always try to do good; I try to be a nice guy, but these bastards take advantage. It don't pay to be nice. They fuck you harder when you're nice. I get all the *farcime e meda* bastards. When they need money, they're beautiful; they smile, *gai focha bruta.* Then after they get

287

what they want—nothing. So first I break their fuckin' heads. Next their legs, and then their arms. I'm tired of being bullshitted. So I'm gonna cripple all slow payers. That's my new rule. Everybody gets a wheelchair for Christmas. No more booze. Then they'll pay; you'll see. Come on, fuck him. It's lunchtime. Let's have something to eat. I'm hungry."

He sat down and opened one side of his desk. They saw cool foggy air come out. It was a refrigerator. He pulled out a couple of pounds of ham, salami, and Swiss cheese wrapped in wax paper. The other two men returned, and Arty made introductions and directed them to set up lunch. One of his men cut up a big loaf of Italian bread; the other sliced a tomato.

"Don't cut the tomato too thin. *Ah capeesh?*" Arty yelled. He looked at Ben as he began spreading a tablecloth over his desk. "He always ruins the tomatoes. He thinks he's a swordsman. He slices them like paper, the bastard. Who likes slivered tomatoes? I like 'em nice and thick."

The guy cutting the tomatoes grinned, as if he enjoyed being talked about.

Ben laughed. "I told you he's nuts. Right, Bep?"

Bepy smiled and nodded; he couldn't believe what he was seeing at this bank.

"What kinda soda you want?" Arty asked. In the same breath, without waiting for a reply, he continued, "All I got is cream."

They began to eat the sandwiches, drink cream soda, and talk about the prosciutto. Arty finally looked up from his sandwich, "Cut up another loaf, make more sandwiches. I worked up a good appetite today. I'm still hungry." Then he turned to his other man. "And you, cut up another tomato, and be careful with that sword, ya *mizadobla.*"

After lunch they got down to business. Ben did all the talking. He told the banker what Bepy needed and that he needed the cars in three weeks without fail.

"It's impossible to get one hundred cars in three weeks," the banker replied. "The loan committee doesn't even meet until next month. By the time the loan gets approved, if it's approved..." and he continued giving reasons why it couldn't be done.

"We don't want a loan; forget the committee and all that stuff," Bepy interrupted harshly. "We want the car deal only. We want one hundred large new cars, delivered to a Brooklyn pier—all with paid bills—in the name of Alley Opolito. I want your bank to process the deal, pay all duties and shipping for us with a letter of credit, and I want you to use your contacts to obtain the cars. You got the contacts, you finance the car dealers. So all you got to do is squeeze them. Call in your favors."

The fat man stared straight ahead while Bepy continued. "Call in your favors; get them to produce. The cars are going to Saudi Arabia. Of course, the letter of credit will never be exercised. It's just a front to make the deal look regular to customs, so it doesn't look like a scam.

"The cars will land in the name of Alley Opolito. Later on, he'll either transfer them to the Arabs or he'll lease them. Do you understand what I want?" Arty still said nothing. "The loophole in the law is there's no limit on the number of cars an American can own in a foreign country. They can't refuse to export the vehicles. And the letter of credit is like a check that never gets cashed."

"Sure, I understand. It all sounds great to me. But why should my bank do all of this for you? We don't know you; we never did business with you. Of course we know Benny, but you're talking about getting one hundred cars transferred, letters of credit, all kinds of bullshit. You want me to call in my favors.

"I did a favor for a guy a few years ago," the banker went on to say. "We gave him a million dollars to set up a car dealership. He sold off all the collateral and equity and then closed down. We didn't control the equity on this bum, and he went into bankruptcy. He took all the cash as personal salaries for him and his family. Now he's worth three and a half million, and his corporation is broke. And what d'ya think? We can't touch the guy.

"He almost cost me my job with the bank. The board of directors was talking to themselves for six months. Of course we sued him, so we could legally take the loss on our books. You know what we got? We got a message from the street telling us that he's connected, so we better lay off him. Look, I'd like to help, but I can't get involved with unprofitable deals. My nerves are getting bad; I'm beating up the bank's clients—all kinds of crap like that. I'm sorry Ben, I can't help you. I wish I could. If the letter of credit happened to get turned in by accident in Hong Kong, or London, or someplace, we'd have to pay on it. My bank would be fully responsible. Why don't you ask me for something easy, like opening up a Christmas Club or somethin' like that, huh? Things like this could destroy me and the bank." When he finished, the room remained quiet.

"Suppose I do you a favor?" Bephino finally asked.

"What kinda favor you gonna do for me?"

"Suppose I collect that million bucks for you from the guy who's connected?"

"How are you gonna collect? We tried everything. You can't touch this guy, believe me. He's got friends." Arty watched Bepy closely as he spoke. Gradually he switched gears and slowed down.

"If you collect that million, you get twenty-five percent for yourself, and I handle your deal for you free. It'll be a freebee, and I'll have one hundred cars in one week ready to go on the pier. I'll even give your grandmother a line of credit. How's that? But, you tell me how you gonna handle a connected guy? It's big trouble. They can make your life miserable, them guys. These guys are family—you know, Mafioso. *Ah capeesh?*"

Ben chuckled, but Bepy answered in all seriousness, "I'll disconnect him. How's that?"

"Well . . . if you got connect . . . OK, then you got yourself a deal. If you collect the million, then we talk seriously."

"Good," Bepy agreed. "You'll deal with me directly or with Benny on all the car details. I'll even send you a cashier's check for one and a half million from my Arab clients, soon as you get the cars. You deposit it in an account in the name of Alley Opolito. The only way any money is to be paid out of the account is if me or Ben calls you.

"Don't fuck us up. We'll do everything by phone—no withdrawal slips. And on the letter of credit, relax. It's only a formality, to show customs what they wanna see. It doesn't mean much."

"Yeah, but it's *cash* we guarantee," Arty replied. "I want it understood that I sign a letter of credit only if you collect our mil."

"Understood," Ben and Bepy responded together. Bepy continued to explain. "In exactly one week from today, the cars must be loading on the pier. Also, make sure you insure the entire shipment. I don't want the ship to go down while we're holding the paper.

"You said the guy got three and a half million personally, huh? I'll have your bank's uncollected million dollars in five days. Now give me the name and address of this guy who won't pay you. I wanna know where he eats, drinks, anything you have on him. Is he Jewish or Italian or whatever?"

"The guy's a fast-talking Italian. He could sell you the Brooklyn Bridge. He seems Jewish, but he's not; he's Italian and smooth as silk. He's got a face that makes you feel sorry for him, so be careful when you're trying to collect. He'll roll his eyes at you like a sad hound dog. This guy's so good he may even try to borrow from you."

Bepy smiled.

"His name is Jack Orio," Arty continued. "Here's a file I keep on him. This'll tell you everything I know. But he's a talker, now, remember."

The men shook hands, and the deal was made. They were headed toward the parking lot when Ben said, "I'll be right with you, Bep. Wait for me in the car." He returned to Arty's office. Five minutes later, he came out, got in the car, and pulled away.

"How come you went back in the bank?" Bepy asked.

"I had to talk to him alone. I gave it to him straight. Now he knows who Bephino Menesiero is. I don't want him to fuck your deal up. Sometimes he gets lazy and don't take things seriously enough. He don't return calls for a month. So I let him know who he's dealing with. It's only fair to him. I explained I don't have a coffin his size, and I told him I wasn't joking either. So he's OK now. The guy is happy to do business with you."

"I can't believe that banker beating up that guy."

Changing the subject, Ben asked, "How do you plan on making contact with this guy Jack Orio?"

"We'll have Alley and Mikey sleep on his doorstep, and when they got him fully under surveillance they'll call. Then I go with you and Alley Oop to notch his fast-talking tongue."

"You mean like punching the coupons on a treasury bond?"

"Yeah, like that. The guy's a fast talker, right? He sells the Brooklyn Bridge for a living. So I'm gonna be fast with the paper puncher on his tongue. Alley will hold his head like he's in a vice. His head won't move—only his eyes and tongue will pop out."

In Las Vegas, Alan Stone was still wining and dining the sheiks. Bepy called him and told him to have the Arabs deposit a million and a half in U.S. funds in the New Vegas Bank and to transfer the funds to Alley Opolito, in care of the People's Northern Point Community Bank, Bronx, New York.

"This must be done right away, because the cars will be shipped in a week or so, and funds must be cleared before they're shipped out of the U.S.," he explained. "Tell the Arabs one hundred large-size Pontiacs, Buicks, and Oldsmobiles will arrive in Saudi Arabia in three to four weeks.

"The money will also cover the Arabs through an insurance policy in case the ship goes down. Everything is being taken care of. I found the loophole we needed to export the vehicles and the people to handle it for us. Everything is OK so far, so pass the info on to your clients that the deal is made."

Bepy, Ben, and Alley Oop waited two hours for Jack Orio to come out of his house.

"I hope this guy's still got the million bucks," Ben remarked.

"He's got it," Bepy replied. "I read his file carefully. He's got *some* investments, this guy. What a financial statement! You wouldn't believe it: trust accounts, mutual funds, all kinds of stuff. All he's gotta do is liquidate a little for us."

Finally, Jack came out and got into his car. They walked over to it while he was warming up the engine and climbed in with him. Alley quickly whacked Jack one time across the side of the head with one of his paws. Ben, on the other side, held a gun to his ribs and ordered him to move over to the middle.

Ben took the wheel so fast Jack didn't know what happened as the car pulled away from the curb. Bepy and Mikey followed behind. Jack, stunned, was holding his head. He was scared, his face sort of pale green.

Ben drove to the rear of a junkyard, parked, then cocked the hammer of his gun and raised it to Jack's head. Jack began to beg for his life.

"Please, buddie. I have three kids. Don't kill me. I'll do anything you say. Anything. Maybe you got the wrong guy," he was repeating as Bepy got in the car.

"Jack Orio, there's a paid contract on your life," Bepy yelled harshly at him. "I understand you're a connected fellow. Well, where're your connections now? Why aren't they here to save your life? After we shoot your brains out, we'll squash you in this car. How do you like that? We're gonna squash you like a fuckin' turnip, ya droopy-eyed bastard."

"Please, fellas, why me?" Jack looked puzzled. "Connected? Who's connected? I'm a financial adviser for my own firm. Why is there a contract on my life? I never hurt anyone, I only make them money. Maybe you got the wrong guy?"

"You know Fat Arty?" Bepy asked. "You fucked his bank."

Jack's eyes widened with fear, "Oh, my God, please don't hurt me. I'll pay Arty's bank the money, I swear. I'm sorry. It was a misunderstanding. Please. I'm sorry. Don't kill me. I'll pay the money. I was so busy I didn't have time to take care of Arty's bank. Now I got plenty of time. Please let me pay it back. OK, fellas? Don't kill me."

"Come on, let's get it over with," Ben said impatiently, trying to scare Jack further. "Let's whack this mutt."

"What's the sense of killing me when I could pay the money back in one day?" Jack was crying and talking now. "I have it to pay. Why kill? Why kill? You'll take a life for no reason," he said. His sad face and smooth talk somehow didn't go together, but his words 'I have it to pay' were just what Bepy wanted to hear.

"OK, Jack. We received fifty grand to hit you. If you pay the million you owe, plus interest, I'll cancel the contract. This is the first time we ever considered canceling a contract, and it's only because you have three kids. But if Arty doesn't get the money by 3:00 P.M. tomorrow, we kill you and your kids, understand?"

"I sure do. What good is money if you can't live to spend it?"

"Now you're talking," Bepy said, smiling. "But to show you we mean business, we're gonna clip your coupon." Alley grabbed him and began to squeeze his head, turning him to face Bepy in the rear. Jack's tongue was soon hanging out of his mouth. Bepy took a paper punch and notched his tongue quickly. Jack screamed and moaned, as blood began dripping.

"See, Mr. Orio. Now when you talk fast, you'll whistle, too. I don't like fast talkers, so I slow them down with a whistle. Today I use a paper punch; tomorrow I use a paper shredder on your fuckin' baggy eyelids. If the money is not at the bank tomorrow, we will kill you and your kids. Your wife we're gonna save." Bepy pointed at Alley Oop. "See him? He fucks her. He fucks her right in her big ass. Could you imagine your wife being banged by a guy like that? Look at him," Bepy yelled.

Jack looked at Alley Oop's rough, smiling face as Bepy continued. "After he fucks her a while, then we clip her tongue, so she will be happy to sign the million dollar check after you're dead. Understand, Jackie boy?"

Blood was dripping all over Jack's shirt and suit. His teeth were red with blood.

"Yes, I understand. Thank you," Jack mumbled, speaking through the mouthful of blood. "They'll get the money. I know what's happening. They'll get the money, I promise you."

They drove back to his house and left him sucking his tongue and crying in his car. As they left, Ben asked, "Did you ever punch coupons before, or is this the first time?"

Bepy, deep in thought, didn't find Ben's question worth answering and didn't bother to acknowledge him. Alley got the message, but Ben, a very persistent man, still talked.

"You know, years ago we'd stop and eat after work. Now we don't even stop for linguine and clams anymore. We don't get fed. We work but no eat. I think Bepy's getting ulcers. He don't like to eat no more."

"Don't mind him, Alley," Bepy said. "He's got a clear head. I'm trying to think about business, and he's busting my balls with the linguine."

The next day, Fat Arty was shocked when the Pioneer Village National Bank of Queens called and said one million two hundred and ten thousand dollars was in their vault and ready for transfer to his bank, by armored car, from Mr. Orio's trust accounts. President Argento was shocked and thrilled. He couldn't believe it had happened so fast. He called the board members. He told them, "Jack Orio's trust accounts, judgment-proof accounts, paid off. We got to him. The money is on the way here by armored car."

Also, the one-and-a-half-million-dollar cashier's check from Las Vegas, to back the car purchases, and the letter of credit for Alley Opolito had arrived by the Western Union and was now in the bank.

Holy shit, the banker thought, I'd better call the car wholesalers and make sure those cars are all in and ready to go. This guy's for real. He doesn't fuck around.

From that day on, the Bronx bank would honor Bephino Menesiero's every wish. His grandmother even got her letter of credit. Fat Arty was a man of his word. The friendship with the banker was to be a long and lasting one. The automobiles were shipped to Saudi Arabia. The Arabs were overjoyed with the smoothness of the transaction, and Bepy and Alan made a profit of six hundred thirty-eight thousand dollars.

"We have six hundred thirty-eight thousand dollars to whack up on the car deal. How do you wanna handle it, Alan? It's still lying in the account at the bank," Bepy told Alan, who had come to New York for business and dinner at Bepy's home.

"Whatever you say, Bepy. It don't matter to me. You did all the work."

"What are you talking about? If you hadn't got the clients, we'd have had no deal. We're partners, fifty-fifty. What are you, a schmuck or what?"

Alan Smiled. "You know, for a guinea, you're all right."

"I'm all right? We're partners, aren't we?"

Dana served dinner, listened, but said nothing while the men discussed business. The children talked to each other. They, too, had been taught never to interfere in their father's business discussions.

The men agreed to put four hundred fifty grand in a Swiss company account they controlled. "I'm sure Arty will handle the transfer for us. It will be safe in a Swiss account. Ben gets seventy-five grand, Alley Oop gets seventy-five grand, and the thirty-eight grand that's left, we split for pocket money between you and me. OK with you, Alan?"

"That's fine."

"Did I hear pocket money?" Dana asked, hearing her cue.

"Don't worry, we'll fill your pocket up, too. We'll always need a good cook like you, Dana," Alan responded. Then, peeking over his glasses, he whispered to Bepy, "Give them," indicating Dana and the children, "give them a few grand outta our pocket money. Let them enjoy, also." Then raising his voice back to normal, he asked, "Is that enough money for Ben and Alley Oop?"

"Yeah, that's plenty for them," Bepy explained. "We're not partners with them. This was your deal, Alan. They're happy whatever they get from these things. They're well taken care of, believe me. They get seventy-five grand each; that's more than they expected, believe me. But I'll give them more from a collection I made for the bank. I picked up a nice chunk, and all I did was clip a guy's tongue. I'll take care of them again on that deal."

"OK, Bep. Whatever you say. As long as everyone is happy."

The next day, Bepy had lunch with Fat Arty, this time at a restaurant, not on his desk. Arty told him he had a quarter-million coming to him on the Jack Orio collection.

"How about interest of two hundred ten grand?" Arty asked. "The bank didn't expect to get the interest. It wasn't part of our original deal with you. We have it in our vault, and I haven't entered it in the bank's records, yet. I waited to speak to you, Bephino." Arty was being cautious. "Do you want the interest plus the quarter-million? It's up to you. I don't want to do the wrong thing."

"You're smart, Arty. You got respect," Bepy commented. "OK, this is what we're gonna do. Have my quarter-million ready to go tomorrow at 10:00 A.M.—big bills, hundred minimum. Have the interest also in big bills. I'll let you know where and what on the two hundred ten grand when I arrive tomorrow. I wanna talk to Benny first."

"OK. That's fine with me. The money is already in big bills."

Bepy wanted to show Arty that Ben was also a respected fellow and should be consulted on this decision.

"The other money, under Opolito, will go to a Swiss bank next week," he added. "I'll tell you about that later."

At ten the following day, Bepy, Alley, and Ben arrived to collect the quarter-million. They also collected the two hundred ten grand in interest. Ben told Arty they would see him that night around nine at his home. "We're stopping over for coffee," he said.

That evening at nine, Ben and Bepy dropped over to Arty's house. Ben loved glory, so he did the honors—putting sixty grand on the table. He told Arty that he was getting sixty grand for his retirement plan in advance, as his share of the interest money. Arty couldn't believe it. It was a gift, he thought; the bank had no claim on it. He never would have believed that Bepy would share the interest payment with him. He thought he would be a hard guy to deal with.

Ben and Bepy split a hundred thousand, and earlier that day Alley had received fifty thousand to split with Monkey—all from the bank collection deal. They were well compensated for their loyalty. This was important to the success in their small family.

16

Bepy received a late night call from Mexico City. "They're still going full blast here." Joey D said, "These Mexicans are getting rich; they're buying new cars and, houses. . . . You know, Bepy, International Amex turned this town around. We really gave them a boost in their economy. They were dead before we came."

"That's good," Bepy replied. "We help them; they help us. Beautiful. Keep them happy, huh, Joey D? We need the merchandise."

"Hey, Bepy. Is Coney Island still there? How's the hot dogs doing?"

"The hot dogs are still hot. Coney's still the same, but the Puerto Ricans are getting close to Bay Fifteen. I hear from the kids there are a lot of fights on the beach now. How's Sheila Diamond?"

"She went to Florida to see her grandmother. The old lady's sick. She'll be there for a month." Joey D paused and then asked, "How's Norma?"

"Norma?" Bepy exclaimed. "Who the hell ever sees Norma? I haven't seen her in years."

"I feel bad for her." Joey D's voice was choked. "She's got the kids and all. Do you think she's all right?"

"What the fuck are you talking about, Joey? Norma? Who the fuck ever thinks of her? It was five years ago I last saw her." Bepy could tell Joey D was feeling low, asking about Coney Island and Norma. "Come on, Bepy, remember when you called her and told her to find Red, you were surrounded by fifty niggers in school, and you needed help."

"How do you know that? I didn't know you in my schooldays."

"She told me the story, Bep. She said that when you were a kid, you always had trouble."

"You know, Joey, I had a feeling you were gonna fuck up my night. Right at the beginning of this phone call; the minute you began to talk and didn't announce yourself with a hello, I knew you were screwed up in the head."

"The operator announced me. I heard her."

Cutting him short, Bepy said, "I'll call you back next week. Goodnight, Joey D." He hung up.

What the hell, is he crackin' up? he thought. Bringing up all that bullshit about when I was a kid. They must be fuckin' up his brain in Mexico. Christ, I don't believe that guy.

He began brushing his teeth, but kept thinking of Joey D and Norma. What a weak bastard! The guy's got everything he wants in Mexico and he's thinking about Norma. Rinsing out his mouth, he kept thinking about Norma. Ah, what the hell. I'll drop over tomorrow to see if she's OK.

He turned out the hall lights and went to bed. Two hours later he still hadn't fallen asleep. Lying there in bed he wondered if Joey D was OK. Maybe Sabu is crackin' up; he didn't sound too good.

Dana woke up and complained tiredly, "You're moving around, Bepy. You're disturbing my sleep. What's wrong?"

"You wanna get laid?" he whispered.

"No-oo. I'm tired. Are you kidding? I'm sleeping. What's wrong with you? It's 3:00 A.M."

"Holy shit. What a night this is gonna be!" He rolled over once again.

The next day Bepy went out of his way, over to Brooklyn. He dropped by Norma's house and knocked on the door. One of the kids opened the door and led him to the kitchen, where Norma was sitting at the table. He was shocked by her appearance: she must have gained a hundred pounds, her hair was in rollers, and she was wearing a torn terry-cloth bathrobe. She had dark rings under her eyes, and her complexion was a sickly yellow.

She had been a tall, good-looking, well dressed girl at one time. He thought of when she used to walk so proudly past the poolroom, showing off her body with an air of importance. She was Red's girl, and Red had been a three-to-five favorite to make it big in business. Everyone in the neighborhood had known Red to be a winner. But an infectious disease—called greed—can destroy more than one person's life; it can ruin the life of loved ones. And Red's greed had destroyed Norma.

Now she was a fat, sloppy person. She sat there eating an orange and spitting the pits out on the table. She seemed unaware he was there.

"Hey, Norma. Are you all right?" he asked softly.

She didn't seem to hear him. She made no effort to reply.

"Norma. It's me, Bephino. How are you?"

He gently put his hand on her shoulder. His touch stirred her to slight awareness. Slowly, her eyes rotated toward his face.

"I was praying," she said. "I like to pray."

Her voice sounded very strange. Then, she smiled. "Oh, Bephino, it's you! After all these years you came to see me. That's nice."

Relieved that she was able to recognize him, he ventured to ask again, "Norma, how are you? Are you all right?"

Looking around the room while he waited for her to answer, his stomach turned. The counter and table were littered with dirty dishes. Something dark brown that looked like a chewed-on drumstick was stuck to a moldy blob he couldn't recognize. Most of the cupboard doors were open, and he could see that they were almost empty except for the cockroaches crawling around.

"I was just praying to God, Bepy. I didn't hear you come in. I was just..." she repeated. Suddenly she jerked her head up and sat tall in the chair and slammed the rest of her orange down on the table, "Damn it! Does it look like I'm all right? Hell, I'm ruined. I'm dead. Look at me! I'm fat and ugly now. I used to be pretty, didn't I, Bepy?" She looked at him. The dark rings under her eyes disturbed Bepy.

"My life has changed so much. Nobody speaks to me on the street anymore. They just whisper stories about me. I've lost my way, Bepy. I'm lost...." Tears rolled down her cheek and mixed with the orange juice dripping from her chin.

"Where's your husband? Where's Red?" Bepy asked, handing her a pressed white handkerchief.

"Thank you," she murmured as she wiped her chin and cheeks. "Red left me five years ago. He ran off with some girl he met from New Jersey. He left me with the kids and flat broke. I eat oatmeal three times a day. I'm getting fat as an elephant." As she talked, Bepy looked for a clean place to sit. Finally, he wiped a chair off with a hand towel and sat down next to Norma.

"Do you know that I suck pricks now to make a few bucks just to pay the rent?" she cried. "One guy brought me an orange last night instead of paying me. Those dirty, filthy men!" Her words were choked by her sobs. "My life is ruined, Bepy. I might as well be dead. I'm living in hell. What did I ever do to deserve this? Tell me, Bepy, what did I ever do that was so wrong? I was a good girl. I was a good girl," she repeated, looking up at him.

"It's the kids I keep holding on for. But what kind of life can they have?"

"Look, Norma," he said in a thick voice. "You did me a favor once. I owe you."

"Yeah, I got Red for you, didn't I, Bep? I saved your life."

Bepy gently smiled at her. "Yeah, I owe you," he said. "That's why I'm here. I wanna help you, Norma. I never forget a good friend—or a bad one. I own a beautiful apartment house six blocks from here. Not far from the Endicott Theater. Remember the Endicott, where we used to neck as kids?"

"There's a three bedroom apartment that just became vacant. Tomorrow, I'll have you moved out of this place and into that empty apartment. Don't pack too much of this junk. Leave the crap. I'll furnish the entire place for you. I'll buy you and the kids all new stuff, new furniture—beds, mattresses, television, everything. Don't worry. Take your kids and go get all new clothes for them. Get yourself a wardrobe that fits you. Stay clean and keep those pigs out of your home. I'll pay for everything."

At that moment a knock was heard on her door. Bepy turned at the hard sound of it, a man's knuckles. Norma just sat quietly.

The knock came again. Bepy walked to the door and opened it.

"Is Norma here?" a large, husky man wearing a peacoat asked anxiously.

"Who are you?" Bepy asked.

"I'm Bobby Greene, from Long Island City. I stop here once in a while. I drive a rig."

Bepy howled, "Get the fuck out of here, you stupid bastard," and slammed the door. Walking back to Norma and reaching into his pocket he pulled out a wad of money. He counted out about two thousand dollars and placed it in front of her.

"You never pay rent again, so you don't need to depend on that kind of man anymore. I'll give you one hundred fifty bucks a week for the rest of your life. OK, Norma? You're Italian; you don't suck pricks for anyone! You don't have to do that. You come from good people. *Ah capeesh?*" he asked, raising his voice.

Bepy felt very uncomfortable; his heart was heavy with pity. He was trying hard to give her respect. He smiled as he spoke, "You're Italian, and you got friends," he repeated. "OK?"

Norma looked up at him. "Bepy, you really mean it? You would do this for me?"

"Why not?" he said with a lump in his throat. "We were kids together, and you saved my life, didn't you? I owe you. Tomorrow, meat and food will be delivered to your new apartment. My men will be there at 7:00 A.M. All new furniture will be in the rooms for you and the kids, OK?" He pushed the two thousand dollars on the table toward her. "Don't worry, Norma; you'll be all right. Leave all this shit behind. If you need anything, call me. Here's my number. If any guys come around to bother you, let me know. I'll take care of them. Here's the address and apartment number. It's yours forever. And there's no strings attached. But if Red shows up, call me. I wanna talk to the bum."

"Thank you, Bephino. God bless you. I'll pray for you. I'll pray for you every day."

Patting her head, Bepy said deeply, "Good, Norma, 'cause I need it."

Bepy went to see Monkey and Little Pauli. They were waiting for him at the hero shop on Wall Street.

"How's everything?" he asked.

"Business is good," Pauli answered. "Everybody's losing, so we're winning. Did you see the books and all the slips I left you?"

"Yeah, I looked them over. Business is good. Pauli, for the next six months drop off the cash at my mother-in-law's house. We'll change the setup for a while, OK?"

"Yeah, whatever you say, Bep. Is something wrong?"

"No. Just do it the way I say, OK? Just tell my mother-in-law to put it away for me in a closet or something. Go there twice a week so you don't pile up too much in your pockets. Are you getting enough, Pauli?"

"Yeah. I'm not complaining. Why you askin,' Bepy? Is something wrong?"

"Look, Pauli, if you need more, take it. But always tell me. Don't ever let me dream of you, Pauli. *Ah capeesh?*"

"That's the last thing I want you to do, dream of me, Bep."

"That's good, Pauli." Then turning to Monkey he asked, "Monkey, how about you? Are you getting enough?"

"Yeah, Bepy. Why all the concern? You know we're makin' good money with you. We never complain, do we? Alley Oop gave me twenty-five grand yesterday. What's that for? He said it was from the Bronx job. I had nothing to do with that job. How come you sent me twenty-five grand?"

"You know, Monkey, I never thanked you for getting those fur hats for Bephino the rabbi years ago. Now I thank you. I give you twenty-five thousand for that job. You're my loyal friend, Monkey. I'll never forget you."

"You paid me for that rabbi thing. Don't you remember?"

"Yeah, but this is your bonus. I forgot to give you your bonus. Remember how poor we were once? Well, we're poor no more. Now we got respect!

"Someday, Monkey, I'll give you a couple of stores for your birthday or for a wedding gift. I'm gonna split these stores with you. When the time comes, you'll be all set. I won't have to worry about you. Why don't you get married so we can have a few little monkeys around?"

Little Pauli was listening carefully. Bepy turned to him and said, "I owe Monkey for many things he has done. I don't forget the good. I don't forget the bad, either. I ask these questions today only to make sure you guys are OK and so you know I'm concerned. I owe Monkey for his unquestioning loyalty. The time has come in my life to try and express my feelings to you. You've done a lot over the years. Someday, I'll make you a partner, too, in all the betting. Don't worry, Pauli. Just stay clean. No dreams, OK?"

"I know what happened with Red years ago," Pauli said. "Greed warped his brain. I'm too smart for that shit."

"*Bene.* I've got something I want done today. It's important to me. You remember those beatniks that rented an apartment in the new apartment house building, the one I bought over in the old neighborhood?"

"Yeah. Near the Endicott. What about them?"

"Tell those creeps their lease expires today. I want them out by four o'clock. Throw them the fuck out! If you have to smack them, do it, but I want them out by four today. Everything they own must be out of the apartment, too. Rent them a truck if you have to, and get them out of the neighborhood. They were a big mistake.

"Then hire some cleaning people to wash down everything. I want the place spotless, because I got all new furniture coming. Mr. Saputo, the furniture guy, will furnish the whole place tonight—new carpets and everything. He's gonna send his trucks the minute you call and work all night. OK, Pauli? So I want the place clean and nice."

"Who's gonna move in?" Monkey asked.

"Norma, Red's wife. She's in bad shape. He left her flat broke. And it's partly our fault that he left town. So we owe her. She'll move in tomorrow. So throw the beatniks out and clean it up. Have the place ready tonight and accept all deliveries until at least midnight. Tomorrow the food will arrive. You guys got a lot of work to do in a short time, so you better call a cleaning service right now and get a crew sent over. I'll stop over later to see what's happening."

"Who's gonna handle the action today?" Pauli asked.

"Let Blubber Head take the bets. He's been running all year for us; he can handle it," Bepy replied.

"Boy, Bep, you're something. You're gonna do all of that for Norma?" Monkey asked.

"We gotta take care of our people, Monkey. We can't turn our backs on old friends. She's been letting herself be abused by perverts just so she can feed her kids. Joey D, who used to help her, is gone, and she's living like an animal. She did me a favor once and I owe her. I don't forget so easy. I'm gonna check on her tomorrow afternoon, after she moves in. Make sure the place is nice and clean for her. I'll see you there tonight. I'm eating over at my mother-in-law's, in case you need me."

"Sure, Bepy. We'll handle it. Don't worry."

About ten, Bepy went to see how the apartment was coming. Three people were washing the place down. He walked in and began checking around. In the bathroom, he found a black woman in her twenties bending over cleaning the tub.

She jumped up at the sound of the medicine cabinet door opening. "Oh, you surprised me, mister."

"Don't let me disturb you," he said. "I'm just checking things out."

She was a pretty girl, her face shiny with perspiration. She smiled and looked closely at Bepy, almost directly into his eyes. After a moment or two, she asked, "Hey, mister, don't I know you?"

He smiled, thinking she was trying to be friendly, and shook his head. "No, I don't think so." And he left the small bathroom.

"I think I know you, mister," she said, following him.

He turned to look at her carefully, with a glitter of amusement in his eyes. "What makes you think I know you?"

She smiled. "I remember ya pretty face, mister."

"Oh, yeah, from where?"

"My late grandfather was Jesse."

Bepy's face dropped down, and his mouth stayed open for a few moments. It was Jesse's little granddaughter, grown into a full-breasted brown beauty. He couldn't believe it! She remembered him from that night. He had almost forgotten all about her, but the little girl had remembered his face even though the hallway was so dark.

He shook his head, grunted, and walked away slowly, as if she had made a mistake, but she called out to him, "Hey, friend! Grandpa was right. You is an angel."

Bepy had to smile, thinking, You just never know who or what's waiting for you around the corner.

One evening Bephino and Alan were in Las Vegas working with the head gift buyer for enormous JPJ Corve, Inc., a department-store chain. They were trying to get him to handle their Mexican product line. The company, the fourth largest in its market, had four thousand discount stores in the United States and Canada. It was a very important deal for still-growing International Amex, and could bring it to the rainbow's end.

Bepy asked Weisman, the buyer, directly to take on their line. Weisman acted coy and reluctant, claiming he had enough vendors at the moment and the time wasn't right for new Spanish products in his kind of store.

"I'm gonna make you a nice deal, so you can retire, Mr. Weisman," Bepy said, a bit carelessly.

"I'm all ears, Mr. Menesiero." he replied.

"Our company, International Amex, has just been listed on the OTC exchange. Our stock is trading at three dollars per share. If you agree to handle our full line of products, our stock will jump to thirteen just on the news of the agreement. Later we'll sign a contract with you for five years, and the stock will run up again, possibly to twenty or thirty bucks. If you distribute our products, I will give you ten thousand shares of stock at three bucks. Your cost—zero. If you agree, I'll make the transfer this week; it will cost me thirty thousand dollars. It'll be worth three hundred thousand dollars to you within a year."

Weisman smiled coldly at Bepy's offer, then said, "I'm gonna be painfully honest with you, Mr. Menesiero. First of all, I couldn't retire on three hundred thousand dollars, and, second, it's not worth it for me even to consider your offer seriously."

Alan began to smile; he knew Bepy had low-balled Weisman.

"How much can you retire on?" Bepy asked.

"I can retire on one hundred thousand shares at three bucks, and hope to God it goes to at least twenty bucks a share. If it goes to twenty, then I can call my boss and tell him to go fuck himself."

"Sounds like you need two million to retire." Bepy said drily.

"Well, if I'm gonna pull a stunt like that, I'd better do it big, because I won't get a second shot at it."

"I don't understand what you mean by stunt. This is a perfectly legitimate deal, with a stock bonus for your extra efforts," Bepy said, acting insulted. "You're asking me to lay out three hundred thousand dollars instead of thirty thousand. That's a lot of bread," he frowned.

"I don't want you to lay out anything," Weisman responded. "I'm not asking for a thing. I just told you how much I would need to retire on. Let's face it, the merchandise you're selling is *dreck,* and it's difficult for me to add *dreck* to the JPJ Corve line. Our stores have class. It'll bounce back at me. Who needs that?"

Bepy smiled cordially at Weisman, but his fangs were really showing. Alan could tell that Bepy did not like his merchandise to be called *dreck.* So Alan interceded. "Let's all think about it. We'll meet in a few weeks to talk again. I think we need a recess." He tried to signal to Bepy to forget it for now. "Let's talk to our accountants first, Bephino."

He wanted to talk to Bepy in private to smooth out their thoughts about handling Weisman. The man had the key; he also had a lot of experience dealing with vendors, and he wasn't going to be bought cheaply. They needed a new plan.

"Look, Bephino," Alan said after Weisman had left, "you got to be softer when you deal with a Jew. I know; I'm a Jew. We get turned off very easy. You gotta handle us softly. This guy is sharp. He's playing coy. Don't upset him. You'll never get him that way." Bepy listened but did not reply.

The next day, Bepy got a telepone call from New York: Don Emilio was arriving in Las Vegas at two that afternoon. Bepy was surprised. The Don never left New York City. Sounds strange, he thought.

Alan thought maybe he wanted to have some fun, but his fun was linguini with white clam sauce and visiting Bephino's Staten Island home.

The Don was happy to see the men waiting for him at the airport. He came toward them with a smile on his lips, but not in his eyes. His eyes were watching every movement around him. He seemed uncomfortable and out of place. His two bodyguards were scrutinizing everyone that came close.

Don Emilio was in his late sixties, but still looked sharp and carried himself well. Watching him, Bepy could feel that something wasn't right.

At the hotel, while relaxing in Don Emilio's suite, Bepy spoke to Big Bubber and Lefty, hoping to discover some indication to what was going on. But they said nothing. The two of them stayed with Morrano even in the suite, which was unusual and made Bepy feel uncomfortable. It was as if they were guarding him against everyone. When Morrano went to the bathroom, Big Bubber's eyes followed him down the hall.

"What's wrong?" Bepy asked hastily.

"Nothing's wrong. Why should anything be wrong?" Big Bubber answered sarcastically.

Noticing Big Bubber's tone of voice, Bepy looked him up and down. Big Bubber was out of line; he had forgotten his respect for Bephino. He knew how close Bepy was to Don Emilio. Why the sarcasm? And why with him—a strong, loyal, close friend for years. He probed Big Bubber once again.

Don Emilio heard the discussion as he came back and told Bepy, "Everything's OK. My wife told me the twins were in Las Vegas on a vacation. So I thought I would come to see them. I came to surprise them. OK, Bephino? That's the reason I'm here. Don't worry."

"If that's the reason, wonderful. Then let's have some fun," Bepy said, looking doubtfully at Big Bubber. "The kids will be pleased to know that you came to see them."

The red carpet was rolled out for the Don. The whole group went to several of the big shows and ate in the best restaurants the hotel had to offer. Violinists at their table throughout the entire dinner caused heads to turn. People readily and casually walked by to view the occupants of Alan Stone's table.

Every time the Don admired a show girl, one of the twins would tease him. "Are you sure you came just to see us?"

He enjoyed their attention and teased back. "Of course. Just to see you two. I'm much too old for the ladies." He'd laugh. "By the way, I'm going back tomorrow. I need to rest. This fast life is too much for me."

Before leaving for the airport he told Bepy privately, "You're smart, Bephino Menesiero. You smell trouble, and you're right. See me in New York when you get back. I'll tell you a little story."

"Why not now?"

"No. We don't spoil our fun. These days we spent together were rare and beautiful. I don't wanna ruin them with terrible business. I had fun with you, Alan, and the children. This was a nice moment in my life, and I thank you. And watch out for your daughter; she's getting to be too beautiful! I noticed too many young men look at her."

"I will," Bepy answered in a low voice. "I'll meet you in New York in two days."

"That's good." Morrano smiled. "I'll see you in Brooklyn." Then, hesitating, he whispered, "See, I told you you needed a guy like Alan Stone. You seem to like Jews now, huh?" he nudged Bepy.

"Alan's topnotch." Bepy grinned. "You're always right, Mr. Morrano. Alan's first-class." Then he added, "I'll see you in two days."

They embraced each other as Don Emilio departed.

"Since you're so close to him, how come you still call him Mr. Morrano, and not Emilio," Alan asked, "and why did you think something's wrong? He seemed OK to me."

"I know the man, Alan—better than Big Bubber, Lefty, and all the rest of them. In the last ten years, I've come to really know him. Believe me, I'm close to this man. If he wants to tell me something, he comes to my home; we talk, we eat, and he watches television with us, then later he tells me the news. He sits on the beach enjoying the ocean; we talk, we smoke our cigars. That's his pattern—bad news after we eat and enjoy. He did the same thing now. Bad news when he's ready to leave. Sometimes he gets so relaxed with me, he even forgets he's Don Emilio Morrano, Boss of Bosses. We are like real family. He loves us. He tries not to show it, but we know he loves us.

"He has trouble, I know for sure. So he comes to Vegas to be near us. It's sort of a sign of weakness in a person. If they see death coming, they wanna be near the strong ones they love. He proved his love to my family, Alan—this is his way of doing it. He has his men: his army, the Capos, the soldiers, but he likes to talk to me. I'm his real strong family. And he only has one daughter and that pinball husband she married. They live in Boston. They're some kind of poetry teachers or nature lovers." Bepy shook his head, then, looking directly at Alan, he added, "I've been calling him Mr. Morrano since I was fifteen years old. It's a matter of respect. I can't get it out of me. Let's go have lunch at the deli. I feel in the mood for corned beef on a bagel."

"Corned beef on a bagel?" Alan asked. "You're supposed to eat corned beef on rye or club, not a bagel. Don't you guineas know how to eat?"

"Yeah. We know corned beef and bagel taste good together. Maybe we should patent this idea and sell it back to the Jews."

"Corned beef on a bagel, huh! A Jew learns something new everyday." Alan grinned.

"Only a smart Jew learns, Alan. Some refuse to learn from Italians"—he winked— "and they stay stupid."

Later, while chewing on a pickle, Alan told Bepy, "One of my buddies from San Francisco has a very serious problem and needs to talk to us. Can we go over to see him today? It's important to him. I told him I'd speak to you about it."

"Where is he?"

"He's here in Vegas. He's a major share owner of the Danube Hotel, on the strip. Can I set up an appointment?"

"Sure. Anytime today. Before I leave for New York. I got Morrano on my mind. You knew that, huh?" Alan nodded. "So you better arrange to see this guy today." Then he asked, "What's this guy's name?"

"Shaggy Goldberg."

"Shaggy Goldberg? What kinda name is that?"

"Would you rather his mother named him Bephino Goldberg?" Alan chuckled.

"You know, Alan, my grandfather had a dog named Shaggy. Boy, was he a hairy little bastard."

"Oh, yeah? Did your grandfather's Shaggy have forty million bananas like my Shaggy?"

"That's why I love you Heebs; you always talk millions. You wanna go over there now?" Bepy asked, wiping his lips with his napkin. "Why keep a guy with forty million waiting."

"OK. I'll tell him we're coming. Oh, remind me. I gotta buy a few shirts. We'll stop by Moe's Shirt Shop after we finish."

At the Danube Hotel, they took the glass elevator to the penthouse suite. "The view of Vegas with the mountains in the background is really something from this angle," Alan pointed out to Bepy.

"Yeah, it sure is beautiful," Bepy answered, staring through the glass like a child visiting the zoo for the first time. "It sure is different from Brooklyn. Look at them purple mountains! Unbelievable."

Alan walked off the elevator and right in like he owned the suite.

Shaggy Goldberg, wearing pajamas, was having lunch: six raw scrambled eggs smothered with chopped lox and raw onions. He was drinking it from a bowl.

"How can you eat lox and raw eggs?" Alan asked.

"I banged a new show girl last night, Alan, and the broad was crazy over Jewish cocks. I'm dead, Alan. She drained all the bone marrow out of my body. I'm like a zombie today. Look at my eyes. They're like two piss holes in the snow. The eggs and lox bring my health back. It's not my favorite meal, believe me." Shaggy grimaced.

"Why don't you drop that mess in a frying pan and make a *frittata*. It's gotta be better than that slop," Bepy said, lighting a cigar.

"What's a *frittata?* It sounds dangerous to me," Shaggy said.

"It's an omelet, and it'll go down better than that gook."

Shaggy smiled at this stranger giving strong, unrequested advice. "A *frittata* goes down better than this?" he asked as he swallowed the mixture in a prolonged gagging scene.

Alan's and Bepy's stomachs turned at the sight. Shaggy Goldberg was a big, sloppy man with wild hair, yellow teeth, and big horn-rimmed glasses. A perfect whale with a shag. He wiped his chin with a linen napkin, neatly draped it over the empty bowl, and lit a cigar.

After a few puffs, he finally shook hands and was formally introduced to Bephino Menesiero. After some small talk, he began to tell his story.

"My wife is an alcoholic. And because she drinks too much, she became vulnerable to the scavengers of the world." He paused. "A tough, dirty world that she does not belong in. She can have anything her heart desires, but the booze makes her a different person. She wanders into ghetto neighborhoods and talks to street people who also drink." He hesitated, "My wife and I do not sleep together anymore. I fuck the show girls, and she can do whatever she likes—provided it doesn't become an embarrassment to me. You know what I mean, fellows? It's the kind of relationship between us. She does her thing and I do mine.

"But my wife met this guy. She slept with him on two weekends that I know of for sure. Then one Sunday night she came home all beat up. I asked her what happened, and she claimed she fell down.

"The woman is no pig. I hope you understand that. She's a beautiful and classy lady with a problem," he added. "She's been well kept, not a mark on her. You know what I mean? She's a tough-looking broad, she's still a beauty in her panties. She shouldn't be beat up.

"So a week ago I noticed she wasn't wearing her nine-carat diamond ring. You know what a fuckin' nine-carat diamond costs? I asked her, 'Charlene, dear, where's your diamond ring?' She said, 'I put it in the vault.' So I checked the vault, but there was nothing there. The next day I asked her again, and she said, 'It'll show up; don't worry. It's around someplace.' Could I believe a nine-carat diamond will show? My father will show his ass from his grave before nine-carats will ever show.

"Finally, one night a close friend of mine says he saw my wife at a San Mateo night club with some guy, and the guy pushed her and then punched her twice in the face. Charlene was hurt, my friend said, but she grabbed his arm and stood by him like a hurt puppy. That hurt me, too, ya know, to hear she was banged around by some stranger. She's the mother of my child. It ain't right. She must have been drunk or nuts to take that shit."

308

Alan and Bepy listened without saying anything.

Shaggy took a deep drag. "You'll never guess what's next, because I can't believe it myself," he said, banging on the nearby bar top. "The fuckin' guy was a *schwartzer!*" His voice rose to a high pitch. "Would you believe a fuckin' black guy? Could you believe my Charlene would do something like this? The guy's a fuckin' coon, and he's with my wife!" Shaggy yelled.

"A *schwartzer?*" Alan asked, stunned. "Why don't you break her fuckin' legs, then cut one tit off? Let her wear the bronze bust. Then she'll learn her place in life."

"I'm not a violent man. You know that, Alan. I hate violence with a passion, but now I heard that the coon has lunch with my wife and daughter and that he's getting real cozy with my daughter. NOW," Shaggy screamed at the top of his lungs, "I'm a violent man. I'm the most violent Jew in the world now. I'm so fuckin' violent I hate myself for fear of what I'm capable of doing. I'll destroy him, I'll . . ."

Bepy smiled at Shaggy's performance and asked, "What do you want us to do? Your wife got herself a black lover. It's not the guy's fault. Let's face it, the guy is doing what all men do."

"I don't mean to be disrespectful, Mr. Menesiero, but I would like to have his black balls cut off and delivered to my wife. Then she'll get the message. Perhaps she'll even stop drinking after seeing his ugly balls in her little jewelry box. Maybe she'll turn to religion or help the needy kids of Israel. Perhaps she'll learn sports or sewing." He looked up at the ceiling. "The woman has caused me an embarrassment," he screamed out. "She broke the rule, and she broke my heart. She crossed the line, and I must take strong action. I'm a violent man now. This is what I want done," he said, taking a deep breath.

Bepy quickly stopped Shaggy from going any further, waving them out on the terrace to finish the contract offering. "Never talk about a death wish in a room; always outside. Now go on with your request, Shaggy," he said.

The big shaggy man looked high up at the top of his hotel. With the wind blowing his silk pajamas, he said, with hesitation, "I want the *schwartzer* dead. Is that all right?" he asked nervously.

"If you have already made your decision, I can understand your feelings. This sounds like an exotic hit. It will cost you two hundred grand. You know that stuff costs."

"Cost? I don't care about cost," he replied softly. "A violent man never cares about cost. Two hundred grand is a fuckin' bargain, and, Mr. Menesiero, I want you to know I appreciate this very much."

"OK. Alan will get all the information you have on this guy. In two to three weeks you'll have your man," Bepy promised, speaking above the wind. "First we have business in New York to take care of. Good-bye."

"It was a pleasure meeting you," Shaggy replied with relief. "Thank you for coming."

After a short stop at Moe's Shirt Shop and Haberdashery, they returned to the hotel. It was 4:00 P.M. In the living room of Bepy's suite, they noticed someone had been drinking at the bar: ice, bottles, glasses, and lemons were scattered about as though a small party had taken place.

"It probably was Alley Oop, having a few cocktails," Bepy suggested. "We haven't spent much time with him since Morrano's visit. He's probably bored and drinking too much."

"It's about that time of day. Shall we have a drink?" Alan asked.

"First, let's check his bedroom," Bepy answered.

The suite had five bedrooms. When they looked through the door of Alley's room, drawn curtains blocked the late-afternoon sunlight. In the semidarkness there were sounds of shuddering and groaning, wet tongues flicking over and under hot flesh. The outline of two bodies was apparent, their features softly obscured. The lovers seemed unreal. Alan and Bepy watched in strict silence. The shadowy figures continued their show, unaware of their standing-room audience.

Alley sat up, balls naked, eyes half closed. He looked like a fat Buddha. Between his fat thighs was a naked woman, sucking and licking. She looked like a groundhog going back under after seeing her shadow. She was so passionate she kept panting and screaming and licking at him all at the same time. Alley, grinning, petted her backside.

Finally, the woman couldn't take any more. She jumped up and demanded that he lie flat on his back. Then she climbed up on his enormous penis and began to squirm her body around, trying her utmost to absorb Alley's huge organ.

With every thrust, she would whimper, "You delicious man, you. You delicious man! Oh, my God, forgive thee." This talk went on for some time. Then suddenly Alley Oop's cock plunged in her so deeply that even Alan and Bepy heard it, saw it, and felt its plunge. As the impact of Alley Oop fully in her became her reality, she stopped in midair, stopped cold by the shock of such a tremendous dick fully entering her body. As she climaxed, she yelled, "Oh, my God! I'm coming. I love it so much. Oh, dear! I'm coming!"

After she fully extended herself, climaxed, and stopped her trembling, she stretched her body over him in contentment. She began to smile and chuckle, and then, finally, she laughed out loud, very loud, not knowing she was on Broadway with a New York audience. "My dear boy, please fuck me! Again and again," she murmured.

"Let's have some fun!" Alan whispered to Bepy. He began applauding. Bepy cracked up and began applauding also. Alan was yelling "Bravo, bravo!"

The woman stumbled off Alley's body and fell off the bed awkwardly to the thickly carpeted floor. Embarrassed, she lay there, trying to remain calm.

The two men were still laughing. Alley Oop got out of bed and took a bow.

Bepy took that as a cue and left, although he couldn't stop laughing. Alan followed him, closing the door firmly to let them know they were now in private.

"Do you believe what we just saw?" Alan howled. "The woman must be some kinda nymph. Did you see how she performed? Where the fuck did he get her?"

About an hour later, Alley Oop and his lady friend came out of his bedroom. She looked like a virtuous woman totally fucked out. She was buttoned up to her collar and wore a black cape and a bonnet. She had freckles on her face and was well into her fifties. She bowed her head and left the suite, walking as though her ass was about to fall off.

"Where did you find *her?*" Alan asked Alley.

"She handed me a pamphlet in the street. I told her she needed a good fuck to get her mind off that pamphlet bullshit. She said God wouldn't like me if he heard me swear like that. She followed me to the hotel, callin' me a sinner. So I said, 'OK, come read me that good pamphlet upstairs.' She didn't want to at first. So I said, 'Ya wanna read me the pamphlet or not?' I told her straight.

"She agreed to the bit about readin' to me and followed me. She kept callin' me a sinner all the way up on the elevator, but when she got here, she forgot all about readin' to me and ordered a double bourbon. She kept pettin' me on my ass while I made the drinks, so I took my cock out, and that was it! She went *pazzo.* She melted like a marshmallow over hot coals. She couldn't control herself; she kept whispering that I was a sinner as she sucked my dick. The woman's another wonder of the world. What d'ya think? Am I right or wrong? Who's the sinner, me or her?"

"Alley," Alan said, still joking around, "did you ever think of joining a circus? You're another wonder of the world yourself."

"Whatta ya mean, a circus?"

"Alley, you're like an art object, you can't be real. I wanna show your cock and balls to the world. We'll get rich. You're not normal; you gotta be a freak."

"Who's a freak? That broad's a freak, not me. Did you see her? Do you call that normal? Did you see that funny hat she wears? You know, Alan, I think you're trying to make a spectator out of me."

Alan, still smiling, leaned over to Alley Oop and, in a serious tone, said, "It's spectacle, not spectator."

"Yeah, that's what I said, spectatacles."

Alan smiled right in Alley Oop's face and whispered, "Give me one of your business cards, Alley."

"I ain't got no business card. You know, Alan, you're a crazy Jewish man. You know that?"

"OK, OK. Don't get so upset. I'm only teasing you," Alan said, patting Alley Oop's back. "You know I love to tease. It's all in fun."

Bepy arrived in New York the next day. He called Don Emilio on his private phone. "I just got in. Everything OK?"

"Yeah, everything's OK."

"When can we meet?" Bepy asked.

"Let's meet at 8:00 P.M. over Lombardi's Restaurant on Coney Island. We'll have some *sfingi di San Giuseppe* for dessert. It's St. Joseph's Day today."

At dinner, Morrano carefully selected an anchovy and a couple of black olives from the *antipasto* in the center of the table. He took time to savor the salty little fish before he said, in a quiet voice, "I have a problem. I smell something and I'm not sure what. *Tu capeesh?*"

Si, io capeesh."

"Frankie Arguilia was knocked off two weeks ago. Three bullets in his chest. Frankie was one of my people."

"I didn't know Arguilia was with you," Bepy responded with surprise. "I've heard of him, but never met him. They say he was a real bad guy, this Frankie."

"Yeah, he was bad, and very loyal. That's why he's dead. He chose death rather than disloyalty. Just before he died, he told some neighborhood guy who found him, 'Tell Morrano there's a contract on him.' Then he died, mumbling. I got the message through the guy who found him. He's from East New York."

Morrano took a sip from his wine glass and looked deep into Bepy's eyes. Bepy put down his fork and waited.

"The way I figure it, it was probably one of the five bosses, who tried to get Frankie to hit me. When they saw in his eyes that he didn't want to, they hit him. Only the bosses knew Frankie worked for me. No one else, understand? They knew I had secret meetings with him. They knew he could get to me alone if he needed to talk to me—like you, Bephino. They know you can get to me alone."

Reaching for a hunk of bread, Bepy asked, "Why should they want you dead? You've always had good rapport with the other bosses."

"Yeah, but things change. Remember what I say: things change, people change. They confuse kindness with weakness, and that's bad. They're like children. If you don't agree with them all the time, they don't let you play anymore. Politics—that's what it is. I'm sure it's only one boss who wants me hit, because he couldn't trust another with knowledge of his vendetta. He'd be afraid the others might come to me and tell me. If it was all of them, I'd be dead already. So it's got to be only one. But which one? That's the sixty-four-thousand-dollar question—which one?

"Be careful, Bephino. Maybe they come to you. They're looking for a man that's not loyal to me. They're searching. They'll watch your eyes for an answer the minute they make their request. Don't forget that. If your eyes give you away, they'll kill you on the spot. They watch the eyes for the answer, not the mouth.

"They must hit me from the inside, because they don't want an all-out war. They can't afford that. They know they will lose."

"Maybe they'll come to me," Bepy answered. "It would be nice for us if they made that mistake."

The hour went slowly as Morrano tried unsuccessfully to enjoy his meal.

"Shall I order the *sfingi di San Giuseppe?*" Bepy asked.

"Nah. I've had enough."

"Me, too." He tossed down his napkin and called for the check.

The dinner and meeting ended. Bepy embraced his good friend and whispered, "Make a novena that they come to me, huh? I'll send them to heaven in style."

Don Emilio grinned at Bephino's remark, then repeated, "Don't forget the eyes. Don't wind up like Frankie."

The next day Bepy took Dana and her sister to Manhattan's Fifth Avenue for some shopping. After a few hours they went to hero shop number four to meet with Monkey, Alley Oop, Little Pauli, Ben, and Augie. While the men talked business, Dana and her sister checked out the cooking area. They were awaiting the arrival of Joey D from Mexico City. He was bringing his Jewish princess, Sheila Diamond, to New York. Everyone had heard about her naked dance, and they wanted to see her. Even Gina was curious to see such a daring girl.

At three a car pulled up. Crazy Mikey opened the restaurant door, and Joey D walked in, wearing diamond rings and a beautiful leather coat. His girl was in a mink coat. Both were nicely tanned. The change in Joey D was unbelievable, everyone thought.

"From a mutt to a baron," Monkey yelled out. "Welcome back! Look at him! He looks like he's doing OK, huh? Sabu has come a long way, huh fellas? No more Vera, no more plastic shopping bags. You're a baron now, Sabu!"

Joey D was smiling, shaking hands, and hugging everybody. Sheila was showing herself off, making herself obvious to all the men by casually opening her mink in order to display her large breasts and sexy hips.

"So these are the Bowery Boys?" Sheila said, smiling at everyone. "Well, I'm glad to meet you. I've heard so much about you guys!"

"We've heard so much about you, too," Monkey said.

"Is that right?" she asked, moving closer to Monkey but looking around at the whole group.

"I heard Joey D lives in a villa," Little Pauli remarked, staring at Sheila.

Sheila eyeballed Pauli up and down. "He certainly does. He's even got a king-size bed," she said, sitting down and crossing her legs in such a way as to expose her sexy paraphernalia to him.

"You can have a villa, too, if you want, Pauli," Bepy interrupted. "Find one up in Spanish Harlem, and the company will buy it for you, OK?" he said, with a stare. Pauli got the message and turned his gaze away from Sheila.

"Yeah," Sheila whispered to Pauli, "Find one up there. I like Spanish villas." Then she turned her head in her teasing style.

"Everyone looks so cozy." Dana's voice echoed across the room. She and Gina were standing in the doorway.

She was about to comment on Sheila's exposed leg, but Bepy cut her short. "Why don't you go window-shopping, Dana. Take Gina with you. Go up the street for a few minutes. I'll be right with you. We gotta meet Fat Arty for cocktails and dinner soon."

Dana's stubborn streak wouldn't give in that easily. She persisted, in a low voice only Bepy could hear. "Who's she? Is that Jewish stripper from Mexico?"

314

"You know who she is, so don't play games, OK?" Bepy replied. "Don't let that girl worry you; she's with Joey D."

"Her worry me?"

"Yeah, you!" He glared. "Go take your sister for a walk and see if you still like that crystal vase you bought that's in the car."

Dana knew Bepy's limit, so she quit while she was still ahead. She gestured to Gina, and they strutted out of the shop.

When he finished his business, Bepy excused himself from the welcome home party and met Dana and Gina outside.

"That Jew is going to be trouble," Dana started in again as they were driving to the restaurant. Bepy ignored her.

When they arrived, Bepy apologized for being late. Fat Arty and his wife were already testing imported cheeses, chunks of salami, and the wines of Italia. Since the car deal, Arty and Bepy had become great friends and often dined in different New York City restaurants. As usual, the beginning of the evening was spent eating and talking about Italian food and money—lots of talk about money. Money was Arty's best subject. He also reminded Bepy that he had politicians in his pocket galore. Opening up his jacket and touching his heart, Arty said, "The bank's got real good connections in New York and Jersey. If you ever need 'em, we got 'em for you."

"That's good to know," Bepy said. "Listen. A deal is coming up very soon, and we expect International Amex stock to shoot to twenty or thirty bucks a share. You should take up a good position in our stock. We're gonna clean up on this deal."

"Is the deal made yet?"

"No, but it soon will be. You can go ahead and buy your shares now, or anytime this month. You'll be rich in a year."

"OK," the banker agreed. "Tomorrow I'll buy ten thousand shares, maybe twenty thousand shares."

"Buy all you want. You'll clean up on this one."

Bepy, the corporation president, was holding one-half million shares for himself and stock in trust for the twins and Dana.

Gina was all ears. "How come you didn't tell me to buy shares, brother-in-law?"

"'Cause you believe in gypsies, that's why."

"What kind of a brother-in-law are you?" she pouted.

"Oh, now I'm your brother-in-law? Years ago I was a hoodlum kid too much of a punk for your sister. Now all of a sudden I'm your brother-in-law."

She began to laugh. She had a beautiful smile and a great sense of humor, but she was naïve as a baby chick on Easter Sunday.

"Don't worry," Bepy reassured her. "I already bought five thousand shares in your name, as a gift, this morning. If you want more, you buy more yourself. Call any broker. But these shares we bought today are a gift from Dana to you for good luck in your new house."

Dana was smiling from ear to ear. She loved her sister and liked Bepy to treat her family nicely. Gina jumped up and said, "I gotta kiss you for that! Thank you, Bephino."

"You got some wet lips, you know that?" he said, smiling.

A few weeks later, Bepy met with Alan Stone and Weisman, the buyer from JPJ Corve. Although he carefully explained his entire new plan to Weisman, it seemed as though he still wasn't getting his point across. The buyer just sat there sipping his drink and looking at his watch.

Alan saw this and said, "I think you should consider very seriously what Mr. Menesiero is trying to tell you."

Weisman gave him a frozen smile, but refused to commit himself. He felt intimidated by the presence of Bepy's associates. He didn't like it at all; it wasn't his style. Finally he spoke directly to Alan, but in a whisper and with a smirk on his face, "Are you people trying to intimidate me?"

Shocked by his direct, candid question, Alan replied, "You just realized that? What are you? A schmuck or what? These guys mean business. You better start being serious about this. Otherwise its *tuffen offen tuche* with your *tuche*."

This got to Weisman. His eyes registered his concern.

"Mr. Weisman, what are your thoughts on this deal?" Bepy asked. "I'd like to get down to serious business."

"I'm going to be painfully honest with you again, Mr. Menesiero," Weisman, staring into Bepy's eyes, replied. "I need one hundred thousand shares, as I said. That's the deal. To talk serious business, we must talk serious money."

Alan, nervously puffing his teamo, sensed trouble.

"This guy ain't budging," Bepy said in a loud voice to Alan. Then, looking back at Weisman, he said, "I'm gonna be a sport. I offered you ten thousand shares. I raise it to fifty thousand. Now that's a serious offer, I'd say."

"Sorry. I can't do it," Weisman replied firmly. "I need one hundred thousand. That's my deal."

"Mr. Weisman, I can't offer you more than fifty thousand. It's impossible. But I will break my rule in this particular case. I will transfer fifty thousand shares to you tomorrow. Then if you buy twenty thousand shares more at market price, I will buy you twenty thousand more. I'll match that with a gift of fifty thousand. That will get you your one hundred thousand shares. You gotta give a little. My reason for that is I want you in, and I want you in with some of your own money. I feel our deal will be safer if your money is in the pot. Do you understand my thinking?"

"I gotta think about such an investment," Weisman said, still hesitating.

"You still gotta think! With an offer like that you gotta think still?"

Bepy was upset by Weisman's hesitation. He wanted a deal tonight. "I'm gonna be painfully honest with you, Mr. Weisman," Bepy told him. "While you sit here thinking about it, I have your fuckin' bulldog. And if you say no to this deal, we're gonna chop his fuckin' head off."

Weisman smiled as if Bepy was joking. Then the smile suddenly froze across his face.

"How do you know I've got a bulldog?" he asked.

"Never mind how we know you got a bulldog. We got him. Keep that in your brain while you're thinking so slowly."

"But he's in New Jersey . . . with my father."

"That's what you think. Your dog crossed the Bayonne Bridge in a limo today. You can believe me. We almost took your father, too."

Weisman's eyes darted around the room, looking at each of the men sitting quietly and waiting. He began to stutter as he realized he was dealing with very serious people.

"You-you can't do that! My father is eighty years old. All he has is that dog."

"All he *had* was the dog," Bepy said flatly. "I told you. It was either your father or the dog. They both wanted to come with us. First we'll chop up that fuckin' mutt; then maybe we'll chop up your father."

"Mr. Menesiero, I live with my father—just the three of us. I bought the dog for him five years ago. He's all we have. I'm not married; I have no kids. My father is sick and old."

"That's why you better get serious," Bepy said, picking up a lighter and flicking it to light his cigar. "Look, Mr. Weisman, we know all that. We know all you got is the dog. We even know what pet shop you bought the dog from—the Pampered Pooch on Staten Island—and we even know what cemetery he's going to, in Newark. Do I have to be so painfully honest or do we have a deal? Are you with us or not?"

"I gotta have that dog!" Weisman yelled, panicking. "Give me my dog! I demand my dog or I will go to the district attorney's office. Show me my dog!" he kept insisting hysterically.

"Alley, get the mutt," Bepy ordered.

Alley struggled to his feet and left the room. He came back carrying the bulldog, petting and hugging him.

"Mommaluca!" Bepy yelled, and continued in Italian, "Stop petting the fuckin' dog. We're supposed to act like we're gonna kill him, and you're hugging him."

Embarrassed, Alley gently put him down. All the men, except Weisman, laughed at the way Alley looked so gentle, but so awkward. Alley was all smiles. "You think I would hurt that dog?" he whispered to Alan. "I would never hurt that dog. He's beautiful. Look at his face and his tongue hanging out."

Alan shifted his eyes. "I know, Alley, but shush about the dog already."

When Weisman saw his dog, he jumped up and hugged him and cried. "I'm in, I'm in. Count me in. We all retire together. You're right. Let's make a deal." He kept kissing his bulldog. "Darren," he whimpered, "are you all right?"

"Oh, that's his name?" Alley said. "I fed Darren raw beef. He liked it. Two pounds."

Six weeks later, JPJ Corve filled all their stores with International Amex products. Sales were strong. International Amex stock began to move upward, based on the leaked tip of a five-year contract being negotiated. Mr. Weisman was looking good on both ends of the deal; executives and corporate officers were praising him for bringing in such a salable line of merchandise. They talked about promoting him to senior vice-president.

Bepy had dinner with JPJ Corve executive officers including the president and vice-president. He cautiously but casually suggested they buy themselves International Amex stock. "We have an exclusive deal coming up in Mexico and Canada soon, which will run the corporation's stock up," he said. They swallowed the bait like sharks.

He had figured that if they bought the stock, they would protect his corporation on all fronts and would be in favor of a five-year contract. They appreciated the stock tip and bought several thousand shares. They were in deeply, and that was Bepy's insurance policy.

Later that week, Weisman called Alan. "I wanna thank you, Alan, for giving me my chance to be part of this fantastic business deal. It's working out beautiful."

"Don't thank me, Weisman. Thank Darren. Because if you didn't love that dog so much. . .the next item on the agenda was a cement mixer making you an overcoat."

The time had come for Shaggy Goldberg to have his wish. Alan had given Bepy all the information for the hit; it was to be in San Francisco. A meeting was held at which Bepy talked to Ben and Alley Oop.

"Here's his picture and address. I want you to handle this. I want it handled this week. Decide what equipment you need and make the necessary arrangements."

"Sure, Bep. Consider it done," Ben said.

"Do it with your own style, Ben, OK? I want you fellows to handle this one without me. Leave tomorrow for California. Study his picture, address, and the car he drives. Study it well. The job pays two hundred grand, no expenses. I keep fifty grand; you guys split one hundred fifty. It's an easy hit, and the pay is good. The guy's a nobody."

"Are there any surprises for us?" Ben asked.

"Yeah, one thing. After you hit him, cut off his cock and balls and mail them to this woman's address. Watch the fingerprints, OK?"

"Do you want these nuts gift-wrapped?" Ben asked.

"No. Just a plain small box. It's important to our client we do it this way. He's paying a lot for these nuts. I agreed, so a deal's a deal."

"I knew there was something more than just a plain old hit. What happened to the plain old shoot-'em-and-run hits?" Ben complained.

"They're still around. Do you want some, Ben? They pay ten and twenty thousand—not seventy-five grand. You're getting top pay for a simple hit. You're hitting a *tutzone.* Anyway, what the hell are you bullshitting about? I wish I had the time to handle it. It's a helluva day's pay. I could have picked up one hundred twenty-five grand. I'd pay Alley seventy-five, and we'd both be happy. Then we'd take three days rest in Vegas and make a party out of a funeral. If you don't want it, go back to your funeral home and wax them mummies' faces, and I'll send Monkey with Alley Oop."

"What the hell are you getting uptight about?" Ben asked defensively. "I'm only joking with you."

"Look, Ben, I've got a lot of things on my mind. I ain't got time to joke around with you. I wish I could go on this hit, like old times, but now we're up to our ass in business. Big business. I have to be here to accept the Corve contract. The timing is critical on this deal. The day I get it, I gotta sign it, and that's the day the figures will be announced. I gotta be around when the stock shoots up and we sell our company to a conglomerate for big bucks. I don't wanna talk any more about it. You got your contract; go do what you gotta do. You're a pro, so take care of it. Report to me after it's done. Use gloves and be careful. No telephones. Good luck." He kissed his men on both cheeks.

Alley embraced Bepy with an extra hug and whispered, "Hey, Bep, remember that Chink, Jimmy Lee? That night we ate them *cappuzelli?* We got even for Monkey, didn't we, Bep? Them guys were like snakes crawling around when we hit 'em. They looked like snakes, right, Bep?"

"Yeah, I remember." They smiled at the memory of a crazy moment they had together.

"Yeah," Alley said. "I still see them snakes in front of my eyes." Then he changed the subject quickly. "I like your new car, Bep. It's a beauty. I like it a lot. Good luck with it. I'm getting you the horns to hang on the dashboard. It's good luck; it keeps the *mulucais* away."

"You like the car? Then it's yours, Alley, when you come back. It's yours from me to you."

"I'm only kidding, Bep. I don't want you to give me your new Cadillac. Only the Boss drives a Cadillac in Brooklyn. I just meant I like it. It's a pretty color, that silver gray."

"It's yours, Alley. I just gave it to you. I made my decision. It's your car. Nobody drives it till you get back."

"You know the rules, Bep. None of the other Mob guys let their men drive Caddies—only Buicks and Oldsmobiles. Ya know that, don't you? I'm not allowed."

"Yeah, well . . . we don't have such rules in our gang. Anyway, you're gonna drive a Caddie. I just gave it to you. You own it already; it's yours. Let's forget the subject."

Alley Oop smiled. "You're crazy, Bep; you know that? Thanks. I'll buy you one when I get back." They hugged and laughed.

"Is this bullshit over with?" Ben interrupted. "I got work to do. And you fuckin' guys got me crying."

"OK, go do what you gotta do," Bepy told Ben with a smile. "And do the right thing, OK, Benny?"

The next day the two men arrived in California. Ben, who loved to be in command, acted as boss. They explored the area, so they could get out quickly when it was over. Finally, after two days of waiting, they saw their man briefly, as he was leaving his house.

Ben laid out the plan so the next meeting would be for the kill. Alley was to grab him and hold him. Then Ben would stab him a few times. After he was dead, they would perform the surgery.

"Are you fuckin' nuts?" Alley Oop protested. "Why we gotta hold this giant? Why not blast him and then cut him up? Let's get a gun, or

320

even a rifle," he suggested. "Why should we have to handle him? He's a fuckin' giant. What kinda hit is this gonna be?"

"Are you serious?" Ben asked. "If we shoot, even at night, we'll have too many people around. How are we gonna have enough time to operate on him? We can't make any noise. We gotta be quiet for this thing. We need time for them nuts. Leave it to me, Alley. I know what I'm doing. I'm fast with a blade."

"We should've arranged to have a silencer waiting for us if you're afraid of noise," Alley complained. "Bepy would've had all this figured out already. You really wanna knife this giant? It don't make sense to me. The guy's a fuckin' monster. Did you see him walkin' down the street; he's like a basketball player."

"Why are you so worried? I've made so many hits and never had trouble. Ask Bepy. He traveled with me to New Orleans. I make the plan to fit the occasion." Ben was reluctant to change his mind.

Alley remained quiet, trying to think things out. They were parked in the street, waiting for their man to return home. The sun had already set, and darkness was closing in.

About two o'clock in the morning, the hit finally arrived back home. Ben yelled, "He's home! That's his car. He's looking for a space to park. You grab him as soon as he gets out, while he's still bending over, so he don't know what's happening. Let's go quick."

The hit was already getting out of his car. Their timing was a few seconds off. In one motion, Alley bear-hugged him and, like a giant eel, the guy slipped out of his hold and stuck him in the chest with a blade of his own. Then he took off and ran like a deer. The knife was still stuck in Alley Oop's chest.

Alley collapsed to the ground and lay there bleeding from what seemed to be a direct hit to his heart. Ben, standing over him with an unused stiletto in his hand, saw that Alley was almost dead. It had happened so fast, Ben couldn't believe it.

With his eyes wide, Alley weakly mumbled, "Momma, help me...."

Ben shook Alley and tried to talk to him, but he had died so fast. "Alley, get up!" Ben shook him again. "Alley, get the fuck up. Please get up." His eyes darted back and forth. "Ya big fuck. Don't do this to me. Get up."

Ben looked around and put his knife back in his pocket. Then he quickly emptied Alley Oop's pockets. He felt sick to his stomach, seeing Alley's body so still. Such a powerful man, and he'd died so fast. He bit his lip as he gazed at his dead friend and made the sign of the cross. His thoughts were self-punishing. What a stupid bastard I am. I fucked up good. How am I gonna live with this? He knew his plan had caused Alley's death.

He made sure he had Alley's wallet, containing identification, to delay any police report of possible New York involvement in the killing. He didn't want to get stopped at the airport.

He left Alley Oop dead on a California street and returned to New York that same night. He had to face Bepy, knowing how he might react. The next morning, fearing for his own life, he took a half-dozen Valiums before he went to see Bepy.

"I got bad news," Ben said slowly.

"Don't tell me you missed your man?"

"It's worse than that." Ben handed Alley's wallet to Bepy. "Alley got killed by the guy. Alley's dead, Bep."

"What! Alley Oop?" Bepy screamed, jumping out of his seat. "My friend for twenty years? How, Ben? How could this guy kill Alley? Alley would have broken his neck."

"Bepy, the guy was big, like a fuckin' giant," Ben mumbled, shaking nervously. "He broke Alley's grip in a split second."

"Grip? What grip?"

"Alley was holding him," Ben said, looking away.

"And what were you doing, Ben?" Bepy asked accusingly. "Why didn't you shoot the bastard?"

"It happened so quick. In the same motion, he broke the grip and stabbed Alley in his chest. He died so quickly, Bep, that blade must've hit him in the heart." He was sobbing now. "It was over in seconds." He paced the floor, twisting his fingers to keep from shaking.

"Ben," Bepy said coldly. "I asked you, why didn't you shoot him?"

"I was using a knife to keep the noise down. I didn't bring a gun. I fucked up. The first time in my life I didn't bring a gun." Ben held his hands to his face and cried.

"Why didn't you at least pipe him first? You should've hit him first, with a pipe, daze him good. Then you hold a hurt and dazed man. You could've controlled the guy better. It's easier. You never try to hold a man that big. They get strength like an animal when they're gonna die. Alley should have strangled him with a wire to maintain control of the guy. What did you try? A bear hug? You should've had a gun ready in case of an emergency. You planned it like an amateur. Ben, you've broken my heart. Alley was my dearest friend. I loved Alley. You're finished, Ben. Stay in your fuckin' funeral business. You're lucky I'm not moving against you for this. I retire you now—today. For old times' sake, I'm forced to let you live, and you're my neighbor. Don't say a word. Don't make me do something you'll be sorry for. We've been through a lot together. But don't ever come near me again, Ben. I knew I should've given you a plan before you left. I knew it. I thought you were a pro. I fucked up. It's my fault Alley Oop's dead," Bepy said, biting his fingers. "I'm gonna miss Alley so much, so very much," he murmured, trying to regain his composure. He quickly changed his voice. "I'll tell Morrano tonight—no hits for you, ever. You're *finito*. You're judgment is bad."

The men looked into each other's eyes, trying to hold back tears of sorrow. In a choked voice, Bepy spoke. "You're an irresponsible scumbag. I can't believe the ridiculous way you handled the fuckin' thing. What happened to you, Ben?"

"I'm sorry, Bepy. I'm sorry. I loved Alley, too. I'm sick over this." Ben began to light a cigarette, but his hands shook too badly.

"Stop that damn shaking! You're making me sick!" Bepy yelled. "Cut it out! Did Alley say anything before he died? Any words at all?"

"No, Bepy. He died very quiet—like a real man." Ben didn't think it was necessary to add to Bepy's grief by telling him that Alley called for his mother as he died. "I can't stop shaking. I took six Valiums a half hour ago, and they ain't helping me."

"Go home and take another dozen. Try to kill yourself. But do it right this time. Good-bye, Ben," Bepy said, dismissing him.

"Good-bye, Bephino. I'm sorry. Believe me, I'm sorry."

The children were away at school, and Dana was shopping with her sister. Bepy sat quietly and watched the ocean for hours. He fought to hold back his tears, thinking of Alley lying in the gutter and the times they'd had together. How loyal Alley had been to him! Now it was over. He knew he was in a dangerous, deadly business—death for himself or his men was always possible. But they had been so lucky for so many years. No one had gotten killed. No one had been arrested. Life was going great, until today. How could Ben plan such a sloppy and foolish way to make a hit? His stupid plan had cost Alley his life. Just when Alley was finally enjoying all the money, fine clothes, new cars, and best broads around. Yet he always gave his mother plenty of cash for the family. He thought again about how he would miss Alley Oop, his very loyal friend for more than twenty years. He fought hard to hold back his tears, but he lost the battle in the evening hours after sunset.

The next day, Bepy sent a message to Shaggy via Alan, who was in New York: "The next time it will be handled differently. We're sorry for this unfortunate delay."

323

"Shaggy understands the hazardous work this involves. Take your time," Alan told him. "Don't get upset. Be careful. We don't wanna lose our valued friends. We understand, so do what you think is right. Please don't let our people get hurt. Maybe we should forget the whole thing?"

"I couldn't accept the loss of another good friend on such an easy contract. The next time, I make the hit alone. I know what's right. Let's go home and eat. Dana and the kids are waiting for us. The kids came home from school because of this. Dana told them. I felt she shouldn't have. Now they're upset, too. They loved Alley Oop."

During the ride, Alan asked, "Where's Alley's body?"

"They're still holding him in the California morgue. His sister went to claim him. We made her report him missing, so the police would know where to place him. Ben took all of his papers that night. The police were waiting for the fingerprints to come back. His sister is sick over this, and the mother doesn't even know yet. We didn't tell her."

"Boy, that's gonna be rough for her."

When they entered the house, Dana embraced them both.

"I'm so sorry about Alley Oop. I still can't believe he's dead. I've been sick all day thinking of him," she said. "He was part of our family. The kids loved him." Then she turned to her husband and said, "Bephino, suppose that was you? Please, Bephino, think. Think what you're doing. You have the twins to worry about. You don't need this shit anymore."

Bepy looked at Alan and back to Dana. "Dana, cut the crap. You know I gotta do what I gotta do."

"No, you don't!"

At that moment, while Dana was pleading, Renee and Patsy entered the room. They embraced their father and Alan and cried when they talked about Alley Oop. He'd been so good to the children all those years, like a big pal. Sometimes he baby-sat and would play games with them, and he taught them how to play checkers and chess.

Don Emilio arrived after dinner to pay his respects. He was very upset about Ben's bad judgment. He asked Bephino over and over, "Didn't they know the *mulanyams* are fast? It's best to hit 'em with machine guns. Never touch a *tutzone;* always make it easy on yourself. Blast them from ten feet away. Chop 'em down." He kept repeating and repeating, "Ten feet away . . . never touch them. They're too fast for us."

A few days later, Alley's body arrived in Brooklyn and was laid out for family and friends to pay their respects. A sudden death in a small close neighborhood, such as Bay Ridge, brings out sympathetic feelings for the person; any anger or bitterness is forgotten. Alley Oop was liked by old and young alike and respected by all families from Mott Street to Bath Avenue in Brooklyn.

Car after car pulled up to the front of Marcella Funeral Home. And the Menesiero gang was out front to accept condolences. They'd chosen to stand outside quietly taking in the fresh air rather than letting the flower fragrance fill their lungs with grief.

Monkey broke the silence concerning Ben. "That fuckin' Ben's full of shit! He's supposed to be such a pro." He paced in a circle, pounding his heels on the sidewalk as he continued to rant. "Pro, my ass! He got Alley killed. How come the big man from Staten Island let this happen?"

"Don't be so quick to pass judgment on Ben," Bepy told him. "He's always been there when we needed him. He fucked up, but he's always been loyal to us." Bepy tried to keep the peace and a piece of Ben's dignity intact.

"Oh, yeah? Then how come he ain't here with us? He should be right here, paying his respects to Alley Oop," Monkey yelled.

Bepy rubbed Monkey's head and said, "It'll be OK, Monkey. Don't worry. Ben's suffering worse than us. He loved Alley, too."

Over the next few days, Ben went totally into seclusion. No one had seen him since Alley's death.

"Poor Ben," Bepy would say while they sat and talked at the club. "I feel sorry for him. Believe me, he suffers worse than all of us. He was such a proud little fellow, and now he probably can't live with himself. I know Ben made a bad decision. It cost us heavily to lose Alley. But Ben is still our loyal friend. Never lose respect for our people. I know his loyalty is unquestionable." But Bepy never called Ben.

Two months later, one night at dinner, Dana said, "You should call Ben. Make him feel better. Huh, Bephino? After all, he's our neighbor. It doesn't look right. I shop with his wife. I can see she's upset, but she says nothing and I say nothing."

"That's the way it should be," he answered. "You both know nothing. So you got nothing to talk about."

"But he's always been your friend, too. You can't be too hard on him. He must be suffering. No one calls him anymore. He don't even walk the beach like he used to."

Bepy puffed his cigar and did not answer her.

The contract with JPJ Corve was signed. The announcement to the public was timed to ensure a buying spree. The stock responded quickly, and the price went wild on Wall Street. Everyone was talking about the big winner that day—International Amex Corporation. Don Emilio made millions on the deal; Weisman was a millionaire now; and the president and vice-president of Corve had more than doubled their investment already. Everyone celebrated.

Bepy and Alan quietly offered the Mexican Product Line Company of International Amex Corporation for sale, through a broker, who quickly offered it to a large conglomerate. The conglomerate jumped at the opportunity, and the deal was made. The company was sold for forty million dollars, to be paid over five years. Financially, all was well in Brooklyn and Las Vegas.

Don Emilio had gotten very rich by knowing Bephino over the years. He set up trust funds for the twins of a quarter of a million dollars each. A gift from him to them.

"Why?" Bepy asked. "You don't have to do that. They'll have plenty when they're twenty-one."

"I made millions via your deals, Bephino," the Don answered. "My heart would hurt if I was so small a man as not to do something for the twins. I must do that for Renee and Patsy. We love them, you know. I'm getting old, and my daughter will have millions. I wonder if she'll know how to handle that fortune? Her husband is a vegetarian; he don't eat meat. Maybe he could buy a lot of lettuce with that cabbage, huh?"

"Yeah, he sure could." Bepy laughed. Then his thoughts turned sad. "We all got rich except for my poor friend Alley Oop. This stock deal came too late for him. He had a lot of it, and his mother won't know what to do with all that money. I gotta help her and his sister. I have to set up some kind of trust or investment plan for them. My God, Alley Oop," he murmured softly. "I miss him so much. I hurt so bad for him."

"Forget Alley Oop," the Don said. "Otherwise you'll hurt inside forever."

Bepy nodded but thought, "I'll never stop hurting."

Joey D married Sheila Diamond after she'd heard about his stock holdings in International Amex. She proposed to him. After a couple of weeks of marriage, she got herself a nose job, and Joey D got the bill. A few months later, she asked for a divorce and half of his money as settlement. But Joey D couldn't control her after her nose job. She was fucking waiters, bartenders, bellhops, gas attendants, even the cook in her favorite Chinese restaurant. She became known in Mexico as the Pig of Calia Beach.

Joey D went to Bepy with his problems. "What do I do, Bepy? She wants a divorce and wants all my stocks and bonds, or she wants the cash equivalent. She knows I made a big score on the International Amex deal. What should I do? She's got a Jewish lawyer calling me."

"Where is she now?"

"She flew back to Mexico the day after she asked me for the divorce. She's staying in a hotel in Puerto Vallarta. Last month's bill was six thousand dollars! She expects me to pay it. I ain't paying anymore. I quit. I went for my lungs on this broad."

"I can't believe she turned on you so quickly. Doesn't she know we'll act on your behalf?"

"She don't care. She says to speak to her lawyer. So I talk to him. He wants everything I got, the bum.

"On my last trip down, I tried to patch it up with her. I asked for her around the pool, and the waiter said, 'La gahoo' is in Cabana 19. I went there and found her in bed with the cleaning woman."

"Cleaning woman?" Bepy asked in disbelief.

"Yeah. A Mexican hotel maid with long black hair. I felt like killing her right there. Then I found out gahoo means pig," Joey D said, bowing his head.

"How come you married her?"

"I don't know why I married her. It was a big mistake."

"Sabu, you know you gotta marry Italian girls only. What the fuck's wrong with you? Didn't your father teach you anything? Fuck any girl but marry only your own kind. Now we got a problem."

"The broad really turned on me, Bep. She's a real fuckin' gahoo pig. I can't believe it," Joey D said, wiping his forehead with a paper towel.

"A pig, huh?" Bepy answered. "Then she must be handled like a pig. Leave it to me. Forget about her lawyer. Don't talk to him anymore."

He picked up the phone and called a contact named Jorge Alverez in Mexico City. "I want to come to New York tomorrow," he said. "I have something for you. Call me at my office when you arrive. I'll be waiting."

"OK, Mr. Menesiero. I'll be there tomorrow afternoon."

The next evening at dinner Jorge asked, "Then you don't want her killed?"

"No. This is a small contract. I don't want her killed yet. I only want her to see what we think of her. She may kill herself and save us the trouble. It must be exotic. She's a Jewish princess, and we must treat her with utmost finesse. I want seven, delivered to her suite." He looked across the table at Crazy Mikey, who was at the meeting to make sure he understood the intentions.

"No sweat, Mr. Menesiero. I will handle it with style. Mikey will see how well I can handle such a thing."

"Leave tomorrow morning. You will be compensated in Mexico by Mikey. Mikey, you'll take care of all expenses involved. Pick up all the tabs. Don't get bills; just tell me what you spend, OK?"

"I'm not worried about the money, Mr. Menesiero," Jorge said, interrupting Bepy. "Whatever you do for us is fine."

The following week Mikey was back in New York. He laughed as he described the details to Bepy and Alan.

"Boy, did it work, Bepy! She looked so bad. The Jewish princess couldn't stand the sight of all that pork; she was like Dracula when he saw the cross. Them red boars were all over her when she woke up. The room smelled like a sty. We were lying by the pool when we heard the screams coming from her cabana. They were loud. The maid opened her door. We ran over with a crowd of people and saw her in her bed screaming. We acted like spectators. We had drugged her drinks good the night before so she'd sleep late and not hear us set it up. When they took her out of the hotel, she was barefoot and bare assed, wearing just that white jacket. Her hair was standing straight up. Boy, did she look bad. And the pigs were running all over the pool area, 'cause the maid left the door open and ran."

Bepy smiled, "Good. That's exactly the way I wanted it handled. You did well, Mikey. Was Jorge satisfied?"

"Yeah, I gave him two grand plus expenses. He was happy as a pig in shit. He thanked me all day long. The Mexican police couldn't figure out how the pigs got into her bedroom. They said there was no evidence of foul play. They finally decided she was just another kinky gringo who let her kinky games get a little out of hand."

"Well, that takes care of that problem. Let's go on to the next. Now that Alley Oop is gone, who will handle the skim from the hotel and the collections for you?" Alan asked Bepy.

"Joey D," Bepy answered. "He's the only person we have available who can be trusted with that amount of cash. He starts next month. You deal with him, Alan, OK? He's the new bag man. And keep an eye on him; he's getting stupid. He's beautiful and loyal, but he's been kinda nervous lately . . . and very vulnerable. Watch him. I've seen this happen to men before. He's getting soft in the head. He married that cunt. Now his eyes show too much emotion. Watch him."

"Sure, Bep. Whatever you say."

"But don't crowd him. Let him be a man."

Book V
1965–1976

17

"Mr. Menesiero? This is Lefty. The Don wants to see you right away...the usual place."

"OK," Bepy replied and hung up quickly. He kissed Dana and walked to the garage to head for Brooklyn. When he bent over to get in his car, a man put a gun to his back. Because he'd been in a hurry, he hadn't checked around for strangers, as he usually did.

The man led him through the brush in his yard to a car parked in a secluded area at the end of his drive. "Get in, Sciacchitano," the guy with the gun ordered.

Bepy hesitated. It had been a long time since anyone had called him Sciacchitano.

"You run fast when you get a call from Morrano, huh?" another said. "Like a rabbit you run." The voice came from the back seat, through a half-open window, into the darkness of the night.

Bepy knew now that this was blood business, but they wanted to talk. Otherwise he would have been dead already. As he climbed into the back seat of the four-door car, he was greeted by Nick, Don Morrano's old friend the Don from Queens. Bepy was shocked. It was Nick, then, who wanted Morrano dead. That's why he was here. Bepy shook hands respectfully with Nick and then half greeted the other two men. He remembered what Don Emilio had told him: "They'll watch your eyes for an answer. If your eyes give you away, they kill you on the spot."

So he acted very warm toward Nick and smiled at the other two. "Why the guns, Nick? I would have come. Can I be of service to you, Nick?" He was trying to gain Nick's confidence while thinking, this is the bastard who wants Don Emilio dead. That's why he's here tonight. He's going to put me to the test, of my loyalty to Morrano.

He stared confidently into Nick's eyes. But he already knew why Frankie Arguilia had been hit. He wouldn't cooperate, so they turned their guns on him. Your eyes, Bep, he thought, keep 'em bright and firm. That's what they'll look at. He continued to stare deeply at Nick. He knew he had to get out of the car. He needed room to operate. It was too confined.

"Why don't we go inside? Come. Come in my house, Nick. Let me show you around my home. It's right on the beach. It's beautiful. Then we'll talk about your business. I'm sure you're here to talk some business, aren't you? That's why I got the gun in my ear, right? Come. Have a nice

331

glass of wine. Bring your boys with you. Let's relax inside, and we talk nicea nice and we make a deal."

"You're all right, kid." Nick laughed. "You're classy. I like that. And you're smart. I like that, too."

They pulled the car around the circular drive and parked right in front of the main entrance. I gotta get outta this car and get them in the open, Bepy thought. I need a gun. Keep smilin', Bep. Don't fuck up. And remember your eyes.

Dana opened the door and welcomed them in a friendly way. She was smiling, but sensed trouble, and couldn't help being scared. She knew Bepy was supposed to be in Brooklyn to meet Don Morrano, but now he was back in the house with these tough-looking men. Bepy is acting too charming to these men, she thought. He never acts weak with men, and now he seems a bit humble, like he's no longer in command.

Bepy got out the wine, the best Scotch, and other booze—the best he had, so they couldn't resist the finest drinks money could buy. He handed out five-dollar cigars, too. "These come from Holland. They're strong. Try them."

The men seemed to be feeling comfortable and relaxed. Dana sensed that Bepy was trying to keep them relaxed. He was hovering over them, like a French waiter, pouring drinks, offering his best cigars, which only he and Morrano and Alan smoked. She noticed he was wiping his hands often with the bar towel. At times his expression changed, but only momentarily. His eyes showed hate, then sudden laughter.

Dana decided to pitch in. "I'm bringing out some cold cuts and cheese in just a minute, fellows. I picked up some imported prosciutto and cappicola today."

The men sat back and enjoyed the hospitality. Stupidly they even eyed Dana as she walked around the den serving them. They grinned and winked at each other to confirm her presence. Dana was beautiful, very firm and sexy looking. They showed it by looking her over too often. Bepy watched their eyes undress her. It didn't matter though; it showed they weren't concentrating on business anymore. Every bite, every drink, every look—he recorded their effects in his mind. He already knew the strong ones of the three. He wanted to gut them right there on his plush, carpeted floor.

He was also hoping Dana would realize that he was in trouble. He didn't want Nick to panic and possibly start shooting in the house. He had to gain their full confidence, so they would trust him and let down their guard.

Before going back into the kitchen for some bread sticks, Dana, who had noticed Bepy never left the room, went into his office, where he kept his favorite gun, a specially made .38 magnum snubnose with a mini handcrafted silencer built into it. He had received this as a gift from Don Santoro in New Orleans. It was priceless. Dana peeked into the barrel to see if she saw bullets. It was loaded. She was frightened, but remembered what Bepy always told her: "Scared people always freeze and die. Brave people survive. Don't ever freeze! It could mean life or death." She had thought she would never have to use that lesson. But now she saw that her husband needed her strength. She was the only person in the house who knew he wasn't acting as he normally did. She walked back into the den and awkwardly asked him, "Do you wanna let them try any of these cigars?"

"Which cigars?" he asked abruptly, knowing they already had his best cigars. He walked toward her, his back to the men. "No. They're no good," he told her. "They're Cuban, and they're not fresh." He looked at her eyes for a message, but she looked away too quickly. She was frightened, so she kept moving. But her looking away too quickly was also a message, Bepy thought.

Dana placed the box on the table just outside the den. Bepy walked over, opened the box, and saw his gun in it. He closed it. "Yeah, they're old cigars. I gave them the better ones already."

Dana felt better now. He knew the gun was there. He took off his jacket and threw it on the table over the cigar box, giving her the answer to her message. "You're so sloppy, Bephino," she said with a laugh. "He throws his clothes all over the house. This morning I found his socks by the TV set."

All the men laughed as Bepy sat down on the couch near Nick. "Are you fellows comfortable? Isn't this better than talking in the car?"

Dana took his jacket and the cigar box into the kitchen. She put his gun in his jacket pocket, then hung the jacket in the back hall closet.

"We have a big problem, Bephino," Nick said, carefully choosing his words. "Don Emilio is getting old. I'm sure you know this."

"Ha, I thought I was the only one who knew it," Bepy said, jumping at the chance to knock Morrano. "And he don't go for spit. A bunch of us at the club complained last week because he was the last one to put up the two-hundred-dollar dues."

"He never votes with me like he used to," Nick continued. "Now he vetos things he shouldn't. You know what I mean? We was *compadra* for many years, him and me. We go back to Sicily. I used to follow him around our town when we was kids. He was older than me. I used to respect him as a kid. Sometimes he would buy me a sweet potato." Nick smiled.

And now you want to kill him, you scumbag, Bepy thought.

"Yeah, I know, Nick. I think the man is aging fast. Last week I talked to him, and he fumbled and dribbled at the mouth. He ruins all his cigars. We talked about money, and he changed the subject. I know what you mean, Nick. Believe me," he said in disgust. "I think he should retire. I even told him that."

"You told him he should retire?"

"Yeah. And he got mad at me. But I feel it's best for all of us if he steps down."

"You're right, kid. You see things right. But he will never retire," Nick said forcefully. "I believe when you can't make a right decision, it's time to hit the rocking chair—one way or the other."

"Hey, some guys aren't lucky enough to hit the rocker, right, Nick? Emilio should be happy to retire before he gets carried out," Bepy said, baiting Nick. "He had many good years. Now he should relax and let us younger guys make the decisions."

"You're right," Nick said. "Like Joe Tortello. You were only a kid when I gave you that contract. But I still call you kid," Nick said with a grin. "You were so young when you made that hit up there."

"Yeah." Bepy smiled. "I was only a kid then."

"You know, Bephino, Frankie Arguilia had to go because he thought very small. The bum was still driving a two-door Studebaker. How big can a guy think in a Studebaker coupe? Huh?" Nick said, directing his eyes to Bepy's eyes.

"I never knew that guy Frankie," Bepy told him, feeling the bead of vision. "Who was he?"

"Ah-h, he was from East New York. He was too loyal to Morrano. We talked to him, but he made no comment, so we knew he was not our man."

Bepy knew what Nick was trying to say, so he moved quickly to satisfy their thoughts. "How much does this contract pay?"

"Ah, that's the boy. Just like old times. Money talks with you, huh?" Nick smiled. "You've always been a guy who'll make a deal for a buck." Looking over at his men, he said, "I told you, if he was in, he'd ask how much it paid."

"Yeah. How much does it pay? It should be big. I only make hits for reasons of principle and for the cash. Not for personal reasons. This is a business to me. But I do a good job. You know that, right? How much is this hit worth, Nick?" Bepy pressed him.

"Ahh." Nick smiled. "That's why I approached you. But why are you so willing to hit Morrano? I thought you were very close to him."

The three men zeroed in on Bepy's eyes, watching closely for his reactions.

Bepy was ready for them. "Well, for the money, for one thing—if it's enough, of course. And because I see you're a much younger-thinking man. He's thinking too old. I'll be better off with a new don, someone I could gain some respect with. I got nowhere with Morrano. I'm still a nobody. When he's gone, who will I be with? Rocco and the others, we don't care for each other. They treat me like an outsider. But the important thing is the money. He should be worth a good price, and I need a score at the moment."

Nick's eyes were pressing hard at Bepy. He removed his cigar from his tense lips and slowly smiled. "You make sense to me. You gave me the right answer. The contract pays fifty grand. How's that?"

"That's too cheap, Nick." Bepy acted reluctant. "He's worth a hundred fifty grand. Morrano's got an army behind him. Fifty grand for him, that's not enough. I got fifty grand for hitting a midget last year."

They smiled at his cheekiness.

Bepy had made a smart move. He showed a willingness, but only for a price.

"It comes out of my pocket," Nick told him. "I'm paying, so I expect a reasonable price from you. I'll make it up to you on other contracts."

Bepy made no comment but picked up his wine glass and took a sip.

"You do this for me and you'll be a made guy with my family," Nick continued. "You wanna be a capo for me? I'll make you a capo. How's that?"

Bepy still hesitated, but wanted to wrap up the deal. He raised his glass. "Saluto! To a better friendship and a new capo. I been a nobody too long," he grunted.

Their eyes were bright. They seemed to believe him. His reluctance over the price had convinced them. His eagerness to be a capo put the cream on the pudding. The two soldiers raised their glasses.

Nick remembered that in the old days, when Bephino was a kid, Don Emilio Morrano had commented, "This kid Bephino is money crazy. He loves to get paid in advance. He'll do anything for money." Nick felt satisfied that he would make the hit for the money. Loyalty to Morrano had become too expensive for Bepy.

Everyone stood up. Nick walked over and embraced Bepy, kissed him on both cheeks, and said confidently, in a low whisper, "You're one of us now. You will be protected by my family."

Why, these rotten scumbags! Protected? Bepy thought. They wanna protect me? Who's gonna protect them?

Dana, watching in a mirror, saw Bepy being embraced by Nick; she had heard the entire conversation from the hall. Knowing Bepy would never turn against Don Morrano, she went to look for the shotgun she knew they always kept loaded. Alley Oop had loaded it and put it on the wall at the top of the cellar steps—so in case of burglars, Patsy would have a weapon nearby. Dana stood eying the shotgun, but did not touch it. She knew the party was over and Bepy had stopped dancing. She was getting ready for war, just in case.

The men finished their drinks. Nick said, "I'd like it done tomorrow, Bepy. It's important to me. Tomorrow, OK?"

"What's the matter with tonight? Bepy answered. "I can get to him tonight. I'll get it over with. I'll hit him with his fuckin' pajamas on. His wife is in the hospital, so he's there alone."

"You're something, Bephino Menesiero," Nick said, smiling. "I'll pay you after the hit. I don't have fifty grand with me."

"That's OK. Your credit is good."

They laughed. As they began to walk to the front door, Dana entered to say good-bye, hoping they would leave her home and never come back. The men thanked Dana for a wonderful time and didn't notice that Bepy had stopped dancing and was making plans to deflate them.

"It's chilly outside, Dana, where's my jacket?"

She got his jacket and returned. The men walked out the front door to their car, and Bepy walked beside them. Holding his jacket, he felt the weight of his gun. Good girl, he thought.

"Dana, go inside. You'll catch cold," he said quickly.

She understood.

One man got behind the wheel and shook hands again with Bepy. "It was nice meeting you," he said. The other one, who had called Bepy the Sciacchitano, was the dangerous one.

Bepy smiled like a weak man, embraced him, and rubbed his arm as though they were now friends.

The men thought Bepy was insecure because he'd jumped at the chance of becoming a capo, every hit man's dream. He wasn't even a lieutenant yet, so his quick acceptance made him look cheap and weak.

They believed he would carry out the contract to save his own life; they knew he had to protect his family.

The man walked around the car, his back to Bepy. Nick, standing by the back door with a cigar stub clenched between his lips, waited for Bepy to open it for him. Bepy smiled and partially opened the door for the Don. Then he started to embrace him, but he kissed only one cheek and backed away slowly, pressing his gun to Nick's chest.

Nick suddenly knew that the deal was off. Bepy had given him the *bocca la morte*—the kiss of death. With his cigar butt clenched tightly in his teeth, he protested. "No. We gotta deal. *Duta lu rispetto,*" he grumbled.

Grabbing Nick by his lapel with his left hand, Bepy spit in his face and whispered, "*Lu rispetto?* My balls. You ain't got no respect. You're as dead as my prick is right now. Ya know that?" Then he pumped two in Nick's chest quickly. Holding up Nick's limp body to cover himself from possible bullets from Nick's soldiers, he crouched, took aim, and shot twice, putting two bullets in the guy on the passenger side. The man's head hit the dashboard, and his big hat, pierced by hot lead, flew off.

The driver turned toward Bepy. He didn't even reach for his gun, just looked up at Bepy with a surprised, sorry look on his face. Bepy had him cold. He had expected this guy would freeze, so he saved him for last.

Nick had a shocked look on his face. His cigar was still in his mouth. He must've squeezed it when the bullets hit. Bepy carelessly dropped him on the ground and ordered the driver out of the car. "Pick up this piece of shit and take him with you."

"OK, OK," the guy said, getting out of the car and shaking like a leaf. He picked up Nick and dumped him in the back seat, thinking he was going to drive away with his two dead friends. "I'll du-du-dump them," he murmured.

Bepy ordered him to get in the back seat and empty Nick's pockets. The guy got in the car and leaned over Nick's body. Bepy blasted him in the head twice.

The three lay dead in the car—two bodies in the back seat and one in the front. The driver's seat had been kept clean. Bepy closed the door with his elbow and wiped the door handle clean. He always worried about fingerprints.

In the middle of this nightmare he glanced over his shoulder and saw Dana standing in the doorway on guard duty, with a shotgun trained on the car. She was white as a ghost, but ready for war. She was so beautiful standing there. Bepy looked at her with amazement.

"Put that shotgun away," he told her. "Do you know how that gun shoots?"

"No."

"It sprays twenty feet around. It's a twelve-gauge shotgun. Did you know that?"

"No. But if they had tried to hurt you, I would've shot at them."

He smiled at her protectiveness and innocence as he walked toward her. What a woman! She would kill for him if she had to. She was scared stiff but relieved that Bepy was all right.

"Everything's OK, Dana," he said. "You can put down the gun. Would you please clear up everything in the den; clean it good. I don't wanna smell the scent these scum might have left in our house." He took the shotgun out of her hand and put one arm around her shoulders as they walked back into the house.

She moved with him, but stiffly.

Bepy leaned the shotgun against the wall and picked up the phone to dial Ben's number. He smiled at his wife as she began cleaning up. She was so strong—to have put the gun in his jacket and come to his aid with the shotgun. "Beautiful Dana," he said, "I love you."

Having already picked up on his end, Ben asked, "You love me? Who's this?"

"Benny, how are you? This is Bephino."

"I'm still living, unfortunately," he replied.

"Come over to my house right now. Right away, OK?"

"Sure, Bep. I'll be right there."

Three minutes later Ben pulled up in the drive, got out of his car, and walked past the car parked in front. Peeking in he saw the shot-up bodies.

"What happened? What did you have, a lawn party? Where'd you get these guys from?"

Bepy told him part of the situation between Don Morrano and Nick. Then he said, with a smile, "I know business is bad for you: so *back and forth, back and forth.* I'll make you have a good year. Here's three customers."

The two men laughed like old times.

"Ben, I need your help moving these guys to a dump spot. Put the car in my garage. Let's hide it for a while. Use the work gloves on the bench. Don't touch the wheel too hard, let their prints remain on it. I kept the driver's seat nice and clean for you. No brains on that side of the car."

"Thanks a lot, sport."

"I'll be inside. We gotta figure out where to dump these guys."

"I'll be right in," Ben replied.

"You want a sandwich and a cup of coffee, Ben," Dana offered nervously when Ben entered the kitchen.

"You got *cappicola?*"

"Of course. We always have it," she said, and fixed Ben a sandwich. "Bepy, you wanna eat?"

"I'll take a cold beer. My tongue feels like cotton," he replied.

"You'd better get those guys out of our drive before the kids come home," Dana said quietly.

"She's gotta clear head," Bepy told Ben. "She's worrying already and I'm still trying to figure out where to dump 'em. I guess if we eat, we can think better. Right?"

"Yeah. I hate to dump bodies on an empty stomach," Ben said, chuckling. "But don't worry, Dana. I'll get them out right after we finish eating."

Bepy drank his cold beer. "How about you, Ben? Do you wanna beer or a glass of wine?"

"No, just coffee. It smells good."

"Who wants pie?" Dana asked.

Bepy looked up at her. "What the hell! Who wants pie? What is this, a funeral or a party? I gotta dump these guys. Hold the pie till we get back, Dana."

Ben laughed. "He's still crazy, huh, Dana?"

"You ain't kiddin', Ben; he's a winner."

As they ate, Ben said, "Did you know in Sicily they always eat after they kill their enemies?"

"Yeah, my grandfather told me that. That meant they were strong people with strong stomachs. But they never offered pie and desserts like those napoletana wives do."

Suddenly and seriously, with his cobra look, Ben asked, "Where should I drop them?"

"Take the Bayonne Bridge to the Jersey Turnpike north. We'll drop them off near Newark someplace. Let them blame the Jersey family for this hit. They'll never believe we would truck them through toll booths from New York to Jersey."

"That's right, Bep. They'll blame Jersey. OK, whenever you're ready, we go."

"After we dump their car someplace, you jump in my car. I'll be behind you all the way. Don't speed, OK? If you use the second Jersey City exit, you gotta drop a quarter in the basket. You got plenty of change?"

"Yeah. How about you? Let's get our coins in order and have the exact amount."

"The bridge we pay only on the return to New York."

"OK, let's go," Ben said, embracing Bepy. "Like old times, huh, Bep?"

"Yeah, like old times, Ben."

"Would you like some more, Alan?" Dana asked two weeks later.

"That was great fettucini, Dana, but I couldn't eat another bite, except for a piece of your wonderful cheese pie." Alan smiled sheepishly.

After dinner, Alan and Bepy moved to the den. Ben stopped over to say hello, and Alan greeted him with an ice-cold smile. When he offered Bepy one of his new Arabian cigars, he awkwardly offered one to Ben, too, but Ben refused.

"How's Shaggy Goldberg?" Bepy asked Alan.

"Same. His wife is still giving the *schwartzer* money, and now he thinks the daughter is into the black stud thing also."

"Is that right? The jig got the daughter, too?" Bepy asked, and Alan nodded as he lit the cigar and mumbled, "I think so."

"I arrive in Vegas Tuesday afternoon. Tell Shaggy it will be over that week. I'm sorry we had to back away for a while. We had to let things cool down."

"I'm sure he understands," Alan reassured him.

Ben, listening to the conversation, asked, "Bepy, you gotta do me a favor."

"Sure, what is it, Ben?"

"Let me come with you. Let me hit the jig with you, like old times, OK, Bep?"

"No. It's out of the question. I'm doing it alone. It's just a plain old rub-out now, Ben. I'm gonna hit him and run. I'm not going to cut his balls off. Fuck that bullshit. I'm just gonna make sure he's dead and blow town. I won't take any chances with the guy."

"Look, Ben, I don't think you should even think of going. You're retired. Stay retired," Alan said firmly.

"Who the hell is talking to you, Alan? I asked Bepy, not you. Don't put your two cents in," Ben spat back.

"I'm putting my two cents in anyway. You got Alley Oop killed and now you wanna get Bepy or yourself killed. Stay home and become an artist or play tennis. You're through as a hit man," Alan informed him.

"Through, my ass. Who the fuck are you? And whatta ya mean 'become an artist'? Who the hell told you I paint?" Ben yelled angrily. "I've been with Bepy for years. I've been loyal, and he knows it, you Jew bastard. I ought to wax you for trying to tell me to paint or play tennis. You got some balls. I wanna do it for Alley—not for me. I gotta kill that guy for Alley's sake."

Bepy listened and smiled. "OK, hold it. Hold everything. After listening to you both, I realize I've got two loyal friends. So calm down, both of you. This is my decision."

"Let me come for Alley, not for me," Ben started again. "I can't sleep anymore. Alley Oop is haunting me. Every night I dream of him. He called me a scumbag last night. I gotta do it for Alley. I feel so rotten."

Bepy interrupted his tirade. "Let me talk. I just made a decision. I've thought it over. OK. For Alley, you've got a deal. I've never refused Alley and I can't refuse him now. Ben, we leave Tuesday. Be ready."

"Give me that cigar now, you Jew bastard," Ben said, smiling.

Alan handed him a cigar. "So even Alley called you a scumbag, huh?" Alan asked with a smirk. "You know, Ben, you're really a schmuck, but I love you anyway." He reached over to light Ben's cigar.

"Good night fellows," Ben said, puffing the cigar as he left.

"Are you doing the right thing with this guy?" Alan asked, staring out the window as Ben's taillights disappeared down the drive.

"Yeah, Benny's OK. He fucked up once, but experience is the best cure for some people. He knows the area and will be able to guide me in and out of town, and he already knows the guy. It'll be much easier for me. Ben is very loyal, Alan. I want you to understand this fully. He's a good man who got a bad break. He made the wrong decision. We all can do the wrong thing at times."

He leaned over, put out his cigar, and took a deep breath. "Let's go to bed. Dana's got your bed fixed, three pillows, as usual, and there's a bottle of seltzer on the night table in case you wake up dry. And Maalox in case your ulcers act up." Bepy laughed, teasing Alan a little, "Dana treats you like a baby. I think she's trying to get invited to Vegas. But I keep telling her she can't come."

"She's beautiful, that girl," Alan answered.

As they walked upstairs, Bepy said, "Oh, yeah, I meant to ask you. How are you getting along with Joey D on the pickups?"

"Joey D? He counts like a computer. I can't cheat him out of a dime. Alley Oop I could cheat, but this guy, forget it. I was ninety cents short, and he knew it. Then, guess what? He warned me he was gonna tell you if it happened again." They both laughed.

"Joey D is OK," Bepy said.

"He's a little fucked up in his head. That's what he is," Alan said. "But he follows your instructions to the letter. You've got a good man there, Bephino, but the guy's got an imagination like a Saint Bernard."

341

"It's the Jew broad, Sheila. She ruined his personality. You saw the job he did for us in Mexico; he's a smart guy. And he learned *ah respecto* a long time ago, when he worked on Wall Street. Joey D is OK. We'll always take care of him."

The next morning, during breakfast, Dana said, "Boy, I wish we had some bagels with seeds. I love bagels with seeds. I've got this fresh whipped butter. We could have..."

"Don't start that shit with the seeds again," Bepy said, lowering the newspaper and glaring at her. Alan looked on, perplexed.

"Alan, I will arrive in Vegas on Tuesday at two on TWA. Have someone waiting at the airport when I arrive, OK?"

"Whatd' ya mean *someone?* I'll pick you up myself. I'm leaving tonight. My plane is being serviced over at Teterboro. It will be ready at five-thirty tonight. So I'll be in Vegas waiting for you."

Bepy pointed to a box on the table. "Take that on your plane and hold it for me in your safe in Vegas."

"What is it?" Alan asked in a whisper.

"Two guns with silencers. I'll use them on the coon. I never thought I would've had to tell Ben and Alley Oop how to handle that job. I remember when we first met. Don Emilio told me that Benny was experienced on out-of-town hits, so I thought he could handle it easily. Now I've lost my good friend Alley Oop. You know, Alan, I didn't give it enough thought because I was busy with the JPJ Corve deal. And I really thought Ben could do it. He really fooled me on that one. I lost a good man when Alley got hit. He was so nice to have around....Ahh, what's the use of crying over spilled milk; it's over."

"He sure was nice to have around. Alley was something else. I really felt for Alley Oop," Alan agreed. "But you're right; it's over with, so forget it already."

"I should have done more. I should have told them to contact our California people to pick up guns with silencers. I blame myself for not working out a plan for them. I should've talked with Ben to see what kind of plan he had in mind. Who'd ever figure they were gonna use a knife? We very seldom ever use a knife. That's the past."

"Don't blame yourself," Alan said. "Some guys you gotta wipe their ass for them. Forget it, OK? Forget it."

Tuesday, Bepy and Ben arrived in Vegas as scheduled. Alan and Joey D were waiting to pick them up.

"You know, Menesiero? For a kid who quit school, you really figured the Corve equation right," Alan joked in the hotel. "Two hundred bucks equals twenty million each." Everyone laughed.

"Yeah, I've made a few good business deals from time to time. I gotta give myself a little credit for that." Bepy grinned.

"We were lucky that Weisman guy was nuts over his dog," Ben remarked.

"I married a dog once," Joey D said. "She had some tits, but what a dog she was! She was such a mutt even a Chinese cook called her 'pig'! She was some kinda dog, that pig."

Alan asked seriously, "Hey, yeah, whatever happened to Sheila Diamond? Mikey said she went crazy down there. Has anyone heard the final story on her?"

Bepy tried to change the subject. "It was the sun—I heard she got too much sun down there and went *pazzo.*" Turning to Ben, he said with a grin, "Now that we're so rich, wouldn't it be a shame, Benny, if this fuckin' coon we gotta hit kills you and me this time?"

"God forbid. What kinda joke is that?" Alan asked, shocked. "That's all that's gotta happen. Shaggy and me, we'll both kill ourselves over this thing yet. You'd better be careful. This *schwartzer* is waiting to be hit again. He's all ready for you. Remember that, huh, Benny?"

"I can't wait to get the bastard. I'm gonna blow his fuckin' head off," Ben vowed fervently.

"Where are we having dinner tonight?" Bepy asked.

"I took care of it," Alan answered. "We're all guests of Sammy Rogers over at El Real. He keeps telling me the next time you're in, Bepy, they wanna host you at dinner. Sammy's good to us. We gotta go for the respect. Is it OK, Bep? Are you in the mood for him tonight?"

"Yeah, that's fine. We'll eat with Sammy tonight. He's good people. And the *osso buco* at the Real is real fine."

Alan's private jet landed in San Mateo, at a small airport for private planes. A car was waiting, supplied by Goldberg. They immediately left for the hit's home in San Francisco, where they sat and waited across the street.

At seven, it was still daylight, and Ben and Bepy were making small talk. Ben sat behind the wheel.

"You know, it's a good thing this is a quiet block. Otherwise, we couldn't sit here and wait like this," he said.

"Yeah. You're right. Do you know your way back to the airport?"

"Yeah, it's easy. Don't worry. What did you tell the pilot?" Ben asked.

"I told him to stay with the plane even if it takes three or four days. I told him we got some beautiful ladies to see in San Francisco. The pilot is OK. He's been Alan's friend for years. He'll eat and sleep at the airport hotel if need be. I also told him not to leave the hotel for any reason. Because when we return we'll be in a hurry.

"By the way, I put wad cutters in both our guns. When he gets hit with these wad cutters at close range, it will look like someone hit him with a hand grenade."

"That's good. Are we gonna cut his balls off?" Ben asked after a moment's silence.

"What balls? Hell, that's where the wads are going. He ain't gonna have any balls left to cut. We lost one man fuckin' around with that bullshit. We put two in his head fast; that should slow down this giant. Then we put the balance—all ten wad cutters—in his balls."

"Look, there he is now," Ben whispered excitedly. "Look at that big mother fucker! He's a fuckin' giant. Look at him!"

"Jesus, he is big."

Bepy was wearing white shorts, a sweater, and white sneakers. Ben was dressed the same way, but in pale blue. Bepy had shaved off his mustache, and his hair was slicked down like George Raft's. Ben had added a pair of pink-tinted sunglasses and color-coordinated sweater tied around his shoulders, to complete their intended gay look. Both had tennis rackets in hand, with their guns stuffed in the covers.

"Let's go get him," Bepy growled. "Remember, act like we just came back from playing tennis—and act a bit gay. It can't hurt. Don't forget these niggers run fast. So when we get close, start pumping. Don't wait for me."

They moved quickly in a jog to catch up to their man. They were laughing, and the black man turned to watch them. Then, quickly, he got into his car and, in one motion, reached under the seat. Slowly, he lowered his window and spoke, trying to size them up, "How'd it go, fellas?"

"Oh, it was just wonderful," Ben replied, putting his hand on his hip and shifting his weight. "We had a grand workout today."

Bepy smiled and leaned over. "Hi, big fella! Where are you heading?" He purposely blocked the guy's view so Ben could get his gun out.

"I'm heading uptown."

Bepy held his warm smile and stepped aside. He knew Ben would be ready to do the honors, and he wanted him to gain back his respect. Ben was waiting with his gun pointed at the man's head. Sup. Sup. Sup. Sup. Sup. Sup. Ben unloaded all six in the guy's head so fast the body didn't have a chance to slump over. Then he shoved the dead man over on the seat and growled, "Lay down, ya black bastard!"

Bepy quickly put his arm in the window opening and pumped six more wads into him, hoping to blow the guy away, balls and all. They quickly put their guns back in the bags, and, acting normal, walked slowly up the street to their car. It was almost dark and not many people were around. No one heard shots or the hiccup of the silencers.

During the flight back to Vegas, neither of them spoke about the hit. It caused a very unhappy moment in their lives to surface again, and they relived it in silence. Alley Oop, their loyal friend, would always remain in Bepy's thoughts. His laughter and the image of his powerful, stout body would always be hanging around the neighborhood. Theirs was a life that could turn on you at any time. They knew it and they had to accept their casualties. But why Alley? Bepy thought. He was such a guy, that Alley Oop.

18

Don Emilio invited Bephino to dinner in South Brooklyn Thursday night at eight o'clock. When Bepy arrived, cars were parked all along 16th Street, so Monkey parked by a fire hydrant. "Stay with the car. I'll be out in about an hour," Bepy told him. A sign, CLOSED TODAY, hung on the door. A man wearing a fedora was peeping out of the window like he was waiting for someone to arrive. When he saw Bepy, he quickly opened the door and greeted him, jumping around Bepy like a yo-yo, speaking Sicilian, and tipping his hat in a style reserved for the Mafia Dons.

Bepy thought the fellow was overdoing the greeting. He was led into the rear room of the restaurant, where private parties were held. It was an ornate room, with a long, U-shaped table. About thirty men were sitting around it. Bepy hesitated for a moment, but then noticed, at the head of the table, Don Emilio. Rocco Borrelli was on his left, and Big Pat Aniello on his right. Also sitting there were the heads of the New York, New England, New Jersey, Pennsylvania, and other regional families—Dons, Capos, and their respective *consiglieri*. In Nick's place was a new don from Queens, Angelo Marandala. He smiled vividly at Bepy as their eyes met. He might have known Nick was going to approach him on the Morrano offer. Maybe he guessed the outcome, Bepy thought as he smiled back.

Bepy walked toward Morrano, who got up and embraced him twice. All eyes were on this outward display of affection and respect. The other Dons followed suit and got up to embrace him and shake hands.

What the fuck's goin' on? Bepy thought. Why are all these men hugging and kissing me? What's Morrano up to? He looked at Morrano's smiling face. He was flushed and happy, as if his son had just graduated from college and he was throwing a party for him.

Bepy sat down next to Don Emilio, where Big Pat now had a chair waiting for him. Morrano tapped his glass to get their attention. When everyone became completely silent, he nodded to an older man sitting directly across from Bepy. The old man started to speak, pronouncing every Italian word and syllable clearly in his strong Sicilian dialect. Bepy hadn't heard the tongue spoken so well since his grandfather had died. The veins in the man's neck were bulging as he talked about Bephino Menesiero, and about loyalty and years of *rispetto*. His voice became noticeably strained as he swore the blood of Bephino Menesiero was pure Sicilian. He knew the Menesiero family, the grandparents and parents of Bephino, from Sciaccia, Sicily, and would take oath to this. The blood is pure, he repeated over and over. He told how he had known Bephino when he was a little boy; he had watched him as a child, even though Bephino did not know him. With his eyes shifting from Don to Don, the old man pointed to his own head. "In my mind," he said, "I raised him. I taught him the ways of our people. *Eo giuramento bestemmia. Ei morte.*"

As the old man wiped his brow, he paused for a moment. Then, his voice soft and his whole face and eyes smiling, he pointed at Bepy and said, "This man named Bephino has proven himself over and over. He is worthy of this honor. His youth will be our future strength. His *famiglia* will be our ally. His blood will flow with our blood. He is a born leader of our people." Then in a deeply forced whisper, and staring around the table, he ended by saying, "What man dare to deny us such a don in our regime as this?"

Don Morrano, who had been making careful and direct eye contact with each person seated at the table, let the threatening question resound in the silent thoughts of these powerful men. The old man sat down, as if to indicate his ovation had settled matters.

346

"I am not asking that Bephino Menesiero be a successor to a don," Morrano said in a strong voice. "I am asking that he be put in our books of the Cosa Nostra and the Mafia as a new don. The youngest ever to be named!" The crowded room heard the release of Morrano's thoughts.

"He would be known as Don Dante, named after Signore Dante, the gallant warrior who fought the French and drove them from Sicily in the year 1283," Morrano continued. "You gentlemen will not need to be confused about his position. He will continue to be unattached. But his family will serve as ally to all families!"

Bepy quickly looked over at him, and he knew that Don Emilio was calling him a gallant warrior. He wanted to laugh when Morrano promised allegiance to secure council approval.

Morrano continued. "Don Dante will be known by all in the Cosa Nostra, and will be sworn to *omerta* on this great day of our lives."

He thus concluded his proposal and sat in silence, staring at the hierarchy of the Mafia. The rest of them focused on Bepy and searched for a decision.

Suddenly a man carrying a knife appeared, a sharp *coltello*. He was *il maschio pavoneggiarsi lo mafia di morte*—the man who carries the knife of death.

This was the way of the Mafia, the only way. The Mafia had lived by the sword since 1283, and little had changed in 1972. Only the Dons were allowed to kiss the pearl handle. The knife bearer circled the table and bowed in respect to each. The *coltello* was kissed by each Don.

Next came the *confidenza*, the acceptance or the refusal. The old speaker picked up the knife, marched over to Bepy, and cut his hand. Then he slowly moved around the table to each Don and requested, with his eyes only, permission to cut their palms.

At the conclusion of that ritual, Don Morrano himself directed Bepy to move around the table and embrace the seven Dons *duo la bocca e faccia*.

If Bepy's embrace was accepted, the Don would then join his cut hand to mix his blood with Bephino Menesiero's. It was known that some Dons had gone as far as the embrace but refused to mix the blood. Mixing the blood was an irrevocable acceptance of Bephino's becoming a don. But if anyone did not mix blood, then Bepy would have to be sponsored again at another meeting. They all knew that Emilio Morrano would see the refusal of his proposal as a personal vendetta.

With a signal from Morrano, everyone stood up and faced Bepy. He quickly understood that he should stand also and go to each Don and request the double sign of welcome. He turned to his right first, to approach the Don from Philadelphia. Bepy leaned over to embrace him and then reached out his cut hand. The embrace was given and blood was mixed. The next three around the table went as smoothly as the first, but when he stepped toward Don Alberto Cirillo, from New Jersey, the Don shouted, "I don't know this Bephino. I cannot accept him." As he sat down, everyone began to speak at once.

In the dimness, Bepy turned toward Morrano for guidance. After a moment of hesitation, the Don waved him on to conclude the ritual. The last council member willingly accepted his embrace and ended by mixing the bloods of five out of six families.

When they separated, the whole room waited to see what would happen next. Counting Morrano, the vote was 6 to 1. It had to be unanimous.

Cirillo sat in his chair and listened while two of the council members took turns whispering to him. Then Rocco Borrelli talked into his ear. Cirillo kept his eyes on Morrano as he listened. Finally, after what seemed to be forever, but was actually less than a minute, he pushed himself out of his chair. When he stood up, he had a slight smile on his lips, but not in his eyes. "I feel like a sheep," he shouted. He walked over to where Bepy was standing next to Morrano. "But I won't be the one to disappoint my good friend Morrano," he said, rubbing palms with Bepy. As relief relaxed the rest of the men in the room, they moved toward the group to congratulate Don Dante.

Don Emilio told Bepy in private, "You have reached a very high-ranking period in your life. Never again in our Mafia will you reach such a peak. Be careful, my friend, be warned, and beware of the same men who embraced you and have drawn your blood to theirs. Those same men may be your destruction. Never compromise your soul at the expense of an ally. Never let your kindness be confused with weakness. If there's a question or doubt, strike first and make peace later with their successors." Morrano then winked and smiled at Bepy. "That's one way to stay alive. Also, you must never use your power to take a friend's wife or daughter, or hurt an honest man. The Mafia hurts only the ones that are to be hurt. Good people must be protected from bad people. We must not manipulate people's weaknesses and prey upon their nightmares."

Bepy, in silence, absorbed the advice.

The Don put his arm around Bepy and smiled. "*Molto, molto bene,* Don Dante."

"*Grazie,* Mr. Morrano, *grazie.*" Then he asked, "Hey, Mr. Morrano, what did Rocco tell Cirillo?"

Morrano grinned as he remembered. "Rocco told him that I had asked to be godfather to his new grandson. He could not deny me that request. So I knew if I made such a request, he could never refuse you the right to be a don and favorite son to me. I only have one daughter, and he knows that. So Rocco relayed the message that I was concerned about his grandson, who lives in Camden, New Jersey. Cirillo would die a thousand deaths with his concern over my concern."

The word hit the streets of Brooklyn that same evening, and the next day, all five boroughs plus New Jersey and Long Island were whispering about the new Don. Word spread to New England, Florida, Vegas, California, Texas, and New Orleans.

Don Dante now had access to the repositories of the Mafia. Although he had his own small army of men, he was assigned ten more soldiers, imported from Sicily. The soldiers were his to command forever. They would be entrusted to his family. His word would be their action. Each New York Don submitted two names of soldiers to be gifts for the new Don. If any soldier proved not to be loyal to Don Dante, all families would endorse his funeral.

Bepy couldn't understand how the word had hit the streets so quickly. Even little kids already knew. He really preferred to be called by his old name, Bephino, but how could he refuse such a gift. To become a don was everyone's dream in Brooklyn. But he felt strange with the new title and name.

Every time he entered the neighborhood club some kid would run up to him and say very respectfully, "Good evening, Mr. Dante." Bepy stopped and looked at one boy's face, flowering out of a polo shirt, and remembered when he was a kid doing the same thing to the neighborhood Boss.

He smiled at the boy and asked, "How are you doing in school, kid?"

"I don't like school," the boy replied. "I hate school."

"Whatta you wanna do, shine shoes forever?"

"No. I'm gonna be a hit man someday."

Bepy was startled by the answer. His eyes twitched and his vision went far beyond this boy, to another young boy, entering a man's private office and asking him for money before he pulled the trigger.

Winter came and huge snowfalls clogged the streets of New York City. "How can you stand this snow?" Alan asked, while they were having lunch in a Manhattan deli. "I haven't worn boots in twenty years. Look at me. I'm like Santa Claus all bundled up."

"You're right. I can't stand this shit either."

Looking over his glasses, Alan asked, "Do you want us to call you Don Dante or Bephino?"

"Come on, Alan, cut the bullshit. You sound like Ben now. I don't care. My name is Bephino, right? That's that." He looked up at the ceiling and rolled his eyes, "Don Dante... I needed that like a fuckin' hole in my head."

Alan stuck a large kosher pickle in his mouth and bit into it. "Shaggy Goldberg has an office in Palm Springs and he wants to see you. He said it's not important. Try these pickles; they're great!" Taking another bite he asked "When can you be in Palm Springs?"

"Why? What's he got, another nigger in his bed?"

"No, nothing like that," Alan said laughing. "It's nothing important. I mentioned that you spend your winters there. He wants you to give him a call."

"OK, tell him I plan on being there sometime next week. I'll call him when I get there."

"Good. You wanna go to Radio City this afternoon? They've got a great Christmas show," Alan said.

"That's a real good idea. I always like those stage shows."

The week passed, and Bepy arrived in Palm Springs. He called Shaggy and made an appointment to meet the next morning.

The next day a receptionist in the foyer of the office building took Bepy's name. "Please have a seat, sir. Mr. Goldberg is in conference. I'll let him know you're here when he's finished."

Bepy waited twenty-five minutes. "Where is he?" He asked the girl. "Did you tell him I'm here? He's expecting me."

"He's still in conference, sir. I'm not allowed to disturb him. You'll just have to wait."

Standing up restlessly, he looked at the receptionist. Her face was young and pimply. He wanted to tell her she needed a good fuck to clear up her act, but he wouldn't say such a thing to such a young girl. Annoyed, he asked her, "What's your name?"

"Myra Silverman."

"Oh, this is great—a Silverman and a Goldberg. That's very nice. A regular fuckin' jewelry center you've got here." He walked straight ahead and pushed open the door marked PRIVATE, DO NOT ENTER.

Silverman followed. "Sir," she called after him. "Sir, you're not allowed to do this. This is a private area."

He walked into Goldberg's office; it was empty. He saw another door marked PRIVATE. He walked to it. Miss Silverman was right alongside with her pad and pencil in hand. When Bepy opened the door, he saw Shaggy flat on his back, half nude, on a leather couch getting aggressively blown by a beautiful young woman in a striped dress. His pants were lowered to his ankles; his belly looked like Bear Mountain, and his tie seemed to be strangling him. His large horn-rimmed glasses were foggy from his hot breath steaming from his mouth, and sweat soaked completely through his shirt. He was coming and saying, "Suck me, you little tramp. You know you love it. Ohh, ooh, eat me, you horny bitch." His big fat body began to jerk and tremble.

The girl was bobbing and weaving and opening her eyes, half grinning at him between gulps.

"You should have been a plumber," he yelled, lying there like an exhausted bull, unaware of his audience.

Bepy watched silently, then noticed that Miss Silverman was in shock. He walked up to Shaggy and said, "And for this you keep me waiting, Shaggy?"

The girl quickly got up, wiping her lips, still trying to swallow the balance of Shaggy. Her tits were like two grapefruit. She moved her big ass around like she was trying to entice the Seventh Army. "My God, doesn't anyone respect a person's privacy?" she said, buttoning her dress.

"Not when it's my time, kid," Bepy replied. "And put your tits back in—you're embarrassing Silverman here."

Shaggy got up, off balance, and pulled his pants over his huge belly, apologizing to Bepy. "OK, honey, go to lunch," he told the girl.

She smiled at Shaggy, "I just had lunch," and she walked out.

Miss Silverman stood there still gaping at Shaggy.

Goldberg asked her, "What do ya want, Myra? Go back to your desk. You're looking at me like a Jew who's never seen a cock before. Myra, stop staring at me, will ya? Go to lunch, go to lunch. Stop looking at me, Myra," he ordered as he tried to tuck his shirt in.

Bepy wanted to laugh at these two freaks trying to mend an impossible situation. "See what you're missing?" he said, smiling at Myra. "You should have lunch with Shaggy tomorrow."

She ran out the door screaming, "You people are sick! Sick!"

"I'm so sorry to keep you waiting like that," Shaggy said, putting on his tie. "The schicksa broad makes me crazy. She sucks cock like you don't know! Did you see those tits? The minute she begins to suck, I lose all control of myself. My ass loves to be kissed with infinite love and affection. Look, my legs are still shaking. Would you believe at my age my legs shake? They shook on my first lay, when I was fourteen. Look, they won't stop. She's unbelievable. She takes everything out of me."

"It's OK, Shaggy. I just witnessed another wonder of the world. I'm glad you had a good time. Sex is still the best part of life. Food is second. Let's go to lunch. We'll talk while we eat. I'm hungry."

Shaggy began to smile. He knew Bepy was more amused than angry.

"You know I already gave Alan the two hundred grand for you," Shaggy said. "Was it enough? You lost a man on this deal, so I'm willing to pay more. I never had a chance to personally thank you, and I insist on paying more for your great loss. I'm sorry about that. That's why I asked to see you. I'm willing to pay more than we agreed on."

"You paid the contract price. A deal is a deal, no matter how many people are lost. You don't owe us anything, Shaggy. You're even with me." Bepy picked up the menu, opened it, and asked, "How're your wife and daughter doing?"

"They're fine. They're afraid to leave the house. They took up knitting and needlepoint, and now the house is loaded with sweaters and scarves. My wife sends the maid out to buy their wool. Boy, this shit really works, huh? Those two women are in shock. Who needs so many sweaters and scarves in California?"

"Yeah." Bepy laughed. "A hit can really change a person's personality."

"Bephino, would you like to join me at the opening of a new night club tonight?" Shaggy asked him. "It's supposed to be something fantastic. It's called Fantasy Mountain. They made a night club in a cave on Mount Sidney."

"Mount Sidney?"

"Yeah, the movie guy from Beverly Hills. He loves to create crazy things."

"OK. I'm free tonight. My wife won't be in until tomorrow. Let's see what it looks like."

"Would you gentlemen care for a cocktail?" the waiter asked.

"No. Instead, please bring a small bottle of Vino de Rosa Fiorenza Cuato."

"Are you ready to order?"

Dana arrived the next afternoon with friends of theirs from Bridgeport. It was a time of the year she and Bepy looked forward to. He really enjoyed being away from the Mob atmosphere of New York, and settled down in Palm Springs to forget New York's dirty business.

They relaxed in the sun, and when Bepy was sure the wives weren't listening he told the men about the Fantasy Mountain. The men couldn't believe it. "It was a world of fantasy, all right." Bepy said, laughing.

One of the older men in the group, Tony Bono, a widower about seventy-six years old, was trying to get the pool waitress to take his order. Finally she strolled over, swinging her body in a provocative manner, and apologized for the delay. She was bursting out of her bikini.

Tony seemed somewhat uncomfortable. As she leaned over to ask him what he'd like to have, he began to pant. Then his left eye twitched a little, and his face became dazed as he looked at her, with the bright sun behind her.

The wives, sitting together, were soaking their bodies in suntan oil, wearing their one-piece bathing suits. They treated their faces with different lotions and creams and at the same time watched their husbands look after the waitress. Most of the men pretended to sleep, but really had one eye on their wives and the other on the waitress. They were looking, but not looking.

Tony had been a lady's man in his younger days, and he began talking with the waitress when she brought his drink. "What's your name, honey?"

"Terri," she answered as she sat down on the edge of his lounge chair and flipped through her order pad.

"You're a beautiful girl, Terri. Do you know that?"

"I've been told. That comes to four seventy-five. Sign here, please."

"Are those things real, Terri?" he asked, pointing to her chest.

She smiled, because she thought he was a cute old man, but did not reply.

"How much are the hookers getting this year?" he asked in a whisper, glancing at the women looking his way.

"I don't know their business and they don't know mine."

"How much are the waitresses getting?"

"For you, love, two hundred a pop."

Tony, a man with probably one pop left, dropped his key on her tray and softly whispered in her ear, through his cigar, "Three, sharp."

"OK, Tony. See you later." She got up and wiggled away.

One of the wives had heard Tony ask the price of hookers. "Hey, Tony, why do you want to know the price of a hooker, huh? What are you, a dirty old man now?"

His face turned red as he tried to suppress the broad grin he felt cross his face. "I was just checking the market this year. Don't worry, I'm too old for that stuff," he said, trying to exonerate himself.

"Yeah, Tony, come on. You're checking the price of what market? You're here to rest. Cut the baloney. That's what you told us in Paris, remember?"

Tony leaned over to talk to his friend Joe. Still speaking through his cigar, he whispered, "What a fuckin' doll that broad is, huh, Joe? Her body can stop a clock from tickin'."

"Be careful she don't stop your clock from tickin', Tony," Joe whispered back, his face expressionless as he tried to keep his wife from noticing his involvement in the conspiracy.

"It's her crotch that get's me, Joe. I could see her hair showing; that did it. I have to have that broad now. Once I see a broad like that, with her hair slightly showin', I'm a goner. I can't see cunt, Joe. It reminds me of my childhood. I made my decision; it's 3:00 P.M. for me."

"Be careful, Tony, be careful. A broad like that can do damage to the ticker—you know what I mean, Tony," Joe warned him.

Later that afternoon Tony got lost. About four-thirty the peaceful sunbathing and splashing in the clear blue water was interrupted by an ambulance and police pulling up to one of the poolside suites. Joe ran over and saw that it was Tony's room. He went in and came out crying.

Outside, talking to the police, was Terri, the waitress. She was crying and explaining that she had been making love to Tony when he died.

Tony's brother yelled, "*Putana,* you killed my brother! What'd you do to him? He looks fucked up. What'd you do to my brother?" he asked her directly.

"We were makin' love. I told him to slow down, but he wouldn't. He kept it up. He wouldn't stop," Terri defended herself. "He was a real man. I just tried to make him happy."

Tony's brother suddenly smiled at her and the policemen. "That's Tony. He loved his women."

"Did Tony need this? See what you men get?" The wives were huddled in horror, holding their beach towels in their arms. "You guys look for trouble. Now Tony's dead."

The men looked at Terri, then back at their wives, their thoughts obviously the same: Maybe Tony was lucky to have died such a beautiful death, instead of the slow death we're in for.

The following months brought new problems for Don Emilio Morrano. His wife died. He was getting old, and his health was failing. Then he had a slight stroke, which changed him to a very meek person. He seemed to be fading fast, and his daughter couldn't take care of him. Bepy visited him every day to see if he was all right.

The new acting boss was Rocco Borrelli, who was chosen to replace Morrano when the Don died or stepped down. Rocco was a very respected

354

man and was close to Bepy. Bepy was glad Rocco was in command, and not Big Pat Aniello, because he felt a closer alliance with Rocco.

"Don Emilio is suffering a deep depression," Borrelli said to Bepy one day. "He can't hack it anymore. He's *finito.*"

These unsympathetic words surprised Bepy. "Depression? My ass is suffering from depression, Rocco. Morrano killed more guys than a German general. He's not in any depression. I don't wanna hear that bullshit. OK, Rocco?"

Rocco knew Bepy was loyal to the Morrano family, so he understood his response and respected him for it. Loyalty, if unchallenged, was not worth having. Rocco knew that. He knew Morrano had lots of confidence in Bepy, so he tried his best to stay friendly and not lose him as an ally.

The Morrano family was huge and spread out across the country. Bephino Menesiero was just a small family of hit men, but he held his title throughout all families of the Mafia. The rank of don was a position of ultimate respect; a boss of thousands. Regardless of division and location, a boss will be respected ultimately by all Mafia soldiers. Bepy was temporarily over acting boss Borrelli, but he would never interfere with Rocco's business unless Rocco called upon him for advice or counsel.

Thinking about this situation and knowing it could never be the same dealing with someone else, Bepy told his wife and children he would like to move to a ranch, possibly down south. He had never forgotten the beautiful ranch owned by Don Santoro near New Orleans. It was time to get out of Brooklyn, he decided.

The twins liked the idea, because they were planning to switch to Miami University. He was surprised, but glad, that they would even consider such a move. They loved big-city life. But it helped his plans.

Dana objected to the move. "No. Forget it," she said. "You're crazy, you know that, Bepy? I will *not* move to a ranch down south, or in Texas or even in California! I am staying in New York. Understand, Bephino? I'm a New York girl. We're not moving. I like New York. My family lives in New York. I was born here," she yelled.

Bepy's eyes worried Dana. She could see that a decision was brewing, and she began to scream at him. "You know, Bephino, I carried a cross with you for twenty-five years, and I'm still carrying it. The cross is so heavy that I'm only four feet tall now. I've got my mother and father in New York. How could we leave? Our whole life is here!"

"I know your family lives in New York," he quietly replied, and the subject was dropped, for the moment.

During the next twelve months, the Don's illness seemed to change the atmosphere of living in New York City. The fun in Bay Ridge seemed to be fading away. Alley Oop was gone, and Bepy still had that empty feeling in his stomach. Things were changing fast. Life was troublesome and aggravating. Nothing seemed to bring Bepy pleasure anymore. Being rich in New York didn't bring the peace and comfort he had thought would come with money.

When he and Dana returned from Palm Springs each year, New York City seemed cold and dirty. It was depressing to come home to such a place after Palm Springs. That's why Bepy liked the idea of getting a ranch, possibly in California. But the kids were on the East Coast. He didn't like being that far away from them, so he shelved the idea. As a feeler, he decided to put the word out to real estate brokers in the Sun Belt that a New York corporation was looking for a first-class ranch, in either Florida or Georgia.

Bepy still made constant visits to Don Emilio, who was all alone except for his nurse and housekeeper. It was a very changed environment in the Morrano household. The Don's lovely wife was no longer there to smile and make him look and feel better. Don Emilio was becoming a vegetable right before his eyes.

He sat and talked to his friend and confided his feelings to him. "We've come a long way, Mr. Morrano, a very long way. We've got the money and we've got the respect. I crawled out of the gutter and I'm on top now. How do I keep myself from being swallowed back up? I'm on top, and there's only one place I can go now—down. How do I survive this avalanche, this fuckin' doomsday, that awaits me?"

He was trying to extract the final bits of wisdom from his dear friend's frail, ill body. He sat and waited patiently for the Don to answer him.

Don Morrano stared at Bephino. His mouth dribbled saliva, he lisped when he spoke, and his voice was low and unclear. "Don't be concerned by my absence. I can see it in your eyes. You will know the way, Bephino. Make your own way, reach your destiny."

19

Soon enough and sure enough, people began to ask Don Dante for special favors. "Can you get my brother out of jail?" "Can you get me a state job?" or "get my case thrown out of court?" Even the parish priest, Father Baviglia, asked Bepy for a favor. He wanted him to meet with the monsignor.

Later that week, when they were to meet, Bephino said to Alan, who was in town, "Take a ride with me. I gotta have a sit-down over at the church. I got a couple of bishops who wanna have a talk."

"I've never been in a church before," Alan replied. "I'm a Jew, you forgot already."

Bepy smiled. "How could I forget you're a Jew!" He pinched Alan's cheek. "You coulda been a race horse."

"I'd rather be a Jew," Alan said.

"Come with me, Alan. This should be interesting."

"For you, I'll try anything—even a church."

They arrived at the office of Monsignor McGee. The introductions that followed were cool and quickly spoken. Father Baviglia was smiling, as usual, and the Monsignor kept a firm, cold face, as usual.

"Befemo, as you know, the housing on this block will be torn down," the Monsignor said. "We have bought all the buildings and are already in possession of the deeds. Mrs. Josephine Magnalari refuses to accept our check and sign over her deed to the church. Last week she told us that you were her nephew and that we shouldn't bother her. What is this supposed to mean to us, that you are her nephew? We aren't interested in who you are or what you do." He stopped to light a cigar.

"Although Father Baviglia speaks very highly of you and your family—ahh, I mean your mother and father as your family, of course." Bepy looked over at Alan, a smirk quickly crossing his face. "We have given Mrs. Magnalari two weeks to vacate or face court action that she can't possibly win. The church has the money to take her through the courts, and we will win. I can assure you of that." Pointing his cigar at Bepy he continued. "She can't afford that, can she? We want her out in two weeks. You understand, don't you, Befemo?"

"I do understand you're taking the people's houses at an unreasonably low market price. That's what I understand," Bepy answered, looking him square in the face. "Those houses are worth twenty-one thousand dollars, and you're paying them only nine thousand. They're scared people who respect the church, so most are selling without thinking. My aunt's an old woman who has no husband. He died two years ago. She's been living in that house thirty-eight years, and she's sixty-eight years old. Where is she gonna go? She just spent six thousand dollars on the house—a new roof, new kitchen cabinets, and all aluminum windows. Now you offer her a lousy nine thousand to get out? Her house now is worth twenty-seven thousand dollars. How can you expect her to move and take that loss? Look, Father"— Bepy turned to Father Baviglia—"if you pay her fair market value for her house, I'll give her a place to live. But she must have at least fair market value."

"Young man, Father Baviglia isn't handling this matter," Monsignor McGee said. "I am. So please direct your conversation to me, if you don't mind."

"OK, but Father Baviglia married me and baptized my twins. He's known my aunt for thirty-six years. I respect him and I want him to know I'm willing to help the church out on this matter."

"Is that so?" the Monsignor replied. "I want your aunt out in two weeks, Befemo, and I'm holding you personally responsible for that. She mentioned your name, and that caused me to ask questions. I have received many different versions of your life style—which could be interesting to the authorities."

Bepy stared at him with cold, contemptuous eyes, "Is that so?" he said icily. "Well, I'm gonna tell you something: I've been beat up, shot at, and even pissed on, but I have never been threatened by a priest before. This is another...You know, Father McGee..."

"Monsignor McGee, Befemo—I'm a monsignor."

"Is that so?" Bepy smiled. "Then you can call me Humpty Dumpty, as you seem unable to pronounce my name correctly. My name is Bephino Menesiero, and I was born in this neighborhood. As a matter of fact, Father, you're operating your chuch in my neighborhood. I remember when I was a little boy, my mother once gave me her last quarter for donation at Mass. She told me, 'Son, make sure you change the quarter before you get to Mass. Put ten cents in the first collection and fifteen cents in the second.' But I forgot to change the quarter—I was only eight years old. When the first collection was passed around, all the kids put their dime in. I only had the quarter. So, not to be embarrassed, I put it on the green plate. Then you yourself came around with the second collection, Monsignor McGee, and I didn't have anything because my quarter was already put in. You looked down and said, 'Whatsa matter? You don't put money for the church?' I was only a kid and I was so proud to have twenty-five cents that day—a whole quarter. And I was bubbling with respect for you. Then you scorned me."

The Monsignor looked away in discomfort. "I never forgot the hurt that you left inside me," Bepy continued. "When I tried to explain, you made a face, just like the one you're making right now. All the kids snickered at me." Bepy hesitated, looking hard at the Monsignor.

"I wanted to be an altar boy, but I knew you loved me only for my money, and I couldn't afford you. So I turned to the streets for love. Maybe I am what I am because of you. After that I was too embarrassed to go to church with the nice kids, so I took up with the bad kids. I have carried that cross all my life. Now it is yours; I give it back to you to carry. You put a kid who wanted the altar into the gutter. Now live with it."

Alan sat through the whole story with an exaggeratedly solemn look pasted on his face. He shook his head from side to side.

"The next week, you showed up at my mother's house with those two giggling nuns you hung around with, asking for a pledge of three thousand bucks. My mother and father didn't even have three hundred bucks in the whole world, let alone three thousand, but you got them to sign a pledge. Before you left you even conned my mother out of her wedding band, for the gold, to make some fancy jewels for a statue, and that night I watched you drive away in a brand-new shiny car. Now you want my aunt out of her nice little house for practically peanuts, just so you can build garages for your fleet of new cars. You hurt me once when I was eight; don't try to hurt me at forty-five. Threatening me would be a big mistake. And, another thing: you're a real gee, Father McGee. I saw you at the race track three weeks ago with those two giggling nuns again and your brother. You were driving a Rolls-Royce. And sure they laugh—your brother drives a Caddie, the nuns got an Olds, and my aunt takes the bus."

"Is that so?" the Monsignor replied. "Are you finished with your childhood memories?"

"Yes, I'm through."

"There's no rule that we can't go to the horse races."

"Yeah, I know there's no rules for you, but you were at the fifty-dollar window. That's kinda steep for a priest, isn't it? You're supposed to help the poor. Somehow, it doesn't look right—those fancy cars and that woman who comes from Philadelphia to see you from time to time."

"What woman are you talking about? What are you insinuating?"

"Nothing. I'm not insinuating anything. But if you wanna pick a fight with me or my aunt, be ready. Because I'll arrange for you to wake up one morning with seven naked big-busted whores swarming around you like honey bees in heat. The Italian newspapers will wire your fame to Rome."

"Is that so?"

"Yes, that's so, Father. And if you don't come down outta that Rolls you're sittin in, you're gonna find the whole neighborhood gone." He pointed at Alan. "See this man? He's a rabbi and he's lookin' for a neighborhood. Don't make me give him yours. Forget about my aunt's house; you can start giving back the deeds, because you're not getting her house. That's a decision I just made. You're not tearing down these houses just to build a garage for you and your all-girl staff. You are a priest. You're supposed to help the poor, not parade in front of them with new cars and fancy broads. Find another place to park your car—and not in my Aunt Josie's kitchen, OK?"

Nothing was said for a minute or two. Then Father Baviglia smiled and served coffee.

"We have another problem that we would like to speak with you about, Mr. Menesiero," Monsignor McGee said. "Last week our jewels—I mean the church's jewels, of course—were stolen. They are worth a half-million dollars. You have the con...I mean, you may know who can help us get them back."

Bepy looked at the Monsignor. "Is my mother's wedding ring melted into those jewels?"

"I'm afraid so." He gulped as he answered.

"OK, give me a few days. I'll put the word out they gotta be returned. Don't worry, it'll be taken care of. Give me a few days."

The men shook hands, and Father Baviglia walked Alan and Bepy to the door, smiling all the time. He seemed to have enjoyed the evening. "You told him well, son," he whispered to Bepy. "He needed that."

"See?" Alan said, grinning at Bepy. "Even he says that about you. You always tell it well."

"Hey, Father, how come you don't have a car?" Bepy asked, changing the subject.

"I enjoy riding the bus with your Aunt Josie," he replied. "I help her with her shopping bags."

Bepy patted him on the back. "That's why the whole neighborhood is loyal to you, Father. Hey, my twins are going to Rome next year. Does this guy McGee have any connections in Rome or is he all talk?"

Father Baviglia smiled. "You get him those jewels back and he'll open all the doors in Rome for the twins—and maybe even the gates of heaven for you, my son."

"You're snowing me, Father. Imagine me going to heaven!" Bepy laughed. "St. Peter surely would like to meet me in person. I've kept him in business since I was a kid. We've got a thing going. You got a deal, Father. In a few days you'll get your jewels back."

"How did you get into that mess?" Alan asked as they drove home.

"My aunt. She loves to tell people I'm her nephew."

"Boy, that was really something. What a story you told!"

"The Monsignor's a thief in a dress, believe me. I hope, after checking around, I don't find out he stole those jewels himself and gave them to that broad from Philly," Bepy said, grinning.

"Is that story true?" Alan asked.

"Nah. I just made it up, to keep him off balance. But did you see his face? Boy, he acted funny about that, didn't he?"

"Yeah. And I almost wound up with the whole neighborhood. Did you really feel so hurt about the collection thing when you were eight?"

"Nah. That happened to my brother, Mario, in Boston. I just put myself in the starring role. My mother never gave me a quarter. I got two nickels for church. But it sounded real good, didn't it?"

"Good? You should get an Academy Award for that! Are ya kiddin'? You had me in tears with that story," Alan said. "What about the jewels? How are you going to get them?"

"I'll go and talk to people at the club. I'll pass the word they gotta be brought back to the church, or else."

One week later a bag lady delivered a box containing the jewels to Father Baviglia, and Aunt Josie never left her kitchen.

Bepy was getting more and more fed up with the New York way of life. No one seemed to be secure. Things seemed to change and were getting worse instead of better. Phone calls day and night, and everyone had a problem and needed help of some kind. Some wanted credit in Vegas, even show and dinner comps for their children's schoolteachers.

In his more reflective moods, he was not listening to Superman on the radio, but was watching the cold ocean waves breaking on the beach, and the oil and debris floating ashore. New York was deteriorating. The oil washing up on his well-kept beach made his stomach turn. He knew there was no more beauty to be had in New York City. In 1974, the dockworkers went on strike, and the oil tankers piled up in the harbor entrance with oil leaking and ruining all the beaches. The sanitation department went on strike, and garbage piled up to the first floor of buildings. The police and firemen were threatening a strike. Bus drivers were calling in sick to support the sanitation workers.

He had always loved New York and had never dreamed he would ever consider moving, but his love affair with New York had come to an end. He made the final decision for himself and his family: they would leave New York City to live on a two-thousand-acre farm down South. A real estate broker had called him the day before and said there was a ranch owned by a man who raised horses and cattle for sale. It was a high-quality place on the line between Georgia and South Carolina. There were rolling hills and green grass year around. It was one of the most beautiful plantations in the South.

"How is the weather in the wintertime?" Bepy asked the broker.

"Warm and beautiful; not at all like New York, Mr. Menesiero, it gets cold, but not like New York."

He decided to talk to Dana once again before he bought it. He walked into the kitchen, where Dana was finishing up after dinner, and said, "Let's talk about tomatoes."

She looked up at him while wiping down the kitchen sink. "What kinda tomatoes—two-legged ones or plum tomatoes?" she joked.

"Plum tomatoes," he replied. "Come here, sit down. Let's talk."

Dana dried her hands and moved to sit with Bepy.

"Dana, I'm getting fed up with the New York rat race. I'm tired of being kissed on both cheeks by old men and women smelling of garlic. The other day, the candy-store lady kissed me, and her whiskers brushed my face. I got sick to my stomach. I'm tired of this life. You know what I mean? I wanna go hide some place. Last month I had a sit-down with a priest, and he made me very upset. He wanted Aunt Josie's house for nothing, I don't want to deal with that sort of stuff anymore."

"You know, Bepy, when I married you, I thought you were a stockbroker—at least that's what you said. You told me you were a big shot on Wall Street."

"Dana, I *was* a big shot on Wall Street. And I still am."

"But you're not a stockbroker, Bepy. You're a . . ." Dana hesitated.

"Yeah, and now I wanna be a farmer. Is anything wrong with that? Look, Dana, someday I'll be the one to get kissed on one cheek. Then what? If I retire a little early from my business, my chances to beat this racket will increase. I gotta play the percentages. *Ah capeesh?*"

"Yeah, I understand. But who the hell wants to be a farmer's wife? You go from one extreme to the other. I think you're *pazzo*, Bephino."

"Look, Dana. We'll only be part-time farmers. I gotta keep my business in New York. I got people to take care of. I could never cut them loose."

"What does this have to do with tomatoes?" she asked.

"I wanna relax and enjoy life. I wanna grow beefsteak tomatoes. The big ones, you know what I mean? I wanna enjoy the simple things in life."

"OK, Bepy, you got a farm upstate, so grow big beefsteak tomatoes up there. Be my guest. Who's stopping you? Grow all the *big* ones you want."

"Dana, I'm talking about leaving New York to grow these tomatoes."

"You know, Bepy, you're really something. I asked you for a garden once, and you told me we live too close to the ocean, our land is too salty, and we couldn't grow tomatoes. We own a five-hundred-acre farm upstate, and I never ate a single damn onion off that farm. Now you wanna leave the entire state of New York to grow tomatoes. This has gotta be a best seller, Bepy. I can't believe I'm hearing this."

"I think I'm getting high cholesterol and ulcers. I'm ready for the pasture. I can feel it in me. Even my feet feel flat."

"Oh, my God. Listen to this bullshit," she said, and laughed. "The guy whacks three guys right on our lawn, sits down, has a beer, and now he's got ulcers, cholesterol, and flat feet, and he wants to put himself out to pasture. Bephino, is this shit for real? The next thing you're gonna tell me is that you and Alan caught Alley Oop's hemorrhoid problems. I can tell you, my husband, that it has not been easy being your wife. I don't know what the next day's gonna be. You always have a surprise for me. It's a good thing *I* raised the children; otherwise, they would be totally *pazzo* like you. Get that caretaker bum to grow you a few bushels of tomatoes on our farm. He sits on his ass all day fishing in our lake. He thinks we bought the farm for him. Let him grow the big ones."

Bepy realized he hadn't gotten through to her. She wouldn't accept reality or the real reason for his tomato story. "OK, OK, honey," he said, kissing her. "Maybe we'll talk another time. I need more time to think. This is a tough decision for me, and you're making it a lot tougher. I'm going to Brooklyn now. See you later."

Later that week, he called the broker. "I'll be down tomorrow to look at that ranch."

She immediately offered to pick him up at the airport. He asked Ben to take a plane ride with him to see the plantation. Ben was delighted to go. They were taken on a tour of the entire farm by jeep. There were cows still grazing in the pastures, but all the horses had been sold off by the owner. The realtor explained that the cows would be included in the price of the ranch.

Both men loved the place. The pastures were green and beautiful. It looked like peace on earth.

Ben asked, "Is this place a ranch or a farm?"

"Sometimes we call it a ranch and sometimes we call it a farm." She smiled at these men from Brooklyn, "This is a first-class plantation or a thoroughbred-horse farm. It's also a ranch because of the cattle. You can call it any of the three."

That same day, Bepy bought the place. He gave the realtor a deposit of fifteen thousand dollars and hired a Hilton Head lawyer to process the final transaction.

That night, at their hotel, Ben said, "Boy, you weren't kidding when you said you liked Don Santoro's ranch. Are you really gonna leave your New York operations? You're a don. How you gonna pull that off?"

"Just watch me, Ben. I'm only one hour and twenty minutes by plane from New York City. It takes me longer to get to there from my farm upstate. Ben, I'm drained by the carnage of my life. I'm fed up with it all. I want at least semiretirement. Peace away from Brooklyn. Can you understand? I want to live my life out on a ranch."

"But are you sure you wanna move here? What's Dana gonna say? She's gonna kill you, Bep. This is too far for her. She loves New York. She loves to shop on Fifth Avenue. There ain't nothing down here for her."

"Yeah. She doesn't wanna leave New York for anything. But she will."

"I know. She'll have no choice," Ben agreed.

"Don't say I bought it yet. I'd better break it to her easy."

They arrived back in New York the next day, and Bepy called Fat Arty. He also called his lawyer and a real estate broker. He gave them instructions to sell everything that wasn't nailed down. "Sell all the real estate I own—apartments, office buildings, rental houses, the upstate farm, everything."

He then mentioned an apartment building in Brooklyn. "There's a tenant living there rent free. Her name is Norma, in apartment fifteen, and she has a couple of kids. She must live there rent free until she dies. Make sure any new buyers know this is part of the deal. If they ever decide to give her trouble, then I will deal with them. Understand?"

He instructed Arty to make sure a check for one hundred fifty dollars weekly continued to go to Norma the rest of her life. "Keep taking it out of the hero-shop account—like she's on the payroll. And continue the Christmas bonus. She'll need the extra cash."

Fat Arty assured him the money had always been sent weekly and would continue to be.

At lunch that day, Bepy brought up the subject of the move once again with Dana, and she rebuffed him with her usual arguments.

"Look, honey. I'm on top. We're rich. Where else can I go now? It's gonna be down—am I right or wrong? When you go up, you gotta go down. It's a fact of life."

"You sound like Alley Oop." She laughed.

"May he rest in peace," Bepy yelled at her. "Always say 'May he rest in peace.' Have respect. Do you want me to wind up like Alley, in the gutter with holes in my body getting pissed on by some young punk? I prefer to be in the green meadows of the South watching my cattle grow."

"I thought you were gonna watch your tomatoes grow. Now we're out of the produce business and into cattle?"

"You make fuckin' jokes at the wrong time of my life; that's your problem, Dana," he said, getting up from the table.

"You know what your problem is, Bepy? You're getting chicken. That's it—chicken," she yelled after him. "You're scared of New York. You're scared of being on top."

He stopped dead and turned his head. The veins in his neck began to swell as blood gushed to his head, and his ears turned red.

Dana realized she had struck a nerve. "You big chicken, me little chicken," she said, trying to be cute. "Bephinooo, you big chicken, me small chicken?" She was almost frightened of her own husband. He had always been kind and generous, but if pushed, his temper could mean spending a week at a medical convention—as a patient. "Bephinooo, do ya wanna bagel?" Her face showed a new design of humor and fear.

He stared at her, trying hard to hold a straight face. But he burst out laughing. He couldn't hold it back. "Look, screwball. Remember that lawn party we had in front of our house?

"How could I ever forget?"

"Good, don't. Because that is what we can expect living here. Nobody's satisfied with what they've got. They always want the other guy's possessions. And they're willing to kill for it. I'm fed up with it. I'm not proud of what I've done, but I got what I wanted. I achieved my goal. But I don't wanna be like the old Mob guys, hoarding all my money and counting it till I die. I realize now that I could've done it without the crimes. But I was a kid. I took the wrong road. I'm not proud of myself, but I have to live with it. I'm not chicken, Dana, and I'm not getting soft. But I'm not staying in New York to have my past haunt me every day of my life. I'm too smart for that shit." He put his

365

arms around her. "I'm sorry I put you through so much. It'll only get worse without Morrano as Boss. Believe me. I'll see you later. I gotta go to Brooklyn."

Later that evening, Bepy talked to Ben at the club. "Dana's giving me trouble. She doesn't wanna move. She's fighting me with the stupidity of a true napoletana."

"You gotta be smooth with them Naples people, Bep. You gotta bullshit her. Buy her something she don't have. Something she can use on the ranch. That way she'll be anxious to use it and she'll soften up. All them Naples people get conned over a gift. Didn't your father ever tell you that?"

"He always told me that they like to spend money."

"Well, that's the same thing. They like to spend and they like to receive. But they love gifts the best. I was humping Carmella for years; she was from Naples. For a lousy belt, she'd fuck all day."

"What can I get her for a ranch?"

"How about a lawn mower?"

"She's already got two she rides all around the place. She's even on the beach with it. You've seen her."

"I know," Ben said, thinking hard. "Buy her a fancy saddle. Let her feel like a cowgirl."

"You think Dana's that stupid? That she'd fall for that bullshit? A saddle without a horse?"

"Tell her the horse is waitin' for her at the ranch. That's gotta work."

Bepy arrived home dragging a saddle, a cowboy hat, and boots for Dana. They were of matching black leather with sterling silver trim.

Dana was lying on the couch wearing a sexy nightgown. When she heard the packages being dragged through the house, she got up to see what Bepy was up to.

"Look what I got for you, Dana," he said with a broad smile. "And your horse is waiting down on the ranch."

"I thought you were dragging in a body," she said. "You scared me." Then she saw the saddle. "You gotta be kiddin', Bepy. Who needs a saddle?"

"How would you like to use this saddle? And this hat and these boots? They're made of pure lizard and trimmed in sterling silver." He was smiling at her, proud of his gifts.

Dana looked at the saddle, boots, and hat. "Where's the matching wristwatch, you kinky old man. What are you trying to get me to do tonight?"

"Nothin'. What d'ya mean kinky?"

366

"You got me boots, a hat, and a saddle. I'd look cute bare-assed in that saddle. It seems kinky, Bephino; I'm telling you."

He was surprised at her misinterpretation of his gifts. Rubbing his face and staring at her, he asked, "How could you think kinky? It's a gift."

"It's easy. It's 11:00 P.M., I'm waiting up for you in a negligee, and you show up with a saddle. I'd look cute in that saddle, wouldn't I?" She smiled. "And you look cute with that five o'clock shadow, cowboy."

"You know what you'd look like bare-assed in that saddle, Dana? You'd look like French provincial furniture in an ultramodern house. That's what you'd look like." He stormed upstairs. "I'm gonna have a shave and a hot bath. Don't follow me upstairs, you kinky bitch," he yelled down at her. "Whatta you, in the mood tonight?"

Downstairs, Dana burst out laughing, put on her cowboy hat, and began to dance. "Bephinooo," she called after him. "You're getting very sensitive lately. That's a bad sign. You know that, don't you?"

A few months passed. Don Emilio Morrano had a massive stroke and became incapacitated. He was too ill for a nurse to take care of at home, so his daughter put him in a rest home in Boston. Bepy felt bad for Morrano. The Don's powerful appearance and classy life style were gone. Bepy stayed in telephone contact with the Don's daughter. She always said, "He's hanging in there."

During that time Bepy's real estate and businesses were sold, and property transfers took place. Dana was kept unaware of all this. Even their house on Staten Island was sold—secretly to Don Rocco Borrelli over a cup of coffee and a handsake. Borrelli had heard that Bepy was moving south and jumped at the chance to buy his beautiful house on the ocean. It was the perfect house for him and for his children to grow up in. He paid the asking price without batting an eye. Bepy liked the idea of his own people enjoying what he and his family had loved so much. It gave him a feeling of comfort.

The time had come for Borrelli to take the oath as a don. He was now in full command of the Morrano family, except for Big Pat, who refused to sponsor him. Big Pat had expected to get the commanding position. He had even threatened anyone who interfered with the internal business of the Morrano family. But Bepy knew that Morrano wished Borrelli to take over, so, at the meeting of Dons, he sponsored Borrelli, rather than Big Pat. As soon as he did, Big Pat walked out of the council meeting, threatening war.

When the room settled down, the oath-taking ceremonies continued. Borrelli swore to uphold the responsibilities of boss of bosses and in an unusual move, asked Bepy to come stand next to him. The two men bound their families together forever by swearing solemnly to *la bocca e faccia*. This oath meant that any enemy of one was also the enemy of the other—a lifetime agreement, sealed with a kiss on the lips.

This type of agreement is very rare in the Mafia, for if it is broken, it can affect the lives of a don's children and grandchildren. The only way such an oath can ever be broken is for the Don breaking the agreement to cut off his own finger in front of the council of Dons and present it to the Don he is breaking the agreement with. The other Don may or may not accept it. If he does not accept the finger, the oath is unbroken. At the death of one of the Dons, the same thing takes place, only it must be witnessed by at least two other Dons and accepted by a surviving *consigliere* of the dead Don. Otherwise the promise and the vendetta will never end.

The other family bosses were surprised when this very strict old Sicilian oath took place. It hadn't been done since the Old Country. This was a tribute to Don Morrano and meant that his family and friends would never be separated.

Bepy met with Monkey and Little Pauli. He told them he was leaving soon. "You guys have a special number, to call me anytime, twenty-four hours a day. If you wanna come visit the ranch or talk business, you'll always have a place to stay. We'll have your rooms waiting. You're my old friends. I don't forget.

"The new soldiers in our command will report to you and Ben weekly," he told Monkey. "I want both of you present when they report. Ben will know this."

"Ben?" Monkey asked in a harsh voice. "You're putting Ben in command of us?"

Bepy looked surprised. It was the first time Monkey had questioned a major decision. He purposely did not answer and continued to explain the new lines of command. But he thought, Monkey's out of order. There always comes a time when even your best will question you.

"Here's a list of the soldiers the Bosses transferred to us. Keep them busy, give them exercise once in a while—let them break a few heads now and then on slow payers, and let them take a few contracts from the other families, if need be. Let them earn their money, and keep the family active. Don't let them get rusty. *Ah capeesh?* If our family gets a contract, let Ben pick the men. I want everyone to earn. Don't forget that. But I want

368

everyone to work for it. I want no free riders. You know the rule. These guys are only workers; they're not old blood. Keep Mikey on top of them. You stay in the shadows from now on, ok pal? You watch things for me."

"*Si, io capeesh,*" Monkey answered meekly.

"You will have the rank of capo in my family, Monkey. You've earned it. But Ben will be my official *consigliere.* Pauli, you are now a lieutenant. No more soldiers; you're all buttons now. We have twenty soldiers total, not counting the old blood. If any of these men ever loses respect for our family, eliminate him immediately. No discussions, only decisions. Quick decisions will always keep our people loyal. Remember, a man who takes time to make decisions usually suffers from paranoia.

"If you're short one or two soldiers, have Don Borrelli transfer replacements to our family. We're a small but powerful group. This is important to him. He wants us strong to help support him, so it works both ways. Never talk to me on the phone about business. Always give me a phone booth number, starting with the last number first. I'll call you back in twenty or thirty minutes. Keep things under control. I will still run our family from Georgia. But Ben will be issuing all my orders to you. Your job will be to carry them out. He's the man from now on. Give him the loyalty you gave me. If you need advice, talk to Ben. I trust him with my life. Understand, fellas? So don't question my judgment."

"Yeah, we understand. Don't worry, Bephino. We'll run the family for you—just like you was in New York."

"Good. That's what I want to hear. Now, I have some more news for you. Pauli, you are now a forty-forty partner with me in the gambling business. Ben will get twenty off the top. You take my share every week to Arty Argento, the Bank. He will handle it for me. OK?"

"Are you sure?" Pauli asked incredulously.

"Yeah, I'm sure, Pauli. That's because you were loyal and I never dreamed of you. You're my partner in the gambling from now on. But make sure Mikey is taken care of properly, or I'll make a new decision.

"Monkey, the same goes for you. As of this week, your name is on all the records of this company. You own half the stock and half of the profits from our six stores. Keep the sandwich business going good. We've come a long way; we're the original heroes, huh, Monkey? We fed a lot of people," he said, trying to cheer Monkey up after his stupid remark.

"Yeah, Bep. We sure did," Monkey said, and smiled.

"Monkey, you do the same with my half of the skim cash. Give it to Arty for me, OK?"

Both men were overwhelmed by Bepy's generosity and they embraced him at the same time, as a gesture of long-lasting unity.

"Joey D goes with me. We're leaving tomorrow morning for the South. He will live with me, but will continue to be the Las Vegas bagman for our family. And, by the way, if I get knocked off or something, make sure my son, Patsy boy, continues to get my cash. If he doesn't, that will cause me to make another decision from my grave."

The men laughed.

"I'll talk to you guys tomorrow by phone," he said, and left.

"Sweetheart," Bepy said to his wife, that evening, "we're moving to our new farm tomorrow. It's on the state line between Georgia and South Carolina."

Dana put down the magazine she was reading and looked at Bepy very closely. "Yeah, tomorrow," she said. "And tomorrow never comes."

"I'm not joking. Tomorrow we leave New York for good."

"What the hell! Are you in the mood to fool around tonight, Bepy? You wanna talk about tomatoes? OK, let's talk again about tomatoes."

"No, honey, I'm serious. I bought a beautiful farm down South. I'm not fuckin' around. I sold all the businesses and rental properties. Everything is sold. A mover is going to pack everything we own—you have nothing to do. So if you have any money hidden in the house, you'd better get it out and in your bags, OK? And tell the kids the same thing; call them at school and tell them we're moving out tomorrow. Give them the new address and phone numbers. Here." He handed her a slip of paper. "When our new house is ready, everything important will be brought down by the movers. For the time being, I'm having a small truck bring only the items we'll need for the immediate future."

She was silent, and her face was white.

"Don't worry. You'll love the ranch," he said, trying to soothe her. "It's beautiful. Two thousand acres of pastures, cows, and horses. It's paradise. I always wanted to live on a farm or a ranch."

He puffed on his cigar and waited for a response. Dana said nothing. He tried another angle. "And we won't be that far from the kids down there at Miami University. And we can easily drive back to New York to visit your mother and father and family. It's a perfect location, Dana."

Her ears heard him, but her heart couldn't believe what she was hearing.

Suddenly, the doorbell rang, and Alan walked in with Joey D. Both were dressed in blue jeans and Western shirts and carried suitcases. "OK, we're ready to ride the bull. What time are we leaving?" Alan asked.

Dana now believed Bepy. She had no more doubts. "You're serious about this?" she asked. "I will never move to Georgia or South Carolina, so forget it." She jumped up, threw her arms up in a gesture of utter frustration, and yelled, "Fuck you, Bephino! You got some nerve telling me I'm moving out of my beautiful home and going to Georgia! I just can't believe you're . . . .! Who the hell do I know down there? Where can I do my food shopping and buy my Italian cheese and olives and canned tomatoes to make the sauce? Are you crazy? I will never move down south, never, never, never! So forget it!" she screamed. "Forget it! Understand, Bepy? You wanna go? Go by yourself!"

When Alan and Joey D heard this, they went to hide in the kitchen.

The following day was very quiet; the only sounds were the light roar of the wind blowing from the south and the humming of the tires along the highway at about sixty miles an hour. Soon a green sign came into view. It read, WELCOME TO SOUTH CAROLINA. The large silver limousine sped past the sign with Bepy and Dana sitting in the rear. Dana was surrounded by shopping bags bursting with all kinds of favorite Italian foods. The driver was Crazy Mikey, and in the car following them were Alan, Joey D, and Ben. Their car was also loaded down with shopping bags of cheeses and olive oil.

The twins were happy and told their father that morning they couldn't wait to see the new spread. Bepy promised them their own horses would be waiting for them. He said they could bring their friends from college and also promised that a large swimming pool would be put in in a few weeks. Everyone was happy except Dana. But Bepy knew that when she saw the place she would change her mind. He knew Dana. She always fought at the beginning. She'd done so when they moved to Staten Island from Brooklyn. But soon she loved Staten Island. In the meantime, Dana wasn't talking.

They arrived in the early evening. The ranch looked isolated but beautiful. Not a house in sight; just rolling hills lit by a gorgeous sunset. Dana's eyes opened a bit, but she remained cool and quiet.

The house, completely furnished by the last owner, was to be temporary living quarters. A new house was planned for another part of the ranch.

Everyone was tired from the trip. Bepy said to Alan, "Why don't you run out and get some Chinese food while we unpack the cars. Get six tubs of soup, some lobster Cantonese, spareribs, egg rolls—get everything. Oh, by the way, Alan, is it OK to order egg rolls, or are you still finding notes in them?"

Alan gave him a big smile. "Seems like a hundred years ago, huh, Bep?"

"Where you gonna find Chinks around here?" Ben asked.

"Let's go have a look in town. There's gotta be a Chinese restaurant," Alan said.

"Go ahead. You try to find one. I slept in this town already, and there ain't nothin' there," Ben told him.

"What town?" Joey D asked. "I didn't see no town for the last fifty miles. I didn't see nothin'. How you gonna live here, Bep? There ain't nothin' around here."

"See what I mean?" Dana said. "They don't even have a Chinese restaurant. How are we gonna live here? My husband couldn't leave well enough alone. He had to move to Georgia."

Bepy, getting nervous about Dana, made a face at Ben and told him, "Go find a fuckin' Chink and cut the shit, OK? I got enough trouble with her. Take Alan. And don't forget the egg rolls."

Ben laughed. "OK. Relax. We'll get a Chink even if we gotta go to Atlanta to find one," he promised.

"Atlanta?" Dana yelled. "That's at least a hundred miles from Savannah and we're thirty-five miles from Savannah. I saw the sign. See what I mean? This place is crazy. I hate it." She sat down at the kitchen table and automatically wiped it with her hand to see if it was clean.

"Dana, after we eat, we'll check out the television programs they have down here," Bepy said, trying to calm the situation.

Joey D and Mikey were unloading the cars, and Dana began putting her cheese, tomatoes, and other Italian groceries away. "I can always make a quick sauce. We can have spaghetti marinara," she mumbled to herself.

"Yeah, spaghetti marinara," Joey D agreed. "It's always good."

"He always pulls some bullshit," she told Joey D. "He can't leave well enough alone. We had such a beautiful house on Staten Island. Right? I think he's going *pazzo,* bringing us to a place like this. Look outside! Not even a streetlight. We had a beautiful beach of our own."

"Yeah, you're right, Dana," Joey D agreed. "It was beautiful on your beach by the ocean."

Bepy heard Joey D agreeing with Dana and looked at both of them and had to laugh to himself.

"Why don't you give me a chance?" he said. "I'm gonna build a beautiful new house and new stables for our race horses. Everything will be new and first-class. Look, Dana, Mrs. Roselli is gonna come down here to our ranch and live with us. She's gonna be your housekeeper."

"I never had a housekeeper before. Why now?" Dana asked.

"Because her husband died and she has nothing, nobody. She's a great cook and a fine lady. You need somebody with you when I have to leave for business trips."

372

"So that's it," Dana said accusingly. "You intend to go on business trips and leave me here."

"Mrs. Roselli's a tough woman. You remember her, don't you?"

"Yes, I remember Mrs. Roselli. She's gonna clean, too? OK, Bephino, that sounds good. When is she coming down? And where does she sleep and watch TV? And where does Joey D live?"

"She'll be ready whenever we send for her. She's afraid of planes, so I'll have the men drive her down. When you're ready for her, let me know."

"You're gonna have race horses, Bep?" Joey D asked excitedly.

"Yeah, of course. And I'm sending you to Kentucky to learn how to be a horse trainer. Then, in the winter, we'll take our horses to Florida and race them. Don't worry, we'll have a good life here. And we're away from all that bullshit of New York. No more chewing gum sticking to our shoes. I like the country and horses and cattle. It's a beautiful life."

"Yeah, it's so wonderful," Dana remarked sarcastically. "No more chewing gum, just cow shit instead. I hope we get the Chinese food in time for breakfast."

Forty minutes later, Alan and Ben returned with two large bags of Chinese food. "It was only twelve miles from your ranch," Alan bragged. "It's a nice little town. They even got a movie house."

"It smells good. Let's eat," Joey D said.

"See, Dana," Bepy teased her. "Now you got everything. Next we gotta find a deli. In case she gets *woolei* for a hot pastrami sandwich on a seeded bagel."

"Look at this guy," Alan said, pointing to Joey D, "What is he, a schmuck? He's biting on his fingers already. Here, here's a sparerib. Chew on that." They cracked up as Joey D attacked the ribs. Everyone felt more comfortable now, including Dana.

"Why am I laughing?" she asked suddenly. "I've been kidnapped by five goons. And all hungry ones at that."

The next day, they all went to town for breakfast. Everyone stared at them.

"Boy, they really stare around here," Joey D said. "They know we're outsiders, huh?"

"Yeah, the Rebels hate Jews and Italians," Ben told him.

"How do they know we're Italians?" Joey D asked.

"Well, in your case," Ben answered, "they think you're Mexican, but they don't like them either."

"No, Ben," Bepy interrupted. "They like Italians, because they know we're crazy, like them. But they hate Jews. There's the Ku Klux Klan down here."

Alan swallowed hard. "Thanks a lot, friend."

"Maybe we gotta join the Klan. Then they'll like us." Joey D laughed.

Dana's eyes didn't know whether to laugh or cry.

While having breakfast, Joey D asked, "What's this mushy stuff on our plates?"

"Those are grits," Ben said, laughing. "I saw them in the army."

"Grits, huh? I don't like them," Joey D complained.

"You gotta get used to the food. It takes a while," Ben explained.

During the next two weeks they bought a four-wheel-drive truck, tractors, and all the things they needed to run a farm. They fixed up the house the way Dana liked it, but she still complained.

"This house will be for the guys when they come down to visit. Joey D's gonna live here. You're gonna love our new house. See that hill? That's where I'm building it. When I finish this place, it will be a beauty!"

Dana listened quietly. Her face seemed sad and unsure. She looked like a spaniel puppy going for its first car ride.

As the months went by, things slowly took shape. The foundations for the new barns were poured, and a new road in to the ranch had been marked off. Dana was becoming more relaxed and interested in the plans. She was starting to enjoy the quiet life. The twins often came barreling up to the ranch with a carload of college friends. They loved the place. Bepy had bought twelve horses for family and guests to ride. He was so involved in his dream ranch, he hardly thought about New York, though he talked business with Ben and Alan about twice a week, and he'd wonder how his old friend Don Emilio Morrano was doing.

Bepy was tagging his new herd of Angus cattle one day when a long black limousine pulled up in the middle of the pasture and parked by the cattle chute. The horn blew. Bepy walked over and leaned down to the open window. "Are you fellas lost?

"We're looking for Mr. Bemfemeo, from New York," the man in the rear explained.

"I'm him. What can I do for you?"

"We would like to speak to you confidentially," the man said, in a slow Southern drawl.

"Well, go ahead. It can't be more confidential than out here in this pasture. Speak. I'm listening."

The man got out. "Look, Mr. Bemfemeo, you came down here from New York for what reason?"

"To retire, if it's OK with you."

"Well, if we find out that you intend to get involved in our business, we will have to move against you and your family. Do I make myself clear?"

Bepy's eyes widened, "What family? What family are you talking about?"

"I'm talking about your wife and children and that old lady sitting at the pool with them."

"Oh, you mean my wife and children. You're telling me you will move against my wife and children? That's strong talk for a man standing in a pile of cowshit. Who the hell are you anyway?"

"God damn!" he shouted, trying to wipe his shoes off in the grass. "I'm Bubba Reed, from Savannah, Georgia, and you're in my neighborhood, Bemfemeo. I've heard all about you. If you intend to do business in the South, there will be herds of trouble. Ya hear?"

"Look, Bubba, I have no intention of interfering with you at all. So don't worry about that; you can put your mind at rest. My business is in New York City. This is your territory, not mine. So you can relax."

"Well, OK, but I'll be watching you," Bubba warned him, walking to his limo but watching carefully where he put his next step.

"Hey, Reed," Bepy said, "how did you get into my ranch and down to this pasture?"

"I asked the sweet young thing in the bikini by the pool. She told me her daddy was working his cows today. Now that's what I call a beauty. Hmm, hmm. She's a beauty. And her mother looks pretty good, too. I saw her from a distance. Goody-bye. Come see us, ya hear?"

The limo pulled out, its wheels digging up the sod as Bepy watched in deep thought.

One morning during breakfast, a few weeks later, Bepy told Dana to make a plane reservation to Newark. "I want you to visit your mother and father. They're getting old; so spend a few days with them, OK? I got business to do in New York and Boston."

"OK. What time you wanna arrive in New York?"

"About five. We'll eat at your mother's house. Tonight's the night she makes eggplant. Tell them we're coming for dinner."

"They'll be glad to see us."

When they arrived in New Jersey, Ben was waiting and smiling. "Boy, you look like two farmers now. You got rosy cheeks."

"Yeah, that's all the fresh air we get." Bepy said.

After two days in New York, he left for Boston. He went to the home where Morrano was staying. A nurse escorted him out to the garden. Don Emilio was sitting under a tree, like a vegetable, in a wheelchair, his head hanging down. His right arm arched in midair. He was wearing an old army jacket, with sergeants stripes, and had a blanket around his legs and a shabby old fedora on his head. He had once been such a sharp dresser in Bay Ridge, and now he was wearing one of his son-in-law's old jackets, probably.

What a fuckin' insult! Look at the stripes on his arm, Bepy thought. It makes him look so unimportant. The man was Boss of Bosses. Now he's wearing the hat of a ragpicker!

His heart beat fast seeing his old friend so docile and ill. He approached a nurse who was checking the patients. "He can't talk or acknowledge you. He's not aware. He can't even raise his head up," she said.

Bepy handed her two hundred-dollar bills and asked her to look out for his old friend and to get him a new hat today. Then he moved a lawn chair closer and sat directly opposite the Don. Morrano's head was tilted down, his eyes looking at the ground. When he sat down in front of him, Bepy noticed Morrano's eyelids flinch upward, but his head was still hanging down. After speaking to him for about ten minutes without any response, Bepy got up and lifted Morrano's head so their eyes would meet.

"Hey, Mr. Morrano," he said gently. "You got any work for me? I sure can use the money. Can you pay me in advance? Let me know you know I'm here." As he slowly released Morrano's head, he noticed that the old man strained to keep it up. He was fighting, and Bephino encouraged him. "Come on! Get it up, get it up! Let me see your eyes."

The Don's whole body trembled with the effort. He managed to raise it just enough to see the person in front of him. They stared into each other's eyes for a few minutes. There was dribbling from his mouth, but no other movement; not a nerve moved in his face. He stared like a mummy. Then, slowly, a tear dropped from his eye. Bepy understood that Morrano was aware that his friend Bepy was once again by his side. It was a very emotional experience for Bepy. He knew of no gift to give his friend but undying loyalty and respect.

"It's so beautiful to be back in the South. I hope I can live here in peace," Bepy told Dana when they returned.

She smiled agreeably.

They sat on their patio watching as beautiful clouds of orange and purple streaked with pink and white lingered before being swallowed up by evening's darkness. The bright full moon seemed to be smiling at them, as if they had finally found their destiny. The evening settled in quietly. The only sounds to be heard were the crickets chirping and the bullfrogs.

Suddenly, the ringing of the phone interrupted the peaceful moment. Bepy reached over and picked it up.

"Hey, farmer boy. How are you?" Alan asked.

"Fine. I'm glad you called, Alan. We just got in from New York."

"Yeah, I know. I spoke to New York earlier. They said you were flying back to the ranch. We miss you in Vegas. It's not the same without you. There's two beauties from Canada staying at the hotel. How about it? It'll be worth your trip. Why don't you come tomorrow? I'll pick you up at the airport."

"I got a guy coming to put up all new fencing around the pastures. Then we have to move the cattle and give them shots and worm them," Bephino explained.

"I don't believe this, Bep. We're talking about working cows. Boy, is our life changing."

"My life began to change when I met you, Alan."

"I hope for the better."

"Ahh, too much kosher food, but for the better."

"Well, if you can't come to Vegas, I'm coming to your ranch. OK?"

"Wonderful. We'd love to see you, Alan. Come on down, y'all."

"Y'all?" Alan asked.

"Yeah, that's the Southern way—meaning, bring a friend along, also."

"Whatta ya got? A crystal ball? I'm bringing my friend Marko. He's a writer. He writes about bad guys like you."

"Oh, yeah. What is he? A newspaperman?" Bepy asked.

"No. He's a book writer, novels. He just wrote a book about one of your people. I'll tell you about it when we get there. You'll love this guy. He's a beautiful person."

"OK. See you tomorrow. Hey, what time will you arrive?"

"I'll call the ranch when I land in Savannah."

Dana was glad to hear Alan was flying in. He was like family and he was getting old now. But he still dressed in real sharp clothes, with gold chains hanging around his neck, diamond rings and watches, high leather boots. He was a cat.

The man has been a good rabbi, Bepy thought. He brought me luck, and good fortune. A rare gift from Morrano, a loyal Jewish gentlemen.

About four the next afternoon, Dana drove the jeep down to pasture eighteen to tell Bepy that Alan was at the Savannah airport waiting to be picked up.

"Let's knock off for the day," he told the men. Then he headed for the airport just as he was, in boots, jeans, and a Western shirt.

"Where's your horse?" Alan asked, happy to see him.

"I always wanted to play cowboys, but in Brooklyn it just didn't seem right."

They laughed and hugged one another. Alan introduced Marko, a short, pleasant fellow, a bit thin. He was wearing a blue suit with sandals, and was smoking a pipe and peeking out of horn-rimmed glasses. Gold chains hung from his neck, too. The guy looked sort of kosher, but was really Italian. He and Bepy hit it off immediately. Alan was proud of his friend and bragged about his new book, which was going to be made into a movie.

Marko was sleepy from the jet lag, so he retired to his room early, and the two old friends watched the late news.

Alan asked, "What do you think of Marko?"

"Ah, that's a beautiful person. I like him very much. He's got a real smile, not like some people we know."

"You're right. I think he may have a few problems with the L.A. Mob. So I want him to be under your family cover. OK, Bephino?"

Bepy nodded as he took a drag on his cigar.

"When they film a movie in L.A., the Mob guys always crawl out of the woodwork with their hands out."

"Marko probably has his own friends, but if he needs me for anything, I will take care of him. Don't worry. Any friend of yours is a friend of mine," Bepy assured him.

"I know that, Bep."

The next day, after breakfast, the three men rode over the ranch on horseback. They watched the ranch hands work the cattle through the chutes and inoculate the calves. Bepy looked so proud of the life he had been able to establish for himself and his friends. It was freedom at last.

That evening, Dana prepared a special dinner: veal from their own stock, eggplant roselli, and a good Chianti Classico. After eating, they relaxed in the den listening to Italian opera and classical records that Bepy had inherited from his grandfather. Marko couldn't believe that a man like Don Dante, raised on the streets of Brooklyn, could find classical music to his liking. Bepy claimed it had been in his bloodline for hundreds of years. His grandfather had nothing but the records, and he had wanted Bepy to have them. "My grandfather was a remarkable man," Bepy said quietly.

Amid the heavy smoke from their favorite Teamos, Alan and Marko talked about a man named Eugene Bolanski. Bepy listened, not interrupting. But he listened with interest.

"How come you let the bastard get away with that?" Marko asked Alan.

Alan didn't answer, but Marko again brought up the subject. "Bolanski just opened up a new studio in California and an office in Manhattan."

"Is she still with him?" Alan asked.

"Yeah. He keeps her under wraps and takes her wherever he goes. He's still fucking her brains out," Marko answered. "He's had her since she was fifteen years old. Now she's twenty-four, and he still can't get enough of her. Her ass is like fine art. You get choked up when you look at her. It's unbelievable the way she moves. It's funny how a guy could get so hung up on a piece of ass."

Alan, visibly disturbed, chewed on his cigar and said, "I hate that son of a bitch. I hate both of them. But him, I hate more than her, because I knew she was stupid. But he was a brilliant man. He knew better."

"What's this all about?" Bepy asked.

"I hate Eugene Bolanski with a passion," he said. "I'll hate him all the way to his grave. I only let him live so I can continue to hate him." Alan reached in his pocket and placed two pills under his tongue quickly. Then he excused himself and retired to his room.

"What's happened?" Bepy asked Marko. "I never heard him talk about this guy Bolanski."

"Bolanski conned Alan's youngest son's wife into a centerfold spread in a hot magazine," Marko said. "He promised her she would become a movie star, but instead the guy fell in love with her. He's nuts over her. And apparently the broad is unbelievable. They says she fucks like a snake. I heard this from Carlo, a headwaiter at El Banco. He banged her one night about nine years ago, when Alan's son got drunk and went to bed early.

"She was only fifteen when Alan's kid married her. Alan bought off her mother so his son could have her. Two weeks after they were married, when the kids were staying at the hotel, Carlo, the horny bastard, had to have her. He couldn't leave her alone. That night he walked her to her suite and they ended up at his room instead. Then he turned on his charm and fucked the kid in her ass. He greeked her, a thousand-to-one shot, and she loved it. They say she never refuses it. It was a new thing for her. She went wild over having sex that way. Carlo, of course, bragged, and Alan heard the story and threw him out of the hotel. Carlo was blackballed in Vegas, so he went to L.A. I guess Bolanski heard the story from him about the young kid who loved to be greeked, so he showed up at the hotel.

"Finally, he sniffed her out. He made her all kinds of phony offers, and eventually she ran away with him. He's had her ever since.

"Then he spread her ass all over the centerfold of a magazine he owns. Alan's son saw her spread-eagled, and became unglued. He's still confined to a head hospital. Alan's hated Bolanski ever since."

Bepy, puffing on his cigar, said, "And he kept this from me? I never knew this was going on in Vegas. I never knew Alan's family that well. It's strange, now that I think about it. This is the first I heard of this. I feel bad, seeing Alan so upset. And I wonder why he's never come to me for help?"

"Alan was ashamed of the broad's having such a drastic effect on his son. Mind, the kid went cuckoo."

"I think it's time Alan stopped hating this Bolanski guy," he told Marko. "Would you let me know the minute Bolanski hits New York? Call me day or night." Bepy wrote a number down and handed it to Marko. "This is my special number. When you call, just give me a phone-booth number and I'll call you back within thirty minutes. Then we'll talk. OK? But don't mention this to Alan. I don't want him to know. He may get upset. I could see it killing him to talk about it."

"Yes, Bephino, I understand. I'll call you the minute I hear something. I know people who are close to him. They'll talk about him when he arrives. He's in New York at least once a month."

"Good. A decision has been made. Let's go to bed."

Five weeks later, Joey D brought Bepy his morning paper and showed him a headline: MAGAZINE TYCOON EUGENE BOLANSKI FOUND DEAD, HIS NUDE, MUTILATED BODY DISCOVERED IN MANHATTAN ALLEY.

Dana was serving breakfast. After hearing about the murder, she said, "It's really a damn shame, people are not safe anymore."

Bepy sat quietly sipping his coffee and reading the sports section. He asked Joey D who he liked in the World Series.

Joey D answered, "The Yankees. Their pitching is much stronger."

As they were finishing breakfast, the telephone rang. Bephino picked it up.

"Hi. How are you?" Alan said in a choked voice.

"I'm fine. How are you?"

The conversation was dry and shallow, not like their usual talk. It seemed as if, for the first time in his life, Alan didn't know what to say. He was stuck for words—perhaps words he couldn't speak over the telephone anyway.

Bepy's brow creased. He sipped more coffee, patiently waiting, but not speaking either.

Finally, Alan, in a low voice, said softly, "I love you, kid."

"I love you, too, Mr. Stone," Bepy whispered back.

Both men were silent for a moment, then hung up. Dana and Joey D looked over at Bepy. Dana asked, "Did I hear you say 'I love you' to Alan? Is anything wrong?"

"Nothing's wrong," Bepy said, looking at her. "What you heard was just a matter of respect."

At that moment the telephone rang again.

Bepy's eyes flickered for a second as he glanced over at Joey D. Then he quickly focused on Dana. He reached out and picked up the still-ringing phone.

"Hello," he said in a still choked voice.

"Is this Mr. Menesiero? Mr. Bephino Menesiero?" a man asked.

"Yes, this is he."

"Well, this is agent Vernon Guilderson of the Federal Bureau of Investigation. We would like to talk to you."

THE END